What people are saying about

To Dance in the Desert

A book that makes me laugh is a joy, a book that makes me cry is a rarity. But a book that moves me to dance is sublime. *To Dance in the Desert* is a spectacular experience. Beautifully written, deeply moving, and warmly engaging—that this is Kathleen Popa's first novel astounds me. That she will quickly be counted among the top caliber of Christian novelists delights me. I simply loved this book.

Kathryn Mackel, author of *The Hidden*

Kathleen Popa creates a compelling vision of a small community's power to coax waning spirits back toward life. This gem of a novel worked on me like a dream. Popa's evocative prose captures the nuance and complexity of transformation with equal parts mystery and truth. She conjures the deserts of Dara Brogan's life with intimate clarity, reminding us along the way of the profound strength of what we take far too much for granted—the deep friendship of kindred spirits. This is a journey worth taking.

Jeff Berryman, author of *Leaving Ruin*

Kathleen Popa's crystal prose captures the desert southwest like a Georgia O'Keeffe painting. Her characters, at once unique and familiar, dance. She shows us a desert of the heart, and then, with wisdom and insight, shows us how to make it bloom.

W. Dale Cramer, author of *Bad Ground* and *Levi's Will*

Every so often a new writer comes along with a distinctive and imaginative voice. Kathleen Popa is just such a writer. Her take on relationships between her unique characters and God as well as with each other is original, vivid, and real. *To Dance in the Desert* is simply wonderful.

Gayle Roper, author of *Caught in the Act* and *Allah's Fire*

There is magic in Popa's words; a quiet, kind beauty that casts the same spell as a desert sunset with its lingering afterglow.

Siri L. Mitchell, author of *Chateau of Echoes*

To Dance in
the Desert

To Dance in the Desert

A NOVEL

KATHLEEN POPA

RIVEROAK®
Good News in Fiction

COOK COMMUNICATIONS MINISTRIES
Colorado Springs, Colorado • Paris, Ontario
KINGSWAY COMMUNICATIONS LTD
Eastbourne, England

RiverOak® is an imprint of
Cook Communications Ministries, Colorado Springs, CO 80918
Cook Communications, Paris, Ontario
Kingsway Communications, Eastbourne, England

TO DANCE IN THE DESERT
© 2007 by Kathleen Popa

Cover Design: BMB Design, Inc.
Interior Design: Susan Rae Vannaman

First Printing, 2007
Printed in the United States of America

1 2 3 4 5 6 7 8 9 10

ISBN 978-1-58919-094-8
LCCN 2007921045

This book is for George.

Acknowledgments

I've been lavishly blessed with the kindness, help, and encouragement of family, friends, and mentors who believe in me. Without them, this novel would not have been written.

Many thanks to Jeff Dunn for getting excited about the story based on my flustered fifteen-minute verbal synopsis, for understanding my vision, and for taking a chance on a new author. Thanks to Jon Woodhams for encouraging and advising me along the way. Special thanks to Cheryl Crews for her hard work, for seeing things I didn't see, and for helping me make this a better novel.

Thanks also to my agent, Janet Kobobel Grant, for her guidance and for always answering my silly questions with wisdom and respect.

The Mount Hermon Christian Writers Conference has made the difference for many writers, and I'm proud to add my name to the list. I'm deeply grateful to Sharon Huffman, my dear friend who convinced me to go; Barbara Curtis, who greeted me on the first day of my first conference and assured me I belonged there; and Gayle Roper, who told me my short story wanted to be a novel, who advised and encouraged me, who rejoiced with me when the news was good.

Thanks also to the people in Gayle's Fiction Mentoring Clinic for their excellent advice. Special thanks to Sharon Souza for her friendship, for the endless hours of proofreading and critique, for her wise suggestions and unfaltering enthusiasm. Thanks also to her daughter, Deanne Barth, for reading the manuscript and joining in to assure me that someone out there would want to read this.

I must also thank Gloria Chunn, Ruth Suski, and Rick and Trinh Stahmann for reading my early manuscript and offering their suggestions.

If I wrote well and accurately about law enforcement, rescue, and medical procedures, it is because people helped me—and if I didn't write well about those things, it is because I didn't listen closely enough to those people. Thanks to Steve Campbell, Jennifer Cash, and Dr. Jerry Hanson* for their gracious advice.

Thanks to my teacher, Dr. John H. Irsfeld, the first author to tell me I could be one, too. I never forgot. And I submitted my manuscript on 100 percent cotton bond.

Thanks to the community at Faith in Fiction for their comradery through lonely days at the keyboard and for helping me think things through.

Thanks to Pastor Mike Suski and the people at Bethel for their prayers and love.

Thanks to my sister, Irene Spaulding, for working late into the night to proofread my manuscript.

Heartfelt thanks and love to my kids: Noah and Julia for cheering me on; and Alex for putting up with my glazed expression, the strange schedule I keep, and the interesting dinners I cook.

I extend my deepest gratitude to my mother, Margaret Conner, who first told me I was a writer, who always encouraged and supported my dream, who told me not to marry a man who didn't understand that I needed to write.

And to George, the man I did marry, this comes with all my love. Thank you for understanding, for sparing nothing to make my dreams come true.

To God, who has so richly blessed me, this book comes with all my passion and all my praise.

*All of the characters in this novel are fictitious. Any resemblance to any person living or dead is purely coincidental—with the exception of Dr. Harry Janson, who is modeled after Dr. Jerry Hanson, who so graciously advised me.

CHAPTER 1

*T*he woman stood atop the cinnamon bluff, her arms stretched to the horizons, her face dry as sandstone, her silver hair blowing like the grass at her feet.

"She thinks she's Moses," muttered Dara, peering through a gap between drawn blinds.

She had meant to have no neighbors. The realtor had played up the view of the bluff and the hills beyond, but Dara had noticed the unmarked dirt road that led there. Just a break in the piñon pines along the highway, the road was hard to find, even if you knew it was there. Once found, it led nine miles through the hills to a valley cloistered from all humankind. So Dara had bought the house.

Now there was a woman on top of the bluff—smack in the middle of her aloneness. What in heaven and earth was she doing there?

Twirling.

She was twirling!

She stretched herself on tiptoe and with those out-stretched arms, began tilting and wheeling, wheeling and gliding, doing a limping reel with one foot flat and the other on tiptoe, first one way and then the other, stretching to the sky, crouching to the earth, tilting, gliding, and laughing.

"Go away," Dara whispered.

But the woman danced on, brushing the wind, stroking the sky, without once bothering to look where she was going.

"If she falls, she'll be blood and bones on the rocks below," Dara said. "Fine with me ... the trespasser."

Still, every time the woman's feet edged nearer the brink, Dara's hands fluttered like birds around her mouth and eyes.

She'd just decided she would have to get out there and save the fool, when the woman stopped dancing and fell to her knees, laughing still and talking to no one there.

"Trespasser," Dara hissed.

The kettle whistled, and she went to make a cup of tea. When she returned, the woman was gone. She glanced at the rocks below the bluff, but the woman hadn't fallen. She was simply gone.

"Huh!" Dara said. "Don't come back."

But she did. The next day she was back again, skimming and reeling as if the sky would catch her to its bosom.

The day after that, as well, and day after day for an exasperating week.

The morning came, at last, when it snowed, and Dara blessed the snow, for surely no one would dance on the bluff that day.

She parted the blinds. The desert glistened undisturbed. She took her tea outside.

It was all she wanted. Nothing but sunlight and meandering snowfall. No one to hurt her and no one to hurt.

She rested against the porch rail, breathed the cold cleanness, and attended the silence.

And the silence spoke.

It said, "Dara, my Dara."

She straightened. Till now she had never heard it in the middle of the day.

She'd first heard it in a dream. No—that wasn't it. She'd felt the tenderness behind it. She'd lain in bed, floating in an unexpected peace—a caressing tenderness, night after night, that one night called her name.

Really, this came as no surprise, in a dream. But it hadn't stayed there. One morning she'd heard it as she lay awake in the blue early light: "My Dara, I'm here."

A voice. Not a voice, but the silence talking, as if the air were whispering tenderness to her.

Not a ghost. Some might have said it was if she had told

them, but at the pivot of her soul, she knew better.

However, there were candidates. Her father used to call her "my Dara," but differently, in a stern voice born of pain. "It's not a safe world, my Dara," he had told her again and again.

It wasn't Kevin, who'd never called her "my Dara." "Mine" he had called her, but that was different, for it preceded other names that held no love in them.

No, it was the air now that kissed her, stroked her face, and whispered, and she didn't know how to answer.

So she set her cup on the porch, shoved her hands into her pockets, and snuffed a great breath. She tramped down the steps and looked around. Get busy. But how?

The snow had picked up. Already a puddle of slush had formed under the dripping faucet by the porch. Maybe she should fix that, but that would require a trip to town to buy a washer. She pushed the thought from her mind.

Anyway, she'd heard on the radio that a serious storm was on its way. She could use more firewood, and there were logs to split. If she got down to business and moved quickly, she might not hear caressing voices she didn't understand.

So the evening found her well prepared, and so she stood at her window, warmed by an extravagant fire, gazing at the storm outside. The snow had gained focus, rushing sidelong in waves, ruffling the piñon pines and obscuring the bluff in the twilight.

She was about to shut her curtain against the cold when she saw movement and color in the storm, something that wasn't wind or snow or blowing trees. She peered closer and groaned.

It was the woman. There she was, fifty feet from the window, her hair frosted stiff, her arms outstretched—dancing!

Dara paced. "Not a safe world," she said.

But if the woman had driven there, there would be no driving out until the storm passed. Besides, a woman who danced in blizzards maybe shouldn't drive at all.

Not a safe world. But she didn't have a phone, and anyway,

from the end of a long and hidden road, it would do little good
to call the police on a night like this.

Not a safe world, but Dara saw only two choices: get her
inside or bury her in the morning. She put on her coat.

When she turned the knob, the wind slammed the door
open, wrenching her right arm and twisting her wrist. She
yelped and let go. The door flapped the other way and caught
her on the elbow.

"Ow!" She lashed out with her fist, but the door swung
again and she hit it on the edge.

"Gaaaaawd ... bless!" she cried. Her father had never
allowed her to curse.

She stepped outside, out of the way of the door, and
yanked it shut. The woman was a gyrating shadow, spinning farther away with each turn.

"Let her freeze," Dara grunted, moving into the storm.

She made her way down the steps, holding the rail with
her left hand, taking care not to fall. An icicle pointed from the
faucet to the slush puddle she'd noticed earlier, now hardened
to ice.

She had to veer left to walk straight in this wind, her coat
useless against the cold. When she finally reached the woman,
she tried to catch an arm midtwirl with her left hand. She
missed and forced an effort to catch it next time around.

The woman jumped at her touch. She couldn't have seen
her coming because her eyes were closed, and she couldn't
have heard her above the screaming wind.

But when she did see Dara, she graced her with the smile
of a duchess at a ball. "Helloooo!"

"What are you doing?" Dara shouted.

"Isn't this splendid?"

"No. It's cold! Would you come inside?"

The woman spotted the house as if for the first time. *As if*,
thought Dara.

"Oh!" she said. "I'd be delighted."

She took Dara by the arm, and they ducked their heads

and walked toward the house.

They were almost to the porch when the woman's foot found the ice from the dripping faucet. Dara went down with her, slamming her ankle on the bottom step. She swore for real this time—but the duchess seemed to find it funny.

Once inside, the woman bustled about, taking off her sweater (only a sweater!), pulling off her boots, rubbing her arms, and crouching by the fire. All the while she chattered, like a guest come for tea, about the "lovely snow" and the "wonderful fire." "So kind of you to invite me in!"

And yet, look at her! The frost had made white dreadlocks of her hair. Her lips were blue.

"It's been so long since I've seen such a snow. My husband, Max, didn't like cold weather."

She prattled on while her melting dreadlocks soaked her shirt. Dara left to get a towel.

"… My brother and I used to build the grandest snow castles when we were young …" She barely took a breath, but when Dara handed her the towel, she stopped midsentence and said, "Thank you, dear. My name is Jane Cameron."

"You have a British accent." She took a chair.

"Yes. All my life."

Dara focused on her folded hands. The babble had ceased. She looked up.

"I'm Jane Cameron," the woman repeated.

"I'm Dara."

Then, sure enough, "Do you take your tea by the fire?"

Take your tea! She'd want it in a porcelain pot—dreadlocks or no.

"Too bad," Dara groused in the kitchen, bobbing tea bags in chipped mugs. The duchess would need a place to sleep, but Dara hadn't thought of that, had she? Dancing women: Did they know when to leave? How would she get rid of her in the morning?

Her hand throbbed, and she pressed it to her lips. She supposed she could at least throw the bags away instead of leaving them in as usual. She poised them over the trash can, then snorted, and plunked them back into the mugs.

When she returned to the living room, Jane had dried her hair and wound it into a bun. She sat with knees and ankles together and smiled at Dara. Still she talked: "And Max and I would take our tea in the tops of trees ..."

She accepted the mug with both hands and said, "Thank you so much."

For the time it took to sip their tea, there was peace. Dara wondered if she'd have to talk. Maybe not. She'd heard enough to know that this lady could carry a conversation by herself.

But Jane showed no such intention. She propped her mug on her knees and asked, "Have you lived here long?"

"No," answered Dara. "Have you danced here long?"

"Ha! Danced! No, not long. I've only lived here a month."

"Lived here? Where?"

"Just the other side of that bluff there. I'm delighted to have a neighbor. I thought there was no one here. You look surprised."

"I didn't know there was another house here," said Dara.

"Oh yes. I've owned it for years. My husband and I were missionaries, and we used to stay here on furlough. This house was always vacant, though."

"I moved in last month."

"You're not pleased to have a neighbor." Jane eyed her gently.

Dara was stuck. No, she wasn't pleased, but there was at least a house to send the woman home to.

Jane smiled.

"Uh—no," said Dara. "No, it's fine."

"It's my little show on the bluff you mind."

"No! You're good—actually."

"I really didn't know I had an audience, or I might have spent more time on my costume."

Dara glanced aside.

"You know, something with veils. Orange and pink and red

ones, I think. Maybe a belly button ring." She lifted her shirt and tugged at her waistband to regard a freckled stomach.

Like a sack of Jell-O, Dara thought, and her laughter burst like fireworks. It felt good to laugh. Who could not like a woman who danced in blizzards?

She wanted to say something just as funny, but she didn't know what. To fill the silence, she asked, "You live there alone?"

"Mm. I came back after my husband died."

"I'm sorry." She stirred the fire.

Jane smiled. "You live alone too."

"Yes."

"Do you like it here?"

"Yeah." She shrugged. "It's quiet."

"And you want quiet?"

"I need it." Dara winced. It was more than she'd meant to say.

"So do I," said Jane.

"So do you what?"

"I need the quiet too."

"Ah." She rubbed her sore hand.

"Where did you live before?"

"Los Cuervos," Dara answered, as casually, she thought, as the question had been asked.

Jane's eyes locked onto Dara's for just an instant, but Dara knew the look and the particular silence that followed. The dancing woman had read the papers.

"Brogan," Jane whispered.

"I go by Murphy now." She had just decided. "My maiden name."

"You've had a hellish time of it."

"That's not missionary talk."

"It is if it's the truth."

She looked away and ran a hand across her nose.

"Oh! You're bruised." Jane stood.

"It's fine."

"Dara, what's happened to you? You've got to get some ice

on that hand; it's quite swollen. Do you mind?" She went to the
kitchen and returned with a bundle of ice in a towel.

Dara flinched as she pressed it to her hand. It took several
tries before she could leave it on. Worse than that was the
duchess hovering with that worried frown of hers. It was too
much attention. "Where were you a missionary?"

"Mexico," Jane said, returning to her spot by the fire.

"Did you like it?"

"Enormously."

"Why don't you go back?"

"You're still trying to get rid of me!"

"I didn't mean …"

She grinned. "It's all right."

"I'm not good at talking to people."

"You're quite good. Wrap the ice around your hand. If
you're going to be my friend, you'll have to be candid."

"I didn't come here to have friends."

"Well you've got one now, so you may as well learn what
to do with me."

"Could you find someplace else to dance?"

"There. Like that. Just say what pops into your head."

"No, really. I mean it. Could you?"

"You want to be alone."

"Yes."

"Because something terrible has happened to you."

Dara didn't answer.

"Because you're grieving and frightened, and … fairly
remorseful too, I imagine."

"Stop it."

"No."

"No?"

"No. I won't find someplace else to dance. Do you have
some aspirin? It'll help the swelling. Don't get up. Just tell me
where it is."

Oh, she had no experience with friendship.

Jane had exited into the storm and most likely pirouetted all the way home. Dara washed the mugs and put them away, then returned to the hearth and fingered the bruise on her hand.

"Not a safe world," her father had told her, and she had learned and kept her distance from it.

Still, she lived in a small town, and even at a distance, the people you see every day become familiar. You think they're your friends because they're familiar.

Then one day you're told you are beautiful. Someone whispers in your ear, and his breath arouses you because no one has ever stood so close. He calls you "mine," and you clutch at the word. Now you note the distant nods and greetings at the supermarket where you work, at the church where you sit beside your father. And you realize it has never been enough.

So you marry him. He calls you "mine" and it's the truth: You are his.

But he's had a tough life, and he can't keep a job—his temper gets him in trouble.

Your father says people think you must have been pregnant, to quickly marry such a man. He asks if it's true. It's not, but now the dispassionate smiles at the checkout counter seem to accuse, and you want to go home.

At home, that word *mine* begins to rot, because it's bellowed now between insinuations about what you do with the men at work. He has stopped calling you beautiful. He says you look like a slut but still he calls you "mine."

At work, when people whisper in line, you imagine they're looking at you. Then you hear them. One says you had an abortion, that everyone knows it. When the register falls silent, the man looks at you and shuts his mouth. But you did hear. You feel brittle, and you don't know how to work the register anymore. You bolt out of the store, you run home, and he is there. You want him to whisper to you, to tell you not to listen to them. You want him to call you "mine."

He calls your paycheck "mine." He calls you "worthless."
Why are you home in the middle of the day?

He hits you. It's the first time.

No, Dara thought when she climbed into bed. She had no
idea about friendship.

She dreamt that night of an earthquake—a wobble that
convulsed to a shattering pulse. She was pitched off balance and
fell down a chasm, her face slamming on rock, slamming again,
and again …

She woke up weeping, as she always did when she had
this dream.

Then she heard it: "My Dara, I'm here." She reached to
touch the voice, and her hand closed on air.

"Stop it!" She scrambled out of bed, reeled, and sat on the
edge. She turned on the light, and when her eyes adjusted, she
checked the clock. It was after two, but if she went back to
sleep, there'd be the dreams—and the voice. She had to find
something to do.

She could unpack another box. A stack of them leaned in
the corner.

She carried the top one to the bed. It was full of linens,
wadded and stuffed. She'd fled her father's graveside service,
decided to leave town on the drive home, and was gone before
Kevin's funeral the next day. It didn't make for careful packing.

She pulled out a fitted sheet. She began refolding, corner
into corner. She felt something hard, and turned a corner inside
out. It was a pink pearl pendant on a silver chain.

She remembered. She'd hidden it in the back of the linen
closet when Kevin started selling things to raise more money. Her
father had given it to her—as a wedding present, she supposed.

He'd met her in the parking lot at work five days after her
courthouse wedding, and two days after she'd wished it hadn't
happened. Her father had cleaned up like he was going to
church, and she wept at the sight of him. They climbed into his
truck for some measure of privacy, and he pulled her to his
shoulder and rocked her till her tears were dry. Then he gave

her the pink pearl in a little box. He lifted her chin so she faced him and said, "Remember the story."

She did remember, now seated on the bedroom floor with the fitted sheet rumpled in her lap. She held the pearl to the light and watched it gently dangle, flawless. "The particular golden pink the sunset wears on the first day of spring," the story had gone. She opened the clasp and fastened it around her neck.

The box of linens could wait. She stuffed the sheet in, put it back in the corner, and climbed into bed. She turned off the light, wrapped a fist around her pearl, and fell asleep.

In the morning, she peered out to see if Jane danced on the bluff. She wasn't there. Dara turned from the window and slumped onto the couch. She inspected the bruise on her hand. The swelling had gone down, and it hurt a little less. Jane, with her ice and aspirin.

Ridiculous how a visit from an imbalanced, prying old woman who caused such irritation at the time could cause something like pleasure when she remembered it.

Ridiculous how she almost wished the duchess were out there now.

A knock sounded at the door. "Dara, it's Jane." She sprang to her feet and rushed to let her in.

"Look at you," Jane said. "Still in your pajamas! Did I wake you up?"

"No."

"Oh, Dara, it's marvelous outside. Let's go worship in the desert."

"What?"

"The air's just filled with gladness out there. Come on. Let's go!"

"I don't want to dance, Jane."

"You don't have to dance. Just being there will be glory

enough. You could wear your pajamas. Who would know?"

"Don't be nuts. I'm not going to do that."

"You don't have to dance, Dara. You don't have to do any-thing but be there."

Dara parted the blinds.

Oh, the white light! Her house did feel so dark.

So she put on her boots, and they went. The first rush of wind was cold, but the sunlight was warm. They wound through the snow and mesquite to a bright spot near the base of the bluff. They turned to look around, their hands pushed in their pockets to brace against the buoyant light. This gleaming world was a joy meant for them, and as they turned, Jane took her hands from her pockets, turned her face to the sky—and twirled.

Dara walked away.

She felt its breath before she heard it speak. "Dara, my Dara."

Oh, it wasn't "mine," this, not the way Kevin had meant it. This was tender love. The breeze brushed her cheek. The wind sounded gentle drums in her ears. She felt fragile as thin glass, but at the moment, she could shatter in this white light and it might be a good way to die.

She gazed at the candescent hills, and her insides began to sway like a silk ribbon. She heard the air say, "My beloved. You are my own."

She took her hands from her pockets and twirled. Just once. Just a little turn.

☙

Her name was Dara Pearl Murphy, so the story was about a pearl. Her father had told it so often she might have forgotten the first time, if he'd told it on an ordinary day. But oh, how she did remember.

She'd been eight years old. It had been four weeks since her mother had wandered off, clutching the family photograph her father had thrust into her hands. "You've got to think of Dara!" he'd shouted, and Dara still remembered standing in her darkened bedroom, flinching at the fierceness in his voice. Worried, she'd peered down the hallway into the kitchen as her mother pushed herself up from the table, then stepped out the back door. Was she barefoot? Dara remembered her barefoot, though it had been January. It was like she just needed to get some air and dry her tears. Who could've known she'd walk through the darkness out the gate and never return? Her father couldn't rightly be blamed for not pulling her back, but the night he told this story, it had been a month, and Dara blamed him.

"It's all your fault!" she'd railed at him. "You made her run away." He gripped her with his arms, but she flailed loose. Trying to calm her, he offered a glass of milk, but she threw it in his face.

She stopped crying and stepped back. He sank to the floor, covering his head with both hands. Milk dripped from his hair and the tip of his nose. She climbed into his lap. "Don't cry, Daddy!" He held her, and together they wept to exhaustion.

He tucked her in that night, and she lay in her bed, limp and heaving from too many tears. He wiped her face with a washcloth, and hesitantly he began:

"Once upon a time, there was a pearl." His voice shook, but he brushed her forehead and continued.

"This was no ordinary pearl," he said, stroking her cheek. "The color of this pearl was the particular golden pink the sunset wears on the first day of spring." He attempted a smile.

"But an evil wizard had thrown the pearl into a foul sea, and as long as she could remember, she had been there.

"When I say she was in a foul sea, I mean the kind of water Daddy gets when he leaves dishwater too long. What kind of water is that?"

"Like snot," she managed between the heavings in her chest.

"Yes! Exactly like salamander snot!" He made a face, and she smiled a little.

"The very ugly thing this water did was that it caused her to calcify. Like the pipe under the bathroom sink, remember?" She nodded.

"Well, the water put layers and layers of this calcifying stuff on the pearl, and it made her look like a rock and not like a pearl at all. And the trouble was she didn't remember ever being anything but an ugly rock in foul water.

"Now, there was a prince who wanted to save the pearl. He dove into the foul sea, and the bad stuff in the water burned his milky skin, but he swam right through it. Way, way down to the deepest, darkest depths he swam, till he found the rock, which he knew was a pearl, and brought it to dry land.

"The pearl was happy to get out of the foul sea. Still, some of the bad water clung to her, so she asked the prince if she might have a bath.

"The prince gave her a good bath in his own crystal clean water, and when he was done, she felt like … a new rock!

"The pearl wanted to put herself to good use to show gratitude to the prince, so she decided she would be a cobblestone on the road that led to the prince's castle. But no sooner had she placed herself on the pile of stones to be used for the road than the prince picked her up and put her in a bucket with other rocks.

"The prince began to shake the bucket, and it hurt her to be tossed around like that. The pearl was confused and upset, until one of the rocks explained—in a hurry as she tumbled by—that they were being polished. Because, you know, when rocks tumble around together they knock the rough edges off one other, and then they all come out smooth and shiny.

"And that's what happened to our pearl. She looked in the mirror at herself and rejoiced at what she saw. She dared to ask if she might even adorn the castle itself, since she really did seem to be a very pretty, shiny rock.

"Well, what do you suppose the prince did?"

"Put her on the castle?" asked Dara.

"You'd think, wouldn't you? But that's not what happened.

The prince did the last thing the pearl ever thought of. He took his hammer and chisel, and began to strike her again and again.

"At first she was so shocked that she didn't know what to think. Then she blamed herself for being so proud as to ask to adorn the castle.

"She cried, 'I'm sorry!' but it seemed the prince must be very angry, because no matter how many times she said she was sorry, he just kept hitting her with his chisel.

"She wailed, 'You're killing me!' Because of course, she didn't know she was a pearl. She thought she was a rock, and it was big pieces of rock that flew off with every blow of his chisel. She thought she must be a very bad rock to make him so angry.

"Then one day, as quickly as he had started in with his chisel, he stopped. She looked up to see only tears and the sweetest love in his eyes. The prince placed her in front of a mirror, and she looked. There, shining in the chinks where the rock had chipped away, she saw a particular golden pink like the sunset on the first day of spring."

It was Dara's favorite story, so he told it often. Once, when she was older, she'd thought to ask what happened next. Did the pearl adorn the castle, or did the prince place her in his crown?

"I don't know," her father said. He turned away and shrugged, as if embarrassed. Then he looked at her and smiled. "I only know rocks."

Chapter 2

*T*he next morning she pushed past the several types of tea in the cupboard to the bag of espresso roast in the back. Five scoops in the filter, straight up. She'd woken at eight, and in all, that gave her what? Five hours of rest?

She'd slept gripping her pearl like an amulet against the nightmares. More or less, it had worked; she hadn't dreamt of earthquakes.

She dreamt of mice. Hordes of them, scuttling through her hair and nudging her armpits. Lumps coursing under the blankets, twitchy fur squirming the floor and swarming up the walls, skittering and scratching.

The worst was she still heard it when she woke up—just for an instant, a little scratch, like the nervous scrape of tiny claws.

She had switched on the light and leaned over to check the floor under and around her bed. She got up and pulled back the bedding, layer by layer.

They can't climb walls, she told herself. She checked anyway. She crawled back in bed, and listened till at last she slept.

All this at two o'clock in the morning.

"Beats the earthquake," she muttered now. She closed the kitchen blinds and poured a cup of coffee. A strand of hair slipped from the shoulder of her tank top to her bare back, and she jumped at the tickle.

Okay, time to think of something else.

She pulled on a jacket and slipped her shoes on without tying the laces, then headed for the porch. She'd drink her coffee outside.

She opened the door.

Something pastel cannonballed toward her and would have struck her in the head if she hadn't ducked. Instead, it hit the door, a spatter of purple snow. She stuck her head out to see where it had come from just in time to catch a green snowball on the forehead.

"Jane!"

The duchess stood beyond the porch in her down jacket, laughing beside a bucket of snowballs dyed like Easter eggs. "Spot on!" she crowed.

She tossed a pink one, and Dara dodged, crouching behind the railing.

"Hold on!" Dara shouted. She collected snow from the drift at the edge of the porch. "Let me get my own." She straightened just enough to hurl the ball at Jane, then lifted her bare cold fingers and warmed them with her breath.

"Watch out for yellow snow!" Jane cried. Her snowball caught Dara on the arm. Dara's next pitch hit Jane's backside as she bent to gather ammunition. "Bull's-eye!" she shouted, both fists raised. Jane's blue snowball hit her neck, dropping ice down the collar of her jacket.

When they were both as wet as they were cold, Dara swept the spilt coffee off the porch, and Jane brought in more firewood.

"Where'd you get colored snowballs?" Dara wanted to know.

"You want me to tell how I make my weapons?"

"You gotta be Martha Stewart's hippie sister."

"A hippie. How decadent! Do you think?"

Dara shook her head. "I've still got coffee. You want some?"

"Oh, please."

"It's strong."

"And hot. Sounds lovely. Only a cup, though. I've got to go to Brittlebush after."

"What's in Brittlebush?" Dara headed for the kitchen.

"My brother. And the grocer's."

Dara stopped in the doorway and spun to face her. "Can you pick me up some stuff? I've got money." If the duchess could eliminate all need to go to town …

"You can't just hermit up here, Dara. It's not good for you."

"Fine." She turned around. "Just thought I'd ask."

They'd barely settled—still wet—beside the fire, when they saw the mouse. A real one, peering from behind the corner chair.

"I knew it!" Dara put down her cup.

"Hello! Look at him!"

"I am looking!" But she'd already headed back to get a broom.

"Oh, he's just a mouse," Jane said when she returned.

"Where'd he go?"

"Not telling."

"Oh Jane! I can't have mice in the house!"

"I had rats in England. Max made recipes for them."

"Agh!"

"Chocolate ones."

"Tell me where he is, and I'll cook him up for you."

"Oh, we never harmed them. It was just his joke. What else could we do?"

"I'll tell you wh—There he is!" She dashed across the room, and the mouse retreated farther into the shadow under the bookcase.

Dara knelt, slid her broomstick in, and swung it back and forth.

The mouse scudded out.

She sprang to her feet and smacked him with the broom. He changed direction, and she hit him again.

He ran into the bedroom.

"Maybe we could make a nonviolent trap," said Jane, trailing close at Dara's heels. "You know, a box with cheese and a spring-loaded door."

Dara looked under the bed. "Sure, and we could decoupage it with violets." In the closet, under the clothes.

"Violets are nice."

Where was he? She beat the broomstick under the dresser. The mouse escaped and fled to the bathroom. "Ha, the little sneak!"

"What, do you mean to bludgeon it with that broom?" Dara shut the door, leaving Jane out.

The mouse ran into the shower. Dara swung and missed.

He ran behind the toilet. She poked him out with the broomstick.

He ran into the corner between the sink console and the white tile wall.

Dara closed in and knelt, her broomstick poised aloft like a spear.

The mouse cringed on his hind legs, his tiny fingers kinked under his chin, his chin tucked to his chest. His eyes squeezed shut.

He shook. Ear to foot, he trembled, waiting to bleed against the white tile.

Dara knew the look of blood on white. She had crouched trembling with eyes clenched, while Kevin pinned her against the refrigerator door.

"Dara?" Jane called from outside the door.

The mouse cried one long, piercing "Eeeeeeeeeee!"

Dara made a low sound of her own: "Eeeee!" She rolled over on the floor and pulled her knees to her chest.

Jane opened the door. "Dara?" The mouse fled between her feet.

Dara covered her eyes with her fists and wailed.

Jane didn't ask. She put some water on for tea. While it heated, she brought a warm washcloth to wipe Dara's face.

Dara melted into the moist texture, the woody smell of the cotton.

"The Bible says Jesus will wipe the tears from our eyes." Jane ran the cloth over first one eye and then the other, then across Dara's forehead, up to her hairline. "I think he'll use a warm washcloth, don't you?"

"He'll need a lot of them."

"I'll bet he has stacks and stacks piled up by the pearly gates. One hundred percent cotton, plush."

"And a faucet."

"Living water. Set to warm, on tap."

When the tears were dry and the tea finished, Jane left to see her brother, to get her groceries and Dara's too. Dara hadn't collapsed to the bathroom floor just to get Jane to do this for her. Still, knowing it had worked out that way made her feel better.

She went to her bedroom to get dressed and open a few boxes. More clothes, pots and pans, towels.

One more box, she told herself, *and then I'll have some lunch.*

She took the next box from the stack and put it on the bed. It was a shabby, much-handled box, and heavy. She'd grabbed it from her father's garage shelf when she left Los Cuervos, on the chance it might be important.

She broke the tape, pulled open the flaps, and looked inside. Yellowed newspaper and pink ruffles. Keepsakes.

She started to close it again, then leaned her weight against it, considering. Keepsakes were memories, and memories were treacherous things. Still, she was curious. She sat on the bed beside it and began.

On top lay a bundle wrapped in newspaper that had not yet gone yellow. She unrolled the paper to reveal a kachina doll, a skirted figure with arms outstretched, one boot-moccasin raised, its face turquoise and black and circled with brown feathers. She fingered the red makeshift armband that concealed a break her father had mended years before. Dara read the faded tag around its leg:

> Morning Singer
> Appears on rooftops
> In the morning, and sings
> To waken the village.

On the other side of the tag was handwritten, "Dan and Clara Murphy, honeymoon, Grand Canyon, June 11, 1976."

She set the kachina on the dresser and returned to the box, then pulled out a bulky manila envelope. She opened the flap and extracted a handful of old photographs. They were all of her mother, every last one. Flipping through them, Dara trembled, hungry for her mother's face. They'd never kept these pictures around—she hadn't even known they existed. Yet there was her mother holding a birthday cake, standing by the Christmas tree, and outside trimming roses.

At last Dara settled on a honeymoon photo of her mother in an aqua sweater, posing with the kachina before the Grand Canyon, a grin flirting around her eyes and dimples. Dara imagined her father behind the camera, saying something funny. Though she couldn't imagine what that might be; her father never told jokes. For that matter, he never laughed. But the day he took this picture, her mother looked like she'd never want to leave him.

Dara remembered the aqua sweater. She remembered a day in the park, sunshine, egg sandwiches, and a spiral slide that dropped her from the sky to circle down like a leaf. She had lain on the grass with her head on her mother's lap, fingering the sweater's pearl buttons, and thinking, *how pretty*.

She set the photos down and pulled out two wooden frames. Oh, she remembered these. She wept, holding them. They'd just disappeared from the mantel years before. She'd thought her father had thrown them away.

The one on top held a Sears portrait of Dara at five years old in a blue dress. The other held a shot of her parents taken the same day. Such a pretty face her mother had and such lovely hair. She was as beautiful as Dara remembered.

She studied the wooden frames' design, remembering how she'd sat with her mother at the kitchen table the day she hand painted roses on them. There was her mother's signature at the bottom corner of each: "CM." Dara ran her finger over the painted letters.

There'd been a third portrait in the set, of the three of them together. It was the picture her mother carried the last time she walked out the door.

Dara exhaled and wiped her tears. This was exactly the kind of memory that made it a bad idea to open such boxes. She started to put the pictures all back inside, then hesitated. There were so few reminders of her mother. What else was inside? She set the pictures on the nightstand and pulled a stack of old newspapers and magazines from the box. The top one was a yellowed copy of the *Los Cuervos Standard*. The headline read, "Teacher Plans Field Trip in Space."

Touching the paper, she could almost feel her mother's warmth at her back. She used to sit on her lap at the kitchen table. They spread the newspaper before them and poured over every detail of Christa McAuliffe's good luck.

"We can watch it together," her mother had said. "You and me, Ducky, we'll watch 'em fly into heaven."

Her mother loved anything to do with space. She loved to show Dara the Big Dipper from the front lawn. She listened every day to *Star Watch* on the radio.

The next item was a *Time* cover story about Halley's Comet, the astronomical marvel scheduled to make an appearance that same year. Dara remembered this magazine too, spread across the same kitchen table. The comet was going to be spectacular: the Star of Bethlehem, the star that attended the birth of Jesus and of Mark Twain. They were going to see that together too.

So much for promises.

She tossed the papers aside and lay back on the bed, closing her eyes. Memories were treacherous things, and they'd gotten ahold on her. What she saw now, even with her eyes closed, was a forked plume of smoke, like a spray of Reddi-wip in a blue sky. She'd watched it alone on the couch while her father sat in the kitchen with two policemen and one clipboard, trying to puzzle out where her mother had gone.

They didn't even notice the explosion.

Not long after that, the big news around Los Cuervos was about a little girl who'd gotten lost on Cuervo Mountain. A search party found her by joining hands and walking through the forest in a line, letting go only to get past the trees.

Months later, Dara watched television with her father as people gathered just twenty-five miles from Los Cuervos to join in an event called "Hands Across America": the entire width of the country bridged by people holding hands. Dara remembered watching them on television from her father's lap and thinking, *If they just started walking, they could find her.*

Halley's Comet had been a bust. At least it seemed so to Dara at eight years old, standing on the front lawn with her father, staring at a dim white smudge in the black sky.

But the shuttle launch was the day children watched their parents disappear.

She remembered a blond-haired boy on his grandmother's lap holding a little flag, screaming skyward with a hand over one eye. His grandmother forced his face to her shoulder, to shield him from what he had already seen.

But nobody shielded Dara from the thing she saw.

The morning had brought too much pain. She looked out the window. The snow had melted in paths between the brush, enough for her to go running, something she'd rarely done amid the inquisitive eyes of Los Cuervos. Today it seemed the only way to clear her mind. How far around the bluff? Two miles? Four? She put on her shoes and set out.

The air was cold, but the sun warmed her shoulders, and the running warmed the rest.

Except for the bluff and the stand of piñon pines that extended past the slope of the hills, except for the mesquite and the occasional low cactus, the desert plain was clean and open. The wind in a place like that rushes through you; it beats once or twice with your heart, sashays, turns, and comes again. And no surprise by now, this wind had a voice that loved Dara.

She ignored it.

On the other side of the bluff, she stopped, breathless, to take in Jane's part of the desert. It looked like her own, except for an odd curve of rocks that extended from a low hill a distance away. She jogged across the plain to have a look.

The rocks presented a short path leading to a curved gorge that cut through the center of one hill. She walked inside. The sandstone walls formed something like a series of attached spires but bladelike, like folded wings. She stretched her arms, unable to reach from side to side—but the feeling was close, as intimate as the cup of a hand.

She leaned her head against the wall and stroked the white rock with curled fingers, waiting for her breath to slow. She almost imagined that the rock pressed back. It felt cool, with the dry smoothness of fine sandpaper. It smelled like rain.

Her eyes skimmed up the rock to the irregular patch of sky telescoped thirty feet above. She saw the pale circle of the daylight moon. Dropping her head back from her shoulders, she felt dizzy, both closed in and exposed. Her breath turned ragged, and in it she heard the beat of her pulse. Unnerved, she got moving. The gorge took two more turns before opening on the other side of the hill. She stepped out, relieved.

A valley larger than her own extended like a wide span of tawny suede stretching off the hills. It looked like it would be soft, if she had a hand big enough to stroke it. A low glint of sunlight revealed a town tucked up against the far mountains. That had to be Brittlebush, where Jane was visiting her brother and buying groceries for the two of them. The highway was a thin black line, like a seam in the suede, with the occasional car skimming along it like a solitary ant.

She turned back to the hill. To her left stood two old shacks, the kind she'd seen from the window of her father's truck along desert roads. Old miners' shacks, probably. She'd never seen one up close.

She made her way through the brush to have a look.

Through the gaps between the unpainted vertical boards on the walls, she could see sunlight shining on the dusty floors through the open spaces in the roofs.

One shack was worse than the other, leaning to one side. She approached to look through the window, cautious lest the whole thing topple. There was an old table in there and an ancient metal bed frame, nearly rusted away. A pale purple bottle glinted in the corner.

The other shack was larger. It seemed just as weathered, but it stood upright. It had more windows than the other, six windows each on the side walls. She looked through the door. Near the back wall stood a small table. Underneath lay a rusted, wrought-iron cross, about a foot and a half long, on a wooden base. Dara cautiously placed a hand on the wall and gave a little push. It stood firm.

She climbed the hill to go home. She didn't want to reenter the gorge, at least not alone. She'd just crested the top when Jane's truck rumbled up the dirt road.

"Jane!" She waved her arms. She sidestepped downhill, slid, then caught herself. "Jane!"

The truck stopped. Jane got out and met Dara halfway.

When Dara showed her the gorge, Jane slowed her step and let out a breath, as of old air stored deep in her belly.

"Guess you danced every place but here, right?"

"I guess I did."

"It's something, huh?"

"It's beautiful." Jane ran her eyes up the curve of a winglike column to the patch of sky at the top, then continued on the path, stroking a hand along the sandstone. When she reached the opening on the other side, she turned to look back where she'd come. She closed her eyes, raised one arm, and began to sway.

"Don't start that." Dara grabbed Jane's other arm, turned her around, and led her out. "There's more."

When they reached the shacks, Jane circled them and smiled. She chuckled, then scanned the broad desert around them.

"Out here in the middle of dirt!" Dara shook her head.

"I suppose someone wanted to be alone." Jane grinned at Dara. "For some reason." She walked forward and pressed on the corner of the shack with the cross inside. "This seems sturdy." She walked in.

"You shouldn't do that."

"I think it's all right."

Dara moved as close to the door as she could without going in.

Jane picked the cross up and ran a finger over the curl of wrought iron. She looked around at the windows. "Do you know what this was?"

Dara shrugged.

"It was a church."

"For who?"

"Whoever lived in the other one, I'd say."

Dara shook her head. "Small congregation. Bad for potlucks."

Jane smiled.

"You cold?" Dara asked. "Let's go have some tea."

Jane ran a finger through the gap between one wallboard and another. She sat on the floor. "I like it."

"Glad to hear it." Dara took a step back.

"What shall we call it?"

Dara took three more steps.

Jane spoke louder. "First Church of the Exceedingly Isolated Valley? I'm certain it's the first."

"Call it what you want. I'm cold."

Jane closed her eyes. "Do you feel something here?"

"Nothing but goose bumps." Trouble was she did feel something, like a breath on her neck ("my Dara"), like an internal drumbeat. "Hey, is my milk spoiling in your truck back there?"

"How could it, as cold as it is?"

"Ha! See? You are cold! Let's go!" She climbed the hill.

Jane did have a teapot with matching cups, saucers, sugar bowl, and creamer, but they were brown and blue clay things, not porcelain. *Missionary souvenirs*, Dara concluded. Jane held her cup with the tips of her fingers, all the same.

Everything was oak, clay, or homespun. The rug looked handwoven—in Mexico, she felt safe to assume. She imagined a woman with long hair that had never gone gray, working a loom passed down for generations, with wool from her own sheep.

Still, the oak furniture was arranged in nice, British symmetrical patterns. Two clay chickens sat on opposite ends of the mantel at precise distances from the mirror in the middle, as if they were porcelain dogs.

"Nice place," Dara said between sips of tea.

"Thank you. Max did it up, mostly with things we found in Mexico."

"The rug?"

"Made by a fourteen-year-old girl, Beatrice, on an eighty-year-old loom passed down from her grandmother."

"You knew her?"

"Oh, very well."

"Bet she raised her own wool."

"No. She got it from her brother-in-law, Jorge. He's got a ranch not far from our compound."

Dara pointed to a wall of photographs matted in glass. There was a close-up of a laughing, dark-haired man, about twenty. A movie star shot. "Is that him?"

"No. No, that's Fernando." Jane put her cup down and walked to the wall. "I have pictures of both Jorge and Beatrice."

Dara joined her.

Jane pointed to a group photo. "That man there, with the cowboy hat, is Jorge. And that's Beatrice in the corner, seated, though I think she was only twelve when this was taken. She's off to university now."

"That's a lot of rugs, to pay for college."

"Yes, and a lot of computer components assembled by her mother. She's going to be a missionary." Jane smiled.

"Like you."

"Yes."

"Wow!" The next photo had caught her eye. The red-haired woman pictured looked like a Vargas Girl dressed in Dale Evans' clothes, red with white fringe.

"Mm, indeed. Wow."

"She'll mop the floor with him." She pointed to the blushing round-faced man wrapped in the woman's arms. His hairline was too far back and his teeth too crooked for a woman like that to give a second look. "She must love him for his money."

Jane laughed. "That would have been a grave miscalculation. He's my brother."

"Oh. Oh, I'm sorry." Dara blushed.

"He does fade in comparison, doesn't he? No one in Brittlebush could believe she married him."

"Is she somebody …"

"Yes. She was most definitely somebody. But famous only locally. Holly sang country-western at all the local rodeos. Tom met her when he was here on holiday, just attended the rodeo on a lark. In two months he'd quit his job in London and opened a little restaurant in Brittlebush."

"So he married her?"

She nodded toward the picture. "Look at him. Of course he did."

"Are they happy?"

"Were happy. She died last June. About the same time as my Max."

"Why? She looks fine."

"She was fine, till a blood clot found its way to her brain. A fall from a horse."

"I'm sorry. Is your brother okay?"

"Well, he's got to be. He's got their little girl now. He stays occupied."

Dara touched the next photo. "That's you in this one."

"Yes. With lovely dark hair. It's rather an old picture."

"Is that your husband?"

"Yes. That's Max."

"He's good looking."

"He was very good looking."

"How'd he die?"

Jane smiled gently and shook her head.

"Sorry." Dara turned away from the wall of pictures and spotted a lone silver frame under a lamp on the table by the couch. The woman in the picture was laughing. Her head was thrown back so you could see the gold crowns on her back teeth. Her hair had come unpinned on one side. "Who's this?"

Jane took the frame from Dara and held it in both hands. For a moment, it seemed she was more with the woman in the picture than with Dara. "That's Lena," she said at last.

"She looks happy."

"Yes." Jane chuckled. "Lena's very happy." She put the picture down. "Well, your milk isn't spoiling, but it may be freezing. Shall I drive you home?"

"Sure."

"I'll be in the loo just a second, and then I'll bring your jacket."

Dara returned to the picture of the red-haired woman draped around Jane's brother. What would it feel like to be "most definitely somebody"? To have a man just drop his whole life, leave his home in London, and move to Brittlebush of all places, just to be with you?

Dara turned from the pictures to wander the living room. She spotted a grouping of colored bottles on the console, shining like a church window in the lamplight. She lifted the red one to her eye and peered through. The effect was surreal, the room ruddy and spiraled through the sculpted glass.

"Try the blue one."

Dara put the bottle down and spun around in one quick movement.

"It's all right." Jane was beside her holding their jackets. "That's what I do with them." She handed Dara the blue bottle. "They're great in sunlight. Look at this one. You're a mermaid, at home in a tropical lagoon."

It was so: Dara could see the underwater parlor, the couches, the tables, and the pictures on the wall. She put the bottle down. "I used to have a green marble I looked through. To find the Emerald City." She shrugged. "When I was a kid."

Jane lifted her chin and smiled. "*The Wizard of Oz*. A story lover."

Dara took her jacket, and they left.

They were just pulling into the drive of Dara's property when they saw the coyote. He skulked past the truck, his eyes watchful of the open window, his shoulders down. He carried something in his mouth. Dara peered at it and saw a gray wad of fur, a hairless tail hanging limp from the corner of the coyote's black lips. The mouse!

Dara jumped from the truck before Jane had finished braking and pitched a rock at the coyote. He'd started running, but she hit him just under the ear. He yelped and dropped the mouse. Dara gave one final chase, and he was gone. She knelt to lift the small body. Jane caught up and placed a hand on Dara's shoulder. "Is he ...?"

Dara rubbed the moisture from her eyes and nose with her free arm. Jane took the mouse from her. "Let's see him."

The mouse was limp but breathing. A wound in his side oozed blood onto matted fur.

"He's not dead, see? Let's take him inside."

The two women poured peroxide on his wound, then made a small bed in an empty packing box. Jane rinsed out a bottle of eye drops and filled it with water to drip into his mouth. Then they settled before the fire with a box and a mouse between them.

At one in the morning, still in her chair, Dara opened her eyes. Jane had evidently tucked the afghan around her shoulders and left.

The mouse was asleep. Dara dabbed more peroxide on his wound, then poked the water bottle into his mouth and held it there until he swallowed. Then she stood and folded the afghan.

She liked Jane very much, and this concerned her. She'd not come to this secret place to find a friend.

She draped the afghan over the couch and went to bed.

The sun did its best to shine through her blue curtains, but it was a feeble daybreak. Dara swung her legs out and slumped on the side of the bed, stood and walked to the bathroom, pressing fingertips into the ache in her neck.

When she finished, she approached the living room, braced for what she might find. The mouse lay where she'd left him. She tilted the box. He moved like a rock, an inanimate thing.

She sank to the floor and wiped her tears with the back of her hand.

It was only a mouse.

She wouldn't go to Jane's today. Hadn't she come here to be alone? It was not a safe world.

Well, what would she do, then? She had a dead mouse.

She found a box of oatmeal in the kitchen and emptied it into a mixing bowl. She found an old dishtowel and returned to the living room. She used the dishtowel to lift the mouse, wrap him, and slide him into the box. She put the lid on and took it out back.

Where?

She looked around. Her yard was plain dirt, not a proper gravesite. She looked farther. The bluff shone red in the morning light. She fetched her shovel from the shed, stepped over the fence, and started out.

If she'd killed him with her broom, she would've buried him deep in the trash. Now, for him, she forced her legs to move, and every step was heavy.

A brush of wind traced her neck.

"Don't you start," she said. "Just go away."

A rabbit darted from a mesquite and zigzagged a distance before vanishing beneath another bush. She gasped at the sight of it, its flashing white fur, its skittering feet. She bent to see where it had gone.

"No!" She righted herself and resumed walking. "You can keep your rabbit!"

She got no answer, and that pleased her.

"What's the point? You wait ..." She was crying, but her rising anger made it easier to walk. "You wait till someone really matters. And then you take them away!"

She had his ear.

"You only let the mouse hang out for a day, I'll give you that. It could have been worse. But it's not enough! Not nearly!"

She kept walking.

"Okay, Dad was my fault, I know. But not my mother! I needed her—you had to know that!" She stopped and dropped her head back to address the sky. "I was a good girl! Wasn't I?"

She walked.

"Okay, but if I wasn't, I was just a kid! And maybe if she hadn't left ..."

She stopped. "Maybe I ..."

She turned around. Where was the bluff?

She'd passed it! She bent her head and caught her breath. When she looked up, she saw the curve of rocks, the entrance to the gorge.

"Yeah." She walked. "Good idea."

A strange place, yes. Full of the voice, and a thousand times over. But that was the sort of place to bury the dead.

She waved her oatmeal box. "Talk to him. I'm through."

There was an enclosure between the curve of rocks and the hillside. She thrust her shovel in. The grave would have to be deep, or the coyotes would dig it up. How deep? Three feet? No, maybe four.

"Dara," she heard.

The dirt was hard, and that was good. She would work hard and fast, and she would not hear her name.

"Dara."

She turned. It was Jane. "Geez! What are you doing here?"

"I like it here." She smiled. "And you?"

Dara held up the oatmeal box.

"The mouse?"

Dara nodded.

"I'm sorry."

Jane took a step forward, and Dara backed away. Jane stopped, and Dara stood, a solitary weeping figure. She put her hands on her eyes. She wrapped her arms around her waist. She pounded the air. What to do with herself?

Jane offered a hug, and she took it.

CHAPTER 3

*T*hey took turns digging. When the hole was deep enough, they broke sprigs of mesquite and made a bed in the bottom. They dropped some in the oatmeal box and put the lid back on. Then they buried the mouse.

Dara smoothed the dirt over the top of the grave. Jane arranged sprigs in the shape of a cross. She stepped inside the gorge and came back with a Bible.

"You just happen to have that with you?" Dara asked.

"I came to read."

"Oh. Sorry."

"Well, come on. Stand here with me."

"You do funerals."

"I've seen them. Come on."

Together they straightened their backs and bowed their heads.

Jane began: "Are not five sparrows sold for two copper coins?"

"He's a mouse."

"It doesn't matter."

"It does to him."

"Not anymore." Jane started over. "Are not five sparrows sold for two copper coins?"

"It's gotta be more than two pennies."

"It wasn't more then."

"Inflation."

"Precisely. Shall I continue?"

Dara fingered her pearl. She didn't mean to heckle, but her mouth was spring-loaded.

Jane started again. "Are not five sparrows sold for two copper coins? And not one of them is forgotten before God."

This one was, Dara thought, but she kept it to herself. Jane closed her Bible and turned her face to the sky. She seemed to be praying, so Dara closed her eyes and bowed her head.

Jane was silent for so long that Dara snuck a peek. Both of Jane's arms were raised. She stood like a crucifix—but a happy one. She smiled, her eyes fixed on something Dara couldn't see. She began to sway.

Here we go, thought Dara.

Jane began a song: "I sing because I'm happy."

Dara rubbed her shoulder. Her hands ached too.

"I sing because I'm free."

She set her jaw.

"His eye is on the sparrow ..."

Dara turned and walked away. *Stupid, stupid, stupid!*

"And I know he watches me."

She hoped Jane wouldn't follow. When she'd gone some distance, she stopped to retie her shoe. She snuck a look behind her. Jane was nowhere in sight.

She didn't want to go home. She didn't know what she wanted to do. Her hands were so tense she wanted to clench her fists till her fingers broke through. She'd gone several yards up the curved slope of the bluff before she knew she was climbing it. She hoisted herself over a rock and kept going. She reached the top quickly and stood panting, for a moment distracted by her struggle for breath and by what she saw.

She could almost see the planet's curve, so far it was across the white dappled valley to the gray and white hills surrounding. An inner part of her stretched to fill the space.

She walked to the edge and sat on a rock where she could see her house. How small, her little secret place. But it had a clean view all around and a door she could lock. This was the safest place she would ever find. This was her best bet.

She leaned forward.

There was a kind of poison, she'd heard, that mice would eat and then go away to die. She couldn't, just couldn't love another mouse.

She would tell Jane to stay away, too. She stood and massaged her hands. She rolled her shoulders and rotated her neck. The Lord gave and the Lord took away. It was his game.

The next morning was as bleak as the one before, but it was as good a time as any to talk to Jane. Then she could get on with her life. She dressed and set out, striding long and fast.

She rounded to the other side of the bluff and stopped. What was that in front of Jane's house?

It was a banner, with long red and yellow flags, flying fifteen feet to the horizon atop twenty-foot poles. Beneath it was a table full of sparkling things arranged on an orange cloth.

Dara stiffened her back. She would not be distracted by whatever it was Jane was up to now. Let her be as crazy as she wanted, but on her own side of the bluff. Dara would tell her ...

She approached the table. There was a teapot on it, a squat yellow one. Beside it were two cups and two saucers, blue and green, and an orange creamer and sugar bowl. Behind these stood Jane's colored bottles from the console, and Jane was right: In the sun, they transformed the morning light into something celestial. Dara reached for one.

"You're early!"

She spun around. Jane was behind her. Her cheeks and lips were red, and she was sweating. She'd been dancing, Dara knew without asking.

"Early for what?" she asked, then winced. She really didn't want to know.

"For my tag sale."

"Your ...?"

"You know, a yard sale."

"You're crazy."

"Why?"

"Who'll come?"

"Well, you came."

"Jane, you didn't put signs on the highway did you?"

"No, I never thought of it. But it might be a good idea—"

"No, please don't!"

"I don't suppose I will. You're going to buy me out of business anyway, aren't you?"

"No. That's not what—"

"Look at the colors of this tea set."

"No."

"You didn't see all the bottles. Look at the green one." She held it out.

"Jane, I want to talk."

"Of course. We'll talk at your place over tea, with your new tea set."

"I'm not going to buy—"

"Did you see this sweater?"

"No, I …" Her breath caught in her throat. No, she hadn't seen the sweater. It was pearlescent aqua blue with white pearl buttons. It was exactly like the one her mother wore in the photograph. Dara took it from Jane. "Where did you find this?"

"I've had it for ages. I dearly loved it fifteen years ago when I was slimmer. I think it might fit you. Try it on."

It fit. "How much?"

"Oh, it's not for money. We trade."

"No, I don't have anything to trade." She gripped the sweater.

"You must have something. You've got stacks of boxes."

"No, nothing you'd want."

"How do you know?"

"I know."

"How?"

"Because. I don't have anything nice like this. It's just plastic containers and towels and stuff."

"You have plastic containers?"

"Not Tupperware. Just cheap stuff."

"I love the cheap stuff."

So they spent the afternoon unpacking boxes, hunting for plastic containers. Jane seemed determined to increase her supply.

Meanwhile, the boxes got unpacked, and painlessly. Jane acted like it was Christmas, delighting over the craziest things, like the old enamel saucepan with orange flowers and a chipped-out bottom from when Dara had left it on the burner. Jane pronounced it "charming." She was welcome to it.

Jane found the yellow curtains that had hung in her father's kitchen. "You know," she said, "these would look nice in your bedroom. You'd wake to yellow light."

"I have curtains in the bedroom."

"Mm. Navy blue. Not a good light. But I expect they'd make a lovely tablecloth."

"They're curtains."

"Says you."

In five minutes, the blue curtains were shaken outside and spread over the kitchen table.

Jane pulled a yellow water glass from another box and put a bouquet of mesquite twigs in it. Dara had never put flowers on her table before. But her mother had.

Jane found some gold foil Christmas paper packed around some coffee cups and crimped it around wire hangers.

"What are you doing?" Dara asked her.

"Go busy yourself elsewhere," she said. "I'm up to something."

"I see that," Dara said, but she pulled a box into the living room to unpack there.

"I found more plastic tubs," she announced a half hour later.

"Great! Bring them here!"

Dara gathered them up and walked into the bedroom. And stopped.

Jane had done a work. She'd pulled a mirror from its plastic frame and set it on the dresser with three bottles of perfume Dara had forgotten she owned. She'd placed a lamp and the kachina doll opposite this. She'd hung another mirror over the dresser.

The hangers she'd decorated hung on the wall, and from them hung Dara's baby clothes. The pictures Dara had left stacked on the dresser were now tucked into the mirror frame.

Dara circled the room. The bedroom looked like it belonged, if not in a magazine, then in a happy home. "Thanks," she whispered, but she thought Jane might not have heard. She cleared her throat to try again.

"You have my plastic containers?" Jane asked.

"They're nothing much. You really need them?"

"Yes, ever so much."

And the barter was made. Jane disappeared with her treasures and returned with the sweater. And the bottles and the tea set.

"No, Jane, you can't," Dara said.

But she did, and when Dara saw the bottles arranged in the sunlight of her bedroom window, and when she saw the yellow pot on her blue tablecloth, she couldn't speak.

So Jane boiled the water, and together they shared a pot of mint tea and a plate of toast. Dara held her blue cup over its saucer with the tips of her fingers like the duchess, and smelled the rising steam.

"A nearly proper afternoon tea," Jane called it. "You didn't ask me to pick up biscuits at the store."

"I'll do better next time," Dara promised, and smiled at her friend.

It was nearly dark when Jane left. Dara went to the kitchen to clean up. When she turned on the light, she saw something vanish into the corner between the refrigerator and the wall. She crept closer and looked along the gap where the thing had gone and saw a mouse sniffing a wad of lint, out of her reach, and unworried. She took the last slice of toast from the table and crumbled it on the floor. She bit into the other half, left the kitchen, and turned out the light.

The morning sun was white, shot with streaks of color from the bottles. She sat up in bed and propped a pillow behind her back. She looked at the green checkered sundress on the wall. She used to like that dress best, she remembered. It was stained a little in front. She'd probably dribbled SpaghettiOs on it. She vaguely remembered her mother coaxing her to wear something else while Dara put her little foot down. This one and no other. Why? With its stains and tears, it was nothing special now, but she had loved it. Who washed it and put it away? Probably her father. Her mother would have gotten all the stains out. She would have known the tricks.

She swung out of bed and walked to the bathroom. The movement felt good. She rotated her neck. No pain this morning. She ran the water till it was warm and soaked a fresh washcloth. She held it to her eyes a moment before moving it over her forehead and scrubbing around her nostrils. Jane was right. Jesus would use cotton cloths. He would know all the tricks.

What should she name the new mouse? she wondered. "Mickey" was too obvious. How about "Mighty"? She remembered watching the cartoon with her mother. It was a good name.

She got dressed and set off to find Jane. There were just small bits of snow beneath the bushes now. The combination of the cold morning air and the warmth of the morning sun made the walk easy. She felt the voice's presence and smiled. Why not let it tag along?

She walked up the steps to Jane's house and stopped. There was a note taped to the door that read, "Gone to church."

Church? It was Tuesday. What church?

Oh, of course. She knew where Jane was.

Dara slowed when she reached the entrance of the gorge, leaned inside, and called out, "Jane?"

No answer. She peered inside the gorge and stepped back. The place seemed too holy to be safe. She climbed the hill and looked down the other side. There was Jane, pulling a board off the smaller of the two shacks. Dara trudged down the hill to meet her.

"Hope you brought your hammer!" Jane flashed a smile over her shoulder.

"Why?"

"The church needs repair if we're to spend much time here!"

"Jane, it's a shack!"

"No, I think it was meant to be a church."

"Maybe. Maybe a hundred years ago."

Jane picked up a hammer and dug some nails from a box. She grabbed the board she'd just pulled from the other shack. She nailed the board over the gap between two wallboards. "We just patch it up like this, see? Then we work out the roof somehow, and we have our church. A carpenter would do it better, I expect."

"A carpenter would tear it down."

"What else do you have to do today?"

Dara didn't answer. Jane smiled and handed her a hammer.

Weeks later, Dara lay at the bottom of the gorge with her arms folded beneath her head, gazing at the turquoise bit of sky atop.

It was one of several spring mornings that had recently softened the desert plain. Modest yellow flowers budded along the mesquite stalks. The hills glowed with drifts of purple tint from the tiniest of flowers massed low on the sand.

The desert had warmed, but the dirt was chilly in the shadows. Still, it was sweet-smelling dirt. It was a fine feeling, being in this place that really did feel like the sheltering cup of a hand.

She heard Jane just outside the gorge, talking on her cell phone to her brother. "Oh, another one quit? Oh, sorry. What? Me? At the dismal wages you pay?"

Behind Jane, Dara heard the wind chimes they'd hung from the eaves: tall copper pipes that rang like church bells, knelling calls to worship at odd moments. The air pulsed with the whispering voice. Dara closed her eyes and breathed it in.

In the weeks she and Jane had taken to fix up the church, she'd gotten used to the voice's breath in her ear. At first she'd whistled, talked to Jane about the weather, discussed the finer points of shanty church decor—anything to drown it out. But she never had been a wellspring of small talk. She just ran out of things to say, and again she was stuck with the voice.

Well, what harm could it do? It was the air, the desert wind.

What if she told Jane about it?

Somehow, she doubted it would raise a ripple. Jane would just go on twirling around sagebrush. *What?* she'd ask in her prim British voice. *You hear only one?*

The duchess probably had a whole crew talking to her. The way she danced in the desert like someone had her by the waist. The way she perched at the edge of the bluff, laughing at some joke nobody in the world had told.

And that was a worry, wasn't it? What do you make of someone who hears voices in her head?

Well.

Dara decided not to divulge.

The chimes sounded a sonorous call. And she was freezing now. She stood and brushed herself off, then walked out of the gorge into the bright morning. Jane turned in her pacing, gave a little wave, and then switched the phone to the other hand. "Well, but then there'd be the traveling again. You've got Clemmie to think of."

Dara entered the church and sat on a pillow. They'd hung Visqueen plastic on the windows, so it was nicely warm inside.

The pillows were outlandish productions—yellow ones, orange and red and fiery green, big pillows, and all in tasseled silk, tossed in the corner. Where did Jane find these things? The place looked like a lovers' hideaway, not a church.

"Shouldn't we have pews in here?" she'd asked.

"Why should we?"

"It feels like we should have servant boys with feather fans to keep us cool."

"Well!" Jane grinned. "If we had any ..."

Dara swung a pillow, and Jane dodged.

So they worshipped on silk and tassels, and it seemed to suit the voice just fine.

Good for the voice.

Dara eyed the pictures they'd hung on the wall, clustered

between the windows like stations of the cross.

She'd seen the stations once, when she was ten. She'd gone with her father on a summer morning, when he finished up a repair in the outer wall of the Catholic church in Los Cuervos.

He told her to wait on the lawn, but it was hot that day, even on the grass, even when she took her sandals off. The cicadas in the trees chattered like rattlesnakes.

She found a side door open, and from it blew a whiff of cool air, scented with something earthy and sweet. She looked inside and found a sanctuary spread with ruby and sapphire light from the windows. She stepped in, and the coolness from the terra-cotta tile rushed into her bare feet like water and washed the heat of the day up through her body and out the top of her head.

She walked down the side aisle toward the front, where a table lay covered with a white cloth, with statues on either side, and behind all, a cross with Jesus dying. This was nothing like the church she attended.

She heard someone clearing his throat, and turned. A priest stood near the open door, smiling.

Had she done something wrong? Her father hadn't said she could come inside.

"Sometimes people come here to pray," said the priest.

"I was just looking at the pictures," she said. She hadn't been, but she felt the need for an excuse.

"They're not just pictures," he replied, and he took her through the story of Jesus' agony, one station at a time. There was one of Jesus being told he must die, one of the soldiers whipping his back, one of him taking the cross. Several of him falling. Fourteen in all, and when the priest was done, Dara turned to find her father there, ready to go. He wasn't mad.

"So much suffering," was all he said. "You'd think they'd let him have his resurrection."

The shanty church was less grand than the Catholic church had been, but the morning Dara found Jane hanging her pictures, it somehow held the same ponderous sense of suffering.

There was Max ... there was Lena ... and Fernando. There was an older couple she hadn't seen before. They looked posed and uncomfortable. Jane held their picture suspended an anguished moment before she hung it on its nail.

Dara didn't ask what the trouble was. It didn't seem she should.

But she knew what she would do. She walked home and got her own pictures: the photo of her parents on their honeymoon, the two portraits from the mantel. She dug out the wedding picture of herself in a white sundress, cheerily half-witted between her haggard father and her insolent new husband.

Her own private stations of the cross.

She hadn't looked at the wedding photo in some time. It made her sick, just holding it. Still, she took it back to the church, hammered the nail, and thrust the picture on the wall.

But later, when she'd walked past a time or two, she took it down. She stuffed it under the table they'd made their altar, beneath the cloth, which hung to the floor, and Jane didn't ask any questions.

It didn't matter. The bare spot between two windows told the story. Dara turned away, reclining into the cushioned corner. The sunlight warmed her through. "My beloved," she heard. She stroked a pillow like it was a hand and then dozed.

She awoke to Jane whistling from just the other side of the Visqueen. Dara crawled out of the pillows, stood, and walked outside.

Jane stood on tiptoe, painting a floral garland around the window. She'd only gotten one daisy done, but it was clear where she was heading because she had already done the door and the other window. It was something a gypsy might have done to his wagon.

Dara shook her head. "When is this place going to look wild enough for you?"

"Wild! That's a fine word, don't you think?"

There was no making sense of Jane. Why try? Dara climbed the hill and sat on a rock, humming. It was a fine day, a fine, broad pastel plain.

Why try to make sense of anything? She'd come to the desert to be alone and instead she'd made friends with a fruit-cake. She'd named the mouse that pooped in her cupboards, and she'd gotten on friendly terms with the voice in her head.

Maybe she was crazy herself. People lost it sometimes, and she had her reasons.

She laughed, realizing what song she'd been humming. It was one Kevin used to sing about a woman who went crazy because her boyfriend left. He used to sing it with his friends, not with her—with a beer in one hand and an imaginary woman on his arm, swiveling his hips and making the song repulsive. Dara tried laughing anyway, just for the attention, and he turned his laughter and his swiveling on her like blades, like *she* was Delta Dawn, and she pulled back, not knowing why she felt pathetic.

But Delta Dawn was a wimp. Her troubles didn't even compare.

Dara clasped her elbows around her head. The memories just waited, ready to spring if she cracked the door. She could slam it shut, but stuff always got through. Like blood on the refrigerator. Like a rusted Toyota truck sailing off a cliff …

She squeezed her elbows tight to her temples.

Crazy was fine. Crazy beat reality to hell and around the block and back again. It was shameful, but she was desperate to be happy, despite the thing she'd done.

Desperate was the word. The smile she practiced that morning before the mirror was hideous with toothy despera-tion. But it was a smile, and she'd take it. In time, it might settle in and get natural.

A light finger brushed a tear from her cheek. She accepted its touch and swayed into the tug and pull of the voice and slowly came to realize that the touch was not the wind, but a real hand, small and light like a breeze—but with new calluses. She turned.

Jane smiled and pushed the hair from Dara's forehead. "In time," she said.

Dara sprang to her feet and strode past Jane and down the hill. "Was I talking?" she demanded.

"No," Jane answered, following. "Why?"

"In time, what?"

"In time ..." They stopped at the foot of the hill near the church. "In time, you'll ..." Jane shrugged.

Dara's hands tensed. Her nails dug into her palms. "In time, I'll accept. In time, I'll understand. In time, I'll ..." She wanted badly to hit Jane. She kicked a small rock a good ten feet. "In time, I'll *feel* better! Right?"

Jane flinched but stood firm. Dara felt a hard pain at the base of her throat, as if she'd swallowed that rock. She tried to choke it down, but everything about her seemed to fold in around it. She choked again, wiping the moisture from her nose and across her cheek. She brushed her eyes with the back of her arm and staggered. Jane caught her by the shoulders. They sank to the ground, and she cried into Jane's shirt in haggard, desperate sobs.

When she was spent, she sat on a rock to rest and watched the sky pale and deepen into dusk, with no awareness of the passage of time. At last, Jane laid a campfire, and the flames caught Dara's gaze.

"Come close to the fire," said Jane. Dara straightened and focused her eyes.

"Come on," she urged. "It's warmer here."

Dara stood and walked the few steps to the fire. Jane put two foil bundles in the flames.

"What's that?" Dara asked.

"Dinner. Beef and vegetables. Hungry?"

Dara nodded. Jane put an enamel coffeepot on the fire.

It was quiet while they ate, soothingly quiet. Jane had made a good supper. It was the food that brought Dara back, that made her aware that the air had turned brisk and the fire was warm, that down her chin dripped a bit of beef juice, which she caught with the back of her hand—that she'd sat on a pebble that was wearing a hole in her thigh. She shifted.

Jane began to hum. Dara glanced up from her food. The duchess ate with her mouth shut, but past that bit of potato she was chewing came music.

"What?" Jane asked, still chewing.

"You're not supposed to hum at the table."

"Oh. We're not at a table."

Dara grinned.

"Who decides these things, anyway?" asked Jane.

"I don't know."

"Why do people like rules so much, Dara? We're obsessed with rules."

"You're a missionary."

"So?"

"Missionaries like rules. Or they're supposed to."

"Supposed to! Yes, I guess we are. But why?"

"Because you're Christians." Dara shrugged. "Christians keep rules."

"Ah. Why is that?"

"Maybe you've never been to Sunday school, but I have. They're supposed to."

"Mm. Supposed to."

"Yeah." She grinned.

"Ah."

That settled, Dara took another bite. Jane hummed.

And then stopped humming. "Jesus, you know," she said as she swallowed the lump of meat she was chewing, "was a consummate rule breaker." She tapped the air with her plastic fork.

Dara tried to ignore her.

"He was. Read the Bible, and you'll see I'm right. A consummate rule breaker. He worked on the Sabbath, he didn't wash for dinner—"

"Yeah, well, when you're God—"

"I'll bet he liked to hum. I'll bet he hummed at the table, and in the loo, and in church …"

Dara took a bite and looked away.

"You know what I'm humming?"

"I'm about to."

Jane sang, her fork beating a waltz tempo in the air. "Look in his eyes you can see what he feels for you, Thence come the swings and the sways and the reels, or you—"

Dara shook her head. "I assumed you'd hum something spiritual."

"Ah."

"Didn't you sing any nice Christian songs in Mexico?"

"Of course. Lena taught me one I like very much." She began to sing. Her voice was boisterously bad, and Dara ducked her head, embarrassed to be sung to, shy of the eye contact. Of course, Jane sang in Spanish, so Dara had no idea what the song was about. She focused on chewing the bit of meat in her mouth.

Something in the song made her look up and stop chewing midbite. Jane had stood and was now singing to the stars. No surprise there of course, but there was something about it all. The song did something that made Dara wonder what was meant by "charged particles," because the particles really seemed charged at this moment. She could almost feel their hidden colors through her skin. The song danced a shindig with all the little bits of air and made them twirl into the stars, do-si-do and promenade.

Dara swallowed her bite. She stood and then realized she had stood. Her hands lifted with the particles of air, and she began to spin, sidestep round the fire, rock, and swing the other way. She caught the words of the song and began to sing along, not knowing what they meant but somehow getting the joyful, loving drift of them.

Jane danced too of course, but the odd thing was that she did what Dara did, at the same moment. Although at the moment, it didn't seem odd at all. Later, Dara would remember tossing her head so her hair swung like a lasso, and catching a glimpse of Jane doing the same. She would remember they both twirled round and round that fire and never once bumped together.

At last breathless, they stood on opposite sides of the glowing coals, smiling in the moonlight. They let the embers cool beneath the stars, staggered into the church, and lay on the pillows. Jane pulled open two blankets she'd left folded beside the pile.

"In time."

Dara heard the whisper. She turned to Jane, but Jane was already asleep. She snuggled into a pillow, wrapped a hand around her pearl, and drifted off in the Visqueen-filtered moonlight.

When she awoke, she clenched her eyes shut against the sunlight shining red through her eyelids. She'd had a dream—something freakish about birds in the kitchen, clapping white wings that smelled of cinnamon. Bizarre, but pleasant.

She rolled out of the glare, stretched, and opened her eyes. Where—oh, she remembered. Did she really dance around that fire? Must have, because here she was, waking up on a pile of silk pillows in a shanty church.

She was losing it for sure.

Well. It was much too cozy, and she'd slept much too well to worry about it now.

But where was Jane? Dara rose and went outside.

The embers had died, leaving a scattering of burnt wood in a fine gray ash, in a charred ring of rocks. A pair of yellow jackets bothered a greasy bit of foil that had fallen into the fire. She shooed them away, picked the foil up by the edge, and put it in the plastic grocery bag they used for garbage.

She climbed the hill to look for Jane. And there was the duchess, quickstepping across the plain, some four hundred feet away. Singing softly, Dara tramped downhill to join her.

She hushed herself, for she'd been singing the Spanish song they'd sung the night before. She had to be careful if she didn't want to find herself spinning round fires again, this time with face paint, maybe. She set her feet down hard as she walked, resisting the lightness, the jubilation pressing in from the air. But some untold joke was just too good, and she laughed aloud.

She closed in on Jane, though the duchess didn't see—her eyes were closed. Why didn't she bump into bushes? This struck Dara as hysterical, and she laughed again.

Jane pirouetted five times in Dara's direction and stopped short, nose to nose with her, before she opened her eyes, her arms still curved above her head like the petals of a tulip.

They regarded each other in silence. Jane's breasts quaked with joy before she laughed aloud. Then Dara laughed, and they collapsed into each other, nearly falling over. They righted themselves, struggling for composure, each trying to suck her mouth into normal position. But then their eyes met, and they lost it, slapping each other's arms in great horselaughs they could not contain. It hurt to laugh like that, so they looked away from each other and brought themselves down by stages, from horselaughs to cackles, to chuckles, to sighs. They wiped tears from their eyes and staggered apart to catch their breath.

Dara loved this feeling. Had she ever felt so light?

"You are my own!" the voice sang to her.

"I am, aren't I!" She giggled.

"My beloved," said the voice.

"My darling," she teased, low and breathy.

"Come away."

She froze in place.

"Come away, my beloved," the voice coaxed. It was serious!

"No," she said.

"What?" she heard Jane ask.

"Nothing!"

"Had breakfast?"

"Come away …"

"No!" Dara said.

"… my beloved."

"Why don't we have scrambled eggs at my place?" Jane walked toward her.

"No." She shook her head and backed away. "No. No!"

"Dara?"

"No!" She ran across the plain, up the porch steps, and into her house. She shut the door behind her. "No!"

Crazy had ceased to be fun. It was just a disembodied voice that didn't know its place, and she'd had enough. She clutched her pearl and yanked it back and forth along the chain, sounding a high, rapid-fire *zip-zip-zip* that helped somewhat to drown the whispers.

She heard footsteps on her porch. "Dara?" Jane called.

"Yeah?" She held her voice steady and pressed her back against the door.

"You all right?"

"Yeah. I'm … I'm okay." The long silence seemed to call for an explanation she did not want to give. "Just a little sick, Jane. I don't think you should come in."

"All right. I'll check back later."

"Yeah. Okay." She heard Jane leave.

She'd get busy. But doing what? The wood was chopped and rechopped. Her house was clean. But clean was not the issue, movement was, so she went to the kitchen and fetched the scouring powder and a bucket of water. She scrubbed the sink, the stove, and the refrigerator, and then she scoured the floor. She scoured the walls, the table, and chairs. Then she moved on to the bathroom and scoured it, top to bottom. She took the shower curtain down and laid it out on the bedroom floor, scoured it and put it back, and then proceeded to the living room. She'd cleaned halfway across the floor when she ran out of cleanser. This struck her as one grief too many, and she collapsed against the coffee table and cried into her sleeve. She crawled onto the sofa and sobbed into the cushion till she slept.

And dreamt.

CHAPTER 4

*S*he felt herself rocking and falling, her face ramming on a rock, slamming, and then the rock became a refrigerator door, and still the slamming. She heard a roar that formed itself into words. "You ugly slut! You hideous piece of ..."

She heard her own voice whimpering, her mouth spread taut from side to side: "Eeeeee ..."

She awoke to find the whimpering real, her knees pulled tight to a belly wrenched in knots. She pressed her face into the cushion. "Eeeeeee ..."

It was too much.

She pulled her legs around and sat up. She walked to the bathroom and splashed cold water on her eyes. The face in the mirror looked salt-burned and swollen.

"You make me sick!" Kevin used to say when she looked that way.

She could see why. She *was* hideous, the saliva spreading wet between her open lips. She backed away from the sight and slid down the wall to the floor.

Whispers. She shook her head. Kevin's voice had once come in whispers. In the vacant lot next to the Shell station, behind an old shed out of the light of the street lamp, he'd whispered into her neck. "Mine," he'd said then. "Mine."

She pushed her head against the tile wall, then pulled forward and slammed it—*bam!*—back again. What was it about a man like that, that makes you breathe by every word he says? That makes you beg him—*bam!*—never fighting back—*bam!*— you just take it—*bam!*—until he's spent. Until he goes to sleep.

Well, maybe he's right. You think of the whispering faces at the supermarket, the knowing smiles. Is there one face in all of it that sees anything in you, one face that would cry with you now?

Yes. There is one, and he must never know. The one face that loves you must never see bruises. What would he do?

Soon enough you find out. One day your father stalks white-lipped into the market, yanks your arm, and pulls you to his truck. His jaw bristles with silver whiskers. "He hits you," he yells. "Why didn't you tell me?"

You have no answer.

"I'll tell you this." He turns the key in the ignition. "You're coming home with me. That piece of scum better keep away from you, or I'll kill him."

At home, your father sits you down and looks hard into your eyes. "They want to know why I let you marry a man who beats you."

You stare at the table.

"They want to know what I did to make you marry him."

You look up at the tears pooled in his eyes.

"Dara," he pleads. "What did I do?"

"Nothing, Daddy."

"They think maybe I touched you. Dara, they think you ran away because I …" He raises his hands, looking for a word clean enough to say. "Because I touched you." His shoulders wretch. Saliva pools like tears at the corners of his mouth. "Just let that filthy piece of dirt come around here. He'll wish he was never born!"

Kevin does come for you. And your father is ready for him—that's what he thinks. But he has no idea the rage in this man.

Kevin looms tall and muscular over your father. He answers threat for threat, ever louder, ever more menacing, and you know well what he can do.

You run to his truck, get in, and plead, Please, please can you go home now? You'll go with him. Please?

He swaggers back to the truck, and his wheels scream as he drives away. He howls filth at you, he calls you "mine," and he drives like a devil.

Everything shakes. Your stomach shakes. You fix your eyes

out the window and squeeze your hands between your knees. So afraid.

Suddenly Kevin falls silent and the truck slows down.

He says not a word. He says nothing for so long it sickens you to think what that might mean.

You glance at him. His lips are pinched, his eyes narrowed to slits.

Outside Kevin's window, your father catches up in his truck. "Pull over!" he bellows.

Oh, dear God. You understand! Kevin is quiet because he is planning!

He doesn't look at your father, doesn't slow down or speed up. He drives past your street, around three corners, through three stop signs, and all the while your father keeps pace, jaw set, lips working, and Kevin has a plan! You open your mouth, but you can't say a word.

The vein in Kevin's temple pulses because his teeth are clenched, but he breathes slow and steady.

The truck crosses the bridge over Myer River and onto the winding two-lane road. On one side is the sheer rock from which the road is cut. On the other side is a hundred-and-fifty-foot drop to the riverbed.

Kevin has a plan! Now he bears down hard on the gas pedal, and you whip around tight corners at eighty miles per hour.

"Please, Dad," you pray, but your father keeps pace.

Kevin has a plan, and his moment comes. At just the right corner, he taps the brake so that your father pulls ahead. Kevin flips his steering wheel sideways and rams the back corner of your father's truck. You watch it go over the edge, out and down, like a bug flicked from a table. As you speed past, you watch your father fall from sight, his fingers gripping the handle over the door, his mouth slack, his eyes fixed on you.

Kevin hasn't planned everything though, and when he returns to his lane, there's a car in the way. It nicks the truck and sends it spinning.

The truck strikes the rock wall on Kevin's side, leaving him with a broken neck. Leaving him dead. And you shrieking in great biting spasms, curled on the seat beside him in a ball.

What is it about a man like him that makes you give him everything you've got to break?

Dara lay back against the wall now, lulled, beyond tears.

There was more to this pain, she knew. She stood and walked to the porch to get some air, and told herself what it was: She alone had given Kevin everything to break. Nothing and no one had made her do it. And in the end, while her husband worked his plan on that road, she said nothing, did nothing to save her father's life.

Hadn't the sheriff's investigator asked her fifteen ways to Sunday if she'd tried to stop Kevin? Well, what had she done? She'd sat beside him whimpering. That's all.

Hideous.

She slumped to the porch floor, bent her head forward, and flung it back—*bam! bam! bam!*—for the hideous filth she was!

She clasped her hand around her pearl pendant and slid it back and forth along the chain. "Remember the pearl," her father had told her. But that was before this thing she'd done to him. She tightened her grip and yanked hard. The necklace broke free, and she flung it into the desert.

She thought she was done crying, but you can cry without tears. She sobbed in dry wracking spasms till she was spent. She traced a finger along the raised wood patterns of the floor beside her.

"And you listen to voices in your head," she accused herself. Voices that called her "mine." She shook her head.

She listened to her breath. It had grown so steady! She felt a gust of cool wind and heard thunder in the distance, a low grumbling sound. Lightning arced over the bluff, and the thunder cracked, harsh and clear.

Something inside had turned resolutely firm. She stood to face the storm.

A cloud flashed on the horizon over the hills, and the thunder muttered.

"You could have caught him!" she answered.

A flash. A roar.

"You could have done it just once for a good man!"

She pictured her father's weathered face, quiet amid clean smiling people who'd never bothered to know him.

"How many times did he sit in your church? He did everything you wanted him to! Everything!"

The thunder growled, low and sullen.

"Because he loved you! He loved you! Didn't you see him?"

Lightning whipped over the plain. To show she was not afraid, she marched herself down the steps.

"I'll tell you one thing," she said. "I am not crazy! There'll be no more voices, do you hear me?"

A grumble.

She took courage. "And I'm not 'coming away,' you understand? I'm staying right here!" She jumped twice to punctuate her words with her two feet on the desert sand.

Three bolts of lightning cracked over the bluff, and the thunder rang loud and long.

"Because!" She fell to her knees and whimpered. "Because I never meant to hurt him. I got it all wrong, and I didn't know what to do, and I couldn't make—it—stop!"

Raindrops began to fall. Little soft ones that traced her cheeks like fingertips.

Thunder rolled like eiderdown, and she said, "I'm sorry. I'm so sorry. Oh please, tell me—did you catch him?"

The rain fell heavy and gentle, as if poured from ladles. As water washed over her, Dara let the thunder have its say, and she knelt on the desert floor and listened.

Oh, the thunder had a lot to say, and really Dara couldn't say exactly what it was. But she heard. In that firm new place, she heard it all.

The next morning the desert gleamed in the aura of a double rainbow. Dara took in the view from her porch step, her hands folded around one knee. It was safe to assume the voice had someplace in mind. "Just please," she whispered, "not Los Cuervos."

She watched Jane swinging between the rainbows, flitting from arc to arc where they touched the sand, pausing to let the colors slip through her spread fingers.

"I guess I should tell the duchess." Dara stood and brushed off the backs of her legs, while Jane twirled sideways like a bent leaf. "Seems to me she'll understand perfectly." She set out to join her friend.

When she drew near, Jane staggered a bit before righting herself. "There you are! Feeling better?"

Dara shrugged. "I'm fine."

"What is it?"

"Nothing."

"Nothing?"

"I'm going away."

"You're going away?"

"Yeah." Dara walked past her.

"Where?" Jane hurried to keep up.

"I don't know."

"You don't know?"

"That's what I said, Jane." Dara didn't want her asking why not, but of course that was next if she didn't talk quick. "You'll be okay here?"

"Well, I won't be here."

"You won't?" Dara stopped. "Because of me?"

"Dear as you are, no. Because of Tom, my brother. I'm going to be a waitress!"

"A waitress. And this excites you."

"Well, I've never done it before. It could be fun."

"You're really lonely, aren't you?"

"No, not lonely. He needs my help."

"Well, good." Dara resumed her walk. "Then I won't worry

about you out here by yourself."

"Nor I you." She kept up with Dara. "But why don't you know where you're going?"

"I don't know, Jane. I don't have everything worked out. I just think it's time to go."

The duchess chuckled.

"What?" asked Dara.

"So do I."

"So do you what?"

"Think it's time to go."

"Well, good." Dara sniffed. "You'll like Brittlebush—it's a nice town."

"Do you think so?"

"Sure. It's bigger than Los Cuervos. It's got a Wal-Mart."

"And how do you like the climate?"

"Oh, the climate?" Dara rolled her eyes. "Why, Brittlebush is warm and temperate, with pleasant weather year-round. The rain falls between eleven and midnight, Sunday through Thursday nights, leaving weekends dry to accommodate the local nightlife." She laughed with the duchess. "You can *see* Brittlebush from the hills, Jane. You've *been* to Brittlebush, Jane. It's the same as here, hot and dusty or freezing cold, with about five minutes in between."

"The nightlife's much the same, as well."

"Right." Dara grinned. "So what are you talking about?"

"I'm talking about you coming with me."

"With you?"

"Why don't you, Dara? You could work for my brother in the restaurant. He can't pay much, but he's got a two-bedroom trailer in his backyard we could stay in, and he truly needs the help."

"I've never worked in a restaurant."

"Neither have I."

"Aren't there actual restaurant people in Brittlebush?"

"Of course! And many have worked for him, but they keep quitting."

"Why do they quit?"

"Because he pays so little. And the lack of business discourages them."

Dara shook her head. "Sounds like a dream job."

"I really wish you would. I'll miss you if you don't."

Dara stopped walking and clapped a hand to her mouth to quiet the emotion that sounded in her throat. "You would?"

"Of course! Won't you miss me?"

Yes, she would miss her. It stunned her to know this so suddenly. She would miss this valley and her home, but mostly she would miss the duchess. She nodded.

"Then why not come with me?" Jane placed a hand on her arm. "If you don't have someplace else?"

"Okay." A whisper was the best she could do.

"Really?"

She nodded.

"Oh, Dara, I'm so glad!" Jane hugged her.

After a moment's shock, Dara responded. "But I won't sell my place," she said.

"Of course you won't," said Jane. "There won't be time."

She pulled back. "There won't? Why?"

"Because we leave tomorrow."

"Tomorrow!" Dara muttered to the surrounding air as she stuffed the washer full of jeans and T-shirts. "All of a sudden, it's a big hurry."

She'd thrown out all her packing boxes, so Jane gave her some of hers. Two, to be exact. "The trailer's furnished," she'd explained. "Just pack the necessities."

Whatever those were.

Two boxes wouldn't even hold her clothes. But she could pack those in suitcases and trash bags. She dumped a quarter carton of milk down the drain and glanced around the kitchen. Jane said there'd be dishes and pots and pans. But she said nothing about a coffeepot. Dara put that in the box on the chair. That and the teapot and cups Jane had given her. She picked these up by the handles, and they clinked together as if a train were rolling by. Her hands were shaking! She folded her arms across her chest and breathed deeply to calm herself. There was plenty to keep her busy, and that was good. She'd pack and repack these two boxes all night if she had to. But she would not grieve for the safety of her desert home. If she did, she might never leave.

She reached for her pearl.

Her *pearl!* Her father's last gift to her, and she'd thrown it away!

She remembered pitching it, watching it hurtle end over gleaming end into the lowering sky. She darted to the front door and burst outside, praying, *Please, please, please.*

She'd thrown it from *here*, sitting on the porch floor. It would've gone …

She scanned the area around the step, descended the stairs, and walked a slow zigzag in front of the house. Nothing. She went out twenty feet. Dara couldn't imagine throwing that far, but given her state of mind the previous night … She searched another ten feet. Nothing, nothing.

Please!

She examined a wide arc from one side of the yard to the other. She looked around both sides of the house. The pearl would have had to turn corners to land there, but she didn't know what else to do.

She picked up a small rock, then climbed the porch steps, sat where she had the night before, and pitched the rock the way she'd thrown her pearl. She watched where it landed and ran to search the area. No good.

She thought of her father's reasoning: If you can't find something in the logical places, check the illogical ones. So she looked all around the house, front and back, five times as far as she could throw. No good at all.

She went back inside and glanced around, then went to the bedroom closet and lowered herself into the crawlspace.

Definitely illogical, but …

It wasn't there. She checked the shed.

And the closets and the drawers in every room in the house.

And the desert floor, ten times as far as she could throw.

And twenty times as far.

At two in the morning she lay in bed before an open window, exhausted. The contents of her kitchen, living room, bedroom, and bathroom were rummaged and scattered—but not packed. She turned from the moonlit breeze that stroked her arm, and cried, "My pearl!"

Hours later she lumbered out of bed and staggered through the living room to answer the door. "What time is it?" she asked Jane, squinting in the light.

"Are you just waking up?" Jane asked as she entered. "It's six o'clock!"

"Six o'clock!" Dara collapsed onto the couch, fingering her collarbone.

Jane scanned the unpacked mess in the living room.

"I'm sorry." Dara shook her head. "I was looking for—"

"This?" Jane dangled the pearl from its broken chain.

"You found it!" She scrambled to her feet. "Where?"

Jane pulled it back from her grasp. "Just a sec." She unfastened the chain around her own neck, slipped the locket off, and dropped it into her pocket. "It was hanging from the faucet outside—rather hidden." She slid Dara's pearl off its own chain and onto hers. "I can't imagine how it got there. A sunbeam caught it just as I approached, or I wouldn't have seen it." She fastened it around Dara's neck. "There now, let's tidy up here, and we're on our way!"

Dara had begun to ponder the thing she'd consented to do.

They were in Brittlebush, but Tom was nowhere to be found. They'd been to the restaurant, gone to his house, and back to the restaurant again. At eleven o'clock in the morning, the place was closed. Jane used her cell phone to leave Tom a voice message, while Dara paced the sidewalk.

The hum and gust of traffic overwhelmed her: cars idling behind other cars waiting for parking spaces, small trucks on big tires gunning their engines. How long had it been since she'd heard this noise? When she came to Brittlebush for groceries she'd always come late at night—when she couldn't get Jane to do it for her. She tucked herself into the shadows near the restaurant door.

Jane snapped her cell phone shut. "I *told* him we were coming!"

"When?"

"The day before yesterday. Well—I left him a message."

"You didn't know I was coming the day before yesterday."

"Well, I told him *that* last night." She rubbed her neck. "In a message ..."

"Maybe he never got them," Dara said. Jane leaned against the window.

The neon sign over the door read, "The Studmuffin Café." The name was circled by a yellow lasso gripped by a curvy red-haired cowgirl. Dara remembered the photograph of Tom's wife. "Is that ..."

"Yes, it is." Jane nodded. "And it looks just like her." She paced, pushing her hair from her forehead. "I wouldn't think he'd just close down his business like this."

"Looks like he did, though." Dara's words were obliterated by the throbbing bass of a passing PT Cruiser, low-slung and black with orange flames painted along the sides. The driver leaned out the window to gaze at her as he drove by. "Jane," she said when he'd rounded the corner, "we could go home."

"Well, I guess we could go back and try again tomorrow. Seems a waste, though. I wonder where he's gone."

Dara had already headed to her car. She got in and watched Jane in the side mirror. The duchess paced once or twice, walked toward her truck, stopped, and turned around. The next moment she opened Dara's car door and slid in to the passenger seat, grinning.

"What are you doing?" Dara asked.

"First, let's have lunch."

"Lunch?" Dara was getting a headache. "We can just get burgers on the way out of town. I saw a drive-through Mc—"

"No, I don't have McDonald's in mind. I know the loveliest place I've wanted to try—"

"Jane, I don't really—"

"My treat," she chirped, as if money were the issue. "Besides, it will give Tom a chance to ring me back. Just turn left at the corner up there."

In two short minutes and four hundred fifty crisply spoken words, Jane had piloted Dara to the front of a blue stucco cottage with a white sign on a wooden post: "The Teahouse." No wonder the duchess liked it. In a town full of rock gardens and parched lawns, this place was straight out of the English countryside. It was not the sort of place Dara went to, but before she could make this clear, Jane had marched inside.

Dara hesitated in the car. The place looked friendly. It had a bay window and double French doors for an entry. Pink roses climbed trellises flanked by spires of blue delphiniums. A flag-stone walkway curved to the door. It looked … too friendly.

What had possessed her to come here? This "Studmuffin Café" where she'd agreed to work was glass-fronted—like a fish tank. Dara Murphy Brogan, the girl in the newspapers, on display.

Back in Los Cuervos she'd come to think she could read people's thoughts in their eyes, could almost hear them. They all passed judgments, about the way she flustered when they asked where the canned beets were. About the loneliness that wafted from her like a stench. Then she married Kevin, and *that* set off a whole psychic talk show in their heads—with widespread speculations about a possible prenuptial pregnancy, in-depth explorations of the effects of her childhood trauma, and grave doubts as to the probable future of a girl like Dara Brogan.

After that day on Myer River Road, there was such an uproar behind their eyes she couldn't hear herself think. People came to her father's funeral, and they bowed their heads, took her hand, and murmured respectful things. But she could hear them. In their heads they accused, condemned, and clamored, and the whole funeral sounded like pots and pans crashing to the floor. She was driven out by it. She bolted as they stood around the graveside, and she sped home, threw some things in the car, and left.

Kevin's funeral was the next day, but she was already gone.

And she had let a thunderstorm convince her to go back among them? A different town, of course, and different people, but hadn't they all read the papers? Jane had guessed who she was in a minute. They only needed to hear her name to know everything about her. Her father's words, "not a safe world," had begun to pulse like a drum at the base of her skull. The last thing she needed was a "friendly place" full of roses and delphiniums and people who knew her story.

A yellow striped cat with an ample bottom strolled around the picket fence and down the walk. The door opened to let the cat in, and an older woman with blonde-white hair peered out and smiled, like the double-chinned mother of the world. Jane poked her head out beside her and waved Dara in. "It's all right," she called. "They said you could come in too!"

Dara glowered at Jane, but the duchess chattered on, oblivious. Meanwhile, the other woman waited at the door. Dara got out of the car and went inside.

And into the arms of Glenda Rawlings, the glad-hearted mother of the world.

"Oooh, do come in and let me take care of you! Harold's just finished a batch of our favorite currant scones, and you've got to try them. Why don't you just sit right here by the window and talk to Algernon, and I'll get your tea. We've got some ginger peach that goes nicely with the scones. Oh, of course, and lunch, too! But I want you to try these on me—they're so good!"

This was no restaurant. This was Glenda's home, full of sunlit polished tables, dusty bookshelves, and rose chintz. There were no other guests.

Algernon was the ample-bottomed cat, and he immediately leapt to Dara's lap. She gawked at him a moment with both hands lifted, then settled them on his back. An easy rumble vibrated through his muscular body. He pierced her blue jeans with his claws, stopping just short of her skin. It felt good.

She'd never owned a cat, or any pet, not in her father's house. Even a goldfish would have been one puckered little mouth too many to feed. He'd loved her fiercely, but she always knew what a burden it was.

Algernon had no burdens. He settled into her, warm and ponderous. She stroked his back and returned his curled pink smile.

Glenda whisked in with a tray set, with a pot of tea and a plate of scones. A bald man in a white apron followed, wiping his hands on a towel.

Glenda set the tray on the table. "I want you to meet my *dear* husband and your esteemed chef. Harold, this is Jane, and this is Dara."

"Pleased to meet you." He bowed.

Glenda took his arm and he patted her hand with his own, large and flour-dusted at the fingernails.

"Harold's a much better cook than I am, but then, he's better than anybody."

"She keeps me company," he said.

"I do. Every chance I get. I sit on a stool and tell him jokes."

"That's my secret ingredient: Glenda's laughter."

Jane bit into a scone and then rested against the back of her chair. "Mmm, good," she murmured. There were crumbs at the corners of her mouth.

Dara forgot to taste hers. She took in the way Harold's fingers played on Glenda's arm, the softness in his eyes.

Those eyes turned to her and caught her staring.

Panicked, she blurted the first thing that came to mind. "They let you have a cat in your restaurant?"

"Well, actually the restaurant's in there." He nodded toward a closed set of French doors.

"This is our living room," Glenda said. "Do you mind?"

"Not at all," said Jane.

"No." Dara focused on the animal in her lap. "I like the cat."

"He obviously likes you." Glenda smiled. "Do you have a cat of your own?"

"No. He's …" She blushed and put Algernon down.

"Dara, you've got to taste the scones," said Jane.

"Yes, do," said Glenda. "They're wonderful, I promise."

Oh, they were, the scones were good, dusted with sugar, kneaded by a kind hand with cinnamon, laughter, and currants—she could taste it.

There was laughter in the lunch too, in the chicken salad sandwiches on freshly baked bread, in the pickled asparagus, in the Earl Grey tea. The Rawlingses served them at their own table and sat down to talk.

Well, Jane and the Rawlingses talked. Dara listened. For a while she ignored their words and just basked in the voices, warm and fervent as a fireplace, bright with an instant, easy friendship. How did people *do* that?

A sudden burst of laughter startled her. She'd missed Glenda's joke. Then Harold told one—about a new pirate movie, very exciting, rated "arrrrr." She covered her mouth, laughing. It wasn't *that* funny—in fact, she'd heard it before. But this time it seemed hysterical. She removed her hand and laughed again, and then the others joined in, and the four of them laughed together. Her father's warning played at the back of her head—*not safe*—but just this once, she pushed it aside. She was having fun.

Jane's cell phone rang. "That will be Tom," she said. She excused herself to the living room, and Dara suddenly felt the weight of silence. What to say?

"More tea?" Glenda offered, and Dara said, "Yes," and wondered what to say next.

"Arrowhead?" she heard Jane exclaim. "Lake Arrowhead? Well, but that's hours away! You forgot me, didn't you? Your beloved sister!"

That simply, any need for conversation disappeared. All

ears had turned to the living room.

"Oh … then you didn't get the messages. That's what Dara thought … She's my neighbor, dear, I told you … Well when can you be home? … Good! Then we'll come by tomorrow … No, Dara's with me; you've got two of us … Tom, it's fine, dear. Don't worry … No, don't bother them. We'll get a room … Good, then. Kiss Clemmie. Bye." She disconnected.

"Fishing," Jane said when she came back. "He took Clemmie and went fishing. Never heard we were coming."

"You'll be all right," Glenda said.

"Oh yes, fine. We'll find a motel. But I would really love your recipe for pickled asparagus before we leave. If it's not a secret."

"No, it's not a secret," said Glenda, pouring tea. "We'll write it down for you. Before you leave."

Algernon resettled himself on Dara's lap. She let him stay.

The conversation picked up where it had left off, while the light from the window crept from one wall to the other, turning from yellow to lavender before disappearing altogether. Dara pretended not to notice, and as near as she could tell, no one else did—except for Harold maybe, who turned the overhead light on.

Meanwhile, lunch flowed into lemon tarts with peppermint tea—which flowed into a dinner of pot roast with red potatoes, honeyed carrots, and blackberry tea—which flowed into chamomile tea with bread pudding—topped with lots of whipped cream, thick and real and sweet as true happiness.

Finally, Jane reached under the table for her purse.

Glenda laid a hand on her arm. "You know, we have a guest room. Why not be our guests tonight?"

Dara exchanged a glance with Jane and blurted, "We'd like that." Jane raised an eyebrow. Dara straightened and turned away.

It *was* a good idea.

CHAPTER 5

*T*he room was in the attic, under a slanted ceiling painted white, with twin beds covered in red toile. The room had an earthy smell that Dara traced to a shelf of old books. There was a table between the beds, with a tasseled lamp. Glenda bustled in and out with a bowl of fruit and a jug of water. Harold stood diffidently at the door to tell them where the upstairs bathroom was. And then they said good night and shut the door.

Jane was ecstatic. "Isn't this delightful?"

Dara giggled, barely able to contain herself.

"And you!" Jane said. "Popping out of your shell like that! 'Oh, yes, we'd love to stay the night!' Who knew you could be so bold, practically inviting yourself!"

"No. No, they invited us!"

Jane smiled and grabbed her toothbrush. Dara dug hers out of her suitcase and followed.

It was embarrassing, the way Jane brushed her teeth, long and raucous, punctuated at last with a gurgle and a splat. Dara watched the door, half expecting the Rawlingses to poke their heads in to investigate.

Back in the room, Jane was out of her clothes and into her nightgown in an instant. Dara blushed to find herself watching. Jane's back was turned, and her underwear were big cotton things, so it was hardly a burlesque. It was the way she put on her nightgown that fascinated Dara. She reached her hands straight up and let the thing slide over her head, and all the way her fingertips stroked the cotton, and her nose snuffed the scent. She hopped in between the bedclothes and smelled the sheets. Leaning against her pillow, she sighed. "You never know what gifts life will bring, do you?"

This was a new thought for Dara. It began a backbeat to her father's words: not a safe world ... what gifts life will bring ... not a safe world ... what gifts ...

Dara changed into her nightgown, for the first time feeling the fabric and snuffing its smell.

When she turned around, Jane was already asleep, sitting against the headboard with her mouth open and a book hanging from her hand. Dara took it from her and put it on the table. Without opening her eyes, Jane slid down, pulled the covers to her nose, and drew a long breath. Dara turned out the light. When she crawled into bed, she smelled the sheets.

What did they smell like? Not soap—something more real than that—like her hands when she pulled weeds—or like freshly sawn wood.

She lay back and watched the stars beyond the silhouetted pines out the window. She ran her toes along the smooth cool sheets, and she wondered at the milky, floating feeling of it all. She felt the familiar presence, and she reached a hand to stroke its face.

"What is it?" she asked, and her answer was the clean, ancient shining of starlight.

She lay swaddled in the cotton sheets for some time before the long river of ginger peach and Earl Grey, peppermint, blackberry, and chamomile surged to join the great wide ocean. She got up to use the bathroom.

There was enough moonlight in the house to show the way without turning on lights. She descended the steps from her attic bedroom and found the bathroom at the end of the hall.

When she was done, she stood at the rail on the landing and looked down into the living room where Glenda had first seated them. The window shone a silver grid on the floor with a cat shadow where Algernon lay on the windowsill.

There was a feeling to this house, thick as whipped cream, that Dara wanted to scoop up and take away with her. A happiness they held so casually.

Her boss in Los Cuervos used to talk about a Russian pilot who escaped during the Cold War, who had spent his life standing in endless lines for bread. When he paid his first visit to an American supermarket, he couldn't believe that all the fresh oranges and peaches, the avocados, the tri-tip, ham, and the bread—sourdough, whole wheat, or cinnamon raisin—that all of that was really there for anyone to pick up and buy. And when he did believe that, he couldn't understand how Americans could hold it so casually.

The Rawlingses loved each other, and they were happy. How did they not hold that with both hands clenched to white knuckles?

She ached to stay, to ask them to be her mother and father, to care for her, and to let her sleep nights in that safe attic bedroom in all this thick happiness you could spoon up like whipped cream.

Algernon stretched on his windowsill, and Dara yawned. She turned from the rail and headed for the attic stairs.

The living room window had guided her through the dark hall to the moonlit landing, but it couldn't guide her back the other way. Still, she saw no reason to turn on the light and break the spell. She knew the stairs were at the end of the hall, and she would find them.

But as soon as she entered the shadow, her face ran— *fump!*—into hairy flesh and the smell of soap. Large hands gripped her shoulders, and she screamed. The hands let go, and she heard a guttural yell as she backstepped toward the landing.

The light came on and there stood Harold in his green plaid boxer shorts, with one hand on the switch and the other pressed to his bare chest.

"Oh!" she cried.

"Dara!"

"Dara?" Jane stood at the top of the stairs.

"What's wrong?" Glenda peered from her bedroom door.

"I … I went to the bathroom …" Dara caught her breath.

"I almost went right here where I stood!" said Harold.

Jane grinned. "You scared the daylights out of me!"

"Scared you?" said Dara. "Oh Harold, I'm so sorry!"

"You're not out of the woods yet, my love," Glenda cautioned, pointing to his knees, which pressed desperately together. He pushed himself from the wall, but then laughed again, which made it all the more imperative that he hold his legs tight.

"All right," said Jane. "Now let's quit laughing so poor Harold can get to the loo." She sucked her cheeks in, but that just made them laugh all the more, and Harold was in dire straits.

"Come on, old man," Glenda said. "We'll just have to make a run for it." She took him by the arm and rushed him to the bathroom, pushed him in, and shut the door.

She sat on the steps below Jane and above Dara, who had crumpled to the floor in a fit of laughter. "Well it's a new carpet," she said. "I don't want it stained."

This made Jane fall over too, and it sent Dara into a holler that echoed across the living room. Algernon leapt from the windowsill and ambled off to a quieter place.

"Glenda?" came Harold's voice.

"Yes, dear?"

"My bathrobe, please?"

"Certainly. We mustn't lead these ladies into temptations of the flesh."

"No. Nor into another fit of laughter at my expense."

This, of course, did exactly that.

When he was safely wrapped in his red flannel robe, he joined them on the stairs.

"Harold," said Jane, "I'd like to compliment you on your fine choice of a lovely green plaid."

"I'm just glad I didn't go natural tonight."

"Oh, pffft!" said Glenda, giving his arm a push. "He never goes natural!"

Dara remembered his round naked belly and blushed.

"But I could for you, dear!" he said.

"Could you? I prefer the bow tie, though."

"And the knee garters?"

"Definitely the knee garters. And the black socks. Always the black."

"Let's not give our secrets away. It's nobody's business what we did last night!"

"Pffft!"

"How long have you two been married?" asked Jane.

"Thirty years last February, and I'm still her love slave." Harold took Glenda's hand.

"That's wonderful. I could tell it had been a very long time."

"Really?" asked Glenda. "How could you tell?"

"The best kind of romance comes only with time, don't you think?"

"Yes," Harold whispered. Then, suddenly stern, "Now let's all get back to bed."

"Oh, but I'm wide awake now!" said Glenda.

"But these ladies have to get up in the morning."

"We'll be fine," said Jane.

"Would you like some hot chocolate?" Glenda urged.

"That sounds wonderful."

And it was. Dara sat in the kitchen with her mug piled up with whipped cream. She listened to the patter, the talk of geraniums, hollyhocks, and recipes for strawberry pie, all in the lilting voices young girls use to talk about makeup and boys. Only in school, she'd never joined in. She still didn't know how, so she listened. It was fun.

For all but Harold. He drank his cocoa like he had a deadline to meet. He swallowed the last of it and said, "Glenda, we should go to bed."

"But I'm not done with my chocolate!"

Well, she wasn't. Not by half. All the same, he took her cup and dumped it in the sink. He said, "It's one o'clock. We're going to bed." He clutched her hand and pulled her to her feet. "Ladies," he said, "you can find your way up when you're finished, I think."

"Good night," she said too softly, and Dara caught a glimpse of her face, her mouth pinched to the side. Harold's jaw was set and trembling.

Back in their room, Jane said, "For one who talks so little, your face speaks volumes."

Dara crossed her arms. "Why would he treat her like that? We were just drinking hot chocolate!"

"That's all we know. There's obviously something we don't know." Jane turned off the light.

Dara lay back on her pillow and tapped her toe on the foot of the bed. Algernon pushed his nose through the door and jumped up beside her. She rolled to the side and stroked his fur, and in a moment, she slept.

When she awoke, Algernon lay by her side. She stroked him, and he stretched, long and longer, till his toes trembled. He yawned, his tongue extended and curled like a party whistle.

She rolled to look at the other bed. Jane was still asleep.

She'd forgotten to brush after her cup of cocoa, and her mouth was gummy. She got up, found her toothbrush, and headed for the bathroom.

The door was ajar, and she pushed it open to find Glenda at the sink, leaning heavily against the tile counter with a glass of water in one hand and an amber prescription bottle in the other. Dara saw the woman's face, pale and haggard, in the mirror.

"You okay?" she asked.

Glenda startled. "Fine. I'll be fine in a little bit. Would you please use the downstairs bathroom?"

Glenda looked like her blood had drained away. Dara stared at her, and her legs felt weak. "Can I get you anything, can I …"

"No." Glenda shut the door.

Dara hurried into her jeans and T-shirt and went downstairs. Harold was in the kitchen chopping bell peppers.

"Glenda's sick," she announced.

"She'll be all right in a bit." He didn't look up.

"She's very sick, isn't she?"

"Just give her a minute; she'll be okay."

"Is it ... like cancer?"

"It's exactly cancer. How'd you know?"

She shrugged. "Just looks bad. I mean, just now."

"She works at not looking sick. She'll come down here looking pretty and happy, like everything's fine. It's a skill with her, and she's good at it." He poured beaten eggs into a skillet. "Well. She's pretty, and I think she's happy. It's not all a fake."

"Can they make her well?"

"No." He focused hard on the eggs, pushing them from side to side in the pan. "You any good with a toaster?"

"Sure."

"You *can* talk. I wondered about it last night."

"I'm not much good at it, I—"

"Oh, for Pete's—you're fine. Haven't we been talking all this time? Just like old friends. You do fine."

"How long will she live?"

He set his jaw and pushed at the eggs.

"How long—"

"See? You're not at all shy." His fingers were tight on the spatula. "Not long enough. I don't know. Doctor says she has six good months."

"Good months?"

"Before she's in bed all the time."

"Don't you wish, Harold!" said Glenda, fully dressed and looking fine. No one would ever guess.

"You're up," he said.

She gave him a kiss.

"Wish what?" asked Jane who walked in behind her.

"That I was in bed all the time. Such a dreamer."

"I was just about to put Dara to work making toast. Why don't you sit down and talk to us?"

"No, I'll make the toast," Glenda said.

"Let me make it." Dara headed for the toaster.

Glenda took her by the arm and whispered in her ear, "He

said six months. I'm going to use them."

"For toast?" Dara hesitated. Glenda winked and pulled a loaf of bread from the cupboard.

"Dara and I should leave after breakfast," said Jane. "If you have any idea of our bill—"

"No charge," said Glenda.

"Oh no, don't be silly—"

"You weren't customers; you were guests. We're no longer in business."

Harold turned off the fire and turned to gape at Glenda.

"You're not?" asked Jane.

"No. Harold and I are going to travel. We've got a motor home out back that's gone to waste long enough."

Harold's gaze had locked onto his wife. She turned to Jane and smiled. "It's illegal to have a cat in a restaurant. So I can't charge you, can I?"

"You didn't want to leave," Harold whispered.

"Now I do," she whispered back and took his hand.

Breakfast was quiet—despite Jane's baffled attempts at conversation and Glenda's attempts at levity. They ate quickly.

Algernon jumped onto Dara's lap and she looked to see if Glenda minded him at the breakfast table.

Glenda had her eyes on the cat—but not in disapproval. Something seemed to wither inside her. When Dara caught her eye, she brightened. *Presto!*—the picture of health. "Dara," she said, "I have a proposal."

"What's that?"

"Why don't you take Algernon with you?"

"Oh, no! I—"

"Well, but he likes you. And you seem to like him. And we can't take him traveling with us. Algernon hates to travel."

Harold bit his knuckle.

"Really, Dara, unless you just don't want him," Glenda said. "I need to find him a good home."

Dara looked to Jane. "We'll be living in your brother's trailer."

"Tom won't mind."

Algernon pushed against Dara's hand. He was a fine, lovely animal. She swallowed hard and saw that a drop had fallen from her eye to his back. She kept her head down and stroked the cat, willing the tears back where they came from.

A hand covered her own, thin-skinned with long fingers, and Dara looked up to see Glenda squatted beside her. With her other hand Glenda brushed the tears from Dara's eyes. "Shhh. Shhh. It would help me, Dara."

"Okay," she said.

Glenda smiled. "Okay?"

She nodded.

Under the sign of the buxom cowgirl, they peered through the window at the Studmuffin's white counter and black stools to the left, and red vinyl booths to the right. A row of chrome tables filled in between, with the chairs set upside down on top. The place looked empty.

But it wasn't. A small movement behind the far end of the counter caught Dara's eye. She looked to see the scuffed soles of a pair of sneakers. These joined two corduroy pant legs, which crawled backward to reveal a large corduroy bottom. The man belonging to that bottom scrubbed the floor with a coarse brush, and on his back rode a small girl, red-haired, in shorts and red cowboy boots.

The man shimmied nearer, scrubbing and pulling his bucket along.

"Dara, I'd like you to meet my brother," whispered Jane.

Dara smiled.

"Come on. I'll show you the rest of him." The door was unlocked, so they stepped inside.

"Tom? Clementine?"

"Aunt Janey!" The girl dismounted and ran to her open arms.

Tom stood and walked toward them with one hand on the small of his back. "Where've you been, love?"

He said "bean." *Of course*, Dara thought. *British*.

"Waiting for you to get your fish caught." The duchess poked his stomach. "I hope you brought me some."

"He didn't try," the girl complained. "We just drove around."

He kissed Jane, then turned to Dara, wiping his hand on his shirt and extending it. "I'm Tom."

He was a big, smiling man with crooked teeth and overgrown hair. Safe. "I'm Dara." She shook his hand.

"You're closed," Jane said.

"Right. I wanted to catch up a bit. Business has been so bad it hardly matters. But I'm always open for you, dear. Had lunch?"

They ate stale sandwiches from paper plates.

Clementine chattered between the two women, fingering Dara's pearl. She pulled a deck of cards from her pocket. "I'll show you a trick." She spread the cards face down on the table. "Pick a card, any car-r-r-d!"

Dara pulled one from the middle.

"Which one is it?"

"The five of hearts."

"Seeeee?"

Clearly the trick was over.

"Brilliant!" Tom smiled at his daughter.

Clemmie's smile was brilliant: fragile baby teeth, gapped and spreading to fill a growing mouth. The girl caught Dara staring, beamed, and spread the cards again.

After lunch they left to see the trailer. While Tom locked the glass doors, Dara stepped into the street, and a black stereo-pounding ZX screeched to a stop before her. The driver leaned on his horn, cursing out his window. Tom grabbed Dara's shoulder and pulled her back. The ZX screeched its tires again and was gone.

"I saw his license," said Tom. "I'll call the police."

"No," she said. "It was my fault."

"He was driving rather fast, wasn't he? Or you would have seen him." He turned back to the restaurant.

"No!" Dara caught his arm. She just wanted out of the open.

"I think he should," said Jane.

"Please don't."

"You're trembling," said Tom. "Come inside. I can—"

"Let's go." She hurried to her car and got in.

Tom's house was a block and a half away, on the corner of Cedar and Roosevelt. The trailer spanned the Cedar Street side of his backyard. Algernon relieved himself in the planter, and they took him inside, where Clementine chased him under the couch.

"Tom, it's fantastic!" said Jane. "You put in new tile."

The trailer smelled like pine cleaner and lemon polish, and the carpet showed vacuum tracks.

Jane walked to the living room window, raised the blinds, and opened the sash. "Such lovely light."

Light, yes—and a front row view of Cedar Street with HandiMart on the other side. A car waited at the light, so close Dara could see the driver pull a drag on his cigarette and flick the ashes to the pavement.

She clutched her pearl. Jane had gone through and opened all the windows. "Dara, come choose your bedroom."

They were both the same: dark paneled with floral bedspreads. She chose the one in back, dropped her purse on the dresser, and glanced out the window. The car had moved on. The store, at least, was a good thing: a mom and pop, but big enough for her needs. She could buy her food and hurry home. She closed the window, shut the blinds, and returned to the kitchen.

"Feeling better?" asked Tom.

"I'm fine." She leaned against the counter.

"I'm very sorry for what happened. It's a bad welcome, isn't it?"

"Is it okay about the cat?"

"I told her you wouldn't mind," said Jane.

"No, I'm just very glad you're here." He sat at the table. "Things have gotten worse."

"How so?" Jane sat beside him.

"There's a new Denny's Diner on Birch Street. My business has dropped by half. Half of too little is—well …"

Jane laid her hand on his arm.

"My cooking's abysmal," he said.

"It can't be that bad. You used to have loads of business."

"They came for Holly. The food was just a necessary penance."

Jane chuckled, and he smiled.

"So, if you ladies wouldn't mind tinting your hair the color of rocket fire …"

Jane shook her head.

"And if just one of you could sing like an angel on steroids, we might just keep afloat."

"We'll never replace her, Tommy," said Jane. "Your chipmunk in there will be just like her one day, but …"

"Not soon enough to save the restaurant."

"It can't be hard. I've been to a Denny's Diner. You just have to be better."

"Of course. What was I thinking?" He dropped his head to the table. "As simple as that."

"Kitty! Here kitty, kitty!"

Dara opened her eyes and glanced from her bed down the hall to the living room, just as a small pair of red cowboy boots crawled from view.

"Here, kitty!"

She turned to check the time: seven o'clock. Her first night in the trailer, and she'd actually slept.

Algernon scuttled down the hall with Clementine close behind. The cat dashed under the bed. The girl stopped when she saw Dara and stood in the doorway with one boot lifted to scratch the back of her leg.

Dara pushed herself to a sitting position. "How'd you get in here?"

"Through the window."

"You shouldn't climb through the window."

"The door was locked."

"Well, you should knock on the door and wait to be let in." She puckered. "It's my dad's trailer."

"Yes, but your aunt and I live here now. You should knock."

"Your cat's under the bed."

"That's okay."

"He's hungry."

Dara leaned over the side to peer at Algernon. He huddled in the far corner with a look of desperation in his eye. "I don't think he's hungry."

"I'm hungry," said Clementine.

Neither Dara nor Jane had gone shopping yet. All she had to offer was leftover snacks from the trip. "How about some Cheetos?"

Moments later they sat in the kitchen, licking orange dust from their fingers. Clementine produced her deck of cards and laid out a game of Concentration—with the cards facing up.

"You're supposed to lay them face down."

"Not the way I play."

Well, that was fine. Dara had to be at the restaurant at eight thirty.

"I go first," said Clementine.

"Be my guest."

The girl picked up two cards, the three of spades and the three of hearts. "Hooray!" She raised a fist in triumph.

Dara reached for the eight of clubs, but Clementine slapped her hand. "I get another turn if I get a pair."

"But you'll *always* get a pair, because the cards are face up."

Shrugging, the girl chose the eight of clubs and the eight of diamonds. The queens of diamonds and hearts, the twos of clubs and diamonds, and in no time the game was over. "I win!"

"Yeah, I'll bet you win a lot."

"I beat Daddy all the time."

Dara ate a Cheeto and licked her fingers. "Does he know you're here?"

"He's asleep. *On* the chair, *in* his clothes! His mouth is open, like this." She dropped her head back to demonstrate a gaping maw. "Last night the TV was on all night."

"Oh."

"He does it all the time."

"What's he watch all night?"

"Nothin'! He just changes the channel, and changes the channel, and watches everything. But you don't see nothin' that way." She wiped her orange-dusted fingers on her nightgown and ate another Cheeto. "One night, I woke up to go to the bathroom, and Daddy was asleep. There was this show on about some stuff called Nads. For taking hair off."

"Off of what?"

"Anything." She pointed at her leg. "You put this goopy stuff on and then you put this thing on top, and then you pull it off, *rip!* And all the hair comes out." She raised her hands, palms up.

"I see."

"Daddy has lots of hair. He has it on his legs, and his toes and his tummy, and on *both* sides of his arms, and on his back. And all the way up his neck—but he shaves his neck." She lifted her nightgown and fingered her navel. "He even has it inside here." She ate another Cheeto. "I think Daddy should get some Nads."

"Clementine?" It was Tom. "Hello?"

Dara retied her bathrobe and opened the door.

"Hello. I thought I heard Clemmie in here."

"Hi, Daddy!"

"What have you got all over you?"

"Sorry," said Dara. "She was hungry and all I had was Cheetos."

"Oh. Well, look at you! You both have orange lips." He flashed his crooked teeth.

She ducked her head and ran the back of her hand across her mouth.

"When we get to the restaurant, I can make your breakfast, if you like." A tuft of hair curled over the collar of his T-shirt.

She blushed. "That sounds nice."

"Right. See you then."

She shut the door and cuffed her forehead. *That sounds nice!* Just as if he'd asked her out. *So stupid!*

She and Jane arrived at the restaurant's back door to find Tom mixing pancake batter in a large bowl. "Janey says you want to work the kitchen."

"She said she'd wait the tables. Is that okay?" If it wasn't, she'd turn right around …

"Right. You're on." He wiped his hands on a towel. "Let's have a look about then."

He briefed her on the morning routine, showed her how to work the dishwasher, and pointed out the "larder," where supplies were kept. When that was settled, he asked, "What would you like for breakfast?"

"Just some toast and tea would be lovely," said Jane.

"And you, Dara?"

"I'll have tea too, and a studmuffin."

"A what?" He bent forward, openmouthed.

"A … a muffin."

"Oh." He straightened. "We don't serve muffins."

"You don't? Why?"

"We never thought of it."

"You call this place 'The Studmuffin Café.'"

Jane chuckled.

Tom ducked his head. "That's not why we call it that."

"Then why do you call it that?"

He turned his head, grinning.

"Tell her," said Jane.

"It's named for me. Uh, my wife's idea."

"She named it 'The Studmuffin' after you?" Dara leaned back in the booth.

Very red now, he turned and did a side thrust with his hip, then walked away. "Perhaps you'd fancy some toast?"

"That sounds nice."

CHAPTER 6

*W*hen the first customers turned up, Dara checked the clock with a measure of relief; it was 9:43. Maybe a little business would give Tom something to do besides babble, and that could only be good. He'd spent the past hour and three quarters telling her every little thing about himself and Clemmie, about Brittlebush, and the state of the world—all of which would have been all right, if he hadn't expected her to keep up her end of the conversation. It must be a family trait, this incessant need to talk.

Still, the open door let in a rush of wind and the clamor of a passing motorcycle, and Dara was glad to stay safely this side of the kitchen wall. She busied herself slicing tomatoes. It wasn't like the restaurant was busting at the seams. She'd do the prep work, let Jane take the orders, and Tom work the grill.

If he ever quit talking. He and the duchess chattered away out there like they had company. She heard Tom making introductions, so Jane didn't even know these people. But when had the duchess ever been shy? Her voice lilted its way right through the cook's window to Dara's headache.

"Oh no, I returned from Mexico some time ago," she said. "We came here yesterday from the desert."

Dara set her jaw. Jane could tell a life story in a matter of moments, and she didn't much like being included.

But the duchess kept on. "We've got houses out there, at the end of a small road just fifteen miles down the motorway from the Carriage Creek intersection."

She'd just given directions! Dara fumbled the knife and nearly caught it by the blade before she jumped back and let it drop to the floor.

Tom poked his head in just as she bent to retrieve it. "Come meet somebody, will you?"

She shook her head and carried the knife to the dishwasher.

"Come on. They're nice people."

"I don't want to." She turned her back to wash her hands and heard the kitchen door swing shut. He'd left. That was good. She finished the tomatoes and arranged the slices in a large plastic container. Just who would eat them all at the present rate of business, she couldn't say.

She heard the squeak of hinges and turned just as Tom led a man and woman in, a short, round-faced couple in matching yellow bike shorts and jerseys. They looked like Olympic gnomes.

"Dara! Please meet my very good friends, Bo and Linda Macke."

Dara narrowed her eyes at Tom, but he seemed oblivious. The Mackes, however, cringed as if *they'd* done something wrong. She gave it up and forced a smile.

"Bo and Linda ride in here on their tandem," Tom said. "All the way from Shannan Valley."

Well, they were quiet gnomes, stooping and smiling.

"Pleased to meet you," she said.

To her relief, they nodded, then scuttled back to their booth.

Tom tilted his head, and Dara could read his eyes: *Is this who you're afraid of? People like them?*

She looked away. She'd seen that look before.

Like when she was eleven, the day *most* of her swim class learned to dive from the high board. She'd been ecstatic. She'd seen the older girls knifing into the water with long, caramel legs, effortless and beautiful as mermaids.

To prepare, she'd shaved her legs for the first time, sudden-tanned them the color of apricots, and painted her toenails ice pink.

At the pool, she climbed the ladder and walked to the end of the board, striding as if her legs were five feet long.

She looked down, and then—oh *geez!* She *couldn't* do this, not for anything! Her bathing suit puckered between her buttocks, her knees cleaved to each other for support, and she was dizzy, and then—oh *geez* what if she fainted and fell! She turned around.

But before she could mouse back along the board and down the ladder, Mr. Stone was there, whispering that the *other* girls had done it, and *they* were okay—that the water was … and then midsentence, he'd shoved her, and she'd hurtled down, sick, grasping for nothing to hold onto, and oh geez, oh *geez!*

And then when she crawled out of the water goosebumped, her chin rattling in cold spasms, Mr. Stone gave her that look: *Now what were you so afraid of?*

Tom didn't get it. She wouldn't be pushed.

She could just go back to her desert.

No, she'd promised, and she had to try. Even here, in this kitchen, she felt the voice's caress.

Like Mr. Stone's arm on her shoulders—just before he pushed her in.

She grunted and hacked her knife into a head of lettuce.

Well, she didn't want Tom bringing people back to meet her. That kind of attention was worse than what she tried to avoid. She'd just meet the customers, shake their hands, and go back to her work.

She peered through the cook's window. Four people out there: the Mackes, Tom, and Jane. The duchess and her brother were so busy talking they hadn't bothered to take the order. She might as well do it herself. How hard, after all, could this be?

She strode into the dining room and pulled the order pad from Jane's apron pocket. The Mackes wanted pancakes and sausage. She glowered at Tom, and he headed for the grill.

Anything in the world was better than the smug glance he shot her as he walked by. She decided to stay in the dining room till he quit grinning.

The next customer was Zita Sanchez, the owner of Time and Again, the secondhand store across the street. She was a tiny woman with masses of black hair fastened in back with a barrette. She wanted "just an English muffin and some tea, please."

She said it with a wave of the hand and a confidential smile. "I think he can handle that."

As soon as Dara delivered the Mackes' order, she knew what Zita meant. The pancakes were pale, flaccid things, rimmed in black with white rings in the middle. The sausages were shriveled black sticks rolling side to side on the plate.

When Zita left, Dara wiped the tables, neatened under the counters, and wiped the tables again. The clock in the kitchen and the clock over the door both ticked, but not at the same time. The place echoed *tick tick, tock tock, tick tick …*

"Don't you have any music here?" she asked. They didn't.

An hour later a man ambled in wearing a straw cowboy hat, sharply rolled at the sides. He was taller than Tom, and older.

"Hooper!" called Tom from the grill.

"Hey, Tom!"

"Scrambled eggs?"

"Like always." He grabbed a paper and sat at the counter.

"Hoop, you've met my sister, Jane. And that's her friend Dara. Dara, meet my father-in-law, also our local printer, cowboy poet, and balladeer."

"You buffaloed these girls into working for you? What'd you do, tell them you had money?"

"Something like that."

"You girls don't want to work for him. He don't know if he's a cowhand, cook, or a limey. He talks goofy."

"I gas off as purdy as you do, old chap!"

"Yeah, but can you talk?"

"I can, and I can walk with both my knees in the same county, which is more than you can say."

"Boy don't know the difference between chips and french fries."

"What's French about them?"

"Not a thing. When *you* make them."

"Dara asked for a studmuffin this morning."

"Well, don't you give it to her. You'll scar her for life."

Jane piped up, "How was she to know you'd name a restaurant for your bum?"

"Why not!"

"Sure, why not? It's a local landmark," said Hooper.

By this time, Dara had gotten intense about wiping down the counters. She turned her face to hide her rising color—but she snuck a smile to Hooper.

When Tom had Hooper's order ready, Jane and Dara both saw what was on the plate. "Oh dear me," whispered Jane.

Side by side they placed it in front of Hooper. He eyed the scrambled eggs and said, "Looks like he chewed 'em up for me, don't it?" He picked up his fork and dug in. He ate his eggs, toast, and burnt sausages, drank his coffee down to the mud, and wiped his mouth.

"Catch you later, Tom! Dara, I'm proud to meet you. Jane." He tipped his hat and left.

Jane nodded. "They came for Holly."

Dara poured herself a quarter-cup of coffee, tasted it, and dumped the rest down the drain. "She must've been something."

They reserved further comments till they got back home.

"He doesn't get enough business to need our help!" Dara said when they'd shut the trailer door. She'd brought the lettuce and tomatoes home.

"That's why he needs our help."

"He's never drunk coffee, has he?"

"I don't suppose he has. Why?"

"I've got an idea. I'm going to the store." And she did—at six o'clock—too full of purpose to care who else was there.

The next morning she was at the restaurant early. She walked in just as Tom started setting up the coffee.

"Stop," she said, holding up a hand. "Let me do that."

She laid a paper bag sideways on the counter and pulled out a black and red foil bag of Italian roast. "The real thing," she said.

"It's a bit expensive, isn't it?"

"This bag's on me. Let's give it a try."

"What else have you got there?"

"These," she said as she pulled a tray from the bag, "are studmuffins. I made them last night. From scratch."

"Did you now?"

"This one's blueberry. This is cheese and bacon. This is chocolate chip. Take your pick."

"What's this?"

"Cinnamon raisin."

He tried it. "Mm, terrific."

"I brought my own pancake batter, too. My recipe. I'll cook them."

"*You'll* cook? What am I to do?"

"Wash dishes." She grinned.

"You'll likely want a raise in pay after this."

"I might. Who knows, you might have enough to give me one."

When the Mackes leaned their tandem against the window that day, they nearly bumped into the sign Dara had put outside the door. It announced, "New! On Special Today! Studmuffin and Coffee, $2.00." They ordered the special.

So did Zita. And when the Mackes left they returned shortly with Bo's brother, who ordered five specials to take back to his real estate office. Zita bought an order to take to her husband at the DMV. By ten thirty, fourteen people had come in to buy studmuffins. Compared to the day before, business had exploded. They sold out.

Dara had begun to think no one would brave her pancakes, but Tom took care of that. When the last muffin was gone, he announced that the same girl who'd made them was also making pancakes, and they were on sale, two orders for the price of one. The older couple in front ordered theirs right off.

"Do you want them with apples, fresh strawberries, or just with syrup?" Dara asked.

With apples. Both of them.

Finally, Hooper came in and ordered the usual. Dara had been waiting for this. While he rubbed his whiskers and gazed at the crowd, she scrambled his eggs and rolled them onto the plate:

butter yellow and fluffy. The sausages came out fat and brown, ready to pop when he cut them open. She arranged the toast on the side and added a twist of orange and a slice of honeydew.

Jane had no sooner pranced the plate past the customers at the counter and set it before Hooper than there were two more orders for scrambled eggs.

Hooper studied his plate a long moment. Finally, he peered squint-eyed at Dara and asked, "What did you do to my eggs?"

They celebrated the morning's success on Tom's patio. He poured Cokes, raising the bottle high over their plastic cups, and everyone cheered like it was champagne. When he poured Dara's cup, the Coke foamed to a half inch beyond the top, wobbled, and rested an instant before settling back to a safe level. As her friends laughed, Dara held a hand to the top of the glass.

"Speech!" shouted Jane, and Dara looked to Tom, who simply grinned at her till she shifted and looked away. She looked up to find Jane and Hooper staring as well.

"Go on," said Tom.

"Me?"

"*Yes*, you! You saved the day, didn't you?"

She denied it, she shook her head, she fought the urge to run to her room. But in the end she said, "I'd like to thank …" All the attention stymied her, but she pushed through. "… my agent and my many, many fans … and let's just get on with things, okay?"

They all clapped as if she'd said something profound, and Dara stood to get some potato chips.

On her grandfather's knee, Clementine hoisted her drink above her head. Hooper raised a hand to steady the cup, but too late; the dark liquid spilled down the front of his shirt. Unflustered, he dried it with the back of Clemmie's dress and held the glass out for Dara to refill.

"Dara," said Tom, "I'll chop tomatoes, wash dishes, and *grovel* if you'll keep cooking like you did today. Promise me you'll make more muffins."

Jane winked. "Twice as many."

"You could stay open two hours later, Tom" said Hooper. "Catch the dinner crowd and that. 'Less you don't need the money."

"I do. I promised Dara here a raise."

"We could dress things up a bit," said Jane. "Put pictures up—"

"Paint the walls," said Hooper.

"Right," said Jane. "Maybe paint it a fresh color."

"Like what?" asked Dara.

"I don't know. Something besides white."

"Blue! I like blue!" said Clementine.

"And flowers on the tables. And curtains. And music on the PA." Clearly, Jane could see it all.

"We don't have a PA," said Tom.

"Well, get a boom box," said Hooper. "Wing it."

Jane continued. "And we could have a grand reopening and expand our hours then. What do you think, Tom?" She leaned forward.

He folded his arms across his chest. "No. I don't want to do that."

"Why not?" asked Hooper.

"I don't know." He squirmed in his chair. "It was Holly's place."

"Ah." Jane looked away.

He gripped the arm of his chair. "The wall color is 'Candytuft.' Holly picked it out." He stood and walked into the house.

Algernon joined what was left of the party and rubbed his nose on Dara's leg. She picked him up.

"Guess he don't like the idea," said Hooper.

"No," said Jane.

"I like it though. Seems Holly would care less for the 'Candytuft' than she'd care to keep the joint afloat. She …"

He looked at his granddaughter and stopped. She had chewed her finger to a glistening shine.

"Rain on him," he muttered. He lifted the girl off his lap and went inside.

Clementine ran to her playground set and bellyflopped on one of the swings to study the foot-worn ground beneath.

The afternoon sun warmed Dara's shoulders. The cat purred and the swing creaked. A breeze rustled through the trees. And from the open window came raised voices, a brief squall that crescendoed once: "Think *I didn't love her?*" It fell off, then crescendoed again: "Folks don't want to eat in a mausoleum!" And then there was silence: the hush of the breeze, the purring cat, the swing.

Tom came out and dropped into his lawn chair. "Okay." He shrugged. "Let's do it."

Jane wasted no time. When the party fizzled (which was quickly, once Hooper stormed off), she headed for the fabric store.

She returned just as Dara pulled the first batch of muffins from the oven. Jane grabbed her arm and led her to the living room. "Come see what I've found."

She pulled a bolt of fabric from a large plastic bag. It was yellow with a pattern of cactus and horses and bits of blue sky. "For the curtains. What do you think?"

"It's … unique. You think Tom'll like it?"

"If he fancies anything we do. It'll go with Clemmie's blue paint."

"He seems upset."

"He'll be all right. Did you catch his face with all those people there today? He was happy, Dara. When his business picks up, he'll be fine."

"How'd he ever get *anyone* in there, the way he cooks? Holly couldn't have been that good."

"Oh, she was something. Tom's cooking wasn't always so bad, either."

"It wasn't?"

"Well, it wasn't the Four Seasons, but it was all right. He's not trying."

"Clemmie says he channel surfs all night."

"He what?"

"He flips channels on the TV. All night. In his clothes."

"What else did she tell you?"

"He has too much body hair."

"Ha! The wicked thing! Just like her mother."

Dara fingered the fabric. "This is nice."

"I'm going to put an announcement in the paper about the grand reopening. I think we can do it in three weeks, if we close for one Saturday to paint. Oh, but with a little more time, I could paint a fresco on the back wall. Maybe our little bluff in the desert."

"Sure, make us feel at home." Dara stood to pull another batch of muffins from the oven.

"You can do that at the restaurant, you know. It's got a bigger oven."

"Maybe I'll need it."

"Perhaps you will."

The next day business was half again as brisk as the day before. They sold out of muffins by ten o'clock. The lunch crowd was big enough, almost, to be noisy.

But Hooper never stopped in. His usual time came and went, and Tom started glancing out the window whenever something moved outside. At closing, he cleaned up quietly and went home.

Jane watched him leave. When the back door clicked shut, she untied her apron and pulled it over her head. "I'm going to Time and Again. Want to come? We might find some pictures for the walls."

When they got there, Zita wanted to hear all the plans, and Jane wanted to tell her. Dara shook her head at the two together, leaning head-to-head over the glass display case, scheming.

Someone had to look for the actual pictures. Dara scanned the walls.

Right away she spotted one, a scene of a saguaro cactus, tall and green against the blue sky, with mesas in the distance. It was a real painting, not a print, and it wasn't bad. Only eight dollars, too. She stood on tiptoe to lift it off the wall.

It was while she was reaching for the painting that she noticed the photo in a wooden frame hand painted with rosebuds on the shelf below. Her breath caught midway out, and she froze for an endless moment before stooping to pick it up.

There was a man in the photo, his dark hair brushed to the side, his face as yet unlined. Beside him a young woman with a broad smile held their small daughter, scrubbed and bobby socked, in a blue dress.

She didn't remember the day the picture was taken. But she did remember the day her mother gripped it in both hands and wandered out the sliding glass door.

Her father. Her mother, just the way she remembered.

Frame in hand, Dara dropped her purse and reeled to the bed in one sweep. The next instant she sprang to her feet and shut the door. Jane could be home any minute.

She sat on the edge of her bed, with the picture held in two hands like a new-fallen miracle from heaven. She shut her eyes. A clatter of reasons came to mind, but only one she could bear, and it walloped her heart to a standstill: Her mother was someplace close! Right here in Brittlebush, maybe.

And she'd given the family portrait to a *secondhand shop?*

It had to be an accident. Maybe the frame just fell from the mantel into the giveaway box.

Maybe Dara had passed her on the street. Would she know?

Dara opened her eyes and gazed at her mother's face. The third photo, taken the same day as the two on the dresser—but a different pose. A different smile, curved in a way Dara had lost the memory of.

Her father looked younger, in ways that had nothing to do with the color of his hair or the texture of his skin. Life had been good for him once.

She stroked the glass, running a finger over her mother's face, over the hand pressed around the child who was Dara.

Algernon leapt to the bed and nudged himself between her face and the picture. She set it aside and lowered the cat to the floor. When she picked the frame up again, her finger brushed something on the back, a white corner protruding where the cardboard tucked into the frame. She opened it and pulled out a slip of paper, a simple watercolor of a white cat against a blue wash, with two initials flicked into the corner: "SJ."

A child's painting? For just a breath, she imagined another girl on her mother's lap, dabbing a brush on the paper. Dara clutched her pearl.

The cat had a black cross painted on its forehead. Someone's attempt at symbolism, she guessed. Would a child do that?

She heard the front door. "Hello!"

The duchess.

Dara stuffed the frame and watercolor into the drawer of her bedside table, and opened the door. "I'll be right out."

She wiped the moisture from her eyes and then smoothed the bed where she'd sat.

Jane stood in the doorway.

Dara faked a smile and spun to face her. "Hi! Find any paintings?"

Jane nodded. "I bought the saguaro you'd been looking at and a nice one of a horse."

"Good." She sat on the bed.

Jane perched beside her and folded her hands. "Odd your family portrait should turn up at Time and Again."

"How'd you know?"

"It's not the first photo I've seen of your parents." She nodded toward the two on the dresser.

She was right. Jane had arranged the pictures around Dara's mirror back in the desert and later seen them displayed in the shanty church. Dara pulled the frame from the drawer and handed it to her. "I don't know what it means."

Jane studied the picture. "Such a lovely young woman. What happened to her?"

"She left." Dara picked lint from the bedspread and shrugged. "Just walked out to get some air. No suitcase, no purse. Just this."

Jane took her hand and stroked it. "Tomorrow I'll ask Zita to check where she got it."

Simple as that, and a thousand reasons would narrow to one.

And what would that one be?

Dara would crack to pieces if she didn't do something. She stood, set the picture between the two on the dresser, and walked away.

There were muffins to bake.

They sold out the next morning.

The Studmuffin filled to capacity with retirees who didn't have to work and business owners who could work when they wanted. But all that mattered in the kitchen that day were the two regulars who hadn't come.

"He never stays mad for long. Don't worry." Tom scrutinized the sidewalk.

Like a dog at the window, thought Dara. Let him think it was his troubles with his father-in-law she had on her mind. That way, he asked fewer questions.

She and Jane had stopped in to see Zita on their way to work, and Zita had promised to look at her records.

How long could it take, she wondered?

Tom called out a greeting, wiped his hands on a towel, and left the kitchen. Dara peered out the cook's window to see who'd come in, but barely noticed the young couple before she glimpsed Zita across the street with a large file box. She scudded to the dining room for a better look. Zita stood at the door of her shop, using her free hand to pull the keys from her purse.

Dara reached back to untie her apron when Tom caught her by the arm.

"Dara, this is Erik and Amy Gunderson. Erik's my minister."

Tom and his introductions! She wiped her hands on her apron and held one out. "Pleased to meet you."

Amy had the hiccups. "Nice—*hic!*—to meet you."

"I'll get some water." Dara glanced out the window as she turned toward the kitchen. No Zita.

Amy drank the water and wiped her mouth with the back of her arm.

After a moment of hiccup-free silence, Erik initiated a round of applause. Amy scanned the room like she wanted to hide.

Dara liked her. "What church do you pastor?"

"Grace Chapel over on Edison," said Erik. "Tom tells me you've single-handedly saved the Studmuffin."

"No." Dara stepped back toward the kitchen.

"Not just Tom," he said. "Everyone's talking about your pancakes."

It was just the ingratiating sort of thing pastors say before the invitation to church. Dara knew the spiel. "I've got to get back to work."

"If you're not going somewhere else, we'd like to have you join us Sunday."

There it was.

Her father had spent every Sunday in church, and until Dara's marriage, he'd taken her with him. Truth to tell, she liked it there, as a child.

There were advantages to being abandoned—well, maybe only one. But a good one: The ladies at church treated her like a lost puppy.

Especially Connie MacAdam, the Sunday school teacher who baked her a cake every year on her birthday.

Dara had gone to church most of her life. It felt safe, and her father had never told her different.

She met Kevin in church.

He showed up one day while they sang "In the Garden." They'd all sung it so many times that their mouths just took over and left their minds free for other matters.

So while they sang of a God who walked with them and talked with them and told them they were his own, their heads turned to the newcomer who strode his way up the aisle in tight blue jeans.

And Kevin played to his audience. He stood in the front pew like an electrical tower, his legs spread and his arms raised, the tail of a snake tattoo coiled just under the sleeve of his T-shirt.

He nodded his head and avowed to everything the pastor said, and by the end of the sermon, he was in tears. Dara could hear his snuffles from where she sat by her father, six rows back. When the pastor gave the altar call, Kevin was the only one to go forward, but it was a conversion to remember, loud and heavy with tears, remorse, and renunciation.

Connie MacAdam liked him.

During the potluck after the service, folks gathered around him like he was the visiting preacher. He bowed his head in humble gratitude for the friendship of these good people, but he lifted it long enough to slip a wink to Dara.

He let it be known that his sins had rendered him jobless, friendless, and penniless. He was sent home with three leftover casseroles, a bag of dinner rolls, and a three-bean salad.

Three men offered him jobs, one of them her father. It took him a month and a half to accept—and lose—all three of those jobs. Mostly due to drunkenness, but in her father's case there was that can of paint thrown through Mrs. Dean's window in a fit of temper.

When the shine had completely worn off his conversion, when the church people had tried and failed to train him in the discipline of godly living, when Mrs. MacAdam finally cast a cold eye his direction, he ceased coming to church.

By this time, however, he'd whispered to Dara that he could turn his life around given time, given someone who understood.

She began slipping out the back door while her father slept, to meet Kevin at the vacant lot behind the Shell station. They picked their way among the weeds and dumpster spillover to a place behind a corrugated shed, out of the shine of the streetlights.

And there he walked with her in the shadows.

And there he talked with her, pressing her back against the aluminum wall.

And there it was he who first told Dara she was his own.

And in no time at all, she was. They slipped off to the courthouse after work, left the marriage certificate and a note for her father on the coffee table, and took a bagful of clothes and her toothbrush to Kevin's apartment, her new home.

When her father came by the next morning, he stood in the doorway and said, "I want you to have a church wedding." Kevin shrugged. And so it was determined that they would say their vows the next Sunday before God and man and purse-lipped Connie MacAdam. They never went to church again.

She tried once to go back. She put on the sundress she'd worn to her wedding and said she was going. He batted her face with the butt of his hand, and she fell headlong into the bedroom wall. Who did she plan to meet there? he wanted to know. A red trickle from her nose stained the white of her dress, so she stayed home.

When the church people stood in line at her counter at the store, their eyes trailed a predictable course from the bruise on her cheekbone to the tops of their own shoes. Mrs. MacAdam stopped coming altogether.

And when the rumors started to fly about her supposed pregnancy and abortion, she knew they had started, developed, and gotten their polish in church.

No, Dara thought when she returned home from the Studmuffin and sat on her bed. On Sunday she would sit things out, find something of her own to do.

She pulled the watercolor from the frame, fingered the initials in the corner, and wondered, *Who was SJ?*

CHAPTER 7

*D*ara heard a knock at the restaurant door, flipped the switch on the coffeepot, and turned. Hooper waited outside with a stockpot.

She unlocked the door and stepped aside. "Where've you been?"

He walked in, set the pot down, and pulled a spoon from under the counter, then lifted the lid and scooped a bite for Dara. "Try this."

"I think you had Tom worried."

"Try it." He shoved the spoon in.

It was beans, meaty and spicy, and a little sweet.

"You like it?"

"Yeah." Her mouth was full. "Good."

"I thought you would!" He crossed his arms and grinned.

"This is what you've been doing?"

"That, and something else." He pulled a rumpled sticky note from his pocket and slapped it on the counter. "This is the recipe. Think you can make more?"

She looked it over. "Yeah. I could do that."

"Good. Keep that pot for today. Put up a special, 'Whistle Berries and Cornbread, $3.50.' I've got the cornbread in the car."

"Whistle berries? You call them 'whistle berries'?"

"Sure, everybody knows that. And if they don't, you can tell them. With a straight face. No, now, I said a straight face."

He loped outside and came back with two pans.

"You said you'd been doing something else."

"Talk at you later, kid. Tell Tom I'll come by when you close."

When Tom saw the sign, he smiled. "Whistle berries."

"It's beans."

"I know. It was Holly's name for them."

"Do you mind?"

He straightened the sign. "Hooper makes good beans. They'll sell."

They did. They sold the last bowl just after four to a roofer who quipped, "Beans, beans, the musical fruit, the more you eat, the more you toot."

"Genius thinks he made that up," said Dara.

"It is a bit crude, isn't it?"

"Quit snickering. It's only the men who say it, you'll notice."

"Holly used to say it."

"A match made in heaven."

"I thought so. But look there." He joined her at the cook's window. A young man at the counter turned to trade jokes with the people in the booth across the way, who bantered with the couple behind them, who contributed to the debate raging round the large table in the middle.

The place pulsed with the ruffle and flam of happy talk.

"I like this," said Tom. "This is why she wanted a restaurant."

"Jane and Hooper want to paint it blue."

"Give me this, and you can paint it purple." He patted her shoulder and got back to work.

Hooper came by just after they'd locked up. "Tom! Get out here a second!" He had a brown grocery bag folded at the top.

"What's in your briefcase?" asked Tom.

"Sit down, and I'll show you. Come on, girls, you too."

He maneuvered the three to their chairs. When they were seated, he opened the bag and pulled out a yellow and green menu. He slapped it on the table like a challenge and waited.

"You've got Holly on the cover." Tom pressed a thumb to his lips.

"Yep, just like the sign out front."

Tom leaned back. "You don't think it exploits her?"

"No, Tom, I don't. I wouldn't treat my daughter that way." Hooper leaned forward. "You gotta understand. It tickled her that people came in here to see her. I wouldn't take nothin' for that girl, but she did love attention. Didn't she love attention? Didn't you love the way she loved it?"

Tom nodded.

"Then let's give it to her! Let's have her all over this place! Don't let it be just another greasy spoon that can't even compete with Denny's!"

"Ouch!" whispered Jane.

"Don't mince words, Hoop. Tell me what you think." At last, Tom smiled.

Hooper relaxed. "People still listen to her music. Folks go by with their windows down, and I hear her on the stereo. They remember."

"I know, old friend. I'm on your side. Let's see what's inside of this." He opened the menu.

Dara and Jane closed in for a look.

"Cackle berries!" said Dara. "Hooper, what's a 'cackle berry'?"

Tom laughed.

"Think about it," said Hooper.

"Cackle berries. Cackle … chickens! They're eggs!"

"Maybe I'll put a picture of an egg in there to clarify."

"Good idea," said Jane. "Look at this: 'Steak and skunk eggs'!"

"Onions." Hooper grinned.

"Brown gargle?" asked Dara.

"Coffee!"

Tom laughed again and brushed a tear away. "She'd love it, Hoop. She would. But you'd better draw some pictures."

Someone knocked on the window.

"Zita!" Dara dashed to let her in.

"Good news, Dara! I've found the name!"

"What name?" asked Tom.

"He doesn't know?"

"It didn't come up."

She glanced at the three seated around the table. "Then, should I wait—"

"No! Tell me now. Please."

"Let her sit down." Hooper pulled a chair from another table, and she took it.

She pulled a paper from her purse. "It was donated two months ago by Carla Martin."

"Oh Zita! Her name's 'Carla'? Are you sure?"

"Why?" asked Jane.

"My mother's name is Clara. Are you sure it's Carla?"

"It's Carla," said Hooper. "She taught piano at the music store."

"My mother played piano!" Dara bounced in her seat. "Maybe she changed her name to Carla!"

"What's this about?" Tom looked from Hooper to Dara.

"Later," said Jane. "Hooper, how long's Carla lived here?"

"I don't know. She might have moved here ten years ago."

Dara clapped a hand over her mouth. "Where's she live? Can I go see her?"

"You can if you don't mind driving," said Hooper. "She moved to Crayton a while back."

"Crayton!"

"What is that, a three-hour drive?" asked Tom.

Hooper shrugged. "Four."

"Her mother disappeared when Dara was a child," said Jane. "And now Dara's family picture has turned up in Zita's store."

"Well, I knew Carla," Hooper said. "Maybe if I saw the picture I could tell if it was her."

Back at the trailer they clustered around while Hooper studied the photo. "I don't know. Carla's a blonde."

"She could have bleached it," said Jane.

"Probably did. She wore glasses. Something about her eyes …"

"It's been a long time since this picture was taken," said Zita.

"I don't know, Dara," said Hooper. "I don't think it's her, but maybe I'm wrong. Why don't you call her?"

He promised to look up Carla's phone number and address, and beyond that, there was little else to say. Everyone went home, and after a time, Jane went to bed.

Dara sat outside on the doorstep. "Can I ask you for something?" she asked the moonlit air. "Can I ask you for this?"

She heard the gentle rhythm of crickets and felt the brush of a cool breeze against her cheek.

In the depths of her sleep, the voices were her mother and father in the next room, the indistinct sound of the lilt and timbre, the closing doors, the murmurs and sighs. Adult voices holding the world together while she slept. Her legs extended, and her clenched hands unfolded like blossoms. In her sleep, she smiled.

Her mother's voice drew near. "We've got to find her," she said. And in that moment, Dara found herself hiding under the bed again, in that secret place tinted ice blue by the sunlight that shone through her bedspread. She heard a closet door roll open a room away and knew they were looking under the clothes. Dara squirmed, ripe to burst with laughter when her mother lifted the bedspread at last.

"I'll let you bang on people's doors," she heard. "I'll drive around the neighborhood and look for her."

They were leaving? But they never looked under the bed! She'd be left alone if she didn't tell them where she was. She tried to speak, but her mouth wouldn't work. She pushed at the words, but they stuck behind her teeth.

She opened her eyes to a dark room in the trailer, with Algernon warm at her side.

It was Jane's voice she heard.

"Has she got favorite houses she goes to, or is it a complete mystery every time?"

"No, it's always different," Tom answered.

Dara heard car keys and checked her alarm clock. It was after two.

By the time she put on her bathrobe, they were gone.

She walked to the living room and peeked through the blinds, just as Jane's truck eased around the corner. There were no other cars, no lights in the houses. The HandiMart across the intersection was dark, except for one light in the back they kept on at night.

She put a kettle on for tea and heard the thrum of Hooper's Fairlane in the drive. She opened the door. Hooper strode up the walk in his jeans and undershirt, with Clemmie asleep in his arms.

"Where's Tom?" he demanded.

"Well—he just left. Why?"

"Boy can't keep his own kid in the house at night." He stepped in and collapsed into the recliner. "I get called at two o'dark in the morning. Bernice Harmon saying my granddaughter's curled up on her sofa, and she can't reach Tom—and neither can I!" His whiskers glinted in the lamplight. "And it's not the first time!"

"I guess they went to find her."

"They're not *gonna* find her, because I've got her right here!" Hooper ran a hand over Clemmie's hair. The girl opened her eyes and closed them again. "Can I put her down someplace?"

"You can put her on my bed." Dara tightened the belt on her robe. "I'll straighten it up for you."

The kettle whistled.

"Don't bother. I'll do that. You make enough water for two cups?"

She had, but it should have been four. She called Jane's cell phone, and before long, Jane had located Tom, and the two were back.

Tom walked in laughing, like he'd been struck stupid.

"Where was she this time?"

"This time!" Hooper stood. "That's just it, isn't it, Tom? *This* time! This time she was at Bernice Harmon's house, and next time …" He shrugged. "Who knows?"

"Oh, Hooper, give over," Tom said. "Bernice could be Clem's granny. Where is she?" He walked down the hall.

"My bed," called Dara.

He returned with Clemmie in his arms, still asleep. "I suppose you think I should give her a good beating?" He shouldered past his father-in-law.

"You might lock the place up," said Hooper.

"I do lock it," said Tom, and he was out the door.

At half past four, Dara gave up trying to sleep. She put her bathrobe on, stepped outside, and settled into one of Clemmie's swings. The grass felt cool under her feet, and the night air rang with the song of one cricket.

She looked for and spotted the Big Dipper. Her mother once showed her how to find the North Star by following the path set by the outer edge of the cup. "For all the time that ever was," her mother whispered, "people have made their way home by that star."

Just a speck in the sky, hardly big enough to twinkle. Still, she whispered, "Please" to the small gray star. "Please, please, please."

The cricket paused as if to catch its breath, and a breeze hushed through the trees.

She wanted to go back to sleep and return to that ice-blue place under the bed long ago. But she'd tried that already, and the path was lost.

The swing hung low to the ground. Dara moved in circles like a deadweight and leaned her head against the chain. She heard a whine of hinges and turned to Tom's back door. Clemmie stepped out and shut it behind her. She walked toward the gate, a small silhouette in a white nightgown.

"Hey!" Dara said.

The girl's arms flung open, and she leapt away from the gate.

"It's only me, Clemmie."

"Well don't scare me!"

"Scare you? You should be spanked. What are you doing out here?"

"Nothing." She joined Dara on the second swing.

"Nothing. Well you can do nothing in your bed."

The cricket started up again.

"Mrs. Harming has a fish tank."

"A fish tank—that's great. And I'll bet she'd show it to you any morning or afternoon you asked."

"Yep."

"You scared everyone tonight, you know."

The girl leaned back and began to pump her legs. "Daddy says maybe we can get a fish tank."

"You like fish?"

"Nope." She was gaining altitude. "You can't do anything with fish."

Dara nodded.

"I used to have a pony when I was little."

"When you were little. What are you now?"

"Well, I'm not *little* little."

"Ah."

"My pony's name was Kansas."

"Why Kansas?"

"Mommy said he was the color of …" She shrugged. "Something they grow in Kansas."

"Wheat?"

Clemmie didn't answer.

"You must miss your mama."

She stopped kicking. Her swing slowed to a soft glide, like a pendulum. She nodded.

"I know what that's like," Dara said.

"Did your mommy die?"

"No. She went away."

"She did?" Her eyes grew round as quarters. "Why?"

Dara looked away. "I don't know."

Clemmie stroked Dara's arm. "She doesn't sound like a good mommy."

"What happened to Kansas?"

"Daddy says I'm too big for ponies." The girl flitted back and forth, her white gown flapping around two tiny legs with tender feet. Her legs went limp. "So I guess I'm not little."

"Your dad says he locks the doors at night," said Dara.

"Yep."

"So how do you get out?"

"He keeps the key on a hook thing."

"Where you can reach?"

"I have to climb on the counter."

Dara nodded.

"I'll go to bed now," Clemmie said.

"I think that's a good idea."

The girl slid off the swing and padded to the back door, opened it, and went inside.

Dara touched the place on her arm that Clementine had touched, a star of a girl in the moonlight.

She walked to Tom's back door and opened it. She turned the porch light on so she could see and found the key on the counter.

She'd give it to Tom in the morning. She locked the door.

Dearest Dara and Jane,

What a blessing that you girls were our last guests at The Teahouse. How better to bring to a close something so dear to me, than a lingering night of laughter with two ladies who were friends from the very start?

I feel fine. H. and I are having a wonderful

time. We've been to Scotty's Castle in Death Valley—got some decorating ideas for our mansion when our ship comes in! Then drove to LA and northward along the Pac. Coast on Hwy. 1. True, true grandeur. Visited several dear friends along the way.

How is Algernon? I'm so glad you took him, Dara. My mind is at ease, knowing I've done well by my dear cat.

I've enclosed the address of some friends in Sacr. we will visit in two weeks. If you write us there, they'll be sure we get the letter.

Love,

Glenda

Jane and Dara,

To my happy surprise, Glenda's health has improved since we left. She sleeps while I drive, so maybe that's why.

I pretend we're taking this trip for Glenda's good, but in all honesty, I know it's for my own. In our thirty years of marriage, I've never had my gadabout all to myself.

But since we've left, we've had great talks. Things we never took the time to discuss. Like the child we lost at birth and why we never had another. About whether deep down we're sorry we married each other, with all our respective faults, and it turns out we're not.

Pardon the smeared ink. I shouldn't write these things when I've only got one page to write on—I drop tears and make a mess.

I'll close, asking you for your prayers.

Harold

Sunday morning while Jane dressed for church, Dara held her position on the kitchen chair in her blue plaid pajamas and gray bathrobe. When Tom and Hooper came, she pulled her bathrobe tighter and retied the belt. She wasn't going.

Hooper brought Carla Martin's phone number and address, scrawled on a yellow sticky note. Dara studied the note. Her mother had a phone number, and this could be it.

Jane emerged from her bedroom and smiled at Hooper. "You're dapper today."

"I clean up good, don't I?" He wore black pants and a black shirt with a plaid yoke and mother-of-pearl snaps. His boots shone with a fresh polish, and he held a black Stetson in his hand.

"That's his cowboy poet outfit," said Tom.

"Have you know, I'm poet laureate of the Brittlebush Rodeo."

"Why don't they call it 'poet lariat'?" Jane asked.

Hooper laughed at this and settled an arm around her shoulders. Tom shot him a look and lifted it off by the sleeve. Jane patted Tom's arm and walked outside. Hooper chuckled, eyeing her every step like … what? He tipped his hat to Dara and left with Tom at his heels.

How long since thoughts of romance—hers or anyone's—had crossed Dara's mind?

It was not a safe world. She slid her pearl along its chain and glanced out the window.

Jane stood near the fence in the sunlight, petting Algernon. She wore a long tunic, earthy pink, her silver earrings mingled in her silver hair. Dara had never thought of her as pretty before, but Jane was a cowboy poet's dream.

An arm around the shoulders wasn't much, was it? Not with Tom around.

Clementine flounced across the yard to her grandfather's arms, in her pink dress and red cowboy boots, a deck of cards in one hand like a clutch purse. A cowboy poet's other dream.

Dara waved them off from the trailer door, the sticky note

curled in the palm of her hand. She took it back to the table for another look.

Carla Martin. The initials were CM.

Like Clara Murphy.

Her mother might've bleached her hair. After what—fourteen years? She probably wore glasses, too.

A piano teacher—of course. Hadn't she taught Dara to play "Chopsticks"?

Carla had to be her mother. Why else would she have the photograph?

But why'd she get rid of it? Why now, after all this time? Dara couldn't think of a single answer that didn't hurt.

Zita had known all about the cat picture. She said it was in front of the photo when she got it. Maybe her mother just forgot the photo was in there. But why cover it up? To hide it? From whom? Dara lifted the watercolor from the kitchen table and stared at the initials on the bottom. Did her mother hide the picture from SJ?

Maybe Dara should just make the phone call and ask Carla her questions. Wouldn't that make sense?

Not really. Carla might deny the whole thing, and what then? How would Dara know for sure without looking?

She wanted to see her. Had to. And there she would stand at the woman's door: *Hi, I'm Dara, the daughter you left, whose picture you discarded.*

She pulled handfuls of hair to ease the tension beneath her scalp.

Her mother might not want to see her. Had she thought of that? She might stand bleach-blonde astride the open door, narrowing her eyes behind those glasses. "You think I've been crying for you all this time? I knew where you lived! If I wanted you, I'd have come back, don't you think? Your father's dead because of you. Get away from me! Out of my sight! Go!"

"Please, please, please, Mommeee!"

Algernon nudged her tear-streaked face and left it flocked with yellow fur.

"Aagh! So stupid!" She lowered the cat to the floor and wiped her nose, then escaped outside to one of Clementine's swings.

"She'd never do that!" she muttered to the morning breeze. Her mother used to bake bread with her, handing Dara a lump of dough to knead and roll with cinnamon and raisins. She used to sing "April Showers" while she braided Dara's hair. She'd tuck her in at night with prayers and a story, *Goodnight Moon*, *Ping,* or *Winnie the Pooh*.

Dara whipped the pearl along its chain. *My mother loved me!* she insisted. Surely it was so: She remembered her mother's love, as true as the other thing she remembered—that her mother had left.

She had left her.

"Take the chance," whispered the morning air. Dara lolled in the swing and listened to the hushing breeze till she was calm.

She had once worshipped with Jane in a place wide and open as all heaven. She missed that. She stood and glanced around Tom's backyard. There was the trailer, the garage, the grass, the trees, the deck, the swing set, and a redwood fence around it all. She walked to a patch of sunlight in the center and twirled. Once. Not the same.

But Brittlebush wasn't a big town, was it? She could get to the desert in just a few minutes. She ran inside and dressed, then got in her car and drove.

In five minutes she was out of town. She pulled her car off the highway down a dirt road, and then she stopped and got out. Off in the far distance lay the hills that surrounded her valley. She couldn't see the shanty church from where she stood, but she felt its pull. "The First Church of the Exceedingly Isolated Valley," Jane called it. She walked several paces and took a deep breath.

Not home, she thought, *but it's something like it, and I can get here anytime*.

Something burst inside like a dandelion, and she felt all the things that troubled her, Carla, Clara, Kevin, her father, and even Hooper's arm on Jane's shoulders—she felt all of it fly off like little bits of fluff. There was something much bigger, and she was lost in it. She twirled. Once, twice, fifty times. She felt airy fingertips brushing hers, and she laughed, closed her eyes, and danced.

"I love you," it said. "I love you, love you, love you!"

"Why?" she cried at the top of her voice and danced to the silent beat of the air.

※

Monday morning, before they opened, Tom asked, "Did you call her?"

"No. I don't—"

"I didn't expect you to. Sensitive matter, isn't it?"

Dara nodded.

"Listen, why not go this week before we start our longer hours? We'd drive there after closing, you'd pay a call to Carla, and we'd drive back. It's a bit of driving in one night, but not so bad if we take turns, eh?"

"Tom! You'd come with me?"

"Well, I think it's a good idea. Don't you?"

"Maybe. But it might not even be her, she might not—"

"Dear heart, if you're not her daughter, she'll adopt you."

She took a breath. "Okay."

"Shall we go, then?"

"Okay."

"Good. We'll go tonight."

※

They were ten miles out of town before Tom said, "It's going to be a very long drive if you don't talk to me."

"I'm sorry, I'm not good at—"

"Talking to people. You've said that. But couldn't you try? For your dear friend Tom?"

"You go first."

He laughed. "Ask me something."

"Okay. Why didn't you want Hooper to put his arm around Jane?"

"Oh, you saw that. Lecherous old fart."

"Hooper's lecherous?"

"Don't quote me! No, he's a fine man. But what if they got married?"

"It was just an arm around her shoulder."

"That's where it starts, right there. And then what? Would Hooper be my father-in-law or my brother-in-law? It gets worse. Would Jane be my sister or my mother-in-law? It's all so incestuous."

"Terrible!" Dara laughed.

"Ask something else."

"Ummm. Okay, why do you channel surf all night?"

"What, do you peer in my window?"

"Clemmie told me."

"The little snitch!" He shrugged. "Excess testosterone. It's a guy thing. Besides, I don't, much."

"She says you sleep in front of the TV, in your clothes."

"She says that? What else does she say about me?"

"Uh, nothing. Nothing much." She glanced at the mat of hair curling under his cuff.

"Ask another question."

"Who taught you to cook?"

"That's it. No more questions from you."

"So ask me one."

"Are you the Dara Brogan I read about in the papers?"

She stiffened.

"Sorry, wrong question. You don't have to—"

"You knew. Did Jane tell you?"

"No. Jane wouldn't."

"But you knew all the same. Everyone'll know. Just like you, they'll all know!" She pressed her head with her hands.

"Hold on there. They needn't know. I never told anyone your last name."

"Soon enough—"

"What's your maiden name?"

"Murphy."

"Ah, no good. Your father's name was in the papers too."

"What are you talking about?"

"Your middle name?"

"Pearl." She fingered her necklace.

"Dara Pearl. There. A lovely name but not a famous one. Your name is Dara Pearl."

"Oh!" She considered. "But my first name—"

"Is uncommon, but there must be one or two more out there."

She nodded.

"Dara Pearl," he said.

She smiled.

"A fine name."

CHAPTER 8

*C*arla Martin was no bleached blonde. She was fair-skinned and tall, a Nordic blonde, born Carla Swensen to Swedish immigrants.

Dara believed her because her eyebrows and eyelashes glinted gold in the afternoon light. She bore no resemblance to Clara Murphy.

"If I can't be your mother, maybe I can help you out," she said. "Come in."

"You collect cats." Tom stated the obvious. Cats slept in the tapestry of accent pillows, lazed in gilded porcelain on the mantel, and peered from the oil painting over the sofa. The corner hutch displayed a grouping of miniature china, wood, and pewter cats. A live calico ambled by on its way to the kitchen.

"That's how I came by the watercolor," said Carla. "My friend Shelly Rimes gave it to me. I used to perform piano recitals with her at Saint Christopher's. I never opened the frame, so I didn't know about the photograph."

"Ah." Tom shifted in his chair. Dara traced the velvet piping of a cushion.

"Come to think of it," said Carla, "Shelly has a recital next Sunday evening. She's on vacation now, but she gets home Friday, and I know she has rehearsal on Saturday. Why not go to the recital? She plays wonderfully, and you can talk to her afterward."

She walked to her desk and pulled a pen from the drawer. "This is a smaller house than we had in Brittlebush. I had to weed out my possessions." She jotted a note. "Here's her phone number and the details of the recital. I'll give her a call and tell her to expect you. It's kind of awkward that I threw out her gift, but if it'll help you find your mother …"

Dara took the paper. "Thanks."

Carla hesitated, one hand rubbing the fingers of the other hand. "I don't think Shelly is the woman in the photo. Still, she must have gotten it from somewhere."

"Why don't you think so?" asked Tom.

"Well …" She lifted the frame from the coffee table. "Her hair is shorter … I don't know. I just can't imagine her leaving a husband and child. She's a very nice person."

They'd taken the first bites of their Big Macs before Tom spoke. "Are you fuming or sulking? I can't decide."

"She said my mother wasn't nice."

"No, she didn't."

"She said Shelly couldn't be my mother because she was nice."

"She could be wrong. Shelly may well be a nice pianist who happens to be your long lost mother with a haircut."

Dara took a savage bite of her hamburger, and another. Tom occupied his mouth with eating, and the silence was a blessed relief. If he'd just stop grinning—

"I hear there's to be a piano recital Sunday evening at Saint Christopher's," he said. "Care to join me?"

"Thanks." She finished her burger and watched him chew his last bite. The minute he swallowed, she gathered the wrappers and napkins onto the tray, dumped them in the trash, and hurried to the car. "Give me the keys."

"Why?"

"You said we'd share driving. My turn."

She knew he was stewing over her. Out of the corner of her eye, she saw him, one elbow propped on the door, the knuckle of his thumb pressed to his lips. She focused straight ahead and willed him to give her some peace. He turned forward and sighed.

She'd been so sure she'd found her mother.

She recalled the moment they parked in front of Carla's house. She'd been so busy checking her hair and smoothing her blouse, so desperate to calm herself, she hadn't noticed the flowers beside the door. Then she glanced out the window, and lost her breath altogether.

"What?" Tom asked.

"Lantana!"

"What?"

Dara pointed to a flowering bush beside the front step. "She had a bush by the door—orange, just like that. Dad let the yard go, but he kept the lantana … or anyway, it stayed alive."

She rang the bell, bouncing on her heels, wishing she looked better, were more of a prize. Her clothes could fit better, her hair could be fuller, her life could be—she winced. Any minute the door would open, and there'd be—

Not her mother. Dara knew right away. Tom explained the situation and asked if she might be Clara Murphy, and Dara listened for the answer. But she already knew, the answer was no.

Maybe Shelly was her mother; Carla could be wrong. Maybe Dara would attend the recital with Tom, and a woman in a long black dress would walk to the piano and turn to face her audience. Maybe she'd search the crowd for one particular face till she found Dara's, and there would be this radiant instant of mutual recognition. The woman would beam at Dara and bow, and then she would play, and in every nuance of her music, Dara would hear something sweetly familiar. Then the woman would play "April Showers," and tears would glisten in her eyes and in Dara's, and when the recital was over, well-wishers would gather around, but she'd break away from them and embrace Dara, and all the stained glass windows of Saint Christopher's, the bewildered well-wishers, and smiling Tom—all of them would disappear, and there would just be Dara and her mother, crying and laughing with so much to say.

Maybe it would go something like that, if Shelly wasn't too nice to be her mother.

The sun slipped over the earth's edge, leaving a pink glow behind the distant mountains, the "particular golden pink" her father had spoken of in his story. She touched her pearl and slid it side to side on the chain.

Thoughts of her father reminded her: She glanced at the instrument cluster behind the steering wheel, as he'd always told her … "Uh oh."

"What?"

"Your warning lights are lit up like Christmas." She came to a stop.

Tom leaned over and looked. "Blast!" He got out and opened the hood. The engine was a mass of loose belts. He slipped a hand down between the radiator and the pulley.

"The bolt's gone."

"What bolt?"

"The main pulley bolt. It holds the pulley to the engine." He rubbed his hand on his jeans.

"Don't suppose you have a spare one in your trunk somewhere?"

"No." He rubbed his nose. "It's big as your thumb. A specialty item." He shut the hood and turned to scan the road. "We're in the back of beyond here, aren't we?"

There wasn't a single set of headlights, not a single lit ranch house window in sight.

"I saw a rest stop about eight miles back," said Dara.

"They don't have main pulley bolts in rest stops."

"We might find a phone."

"I could call Jane, let her know where we are. Maybe the highway patrol. You want to wait here? I'll go."

Dara considered the road, still empty and getting dark. If a psychopath wandered by … "No," she said. "I'll come with you."

He pulled a flashlight and blanket from the trunk. "May as well wait for the patrolmen at the rest area."

The pink glow behind the mountains had turned deep

persimmon against a cobalt sky, but a full moon was out. It wouldn't be a dark night.

"We might watch the road as we go," he said. "It's a big bolt. We might find it."

"Oh, right," said Dara. "Somewhere between here and Crayton."

"It had to fall off within the last few miles. The car overheats without it." Tom turned the flashlight on and scanned across the pavement. "Keep your eye out."

They did not, however, find a main pulley bolt in the road. Neither did they find a pay phone when they finally trudged into the rest stop.

"What they do have here is a toilet," said Tom.

"You sound desperate."

"I am."

"My dad always just went off in the bushes."

"It's only our first date." He winked and disappeared behind the cinder-block wall covering the bathroom door.

"Not a date," Dara muttered, walking a circle under the lights. What made him say that? She hadn't done anything to make him think that. She'd bought her own hamburger. Taken a turn driving.

She paced.

It was not a safe world. She didn't want to date anyone. She wanted to have a quiet life in her backyard trailer with her cat and her job behind the window at the Studmuffin. She'd be Dara Pearl to the few who knew her at all. She wanted her safe friendships with Jane, Clementine, and Hooper. And with Tom. He was her friend too.

Wasn't he?

Maybe he was joking—he'd joke about a thing like that. She wouldn't bring up what he said. If he brought it up, she'd put it down. If he wanted to buy her dinner or drive her home, she'd say no.

The recital! She had said she would go with him. He probably considered that a date. She'd just tell him she changed her mind. She'd go alone.

Tom emerged from behind the brick wall in front of the bathroom doors. "What shall we do?"

"Nothing!"

"What?"

She walked away.

Tom kept up. "By the looks of things, it could be some time before we see anyone. Maybe morning."

"Great."

"Well, there are ranch houses. I saw them on the way to Crayton. But they're all down little roads here and there. Worst case, we can find them in the daylight."

"Oh! Just great."

"Yeah. Well. So we either wait here or in the car."

"Might as well be here." She plopped down under a tree.

He sat next to her and spread the blanket over their legs. "If you want to sleep, I'll keep watch for cars."

She leapt to her feet.

"What's wrong?"

"Let's go back to the car." At least there they'd have a stick shift between them.

Tom shrugged, rolled the blanket, and tucked it under his arm. He turned on the flashlight, and they set out.

Dara's strides kept pace with the *creak, creak* of the crickets in the brush beside the road in the moonlight.

They'd walked a long way when her feet began to cramp. She yawned. "Talk to me."

"Tell me about your mother."

"My mother. I was little when she left. But I have really good memories of her."

"Tell me."

"She loved me. My dad did too, but he worried about every little thing—that's how he showed it."

"How'd she show it?"

"Sometimes she'd turn and look at me and then—I'd been there all along, you know? But she'd let out a yell like … like she was at the airport. You know when people meet at the airport and they run to each other? She'd run at me, sweep me up, and swing me in a circle, screaming, 'My baby! My sweet, pretty baby!'" Dara shouted this, twirling with her arms wrapped around herself to show just how it was. It crossed her mind that she was getting punchy.

"Strange that a mother like that would leave." Tom slapped his forehead. "I don't mean anything bad by that."

"No, I know what you mean. It is strange."

"It must have hurt you badly."

"Yeah. It hurt." She was too tired to fight the tears.

"No idea why?"

"I think Dad blamed himself. But I don't know why. I can't think why. Unless he said 'not a safe world' just one time too many." This struck her as intensely funny, and she laughed.

"He said that?"

"All the time."

"And you believe him?"

She walked several paces. "Yeah. I do. I sure believe him now."

"I suppose I'd think so too, if I were you."

"What do you think? Is it a safe world?"

"Ah. Good question."

When he'd been silent a long while, she demanded, "Well?"

"No, I don't suppose it is. But it has its moments."

"You and Holly were happy."

"Yes. We were very happy."

"Tell me about her."

"Oh, there was so … *much* to her! You know, she sang beautifully—"

"Like an angel on steroids."

"Yes. And she was really beautiful. But more than all that … *beneath* all that there was this great well of feeling. It came out in her music and in the way she talked to people in the restaurant, the way she cared for Clemmie …" He walked several paces before continuing. "I just wanted to give her a safe place to do all that."

"Did you?" Dara could only whisper the question.

"Well, there was that fall from the horse."

A rabbit flicked through the flashlight beam not eight feet ahead. Startled, Dara leapt back, laughing.

Tom steadied her with a hand on her shoulder and continued.

"I think you would've liked Holly. I think perhaps she was very much like your mum."

"My mom?"

"Yeah, you said she swept you up. Holly was spirited, and … boisterous like that."

"Did she sing to Clemmie when she fixed her hair?"

"Yeah. Your mum?"

"Yup! And did she teach her how to make cinnamon bread?"

"Ha! No! I was the cook in the family."

"Oh, no."

"Oh, yes! Holly taught Clemmie to ride a pony."

"You'll have to teach her now."

"No. I won't teach her that."

"Why?"

"It's not a safe world."

She glimpsed his smile and staggered on, too tired to know why it bothered her. "How'd the accident happen?" she asked, and winced. "I shouldn't ask that. I'm sorry."

"It's all right."

He was silent a long time, and Dara thought he wouldn't answer.

"What's the big question? 'O Death, where is your sting?' I can tell you where it is." He raised his face, as if addressing the sky. "She took a fall during a barrel race at the rodeo. The doctor looked her over, and she seemed to be all right. Two weeks later a blood clot found its way to her brain. We'd gone to the stables to groom her horse. I left to get the thermos from the car, and when I got back, she was on the floor."

"That's it?"

"Yeah. Doctor said it was instant and painless, isn't that nice?"

"You see?" she shouted. "It's not a safe world! People … people *matter* to you, and they come along, and they step on your soul! And they don't mean to, they're just not paying attention. But it hurts you just the same. And that," she said as she poked the air with her finger, "that's if you're lucky! If you're not, they squish you under their work boots." She stomped the ground while Tom stood gaping at her. She twisted her foot back and forth and continued. "They grind it in, and they mean it to hurt, they hope it hurts long and hard, you know? And even if they're perfect little cowgirl angels like your Holly, even if they do nothing else to hurt you, they *die!*" She kicked a rock and sent it flying, but when it hit the blacktop and bounced, it went *clink!* It bounced twice more—*clink* and *clink!*

"What was that?" asked Tom.

"Shine your light. Over there, I think."

Tom shone his light where she pointed, but there was nothing there. He scanned it in a circle and stopped. Black against the pavement something wobbled. "Is that it?"

Dara jogged ahead and picked it up. It was a bolt half again as big as her thumb. "Yeah. I think it's our bolt."

"Amazing."

"Had to be here somewhere."

He laughed and collapsed on the road, spread-eagle on the yellow lines.

"What are you doing?" She giggled.

"I'm tired!"

"You'll get run over."

He arched his neck backward to look up the road, then raised his head and peered between his feet. "Nah!" He lay his head down.

Dara's legs buckled, and she sat beside him. "So what do we do, take a nap here?"

"Sounds lovely."

"The pavement's hard."

"It is rather, isn't it?" He didn't move.

She lay beside him on the road and held the bolt in both hands like a lily.

He chuckled. "You were a bit worked up back there, weren't you?"

She didn't answer.

"You know why I watch the telly all night?"

"Why?"

"I can't think how to go to bed without her. I manage during the day. I get Clemmie ready for day care, pick her up in the afternoon, feed her, spend time with her and all that. And I have the restaurant. But at night, once Clemmie's in bed, once I turn the telly off, it's just me. No Holly stringing me along, bouncing on the bed on her knees, telling me all her plans."

"She did that?"

"Never grew up. And never got tired. She was awake or she was asleep. Click, like a light."

"Isn't it hard at the restaurant?"

"Sometimes."

"Why do you keep it? To preserve her memory?"

"That's not all of it."

"So?"

"You really want to know? You won't laugh?"

"Why?"

"I like to watch people eat."

She laughed.

"Heartless! I trusted you!"

"Why do you watch them eat?"

"Because when they eat, I can see into their souls."

"You're nuts!"

"You watch them sometime. Catch them eating alone, when they think no one's watching. They're positively transparent."

"Okay. What do souls look like?"

"Well it's like this: You watch a man sitting alone, and he's eating a bit of potato. He puts it in his mouth, and his eyes close a little because it's good, and something childlike crosses his face, something like the baby with his mother. It's just for an instant. But it's there."

"That's it?"

"No. You look deeper. There's more."

"Like what?"

"Like sorrow. Everybody's sad, Dara. Ever notice that?"

"Yeah. I can buy that."

"And a kind of … of resigned disappointment. Nobody's okay with themselves. No one."

"Hooper is."

"Watch him. Not even Hooper."

"So why would you want to see all that?"

"Because of the other thing I see, deeper still."

"What's that?"

"A kind of … luminescence. People may not like themselves, but somebody does like them. And if you look close enough, you see why. Take a fat woman in a dirty dress who spills down both sides of the chair, who orders pie à la mode and then hopes against hope no one sees her eating. Forget the magazines. Look deep enough at her, and you'll see the beauty God sees."

Dara had lost the will to answer him. Her head rolled to one side, and her breath flowed heavy and rhythmic as ocean surf.

"You're falling asleep," said Tom.

"Mmm."

He rolled on his side. "If we sleep here, a semi will come along in the morning and run us over."

"Mmm."

"Come on." He stood and stretched an arm to her. "Let's go."

She opened her eyes and took a deep breath. She accepted his hand, and he helped her up. *Sweet Tom*, she thought, *sees people's souls.*

He slipped his arm around her waist, and tired as she was

she let him. She almost didn't have to wake up, her head resting on his shoulder. They trudged along. "Almost there," he said at length. When they got to the car, he asked, "What do you say we rest a bit before making our repair?"

"Good idea."

She fell asleep the moment she pulled the lever to lower the back of her seat.

And she fell—*bam! bam! bam!*—down the rock ("you slut!") and down the white refrigerator door ("you hideous, worthless slut!"). He slammed her head, and it hit the chrome handle. A thick liquid tickle coursed past her ear.

He grabbed her nightgown collar in a fist and yanked, and she glimpsed the arc of red smear on the white enamel door. He jerked her toward the living room and drove her face down onto the couch in the blue television light, her hair smeared and plastered to her face, as the top of her head rammed again and again against the arm of the couch, and she swallowed the spoiled-meat taste of blood.

She felt the pressure of a hand on her shoulder and in a flash of panic knew that the hand was not part of the dream. She heard the animal shriek of a lion and realized it was her own voice, and her eyes snapped open to blinding light, and her hand tore through the air and was caught by the wrist. She fought and was released, and she heard Tom's cry. "Dara! What's the matter with you?"

She bolted upright and looked to the driver's side of the car. He wasn't there, so she turned her head to the other side, where she found the door open, and Tom squatted beside her. Blood seeped from between the fingers he pressed to his face. He removed them to reveal three livid scratches across his cheek.

"What are you doing?" she cried.

"What's wrong with you?" he repeated. "I was waking you up, that's what! You were crying."

She got out of the car and walked into the brush, quaking, brittle, struggling to separate the dream from the morning, the blood on the white enamel from the blood on his cheek. She sat on a rock and caught her breath.

She turned to him. He stood apart, wiping his face and fingers with a red shop rag. She groaned. "I did that?"

He half-nodded, trembling himself, and stuffed the rag into his back pocket. He stormed to the open engine compartment and bent in. She went to stand beside him. The bolt was in position, and he jerked the wrench to secure it in place.

"I'm sorry, Tom."

He slammed the hood shut. "Forget it!"

"You're still bleeding."

He yanked the rag from his pocket and held it to his face. She smelled engine grease.

"That's dirty."

He rolled his eyes and clenched his teeth. She flinched. He walked to the driver's side. "Would you get in?"

She did, and the two sat together, her head bowed, his breath heaving. She waited for him to start the engine. She waited a long time and finally peered to the side.

He grabbed her chin in his hand and twisted her head to face him. "Look at me. Sit up. Straight! Sit up straight!" His voice was intense, his jaw tight. "Don't you ever let anyone make you feel like this. Not me or anyone. Sit up, and look me in the eye!" She did, trembling, and he turned to face the steering wheel.

He touched his cheek and looked at his fingertips. The bleeding had slowed. "This doesn't matter. It'll heal. But whatever that was about just now ..." He wiped his eye with the back of his wrist. "I would have killed him."

She looked out the window, remembering her father's grizzled jaw. "Or he'd have killed you," she whispered.

He shrugged. "Besides, your father succeeded after all, didn't he?"

She had seen her father's face as the car went over. A look of resignation. She saw it all again and thought she would fly to bits if Tom didn't shut up. "Can we go?"

"I ... I'm doing this badly. I'm sor—"

"Please, can we go now?"

He started the engine. "Let's go get some breakfast. I should call Jane."

Just before they pulled into the truck stop, they saw Hooper's Fairlane speeding the other way. Tom honked his horn, the Fairlane wheeled onto the ramp, and the two cars met in the parking lot.

Both Jane and Hooper emerged from the Fairlane. Tom opened his door and got out.

"Where you been?" called Hooper.

"Tom! Your face!" Jane ran to him.

He held up a hand and shook his head, then hugged her with one arm.

"Where's Dara?" asked Jane.

"Right here." She got out of the car.

"Zita's picking Clemmie up from school. When you didn't come home, I closed the restaurant."

Hooper eyed the two of them. "What happened here?"

Tom ducked his head. "It's a long story."

"It's my fault," Dara said at the same moment.

"Let me buy you breakfast," said Hooper, "and you can tell me all about it."

Dara turned to Jane, fighting tears.

Jane took Hooper's arm. "Or not. We can talk about something else."

Breakfast was interminable. Hooper chewed his sausage and eggs with his eye on Tom's wound and Dara's bowed head. Jane babbled about Clementine's card game and the cowboy wall clock Zita found for the restaurant. Finally, Hooper cleaned his plate, and Tom and Dara pushed theirs away. Jane washed down the last of her toast with a swallow of tea.

She drove Dara home in Hooper's car. Hooper rode with Tom.

CHAPTER 9

When they pulled into the driveway, Dara trudged past Tom and Hooper where they mumbled under the shaded carport, past Jane where she chewed her thumbnail in the sunlight. She stepped up the metal stair, into the trailer, walked through the living room and down the hall, into her room, where she lay with Algernon on the bed.

She had told Jane what had happened. She had to if she didn't want her to draw the wrong conclusions.

Doubtless, Hooper had gotten to the bottom of things. Tom would've told him the whole story.

Had she said anything in her sleep? How much did Tom know?

The sordid story of Dara Brogan! Not enough that people could read it in the papers; it would be retold and embellished again and again. For how long?

She pressed her face to the wall beside the bed. She wanted to be Dara Murphy again, Dan Murphy's daughter, back in that sad little house with her father's wary eye on the world. This time she'd lock the doors and windows, and this time she'd take her turn at the lookout.

But Tom was right. The name "Murphy" was part of the story.

From now on, she was Dara Pearl. She gripped her pendant in a fetal fist. She'd tell Jane …

Later.

She was so tired.

She awoke when Jane sat on the edge of her bed. "I've poured you a bath." She brushed the hair from Dara's eyes. "Dinner will be ready in half an hour."

Dara smelled roast chicken and lavender bath salts. "Are we having company?"

"No. I thought you could use some mothering tonight."

She sat up and leaned against the wall. "It wasn't Carla. Did I tell you?"

"You'll find her."

"Maybe she doesn't want to be found. We never moved. If she was as close as this, she could have come anytime. If she wanted."

"Some things you'll never know till you ask her yourself."

"Jane?"

"Mm."

"I'm going to go by Dara Pearl, now."

"Yes. Tom told me."

"Tom." She cupped a hand to her forehead.

"Tom's fine."

"I didn't mean to scratch him."

"I didn't think you did."

"He knows all about me now."

"No one knows all about you. Not even you."

"Okay then, just the worst. He knows my father's dead because of me. He probably knows Kevin warmed himself up by watching me bleed. I really hope that's the worst of it, Jane."

"Dara?"

"What?"

"There was a time when I would have had some advice for you. I went to good schools. I studied systematic theology. I was trained to know things. So I would have told you just what God was doing, and what you should do in response. But …" She shrugged and smiled. "I know less now than I once did. So I have no advice. I don't know what God is doing, and I don't know what you should do." She stroked Dara's hair. "But I think he knows, and I think you'll know."

Dara studied her friend's face. There was a weight in the skin around her eyes that was more than age, and a buoyancy in her smile that was more than youth. Would she ever understand this woman?

"I bought you something," said Jane. She handed Dara a bundle tied with green ribbon. Dara slid it off and unfolded a blue nightgown. The fabric was light cotton, the kind to skim with her fingers as it slipped over her head.

"I like it." Dara spread it across her lap and stroked the fabric like a cat. "Jane?"

"Mm?"

"I … I hear voices. Or *a* voice."

"I know." She stood. "Don't let your bath get cold."

While Jane put their plates in the dishwasher, Dara raised an arm to her nose and smelled. Her skin was still fresh with the clean scent of lavender, and her hair rested damp and cool against her neck. Her nightgown smelled of new starch. It all felt sweetly unfamiliar, like trying on a brand-new life.

Jane had served the roast chicken on a bed of wild rice. It broke open when she cut it, brown and glistening, and speckled with rosemary. Dara rested slack in her chair.

With her hand, she slipped an asparagus spear from the platter and ate it. Jane smiled and pulled up a chair, plucking one for herself. She bit the elfin flower off the top and leaned back.

The trees rustled outside in a warm wind, and a breeze whispered through the window.

"You know," said Jane at last, motioning with her asparagus at the evening sky, "I really miss our desert sometimes."

"So do I." Dara rested her head in her hand, gazing at the woven pattern of the tablecloth. "Last Sunday, I drove out of town a ways. It was almost as good."

"Oh? Does Brittlebush have a desert as well?"

"Well, yeah." Dara suddenly caught the meaning of Jane's grin, and sat up. "Yes, it does," she said slowly. It was a great idea.

"We've still got a bit of daylight left." Jane was on her feet.

"I'll change clothes." Dara stood and snatched up the plate of asparagus to cover it with plastic.

Jane took it and gave her a nudge. "Don't bother changing, just put on your shoes."

"Right!" Where they were going, no one would see her in her nightgown. Dara dashed to the bedroom.

They left with the plate of asparagus propped on the emergency brake between them. They rolled their windows down to catch the warm air and skimmed past houses and parks, past trees buzzing electric with cicadas, past motels and fast-food restaurants and auto repair shops. And then they were on the highway.

Dara hung her arm out the window and let the rushing air dance on her open palm in figure eights, playing over her fingers like a silk scarf.

They pulled onto a dirt road and followed it over three hills and two bends until Brittlebush and the highway were out of view. Jane cut the engine. Dara removed her sweater and left it in the car.

There was no sound at all, except the wind. Dara listened for the voice but heard only a long contented sigh, an uncomplicated silence. Jane walked the dirt road farther, and Dara followed. They left the road and set off through the brush till they came to a tumble of boulders. They wound their way through to the other side and onward till the car and the highway were lost from view.

They walked to the top of a gentle rise. Evidently the hill sloped lower on the other side, because from where they stood, they saw miles and miles of undefiled space—hills, rocks, and valleys dotted with brush. The wind whipped Dara's nightgown around her legs, and she sat on a rock to rest. Her hair was nearly dry, and it played in cool strands around her face. She combed it away with her fingers and caught the faint scent of water and soap mixed with the mineral smell of the desert air.

Jane walked farther to where the melba sand gave way to rocks the color of pomegranates. She stepped around them and stopped. Her arms floated, as if lifted by the drumming wind rushing upward from the ledge at her feet.

Dara saw the woman she'd seen that first day on the bluff—but closer this time, and more clearly. She stood like the cross of Christ, like a phoenix at takeoff.

In the pound of the wind Dara heard the fire she rose from, flaming, beating like a distant conga, like a bodhran, like her own heartbeat.

And then began the dancing, the gusts of wind that set the woman maundering and swaying, minding nothing but the beat of the air. She soared.

Dara lifted her arms and let the wind dance her around. "Oh, my love, my love, my love," it sang, and the fire and the love all but consumed her. She staggered and opened her eyes.

Jane stood three feet from the edge.

Dara walked closer and looked down, maybe fifty feet, to the dry creek bed below. A hundred glinting flecks of memory shot through her like shrapnel. She staggered backward, remembering how her father had gripped the handle above the door as he fell. She heard the wail of her own voice. "Come back, Jane."

Jane stood with her arms out, her hair streaming in the wind. "I'm all right."

"Jane, come back now!" she shrieked.

Jane turned and rushed through the rocks to wrap Dara in her arms. "I'm so sorry," she said. "Oh, Dara, I'm so sorry."

The two dropped to their knees on the sand.

She knew the morning chores well enough to accomplish them while her mind was five days and four blocks away at Saint Christopher's, where Shelly Rimes would hold her recital.

When it wasn't across the street at Time and Again. If her mother donated the picture, maybe she stopped in there once in a while.

Dara glanced out the window. Of course no one was there. It was six thirty; everything was closed.

She dipped a rag in bleach water and began wiping the salt and pepper shakers.

Truth was, her mother could be any one of a hundred women walking past the window every day. Had Dara seen her already? She glanced out the window again.

And there stood a cowboy, big as John Wayne.

She jumped.

"Hooper, don't do that!" She unlocked the door.

He entered, with a large Gallo wine box under his arm.

"What goes on out there?" called Tom from the kitchen.

"Your girl's pretty jumpy today. Just what'd you do to her, Tom?"

"I'm not his girl. What's up?"

"I want my breakfast."

She locked the door behind him. "A little early."

"Well, and I brought something for the grand reopening." He set the box on the counter.

"We don't serve alcohol," said Dara.

"Well now, that's real good. Neither do I." He opened the box.

Tom emerged from the kitchen and sidled next to him.

"Sound system," Hooper announced, "compliments of yours truly." He pulled out the CD player.

Tom pulled out four small speakers. "I suppose you've got the music picked out."

"I do." He pulled out several CDs and set them on the counter, then pulled one from the middle of the stack and set it on top. On the cover was a laughing redhead in a fringed denim shirt. The album was titled, *Holly Laurel.*

"You all right with that?" Hooper squinted.

Tom nodded.

"Your customers miss her."

"So do I."

"It would honor her memory, Tom."

"No need to belabor the point."

"No need at all."

Tom shifted.

Hooper took a breath. "Well, you two have work to do, and so do I. Go on and make my breakfast, and by the time you do that, I'll have this all set up. Tom, you know how I like my eggs."

"Coming right up, old chap." Tom headed to the kitchen.

"Old chap!" He shook his head.

Dara turned back to her salt and pepper shakers, and Hooper caught her by the arm. "Listen." He leaned in and hushed his voice. "Whatever happened the other night, well, I've never known Tom to do anything mean or … or improper in his life. I'm sure he didn't mean to—"

"No." Dara stood slack-jawed. Hooper had no idea! She glanced into the kitchen.

Tom snuck her a wink and turned back to the grill.

"No," she repeated. "He didn't do anything wrong at all." She walked into the kitchen.

Tom kept his back turned. "We still on for the piano recital? We'll walk, and I'll mind my manners this time."

And so it was that Dara sat beside him at Saint Christopher's on Sunday night, whipping her pearl back and forth on the chain, with Tom saying, "It's all right, it's all right."

He clapped his hand over hers midslide. "Stop," he said, and pried her fingers from the pearl. "If this lady's your mum, great, but if not, we'll learn where she got the picture. Just follow the trail. We'll find your mother, Dara."

The lights dimmed and the room quieted. Here it came. Any moment now Shelly Rimes would step onto the platform and walk to the piano. Would she scan the crowd for just one face? Dara lifted a hand to finger the pearl.

The minute Shelly appeared, Dara knew she was not her mother. This woman was taller than Clara, with a bottom twice as wide.

Shelly did scan the crowd for Dara's face, then smiled, and bowed. Why? Was Dara mistaken? Maybe her mother had somehow grown ten inches from head to toe, or maybe Dara just remembered wrong.

But no. The woman's granite cheekbones were all wrong, and the flinty twinkle in her eye. She was too old to be Dara's mother. And she didn't play "April Showers."

She played Chopin's "Scherzo in B Minor" and Bach's "Prelude and Fugue in C Minor" with a majesty the small church strained to hold. Dara gave her pearl a rest and lost herself in the music, and when she closed her eyes she found herself in the holy darkness behind her eyelids, dancing with the voice that whispered in her ear, "It's all right … It's all right."

All was grand and significant, and everything was certainly all right.

Dara nodded forward, and Tom caught her head with one hand and guided it to his shoulder. She slept until Shelly ended with Beethoven's "Moonlight Sonata." She heard the applause and lifted her head.

She stretched.

"Not your mother?" Tom stood.

"No."

"Let's go see what she knows."

They walked to the front and waited while Shelly received her friends. She spotted them over a woman's shoulder, broke away, and greeted them.

"Are you Dara? Carla told me about you!"

"How'd you know it was me?"

"It wasn't hard. No one else was so intense, you poor thing. I'm glad my music had a calming effect."

"Your music was magnificent," said Tom.

"Thank you."

"I wonder, can you tell us where you got the picture?"

"You're in luck. I remember, and at my age you can never assume. I found it at a yard sale on the corner of Broadbent and

Birch—a barn-red house with green shutters. It was just a picture of a cat as far as I knew then, but Carla collects cats. Can you believe her throwing out my gift? When I paid seventy-five cents!"

"Broadbent and Birch," Dara repeated when they got outside and away from the crowd.

"A red house," said Tom. "I suppose her favorite color was red."

"I think it was green. We had a lot of green stuff in the house."

"Green shutters! There you go! Let's pay a call."

"Tom, it's ten o'clock!"

"We'll just look, then."

When they got to the corner of Broadbent and Birch, the porch light was on, and so was the lamp in the window. A green Forester was parked in the driveway.

Tom strode to the front door.

"What are you doing?" Dara whispered.

"There's her car. It looks like she's home." He rang the doorbell. A dog barked inside.

"Tom, she could be asleep."

"Not anymore, not with that dog." He rang again, and the dog doubled its efforts. "Besides, her porch light's on."

"For safety, Tom! So no one can hide in the bushes."

"Dara."

"What?"

"Stop whispering."

"*What?*"

"She's not home."

"Oh." She sighed. "Well then, come away from there."

He took Dara by the arm, led her across the street, and sat on the curb. "Have a seat."

"Why?"

"Just sit down here."

She sat.

"Now tell me, Dara. What would your mother's house look like?"

"I don't know. It'd be clean; she was always cleaning house."

"Like that one there?"

"Maybe."

"Look at the nice little wreath on the door, the white iron furniture under the tree. Does your mother do cute?"

"I think she might. I had a stenciled butterfly border in my room. Doubt if Dad put it there."

"Ha! We've got her this time! The woman who lives in this house is just the sort to stencil butterflies! Let's come back tomorrow."

"Tomorrow's the grand reopening. Did you hear Hooper's ad on the radio? We might have a crowd."

"You could break away."

She clapped a hand over her mouth. This house maybe, and maybe tomorrow. For better or worse, the truth. "What if it's her, Tom? What if she's spent all these years waiting to brush my hair and tuck me in and keep me safe?"

"You'd like that?"

"Oh, yeah. I'd really like that."

"*What*, Jane?" Dara slammed her knife down beside the onion she'd just hacked to confetti.

Jane gawked from the other side of the cook's window. She'd been doing it all morning, casting glances like Dara had a live fuse on her head. "Are you two all right?"

Dara glanced at Tom, who stood beside her slashing potatoes into french fries. Two eyes, a nose, and two pale lips pressed white to his crooked teeth. Same Tom.

"We're fine," she said.

"It'll be a lovely party tonight!"

"That's why we've got work to do!" Dara mimicked the lilt in Jane's voice.

"I thought the two of you were building a house in the kitchen, for all the rapping I hear."

"If it bothers you, go dance somewhere."

Jane retreated and hung the curtains she'd made.

Dara wiped her eyes with the back of her arm. She plunged her knife through the center of an onion and split it in two, then whacked away at the two halves. Tom gashed open a potato, and the noise continued: *Knock! Slam! Whack!*

Tom stopped to examine her. "*Are* you all right, really?"

She rolled her eyes. "Just chopping onions. I'm fine." She snuffled and chopped away.

"You're breathing oddly for someone who's fine."

"*Breathing* oddly?" She tore the skin off another onion and drove her knife in.

"Something's happened."

"Stop peering into my soul, Tom. There's nothing there." She fetched bell peppers from the back room. There was plenty to do.

She swallowed a lump so big it bruised her throat. But she swallowed it good. For this one day, she'd turn her mind off and just work.

Above all she wouldn't tell Tom what had happened that morning. If she did, she'd never make it through the day. The grand reopening was tonight, and all she wanted was to drag herself back to her desert, dig the grave, and crawl in.

She'd stopped by the red house on her way to work, just to get another look, to imagine living there.

But the front door was open, and a dachshund scampered out, barking and jumping at the fence. A young woman emerged with a diaper bag over her shoulder and a small boy on her hip. "Shultzy, get back!" She smiled over the boy's head and opened the door to the Forester. "He's all bark," she called. "He won't bite."

Dara slipped her hand into her purse to retrieve the frame.

The woman was no more than thirty years old. Still, she'd gotten the picture somewhere. Dara showed it to her and asked.

"Oooh," the woman said. "I remember this. It was the strangest thing. You wouldn't believe how I got it."

"I might believe it." Dara steadied her voice.

"Well, I don't know if I should tell you. Did you buy it from me?"

"No. I, uh, got it from someone who did."

"Oh. Well, why do you want to know where it came from?"

This woman was driving her nuts. "I'm just curious about its origins."

"Its origins, huh? Well you might not like what I have to say."

"Please." Dara took a breath. "Please tell me."

"Well, to tell the truth, I was dumpster-diving."

"What?"

"I pulled it from a dumpster."

"A dumpster?"

"Years ago. I was out behind Safeway, visiting my boyfriend at the time—we're married now." She nodded toward the child in the Forester. "He used to work in produce, and he took his cigarette breaks out back. I saw this bag on top of the dumpster with these curtains peeking out, real vintage. And I love vintage, you know? So I pulled the bag out of the dumpster and there was all kinds of stuff in there, old linens and some of that painted Pyrex—and there was this frame." She wrinkled her nose. "So it was in the dumpster. But it wasn't dirty. Probably some lady told her husband to take the bag to Goodwill, and he just …" She waved her hands. "You know men."

"The dumpster," Dara replied.

The dumpster! She thought now at the restaurant, chopping so hard the two halves of a bell pepper tumbled from the knife.

"Yeah," the woman had answered. "But *I* didn't mind. It used to have this darling watercolor of a cat. I had it in my bedroom for a long time. I've still got the curtains in my living room, see?" She pointed toward the window, and Dara peered around her. The curtains were a Hawaiian print bark cloth, maroon orchids on a green background.

Too old and too tacky. Definitely not my mother's. Dara split open another bell pepper with one deft blow of the blade.

"I suppose green peppers make you cry as well," Tom said.

She turned around.

He charged out the back and slammed the door.

What was that about?

Before she could figure it out, she heard a knock at the glass door and looked through the cook's window. A woman stood outside with a bouquet of yellow daisies, tapping her foot. Dara glanced around the dining room. Where was Jane? She dried her hands and went to the door.

The woman wore a gray suit and white tennis shoes, like she'd been power walking with her bunch of flowers. Thankfully, she seemed in a hurry.

"I wanted to drop these off myself," she said, thrusting the bouquet at Dara. "But I'll be back tonight. Tell Tom I wouldn't miss this party for the *world!* It's so wonderful what he's done with the restaurant. And Holly was *such* a special woman! I listen to her music all the time, and it has really changed my life."

Nodding, Dara put her hand to the door, but the woman was crying now. "I mean *really*—changed it, you know? I remember the first time I heard her sing," she squeaked. "It was really a bad time for me." And she proceeded to tell the story of her divorce and her deep depression, and overall what a devastation her life had been, and how Holly had managed to turn it around with a song.

A long story, but the woman told it quickly; Dara had to give her that. She said, "I've got to get going, or I'll be late. I'm Patsy Carson. And your name is?"

"Dara Pearl," she mumbled, grateful for Tom's idea. The woman left.

Dara locked the door behind her, set the flowers on the counter, and headed for the kitchen.

Her hand touched the swinging door, and she heard another knock behind her. Another bouquet of flowers, red carnations, delivered by a man in a tank top, jeans, and cowboy boots. He, at least, had little to say. He handed the flowers over and scratched a tear away like his eye was itching. "Tell Tom I'll see him tonight."

Two more bouquets arrived right behind him. Luckily, Jane came out of the bathroom, so Dara didn't have to take them both. The lady with the sunflowers hugged Dara. "Oh, sweetie, I'm so glad you folks are doing this. Did you know Holly? She was just the most beautiful woman, just stunning. And she and Tom were so in love. So sad."

And she was gone.

Meanwhile, the lady with the yellow roses sat in a booth crying while Jane held her hand. *Next, she'll be getting her tea,* Dara thought. She checked her watch: less than two hours left. She hurried to the kitchen.

Tom stood at the counter, banging his knife into a bunch of green onions like he was killing chickens.

"You got some flowers."

"I know."

"Tom, I'm sorry I snapped at you—"

He held up a hand to stop her.

Fine, then. A lousy mood might keep him out of her business.

Hooper kicked open the back door and nudged his way in with a box.

Tom rushed to help him. "What's that?"

"Sour cream carrot pies."

"Quite a lot of them."

"This is just the first box."

"How many did you bring?"

"Four boxes. Sixteen pies."

Tom ran out to Hooper's car and returned with a box in each arm.

"Don't you drop those, now," said Hooper.

"Are they all carrot?"

"Yep. My own recipe. They'll love it." He walked outside for the last box.

"They'll have to, if we're to sell sixteen pies."

Hooper handed Tom a cardboard sign. "How about you hobble your lip and make yourself useful. Go stick this sign in the window."

It read, "Free Slice of Sour Cream Carrot Pie with Every Dinner Order."

There was a knock out front again. Tom looked to see who it was and groaned. More flowers. He handed Dara the sign. "Please," he said. "They'll want me to talk about her."

Hooper and Jane pitched in to accept the bouquets.

Dara glanced at the clock. An hour and a half.

Still more flowers. And more promises to return that night. She had picked up from Jane and Hooper what to do: She smiled, nodded, and agreed with everything they said. They left quicker that way.

But they kept coming. It was fifteen minutes before she got back to the kitchen.

And there was still work to do, soups to make, and last-minute setup.

She heard raised voices out the back door just before Hooper busted in with a box.

Tom followed at his heels. "You said people didn't want to eat in a mausoleum!"

"It doesn't make the place a mausoleum to play her albums, Tom! How long since Clementine heard her mother's music in your home? You ever play it?"

"*No*, I don't. She deserves to be happy." Tom trailed him to the dining room.

"Oh, your house is a *real* happy place! That's why she crawls out at night."

Dara peered through the cook's window.

Hooper reached into the box he carried, pulled out a framed photograph of Holly, and set it on a table, then moved to the next booth. He had a picture for each one.

Tom snapped up the pictures as quickly as Hooper set them out.

"Put 'em back, Tom," said Hooper.

"No!"

Jane moved beside Dara to watch with her, but Dara hardly noticed. She stood dumbfounded by what she saw.

Tom was crying.

He slumped over his wife's photograph and turned his back, as if for privacy. "I can't look at this."

Hooper put a hand on his shoulder. "Yes, you can, Tom. I'll help you." He wiped his eye with the palm of his hand, and his lips mashed together, crying. "Let's walk."

They grabbed napkins from a dispenser and wiped their noses, then left out the restaurant's glass door.

Jane closed her eyes and sighed.

Dara stirred the whistle berries, too numb to think.

CHAPTER 10

*W*ithin two hours people were waiting at the door for tables. Hooper put on an apron and set to work.

No one had time to talk, and that was good.

At four o'clock someone asked for sour cream carrot pie, and the pies moved quickly after that. So did the burgers and whistle berries and the various dinners, and that was just what Dara needed. The faster she moved, the less she thought.

It was eight thirty before she had time to look up from the grill.

In the booth by the window, a man hollered, "You've missed your calling, Hoop! You make better pie than my mother!"

Hooper reached behind himself to flip an apron tie at the man and continued talking with the couple he'd just seated.

Jane shared a joke with the group in the front booth, and Clementine went table to table with her deck. "Pick a card, any car-r-rd."

Tom interrupted it all by tapping the microphone. It whistled. "I'd like your attention, everyone." He pulled the mic from its stand and stepped onto a chair. "Excuse me; I'd like your attention, please."

The crowd simmered down.

Tom cleared his throat. "It means more than I can say to see all of you here tonight. I'll state the obvious, that if you find anything worth coming back for, and if you find anything to eat you'd care to experience again, then it certainly has nothing whatsoever to do with me."

There came a general shout of assent from the crowd.

"I'd like to thank my sister, Jane Cameron, our interior decorator and your waitress."

Jane took a bow to grand applause.

In the kitchen, Dara'd crept from view, but it did no good.

"Also our extraordinary chef, Dara Pearl." Tom shouted this, as if to reach in after her. "Come take a bow, Dara."

She cursed, went to the window, and waved.

"I'll now turn the mic over to a man who's not only my father-in-law, but my dearest friend, as well." He took a deep breath and continued. "He's responsible for the menus, as well as the whistle berries and carrot pie you're all enjoying." He waited for the applause to quiet. "He's also the Brittlebush Rodeo's poet laureate, and he'll share a poem tonight. Ladies and gentlemen, I present to you …" He grinned. "Marion Gayle Hooper!" He stepped off the chair.

Hooper took the mic and kicked the chair away. "I brought my own altitude, shorty. And by the way, I think it'd be in the best interest of all concerned if you all would just call me Hooper."

"I like Marion Gayle!" a man called from the corner.

"Like I say, Randy, it'd be in your best interest."

When the laughter quieted, he turned a dimmer switch to lower the lights and flipped another one to shine a recessed light over the place where he stood.

"Poet laureate deserves a spotlight, don't you think?" He turned serious and waited for the room to quiet. "This night marks a milestone for me, for Tom here, and for most of you folks too. Lot of you were regulars when my daughter, Holly, was with us. I think she ran this place just so she could shoot the breeze with good people like you. And I guess when she left us, the Studmuffin just became pretty much a place where Holly wasn't. I don't blame you for wanting to stay away. My Holly's right where she belongs today, teaching the angels something about music. But a big part of her is with us here tonight. And she …" He touched an eye with his knuckle. "She couldn't stand to see her restaurant turned into—a sad place. She never was about being sad. That's why tonight we're gonna let a fresh wind blow her spirit around." He motioned with his hand and shrugged. "You know. We're gonna listen to her music and eat good food and enjoy each other's good company! We're gonna be happy that we had Holly around us at all." He waited out the whistles and cheers, and said, "First though, if you'll indulge me." He pulled a yellow paper from his pocket, and began:

> I oughta seen it comin' on that snowy winter
>   morn,
> For the starry sky gleamed brighter when my
>   tiny girl was born.
> And the sun sat up and noticed when we
>   brought her to the farm,
> And even hardened waddies turned to puddin'
>   by her charm.
>
> Her first gurgles in her pablum served to lead a
>   lively dance,
> And before she learnt to walk she'd taught her
>   pony how to prance.
> But we never guessed just who we had, though
>   it seems strange to say,
> Till she sung her first words in the barn one
>   cheerful summer day.
>
> Now most folks start to talkin' first before they
>   sing a song,
> But let no one ever make you think my darlin'
>   got it wrong.
> For if you had heard her sing, it wouldn't be
>   long 'fore you knew
> That to speed her music to us was the proper
>   thing to do.
>
> For the horses in their stables and the heifer in
>   her stall
> Knew the song that she was singin' weren't no
>   childish caterwaul.

For her voice was like a fire and her song a
     solar flare,
And before we knew, the stallion started
     spoonin' with the mare.

None recalls how they got out—you see it was
     a great distraction
When the horses took a mind to put some
     hooves to their attraction.
But the next thing that we knew, the two was
     dancin' in the pen,
A fandango, then when they were done, they
     danced it round again.

Well, you can't dance the fandango well without
     some castanets,
So the chickens went and got some for the
     amorous duet.
And the pigs found my guitar inside the cab of
     my old pickup,
And my darlin' had her first band—but that's
     when she got the hiccups.

The horses were so happy and the pigs were
     playin' fine,
And my darlin' was reluctant to call off a lively
     time.
So she kept right on singin', and in truth she
     couldn't know
'Bout the strange effect hiccups would have on
     magic songs, and so …

When the horses' nostrils started puffin' smoke,
     she gave no thought,
She was just a baby, after all. Now you might
     get distraught

When you learn what happened next, so please
  just listen to the end,
For this story will get better, and I don't mean
  to offend.

Well, the horses just danced faster as she
  hiccupped through her song,
And the more they danced, the more they
  smoked. It weren't so very long
Till their manes became a fire and their tails a
  flamin' torch,
And their dance flared up like fizgigs and their
  hoofprints left a scorch.

But that only made them want to hoof their
  wild dance faster still,
And they danced and burned and burned and
  danced their brightest dance until—
Now I know what you're a-thinkin', that they
  turned to ash, but no,
What they turned into was stardust, and they
  danced still, all aglow.

Well, the stardust spun in two bright spheres to
  orbit one another,
For I tell you folks, my child sang at that young
  age like no other.
But the hiccups kept a-comin' and the spheres
  began to whirl
Ever tighter, ever brighter for the song of my
  small girl.

Then they slowly rose into the sky to join the
  mornin' sun,
And it seemed that day we had three suns up
  there instead of one.

It was then we thought to get inside the
    farmhouse with my daughter,
For she still had hiccups, and we thought she'd
    better drink some water.

Now you may figger this is so much bull and
    ballyhoo,
And if that is what you think, I guess I'll think
    no less of you.
But if you'll just look beside the moon when
    you turn in tonight,
You'll see two horse stars there, to your amaze-
    ment and delight.

Well, to sing with so much fire requires some
    stardust in your soul,
And it's plainly clear she had some by the story
    I just told.
So you'll understand my thinkin' that a star was
    born that night,
When we thought we had a baby in the wild
    celestial light.

Now, even stars don't last forever, and my girl
    has left us now,
But my faith says she's still with us, though I
    couldn't tell you how.
I've heard tell that when a star goes out, it
    leaves some fire and dust
To start new stars with when it's gone, and that
    is what I trust.

So, Holly, in your songs tonight we'll shine your
    light again,
And the fire and dust you left us might just
    start to burn, and then

> Some heart may find it has to dance a light
>   fandango too,
> And I don't know a better way to please and
>   honor you.

The crowd applauded as he pushed a button on the CD player. Then he picked up Clementine and took a chair.

And there was Holly's a capella voice, singing "Amazing Grace."

Dara stood transfixed in the far corner of the kitchen. She had never heard Holly's music. It started slow and soft and built to a butter-smooth crescendo that shook the walls.

When the song finished, a steel guitar struck a chord, and Holly's voice began anew. Dara leaned exhausted against the counter to listen.

Her gaze drifted out the cook's window to the boisterous crowd in the dining room. People full from their dinners rocked back in laughter or leaned forward in the red candlelight to talk. All in motion, and all happy.

All but one. Dara moved to get a closer look.

In the back corner, a woman sat alone, just a shadow in the dim light, with a halo of short blonde hair. She'd come in at lunch and never left, except to smoke a cigarette out front. Dara had caught her staring several times. Till this moment, beyond an unacknowledged edginess, she hadn't given her much thought. But there she was still, alone in the corner.

The woman locked eyes with Dara.

Chilled, Dara forced her gaze to the other end of the room. In the orange neon light streaming through the window, there stood another solitary figure. Tom hugged his arms across his chest, his face drawn, his eyes shut. Almost imperceptibly, he swayed to the beat of Holly's song:

> I never knew that there were angels in a
>   passing glance,

Or that God would work his wonders in a
    happenstance,
That his light would shine out through your
    eyes to sanctify each ordinary day.
I never knew he'd work his miracles that way.

Holly had written this for Tom, Dara was certain. She could see it in the way he lifted his eyes to no one there, as if Holly appeared to him alone.

How different their marriage must have been from hers. She'd never felt a moment's grief for Kevin. Even in her nightmares he had no face.

What must it be like for Tom, to love someone the way he loved Holly and lose her?

Still, he was lucky. She'd died through no fault of his own, so there was no remorse, no biting self-hatred.

Only, just now he didn't look lucky. He looked like he was dying.

His eyes met with Dara's. She looked away.

And caught the eye of the woman in the corner.

Dara turned to wipe down the kitchen counters. One more time. With a vengeance.

Who *was* this woman?

Her skin prickled with a new idea. Oh … Oh! Not her mother! She couldn't be!

Dara went to the dining room door and opened it a crack. The woman stared into her coffee cup, her bleached hair fluffed out like a thistle. Almost—*almost*, Dara could wish she was.

But there was no resemblance at all.

Dara wasn't going to find her mother; she needed to settle into that. Her search had led to a dumpster, and dumpsters don't answer questions.

The woman lifted her eyes to the cook's window, searching. Dara eased the door shut and pressed her head to the wall.

She couldn't breathe for sadness. Hidden by the darkness and noise, she let her grief out in surging, childlike wails. She turned toward the sink, lifting an arm to wipe her eyes. Tom was there, so close she felt the warmth of his breath on her upraised arm before she saw him.

A tear coursed down his nose, and Dara's own tears surged again. Sorrow was a wave that rocked between them. Her knees gave, and she rested against him. He lay his head on hers, crying as she wept into his shirt. He held her so tightly her shoulders pressed toward her neck, and they wept until their tears were spent, and still, in the darkness, they held each other up. He took her hand that was pressed to his chest and said, "Dance with me."

And so they did, in the darkness there, to the din of the restaurant crowd, to the grace notes of Holly's song:

> With his hand twined in yours and his right
>   arm behind you,
> You join in the dance and with him there you
>   find you
> Can slide, you can glide like you know what
>   you're doing.
> You don't—that's the fun, and him all the while
>   wooing you, loving, pursuing you …
>
> Look in his eyes, you can see what he feels for
>   you.
> Thence come the swings and the sways and the
>   reels, or you
> Rest on his shoulder and hear his heart beating,
> His breath in your ear as he whispers, repeating
>
> Things gentle, so tender, it's hard to believe
>   them,
> But do, listen closely until you perceive them
> The truest things ever that rang in your soul,
> Till you really believe he can dance the world
>   whole.

And then don't try to help him, just move
    where he leads
You—don't look at your feet, your own needs,
    your own deeds,
You can dance so much better by watching his
    eyes,
By hearing his whispers, the tender surprise

Of a prince who so loves you, a life you were
    made for,
A dance so much sweeter than your own
    parade,
For you never will march anyplace that's worth
    going,
Not knowing the Lord of the Dance and him
    knowing you—

Listen: The tune has begun; take his hand,
As he calls all creation to strike up the band.

"Stupid, stupid, stupid!" she whispered to herself on the walk to work.

The sunlight slanted warm and yellow over the rooftops, past the shadowed lawns to the sidewalk. Dara yanked the hood of her sweater over her head, taking deep breaths to fight the tears. "Stupid, *stupid!*"

After last night's dance in the darkness, Tom would think they'd started something. With the new schedule, he'd spend ten hours a day presuming he could stand close as a lover as they worked, could brush her arm, could stop by the trailer after closing. Unless she told him not to. And she would. She'd say, "Tom, I'm just not ready for a relationship …"

"Stupid!" He'd joke about it! He'd ask if she was ready for maybe just a flirtation or something, and she'd feel like a fool.

No. He wouldn't joke, not Tom.

He'd fold in the way she'd seen him do the night before: shrunken, like grief had siphoned the blood from his veins. And she'd *be* a fool, an unforgivable fool to make him feel that way.

She turned into the alley and plodded past concrete steps with bicycles chained to the handrails. A feral cat darted under a dumpster and crept to the edge of the shadow to watch Dara pass by.

Who was she kidding?

It was *Holly's* song they had danced to. Dara was just a substitute for a neon Vargas cowgirl grand enough to fill the Studmuffin to capacity—despite Tom's runny eggs. A dazzling, beautiful woman more alive to him than Dara was, trudging through the alley to work, hidden in the hood of her sweater. "Stupid!"

She wanted her mother.

She pictured an older version of the woman in the photograph, hair shortened to a bob, streaked blonde to hide the gray. Softly veined hands smoothing the furrows from Dara's brow. "*Looks aren't everything,*" she'd coax. "Personality *isn't everything either.* Virtue *isn't everything. You have so many other qualities for a man to love.*"

To which Dara responded with the burning question: "*Like what?*" and her mother's face went slack. Apparently none came to mind.

"Kinda drawing a blank, myself," she muttered.

The voice walked beside her, companionably silent.

"Why can't I find her?" she demanded. "Why even bring me here to find the picture if I can't find *her?*" She shook her head. "Stupid."

She stopped at the back of the Studmuffin and climbed the two steps to the door, groping in her pocket for the keys. Before she pulled them out, the door swung outward. Jane held it open with her backside and swept a pile of dirt onto Dara's feet before she noticed Dara standing there. "Oh!" she laughed. "Sorry! Here, I'll get that for you." She swept the toes of Dara's tennis shoes. Dara pushed past her and hung her sweater on the hook.

"A smashing success last night, don't you think?"

"Lot of people." Dara put her apron on.

"Everyone raved about the food. How would we have done it without you?"

"You'd have done fine." Dara smelled coffee brewing. Good. She could use a cup. She lit the grill, peering into the empty dining room.

"He's not here yet." Jane frowned. "He had a bit of a situation this morning. He's fetching Clemmie from the Baxters'—on Cottonwood Lane."

"Not again!" She turned to Jane. Cottonwood was two streets from home.

"Afraid so."

They heard Tom's car in the rear lot and turned to the back door, waiting. The door opened, and Tom walked in and stopped, looking from Dara to Jane and back again. "What?"

"Is she all right?" Jane propped her hands on her hips.

"Clementine? Sure!" He laughed and reached for his apron. "I'll have to replace their window, though. Seems her foot caught it on the way in."

"It's not funny, Tom!" Dara followed him to the sink. "She'll get hurt if she keeps it up!"

"Nah, it's always people we know. They almost expect her to pop in from time to time—"

"She's out wandering at night—" Jane said.

"Morning," he corrected. "John was having his breakfast."

"John works the early shift," Jane pointed out. "So what time does he eat his breakfast?"

"Four." Tom ran a hand through his hair and scratched his head.

"*A.M.?*" Dara leaned forward. "She's out climbing in windows at four a.m.? She—"

"Look!" Tom put a hand up to stop her. "Clemmie and I are coping as best ..." He leaned on the counter and dropped his head. "I'm doing my *utmost* as her father, and I'd thank the two of you to back off."

"Your best should be better, Tom!" Dara softened her voice. "It's not a safe world. What if it wasn't someone you know?" She reached a hand to his shoulder.

"Well it is!" He spun to face her and she yanked her hand back. "I can't deal with the what-ifs, and I can't—" He quieted his voice to a rasp. "I can't deal with you!"

Dara stepped back. *Stupid!* She spun and walked to the refrigerator to start her prep work. But once she opened the door, she couldn't think what to do next.

Jane leaned close and whispered, "Help me wipe the tables?"

Good idea.

In the dining room, she glanced at the metal bolt in the gap between the double glass doors. Still locked. She clutched her pearl.

Something in Tom's voice told her he wouldn't be stopping by the trailer anytime soon.

Just as well. She swallowed the lump in her throat and scrubbed the counters, till Jane stood beside her, smiling. "We're just disinfecting, dear, not polishing the pattern off."

Dara slumped. "I didn't …" She shook her head. "But he has to protect her! She's just a little girl."

"Agreed. But Tom's a good man. He'll figure it out …"

Jane's voice fell off at the last word as if someone had pulled her plug. She stood, slack-mouthed, her eyes fixed out the window.

Dara turned. An older couple stood near the door, their heads bent to read the Studmuffin's hours of business.

Well, they'd see the restaurant was closed for another two hours. Dara turned back.

Jane's eyes darted toward the kitchen door on the opposite side of the counter. "Hide me," she whispered, sidling behind Dara and gripping her arm.

"Why?" Dara looked again. The couple was still there,

checking their watches. There was something familiar … *Ouch!*
Jane's nails pressed into her flesh, twisting her shoulder to form
a better block. She really was trying to hide.

But too late. The woman outside peered into the restaurant and brightened, grabbed the man's arm, chattered, pointed,
and waved.

❦

Jane put on a good act. She squealed, spread her arms, and
wrapped them around these two, one by one, crying, "Finis! Ivy!
What are you doing here?"

No one would've guessed at the fingernail bruises still
smarting on Dara's arm.

Dara knew where she'd seen them before—in a photograph in the shanty church, the frame quivering in Jane's hand
before she thrust it on the wall.

They looked better in person. Finis had less hair, but what
he'd kept was something to see—like the silvered pages of her
father's Bible.

Ivy's hair was brown curls arranged in choreographic
swirls. Dara wondered if she'd just come from the salon or if she
always looked that way. Judging by her ladylike smile and the
gold stars on her blue espadrilles that matched the gold stars on
her blue sweater set—Dara guessed that both were true: The
woman always looked that way *because* she had always just
come from the salon.

Dara rubbed the little bruises on her arm.

"I can't believe I'm looking at you two!" Jane said. "What
brings you here?"

The man held her two hands. "We're here to see you, kid!"

"How did you find me?" asked Jane.

He winked. "We have resources."

Dara saw movement out the corner of her eye. She turned
and Tom was there, wiping his hands on a towel. He sidled up,
though not close enough to brush an arm. "She knows them?"

"Evidently. *You* know them?"

"Amy's parents."

"Who?"

"Pastor Erik's in-laws."

Jane had moved the couple to a booth. "Tom! Dara! Come meet my friends!"

"Oh, we know Tom!" Ivy said.

Tom stepped forward to shake their hands.

"You do?" asked Jane. "One of your resources?"

"Not me," said Tom. "How do you know Finis and Ivy?"

"Where are your manners, Tom?" Finis grinned. "First introduce your young lady."

Dara blushed and stepped away from Tom. "I'm not—"

Jane grabbed her arm and pulled her in. "Finis, Ivy, this is my dear friend Dara." Tom crossed the dining room to get some coffee cups. Jane scooted over, and Dara sat beside her.

"We had no idea Tom was your brother," said Ivy.

"Finis and Ivy are Amy's parents," Tom explained, setting out the cups. "They come to visit every now and again." He poured coffee and set the pot on the table. When Dara didn't move to make room for him, he pulled a chair up and straddled it.

"Really," said Jane. "Finis was my professor in seminary, and then he was my field director in Mexico—mine and Max's."

"Now I'm just her spiritual guide." Finis winked again, laying his arm around Ivy.

"Then have you come to guide me?" Jane asked. The table fell silent. Finis's eyes locked onto hers.

Ivy patted Jane's hand. "We just stopped by to say hi. We didn't know you were in Brittlebush till we saw you in your truck yesterday. And Amy said you were working here." She smiled. "But then you did have a home nearby, someplace, didn't you?"

"I didn't know you had a daughter."

"Two," said Ivy. "Amy and Stacy. They're why we're back in the states! We're having a bit of a reunion for Finis's birthday. Which we hoped we could have right here."

"Of course," said Tom.

Jane smiled. "But isn't Finis's birthday—"

"Not for another six weeks, I know," said Ivy. "But this one took some doing, so we got an early start." She patted Finis's hand. "And Finis can use the time to make progress on his book."

"Oh Finis, how wonderful!" Jane touched his arm. "You've always wanted to write a book. Tell me all about it!"

"Well." Finis stirred his coffee, a grin pulling at one corner of his mouth. "It's about the Ten Commandments."

Jane nodded.

Ten Easy Steps to Turn the Hand of God," said Ivy. "That's his title."

"To turn the hand of God," Jane repeated. "Sounds ambitious."

"It's about the way God honors an obedient life," said Finis. "You'd remember from your days in my class."

"I do remember."

"I figure the book should write itself."

"Undoubtedly. But …" She ran a finger around the rim of her cup.

"But what?"

"Do you really think they're easy, Finis—the Ten Commandments? I've never found them easy."

What was she saying? "Sure you have," Dara blurted. The others turned to Dara, and she blushed. Still, the worst thing she'd ever known the duchess to do was to put little bruises on her arm—and Dara figured she had her reasons.

But Jane was serious. "No, really. I haven't."

"What's hard?" asked Finis. "They're all 'shalt nots': things you don't do."

"Ah. But I wonder why Christ troubled himself to hang on the cross then?"

"To give us a second chance, and of course you know that. Why are you fooling with me?"

"I'm sorry, Finis. I really hope the best for your book." She raised her clasped hands to her chin.

"So tell me about yourself, kid. What brings my protégée to

Brittlebush out of the mission field God called her to?"

She dropped her gaze but held her smile, and offered no reply. Dara counted the ticks of the wall clock, to see how many seconds it would take before someone broke the silence.

Eleven.

"Maybe you'd like me to change the subject," said Finis at last.

"I'd like nothing better," Jane replied.

Tom cleared his throat. "Which birthday did you say this was?"

"Mine." Finis glowered.

"His sixtieth." Ivy gave a slow nod. "It's going to be a very special occasion." She teared up a little. "Our daughter Stacy's coming, and she's bringing our granddaughter, Talia, with her. We haven't seen either one since Talia was a baby."

"How old is she now?" Tom asked.

Finis took a breath.

"Sixteen," said Ivy firmly.

"Sixteen." Tom nodded.

"Well, since you bring it up," Finis said, "this little reunion illustrates the premise of my book."

"I'll take the bait," said Jane.

He laid his hands on the table. "Stacy's been estranged from us from the time Talia was on the way." He glanced at Ivy, who had petrified into a tight smile. "Things were said," he admitted. "She was eighteen, and there was no daddy, no …" He shrugged. "She was on drugs. Then she moved and didn't tell us where she was going. For oh, *years* we didn't know where she was." He finished off his coffee, and Tom refilled the cup.

Dara leaned forward. "How did you know she moved?"

Finis looked at her, and she tried to clarify.

"That someone didn't …" Dara shrugged and shook her head.

"Well." He sighed. "She'd turned the key in to her landlady, and all her things were gone."

Dara nodded. Her mother had only taken the picture.

"I thought one day the phone would ring and it would

be …" Finis took a breath. "The morgue someplace or other—
you know, if she left any indication we were her parents. And
they'd maybe tell us where to find Talia." He paused, swallowing.
"I prayed." He choked and swallowed again. "I prayed very fervently that God would bring my daughter back to me. *Very*
fervently." He shook his head. "But to no avail."

A small cry escaped from deep in Dara's throat. No one
seemed to notice. She held her face rigid.

Hadn't she prayed a few fervent prayers herself? As a girl,
she'd knelt by the side of her bed and folded her hands, zealous
to do it right.

Finis cleared his throat, and Dara could almost watch him
pull himself together. He sniffed and straightened his back, and
began again. "The Bible says, 'The effective, fervent prayer of a
righteous man avails much.' Well I had some thinking to do,
didn't I? I mean, if the fervent prayer of a righteous man avails
much, and this old boy's prayers availed *nothing*, then only one
element could be missing: I hadn't attended properly to my own
righteousness. Amen?"

Dara nodded.

"So here's what I did: I looked at the Ten Commandments
and made a list of all the ways I was breaking God's law—or had
broken it." He pounded a fist into the palm of his hand. "Then
one by one I started to rectify them."

"And what happened?" Dara asked.

"Well, then I got a call. Stacy …" He took a deep breath and
tried again. "My daughter called from a rehab center. She wants
to go through the program and then come to see me for my
birthday."

Dara wiped her nose on her sleeve and looked down,
struggling to hold her composure. "It worked," she whispered.

"Yes," said Finis. "It worked."

The Ten Commandments. Of course. Dara wiped her nose
again. Her hands trembled.

It seemed fair. Wash God's back, and he would wash hers.
It made sense.

"Young lady?" Finis asked.

She looked up.

"Perhaps *you* have a prayer you'd like God to answer?" He leaned forward and put a hand on her arm.

"Yes," she said. "I do."

Finis had worksheets. Dozens of them, it seemed, all hole-punched and bound together with a black binder clip. He also had, still in their blue plastic Wal-Mart bag, a red binder, multicolored tab dividers, and a four-color pen with little sliders at the top, one for each color: red, blue, black, and green.

When he and Ivy arrived an hour past closing, Dara was ready. All the cleanup was done, and a pot of coffee had just finished brewing. There was one light left on in the restaurant, near the back wall.

Finis scooted far into the rear booth to make room for his briefcase on the seat beside him. Ivy sat opposite. Dara brought the coffee and pulled a chair to the end of the table, while Finis laid his worksheets out like some giant game of solitaire.

"Looks like we're doing taxes." She fingered her pearl. Ivy grinned.

"Don't you worry, this'll be easy," he said absently, adjusting his glasses and aligning the edges of the papers with a tap of his finger. "It's 'Ten Easy Steps,' and it's going to get you your mother back. Isn't that what you want?"

Dara nodded.

"Well, all right then." He leaned back. "And just to help you keep that in mind, when you get home tonight, here's what I want you to do." He put his hand on Dara's. "I want you to take that picture of your mother out of its frame. Can you do that?"

"Why?"

He held the red binder up and slipped his finger into the clear plastic sleeve on the cover. "You see this? I want you to slide that picture right in here, so any time you wonder why you're doing all this, you can just look at that picture and say, 'That's why I'm doing it—so I can find my mother.' You see?"

Dara nodded.

"Don't stop there, though. Get some old magazines. Maybe find a picture of a woman that looks like your mother might look right now. And get creative. Put it together with a picture of yourself so it looks like you're standing side by side with her, because that's just what you want, isn't it? Put that in there too. And that'll leave plenty of room so you can cut out other pictures, maybe places you'd like to go with your mother, things you'd like to do. And then when you go to bed at night I want you to put your hand on these pictures and say, 'Lord Jesus, that's what I want. I want you to give me my mother back so we can spend time together, make up for all those lost years.' Isn't that what you want?"

"Yes." Dara fingered her pearl and nodded.

"All right then. Now what are we going to put inside your notebook?" He scanned the papers laid before him. "We'll start with step one." He pulled out a sheet and read from the framed box at the top: "You shall have no other gods before Me." He laid the paper on the table in front of Dara. "It's appropriate here to ask yourself what really matters to you."

Dara shrugged. "My mother?"

"Well, that's fine. One of the commandments says to honor your mother and father, as you'll see. But there are clues in your life that will tell us what things are really important to you deep down. For instance ..." He pointed to a sub-bullet on the worksheet. "Where do you spend your money?"

"You know, you could have a future with the IRS." Dara rubbed her neck. Ivy chuckled, but Finis gazed at Dara till she felt chastened. "I don't buy much. Groceries. Jane and I split the utilities."

"Do you give to the church?"

"I don't go to church."

"Huh. We'll get to that one later." He pointed to the second sub-bullet. "Where do you spend your time?"

"Here. And at home." Finis seemed to expect more. "Sometimes I drive out into the desert with Jane."

He leaned forward. "And what do the two of you do in the desert?"

"Well we're not smoking weed out there or anything. We just … Well, Jane calls it worship, so I guess that's church, in a way, right?"

"No." Finis cupped a hand to his forehead. "Look. I won't gossip about Jane. But back in Mexico after her husband passed, she kind of went off the deep end. She got hooked up with this pagan woman—"

Ivy shook her head. "You don't know she was pagan."

"Well, she was something." He held a hand up as if to hold her back. "Wild-haired and crazy. We used to see her in the desert around the church, out there gyrating like some kind of mime on truth serum." He wagged his hands above his head.

"Finis," Ivy said.

He turned to scan his papers. "Just you mind where Jane leads you, is all I'm saying."

He pulled out a lined sheet titled "Things To Do Now," and wrote on the top line, "Go to church." Underneath he wrote the name "Grace Chapel" and the address "512 Edison." He tapped the paper. "Church is a nice little blue cinder-block building with an address. It's not out communing with nature some-place."

Dara snuck a glance at her watch under the table. It had only been fifteen minutes.

Finis pulled out step two. "You shall not make for yourself a carved image," he read.

"Well that's one I never did. Let's skip to the next."

"Not so fast. Do you *possess* carved images?"

"No!"

"Are you sure? A lot of people have things around their houses just for decoration that they got on some trip somewhere, and they never knew they were pagan idols. Folk carvings, masks, dolls, and whatnot. Do you have anything like that?"

"Like a kachina doll?"

"Do you have a kachina doll?"

"Yeah, but I don't bring it flowers and fruit. My parents bought it on their honeymoon at the Grand Canyon."

"Your parents began their marriage by acquiring a pagan god?"

"No! They bought a souvenir."

"That was their intent. But what was the effect? What happened to your family once they brought that thing into your home?"

Dara opened her mouth to speak and then winced at the images that flickered in her mind. She clutched at her pearl. "Okay. I'll get rid of it. What's next?"

"Just a minute." He pulled out the list he'd started and added "Get rid of kachina."

"Best you destroy it utterly. Don't leave it for someone else to find and take home with them."

Dara nodded, sliding the pearl along its chain. "Let's go on to the next one."

"What's that in your hand?"

"What's what?"

"On the chain around your neck. What is it?"

She opened her fingers and pressed the pendant against her throat. "It's a necklace—a gift from my dad."

"Finis," said Ivy.

Dara looked to the woman for defense.

"She clutches that thing like a security blanket. It's more than a keepsake."

"Finis," Ivy repeated. "Stop."

Finis thrust his jaw forward. Ivy shook her head firmly and held his gaze. He sighed at last, turned his attention back to the papers spread before him, and pulled out the third commandment.

"Like a robot with a flair for fashion": That's how her father described the kachina when she was fifteen, the day she broke its arm. Dara held it in her lap now, sitting on the moonlit doorstep to her trailer.

She'd been leaning against the mantel when it happened, her face pressed against her folded arms. She refused to look at her father because he wouldn't let her go to Amber Wiley's party. She couldn't believe Amber had even asked her to come.

"It's not a safe world," her father insisted. It was his reason for everything. "Not a safe world," so she couldn't walk to school alone. "Not a safe world," so she couldn't go to dances. She was sick to death of hearing it.

He touched her shoulder and said there'd be other parties to go to, ones with parents there to chaperone. "No there won't!" she squalled, shaking his hand off. Her flailing arm caught the kachina and sent it flying off the mantel, landing on the floor six feet away. It bounced and landed again in two pieces, this thing that had always been part of the home she lived in—or what was left of it.

There'd been moments in her life when Dara wished she were dead. That moment, when the kachina lay fractured on the floor in a dust of red clay, was one of them. She knelt beside it mourning. Everything was broken, everything, everything.

Her father squatted beside her. "It's okay," he said. "I'll fix it." And he did—sort of. But there were pocks around the seam where bits of clay had crumbled off, so he cut a piece of a red shop rag and knotted a tiny armband around the break. "There now, see?" He displayed it with two hands like he was making a ketchup commercial. "Looks like a robot with a flair for fashion, don't it?"

Her father had always had his own special way with words. How did she answer him that day? She didn't remember. Safe to say at fifteen she didn't say what she wished she'd said: that he should write books maybe, even if he hadn't finished high school, instead of painting houses, trying to keep up with men half his age and twice his size.

But he was right about the kachina. Dara shifted on the

step to hold it to the light from the living room. Its face was painted turquoise, with black lines resembling coin slots for its eyes and mouth. It wore a white rabbit-fur ruff, a leather skirt with a painted sun symbol, and cuffed boots like a musketeer. The tag said it sang in the mornings to wake the village.

What did Finis find so wrong with that? Did the Hopi light candles at its feet for prayers? Did it demand they sacrifice their children for rain?

Dara didn't like Finis. She didn't like the cadence of his voice or the way he looked at her like he would a piece of real estate. She didn't like the sick way he made her feel, like she was going to take home a turbocharged red-binder life plan with a clear plastic sleeve, whether she wanted to or not. She didn't like the calendars that told her when to go to church, not just Sunday mornings but Sunday nights too, the midweek Bible studies, the women's ministry meetings, and any other special events they could dream up down at Grace Chapel.

She didn't like the daily goal sheet, where she was to give herself a score each night: plus five if she did a kind deed, minus five if she swore, plus ten if she brought someone to church. She didn't like the progress chart, where she was to graph her daily scores with a red line to see how close she was to finding her mother. She especially didn't like the list with "Get rid of kachina" written second from the top.

Well, she didn't have to do what he said. If she wanted, she could go the other way just to spite him. She could recite from the script of *Snatch* every morning like the pledge of allegiance, and take off five points for every bad word. In fact, most of those words might even rate a minus ten; she'd have to ask. She could make that little red line slide right off the page, and see what Finis thought of that.

She leaned on the metal handrail, straining to enjoy her own cleverness, but it was no good. The moment she pictured the red line dropping off the page, she slid down it herself, falling farther and farther away from her mother.

She ran a finger over the brown feathers that fanned from the kachina's head.

It wasn't only bad things that had happened since her parents brought it home. Everything had happened; good things as well. She'd listened to her mother play the piano, helped her make decorations for a party, and read the newspaper from her mother's lap. She'd heard her father tell the story of the pearl countless times and sat on the stool in the garage while he mended things.

It was a short list for a whole lifetime, but it was no use trying to make it longer. She could avoid the obvious bad memories, but in the end she was left with long days of loneliness, the color of dust, and the sound of a ticking clock.

Her grip on the kachina tightened till her knuckles turned white. The little clay arm snapped off a second time, and the red armband fluttered to the ground between her feet. A sound rose in her throat, her face grew hot, but she would not cry. She stood and slammed the kachina against the handrail, and its head flew off. Panting in little groans she slammed it again and again, and it seemed that blood spattered in the red clay till there was nothing left to slam, just the musketeer boots in her hand.

She scooped up the pieces, the ruff, the armband, and the leather skirt, and walked them to the trash can. Then she went inside to slip her mother's picture into the plastic sleeve of her new red binder.

CHAPTER 11

*C*offee?" Dara stood in the trailer door the next morning, smiling like a stewardess.

"That sounds lovely—I'll be right in." Jane stood outside in her bathrobe hosing red dust off the metal steps. "I wonder what this stuff is."

Dara withdrew to the kitchen. If she didn't answer, it wasn't a lie.

Jane liked her coffee with milk and sugar. Dara tried to remember how much of each. She'd always left it black—the sugar bowl was on the table, and the milk in the fridge. But she got points for kindness. She dropped a sugar cube in the cup, poured the coffee, and added milk till the color looked right.

Jane joined Dara at the table. "You look very pretty."

Dara stood and held her arms out. "Do I look okay? This is an old dress."

"But a lovely one—it accents your eyes. Where are you going?"

"To church! Aren't you?"

Jane gazed at her a split-second too long before answering. It was one of those things she did that annoyed Dara most. "Of course," said the duchess, at last.

Hooper provided the ride again, and Dara rode in back with Tom. Clementine sat between them in her green challis and red boots, reciting aloud her memory verse, while Hooper, Tom, and Jane smirked out their windows. "Blessed are the meek," she announced, "for they shall inhibit the earth."

No one spoke up, and Dara thought it must be worth a point or two to correct her, but there was no time. As soon as they rounded into the parking lot at Grace Chapel, they were escorted by three girls in jeans, T-shirts, and heavy makeup who seemed to know all about the little cowgirl. Or else about Tom. "Hi, Clementine!" they cooed. One of them, a little older than the rest, looked from Dara to Tom and back again, and flashed a smile. Dara forced herself to flash one back, but the way she felt at the moment, she doubted she'd earned any points.

The blue cinder-block church was infested with people, and there was no cook's window to hide behind. There were at least three couples chatting in front that she had to walk through to get to the door. Then in the foyer, there were twelve or fourteen people more. When she walked in they turned all their smiling eyes upon her, and she hadn't even gotten to the greeter. Why did churches have greeters? This one was a bearded old man with false teeth who took her hand in both of his and wanted to know her name.

"I'm Dara Pearl." She winced. That was five points off for lying. She was going to have to give out her real name, and that was more than she could think about just now.

Everyone prodded Tom to introduce them to his "friend." They all raised their eyebrows when they asked, and Dara knew they assumed she was more than that. She meant to sit next to Jane, but the duchess, Hooper, and Tom all slid into the pew before she had the chance. She had Clemmie sit between her and Tom, but that was almost worse. Especially since Clemmie laid her head on Dara's shoulder and held Tom's hand like the three of them made a family.

Besides, within the half hour all the children were dismissed to children's church. Time for Clemmie to explain to a Connie MacAdam on her own how the meek would inhibit the earth.

And that left Dara side by side with Tom. She scooted six inches the other direction and shot him a look—which he missed.

There was Finis and Ivy in the front row opposite. When it was time to take the offering, it was Finis who stood at the end of Dara's pew, nodding approval that she was there, and that she had an envelope stuffed with two twenties and a ten, all ready to drop in the velvet offering bag.

Amy, Pastor Erik's wife, was at the piano. She gave a little wave between praise choruses, subtle enough not to draw attention, and Dara was grateful.

But Pastor Erik let fly from the podium that they had a visitor there with them today, and he asked Dara to stand. Dara lifted herself a half-foot from the pew and sat down again. Then Tom stood, pulling her up by the arm, and announced, "I'd like you to meet my dear friend Dara Pearl. This is her first time with us, so I know you'll all want to say hello after the service."

When she sat down she kicked him, and *that* he caught.

"Ow! What was that?"

Jane and Hooper chuckled, two women in front of them turned to smirk at Tom, and Dara wanted to crawl home. She'd probably lost points for the kick, not to mention Tom's lie about her name. That probably went on her record as well.

She turned to a woman who tapped her shoulder and shook her hand. "Pleased to meet you," Dara cooed, just as sweetly as anyone else with their church smiles on.

Pastor Erik stuttered through the first five minutes of the sermon. He kept looking to the right front pew, where Finis sat taking notes in a steno pad with his four-color pen. Something about the way Finis leaned back peering slit-eyed over his glasses made Dara think he wasn't recording spiritual insights gleaned from Erik's preaching.

"For by grace you have been, um …" Erik looked to Finis, then down at his notes. "… saved through faith …" He cleared his throat. "Says the Word of God."

"Amen!" shouted a powerful voice directly behind Dara.

"Oh God!" Dara leapt, and her purse launched from her lap like popcorn, landing wrong side up on the floor.

"You preach it, boy!" bellowed the bass trombone behind her.

Tom chuckled and leaned over to help Dara gather her change purse and checkbook. "Erik's granny," he whispered while they had their heads down. Dara sat up and gazed casually off to the side, up at the ceiling, and over her shoulder, like she was watching a fly. The withered woman behind her flashed a toothy smile. Dara wanted to look away like she was still following that fly, but for a split moment, it was impossible.

This woman was something to see. *Withered* was the precise word because she looked like a deflated southern debutante. She wore a yellow off-the-bony-shoulder dress with a red rose at her bosom. She showed an inch of cleavage, but it might have been just a fold of skin—there were lots of those. Her hair showed vestiges of a youthful blonde, and she'd rolled some into a knot at the top and let the rest hang free. Her hands, clasped on her lap, were heavy with rings bigger than her knuckles. Her nails were painted pink.

She flashed a second smile. Dara blushed and turned her attention back to Erik.

"I'm not so sure this verse, uh, always *sounds* to us like good news. What do you make of a God who will take charge of something so ... so clearly up to us as our salvation? How do you control a God like that?" At last he gathered a wisp of steam. He leaned over the podium and pointed into the air. "And control has always been the issue!"

"Oh baby, you tell 'em!"

Erik smiled at his grandmother and blushed. Finis clicked his pen and wrote a note on his pad.

The sermon didn't go as well after that, but you couldn't have proved it by the blonde bombshell. Her voice was brazen with pride and bravo, and maybe cigarettes.

Erik wrapped things up quickly. No one came forward, so he slipped out while Amy played the final chorus.

Dara didn't blame him a bit for running. While he left out the back, she slipped through the side door and crossed the lawn to the parking lot. She'd wait in the car.

She waited a long time, watching the door through the rearview mirror. Exactly two people left after the service, and she watched them drive away. She looked at her watch. It had been ten minutes. She watched the mirror.

Finally, the double door cracked open. Good. She buckled

her seat belt and looked again. The door was closed, and a lone woman walked across the parking lot. Dara rolled down her window, and Amy bent to talk to her. "Would you like to join us in the fellowship hall? We've got coffee and cookies."

"Oh, is that where everyone is?"

"Well, a bunch of our ladies made the cookies from scratch. Chocolate chip. Not many people can pass 'em up."

"I think I'll just wait, thanks."

Amy looked at the sky. "I don't blame you. It's nice out. Mind if I sit in your front seat?" Dara shook her head, and she pulled the door handle and sat sidesaddle, with her legs crossed out the open door. "I think Erik's gram scared the piewadden out of you."

"I'll bet that happens a lot."

"It happens all the time!" Amy laughed. "She thinks Erik hung the moon, but with her on one side and my dad on the other, well, you can imagine."

"Is she visiting?"

"No, she lives with us! She doesn't get along with Erik's folks, and she can't live alone."

"Does she get along with you?"

"Oh sure! I think she's fun. Just an excess of personality, that's all. Years ago she was a lingerie model. She's still got better underwear than I do. I'm scared to death Dad will get a look at her closet some day because she's got all her old glamour shots in there."

"He doesn't live with you, does he?"

Amy nodded. "He and Mom have a motor home in our driveway, but that's close enough to have opinions."

She peered around the headrest and grinned. "Know what Gram does? You're not going to believe it."

"What?"

"She freaked me out one day. It was time for her morning pills, and I knocked on her door, but she didn't answer. So I cracked it open just a little and about fell over, because there she was with her long gray hair fanned out on the pillow like the Lady of Shalott. And her hands folded on her chest—with a lily! And her face all sunk down like a badly made bed. I swear, my first thought was ..."

She started giggling and couldn't finish.

Dara cupped a hand over her mouth to contain the revulsion. She saw too clearly the flesh-draped skull sunk into the pillow, the jaw hung open ...

"And then she let out this *long* snore,"Amy continued, and Dara choked. "She wasn't even embarrassed that I'd caught her! The lily's silk, and she keeps it in a vase by the bed. She said, 'It's gonna happen one day, darlin', and I mean to look good when it does.' She says, 'All it takes is a little planning!'"

"Amy!" The bellow was unmistakable. Dara peeked over her shoulder and there at the door was the bombshell, in—for heaven's sake!—white stiletto heels.

"Oh!" Amy ducked behind the front seat and snorted. They heard the heels clop their way across the parking lot.

Amy sat up. "Hi, Gram."

"Where are you? What are you doing with your feet stuck out the car?" She peered into the backseat. "Oh, hello!" She reached to shake Dara's hand. "I'm Una Gunderson."

"I'm Dara."

An odd look crossed her face, and then she brightened. "Are you Jane's friend? Lucky you. Jane is just the most wonderful woman, isn't she?"

She turned to Amy. "Did you hear about Clementine's memory verse in children's church today?"

"No."

"She said, 'The meek shall inhibit the earth.'"

The two cackled as if they were used to laughing together. Dara studied them till Una turned to study her.

"So, you're Dara ..."

It was as good a time as any to tell the truth. "Brogan," she answered quietly.

Una nodded slowly and softened her voice. "I mean it, honey, you hang on to Jane. Amy here's a good friend, and her mother's got great potential, but ..."Amy made a face and grinned at Dara, but Una's tone was serious. "Women like Jane just don't come along every day." She locked eyes with Dara as if to be sure her meaning was clear. Dara didn't know that it was.

"So are you and Tom …" Una finished her question with a smile.

"No."

"Oh, too bad. Because Tom's got potential too."

"Amy!" Another unmistakable voice. Dara turned, and Finis was already halfway across the parking lot.

"Finis!" said Una, but his attention was on his daughter.

"Amy, you've got people in there!"

"She's got people out here." Una raised an eyebrow.

"Well then, why don't we all …" He spread his arms and flipped his hands toward the church.

"We survived the day." Jane shut the trailer door behind them and flopped onto the couch.

"Yes." Dara sat beside her. "We did."

Finis had strongly implied that she would lose at least twenty points if she didn't get herself into the fellowship hall. She had no sooner gotten back in the church than he pulled her to the side in the hallway.

"Don't take Una too serious. She's got a very fine testimony, I'm sure, but I doubt it would be for the children's ears, if you get my meaning." He touched his head. "The Lord salvaged all he could." He patted Dara's shoulder. "Why do all the crazies gravitate to you?"

Dara escaped from this one man to the relative comfort of a room full of church people.

Tom sat near the door with Ivy. By the sounds of things, they were planning Finis's birthday party. Una and Jane sat in the corner howling over something, slapping each other's arms. Dara hadn't seen Jane laugh so hard since that day in the desert—back when all she had to worry about was the voice in her head.

Finis headed straight for the corner. He said something to Una, and Una left him alone with Jane. It looked like he was drawing a picture in the air for her, the way he poked and motioned with his hands. He did all the talking, while Jane nodded and rubbed her head and offered the occasional smile.

Everybody else was quiet and pleasant, and Dara observed their gentle nods and small talk and fed them back like she was learning a foreign language. It wasn't so hard.

And it didn't last long. Una went and talked to Hooper, and tall as he was, he peered over all the tops of heads between him and the corner. He excused himself from the man he'd been talking to and broke through the crowd to take Jane's arm. He nodded to Finis without smiling, gathered Tom and Clemmie, motioned to Dara, and they left. Clemmie had to fill the silence on the way home, but she did a fine job.

It was good to be home.

Jane turned her head against the back of the sofa and sighed. "You know what I'd like?"

"What's that?" Dara asked.

"I'd really like to go to the desert. We'll stay away from steep rocks this time. Why don't we?"

Dara's skin tingled with the memory of desert air, the place to stretch her arms out and feel the whispering love. A soft wind brushed at the window. The living room weighed dark and musty around her shoulders.

But she remembered what Finis had said about Jane. "You go on ahead."

"Oh, are you sure?" Jane pleaded, though she seemed too tired to lift her head from the sofa.

Dara swallowed hard. "I've got something to do."

She got up and walked to her room. Had she taken the Lord's name in vain when Una thundered behind her or merely uttered a prayer? It was negative ten points or positive ten, and on this day she'd be lucky to break even. She decided she'd been praying. She needed to record the day's scores on her chart before she forgot what they were.

Dearest Jane and Dara,

We had such a good time in Sacr., we stayed three wks. Now we are on our way north again. We stayed the night in a little town called Yreka (yes I spelld that right). Bedded down in the Wal-Mart parking lot—good view of the store from our window.

We hope to make it to Victoria, BC in a week or so.

> Love,
> Glenda

Jane and Dara,

Sacramento was not so great that we wanted to stay three weeks. Glenda's in Wal-Mart buying toothpaste, so I will tell you, she spent those weeks in the hospital.

She's walking across the parking lot, so I'll seal this in the envelope before she sees it.

Pray.

> Love,
> Harold

*A*mazing how few people kept up on things. Dara had taken her turn at the tables every day for weeks now. She'd made a point of giving out her name—her full name. Really, it hadn't raised a ripple.

Of course, Jane and Tom knew who she was, and so did Una, safe to say. But Finis, who took such pride in his erudition, had somehow missed the cautionary tale of Dara Brogan.

So had the dimwitted lady who breezed in that first Monday morning after Dara started the Ten Easy Steps program.

"Do you remember me?" the woman trilled. "I'm Nancy Sweet. I was here for the grand reopening. I had so much fun I brought my friend Tracy with me today. You're the shy little gal in the kitchen, aren't you? Uh, let's see, your name's Pearl ..."

No more lying. She told the woman her real name and waited.

"Oh! Dara Brogan! Well, Tracy, she cooks a fabulous steak and the most wonderful coffee—can we seat ourselves? They call it 'brown gargle.' Isn't that cute?"

Such idiotic, perky blather—but Dara slapped a smile on. Surely niceness got high marks in the Ten Commandments somewhere.

She turned from Nancy's table and found herself face-to-badge with a sheriff's deputy. One look at the khaki brown uniform with the black gun holster, and her mind flooded with memories of the interrogation after that day on Myer River Road. Her newly affected smile slipped right to her shoes.

"You say your name's Brogan?" asked the deputy.

What did he want from her? Did he come with more questions? He waited for his answer. She nodded.

"My wife's got a cousin, name of Cory Brogan, in Idaho. You know him?"

Incredible. "No, I don't think he's related."

"Ah. Well, I'm Lonnie Santiago." He made a motion as if to tip his hat, though he already held the thing in his left hand.

"Why are you here?"

"Uh, because I want some breakfast."

"Oh. Right." She slapped on her smile. "Why don't you take a seat right there …"

The deputy did as she told him. He sat in the empty booth and pulled out a well-worn crossword puzzle book. When she brought his menu, he sucked his pen and asked for a ten-letter word for "beyond belief."

Incredible.

A couple brought in a newspaper and had it pulled apart by the time Dara brought their menus. The man read the comics while the woman read aloud a recipe for chocolate cake.

Who reads recipes out loud?

"I'll be your waitress today," Dara chirped, taking a cue from Nancy Sweet. Perky and nice seemed to go together, and she thought she was getting the knack.

"My name is Dara Brogan," she continued.

They smiled and opened their menus.

"D-a-r-a." She spelled it for them.

"Well, that's a very pretty name," said the woman, without looking up.

Didn't anybody actually *read* the papers?

Safe to say the thistle-headed mystery woman did. Ever since the grand reopening, she'd come in morning and evening— evidently just to watch Dara work. She ordered black coffee in the mornings and a grilled cheese sandwich every night.

One day Dara introduced herself to her, half-hoping she'd recognize the name, get the shudders, and leave. And sure enough. The woman turned so white her bleached hair looked dark. She paid her bill, hurried out without finishing her sandwich, and didn't come back.

Till the next morning. She was still pale as skim milk, but there she was, back at her station, wanting coffee. Tom went out for a chat and came back with no more than her name: Sophie Cook. But that was more than even Jane had been able to glean— and Jane was good at gleaning. This woman was locked up tighter than Dara had ever been. She could use a few lessons in perkiness.

She was out there now, sitting in front of her usual evening meal. Dara glanced out the cook's window to the dining room, and caught her eye. Sophie dropped her gaze to her coffee cup. What *was* her deal? Dara shook her head and turned the four burgers on the grill.

Any minute now, Sophie would go outside for a cigarette and return five minutes later. That's how much a part of the furniture she had become; Dara could tell by the way she gripped her cup, when it was time for a smoke.

Meanwhile, the only indication the Ten Easy Steps program had worked any change at all were the smarmy looks Tom kept throwing her way. About the time she learned the art of perkiness from Nancy Sweet, he started eyeing her every time she passed by. Right this minute he was casting glances, scooping fries onto four plates, turning to face her, running a knuckle under his chin.

"What is it, Tom?" she asked, scraping the grill.

"How do I say this?"

"You'll find a way." She reminded herself to be nice.

"You keep baring your teeth."

"Baring my teeth? I'm smiling, Tom."

"Ah. Is that it?"

She looked into the restaurant, then out the window to the sidewalk where Sophie paced, pulling drags on her cigarette. "Jane smiles. Why can't I smile?"

"You can, it's just …" He cocked his head. "I'm not sure that's quite the smile God gave you."

"You're snooping in my soul again, Tom!" She bared her teeth, and then glanced out at the sidewalk, back at the booth, and outside again.

"Is Sophie bothering you? I can tell her to stop coming in."

"Not now you can't," she said. "She's not here."

"Of course she's here; we're not closed yet. She's probably gone to the toilet."

"Not unless she was in there with Jack Fry. He just stepped out."

"Well, she's outside then."

"Do you see her?"

He looked. "Huh! Perhaps the problem's solved itself. All that tooth-baring you've done."

The back door opened, and Hooper came in with a box. "Hey, Dara! Tom, I brought your inserts." He nodded to the dining room. "Jane out there?"

"She is." Tom pulled a sheet from the box and inspected it. "Do you have a reason to ask?"

"Thought she might like a candlelit dinner on my patio Sunday night—if you must know."

"She's been looking at your whistle berries for weeks!"

"Well now, I might know how to cook something you don't serve in your restaurant. Ever think of that?"

"Not once. You plan to ask my blessing one day?"

"Maybe. When I think you might give it."

Tom chuckled.

Hooper headed to the dining room. "But I gave you mine once," he said. "Don't forget."

What kind of way was this to find a mother? Virtue wasn't Dara's gift.

She trudged home, too drained, almost, to lift her feet. The afternoon heat that cuffed her face when she opened the Studmuffin's back door now seeped from the sidewalk through the soles of her shoes.

She had worked hard that day. She had cooked, waited tables, and cleaned. She had smiled, prattled, and cooed at babies like a politician on the make. She had told her name to several customers, though by now she knew how little credit there was in that. Most people, it turned out, were too busy with crossword puzzles and comics and recipes to care who Dara Brogan was.

Still, she went to church and dropped money in the bag. She quit dancing in the desert with Jane and kept her distance from Una. She wasn't swearing, was hardly ever sarcastic, and she'd learned to be perky and nice as any good Christian you could name—despite Tom's annoying, squinty little grin.

The red line on her chart practically soared off the page. She'd come a long way. And yet, not a single new lead on her mother. It just wasn't working.

Finis said to be patient; the answer would come suddenly, when she wasn't looking. But that would be hard, wouldn't it? Because she looked all the time. Anytime the phone rang, it could be her mother on the other end. Any day's mail could bring news.

She rounded the corner onto Coolidge Street and saw a blonde woman twenty feet down the walk.

"Sophie." She faked a smile and glanced around. Nobody else on the street. The heat had driven most people indoors, and the two were alone.

Not a safe world.

Sophie dropped her cigarette and ground it out with her foot.

Dara tried to think of a public place to go. She didn't want Sophie following her home. The gas station?

When she drew nearer, though, something stopped Dara's breath in her throat. Was it a movement Sophie made, the way she held her shoulders? In an instant Dara imagined she knew everything this woman felt: the terror of another face, the sickening belly-weight of self-disdain.

Without her cigarette, Sophie seemed unsure what to do with her hands—or her eyes. "The restaurant's closed?" She glanced at Dara, then back to the sidewalk.

"Yeah. You okay?"

"I really wanted ... some coffee." She seemed short of breath. "Would you like some at my place? I could make you some." She looked up and smiled, then closed her lips as if to hide bad teeth.

Back in Los Cuervos, Dara had never asked people over for coffee. This was a brave move for Sophie. "You live around here?"

Sophie shrugged. "Just a room at the Little Oasis."

She had seen the Little Oasis, a sorry little paint-chipped place with a faded sign under a neon palm tree, half burnt out. It advertised one bed for twenty dollars. It didn't look like it was worth ten. "You here on a work thing?"

"No."

"Just had to take in the sights of Brittlebush, huh?"

"I've just got instant coffee." Sophie shrugged.

Dara saw Sophie's pleading look and drew a ragged breath. "I'll come."

The motel room was cleaner than Dara expected—much cleaner, given what she'd seen outside—the thick algae in the swimming pool, the faded cigarette pack in the yellow grass.

Sophie took the wrappers off two glasses on top of the refrigerator in the corner. She opened a small jar of instant Folgers and used a plastic spoon to portion some into each glass. She disappeared into the bathroom, and Dara heard the faucet.

In the corner she saw the ice bucket, stocked with window cleaner, pine cleaner, and lemon oil, with a rag spread neatly over the top.

"You clean this room yourself?"

The water stopped, and Sophie walked out with their coffee. She nodded to the side like it was something she was ashamed of. "Go ahead and take the chair." She sat on the edge of the bed.

The plastic headboard shone with lemon polish. The bedside table was yellowed maple, with cigarette burns along the edge. A paper towel served as a doily in the middle, with a potted fern and a picture on top.

"The water from the tap's pretty hot," said Sophie.

Dara sipped her coffee and suppressed a grimace. "It's fine."

Sophie stared into her glass.

Dara pointed to the picture on the table, of Sophie and a woman standing arm in arm.

"Is that family?"

"No. Well, all the family *I* have. She's my sponsor."

"Your what?"

"I'm in AA. I've got six months. That's Marie."

"Oh."

"A sponsor is someone who, uh …"

"Helps you?"

She nodded and turned her eyes back to her coffee. "She calls me every night at ten. She knows I can't afford a phone bill."

"Six months. That's a long time."

Sophie shuddered. "I fight it every day."

Dara nodded.

"Marie's been sober ten years." She smiled, then closed her lips.

"Why do you hide your smile like that?"

"What?" Sophie frowned.

"Your smile's perfectly good. Nothing wrong with your teeth or anything."

"No." Sophie shifted. "I've been lucky with my teeth."

"So you shouldn't shut your mouth when you smile."

She shrugged. "I'll write it on my inventory."

"Your inventory?"

"Step four: a searching and fearless moral inventory." She opened the drawer to the bedside table and pulled out a card printed with twelve steps. "It's something we do in AA."

"Oh." Dara looked at the card. "I'm doing something like that."

"Are you in a program?" For the first time Sophie looked into Dara's eyes.

"I guess I am."

"Well, God bless you then." She looked away.

It was dark when Dara got home and somewhat cooler. Walking up the moonlit drive, she heard bursts of muffled voices. Finis and Jane.

She stopped within the light of the window, then backed away.

"I'm a widow, Finis!"

"And you think Max would want you traipsing round with this cowboy?"

"I don't know what he wants; he's dead!"

"Jane, the man spends his time writing bad poetry. You, however, have a calling!"

"And you know better than I what that calling might be?"

Dara crept to the swing set and tucked herself into the shadows, where the stars flashed through the fretting leaves. Even from here, she heard fragments: "responsibility" intoned in a masculine voice, "grace" pled in a feminine one. "Your work undone!" against "time to rest!"

The door finally opened, and Finis stepped out, then turned back. "That pagan woman is filling the vacuum, Jane. Every day we lose people to her." He descended the steps, stalked down the drive, and was gone.

Dara thought of going inside like she hadn't heard a thing, when the door opened again. Jane padded barefoot down the steps to a moonlit patch of grass. She stood, motionless as stone, with her face to the stars. In the moonlight her silver hair shone like a trout in water. From her open mouth came a keening, wordless song, and Dara felt the crushing weight of it. Then Jane quieted, and the wind whispered undisturbed for several moments before at last she snuffled and drew an arm across her eyes.

Dara whispered, "Jane?"

Jane turned to the swing and sighed. "I didn't see you there."

"Sorry."

"May I join you?" She sat in the other swing and rested her head against the chain.

"I didn't hear much."

"I don't mind." Jane turned to Dara. "Finis is … a good man, Dara. He's a very responsible man. He cares deeply for the mission in Mexico, and he wants me to be … responsible."

"You are responsible."

"I used to be."

She was silent so long Dara thought the conversation had ended. Then Jane breathed deeply and began.

"Before Max died, there was so much to do, so many in our church were sick. Everybody was sick, *we* were sick, but there was the work. Max and I had begun fighting. We'd never fought like that. We were very close, but we were so tired. In the middle of a terrible row, he got a call, and I shrieked at him …" She cuffed a hand to her mouth and moaned. "I ran beside his truck all the way to the road, screaming at him not to go. But he did go, and that night his car ran off a bridge. And I don't know … It might have been an accident, but I don't know."

Dara bowed her head, unable to speak.

"Finis doesn't know about the fight. I returned to England for the funeral and went back to Mexico the next day. I thought it was what Max would want, and Finis said the mission needed me. I just don't know how to tell him."

"Can't you just say it?"

Jane stared into the stars. "One night I felt like the breath was crushed out of me. It was late. Everyone was in bed. And anyway, who could I tell? I tried to make it to the church, but I fell on the steps, and I couldn't get up."

"Did you faint?"

She shook her head. "I remember the moonlight and …" She laughed. "And a dog that stopped to mark the steps. It was very cold, but … it was the end."

"The end?"

"Well." She shrugged. "Lena found me and took me home. Finis was angry because he didn't know where I was, but for days I just sat by her fire. And she took such care of me."

"Well, you were sick—"

"Finis says she should have taken me to the hospital. But she took me to the hills around her house, and she began to dance, just the way we had always seen her do off in the distance. But that day …" She shook her head. "It was as if the sky bent down to give me back my breath. When I was well enough, she told me to go home. And I did."

Dara started to speak, but the wind brushed her lips, and she stopped.

"Max and I were all the world to each other, Dara." She rocked fitfully in her swing and wept with her face to the sky. "But if you could have heard us that night and for the weeks and weeks before that …" She choked, and in the moonlight, her lips stretched taut to a grimace, and still she rocked.

Turning in her swing, Dara reached a faltering hand to Jane's arm. She stroked it a long while, and Jane wept in the darkness. Then, knowing nothing better to do, she went inside to draw a lavender bath for her friend.

The next morning, while Jane sat at the table in her bathrobe, Dara stopped a run in her hose with clear polish. "Tell Hooper I won't be riding with him. Sophie's coming to church today, and I said I'd walk with her."

"Sophie from the restaurant? She talked to you?"

"I had really bad coffee with her yesterday, in her room at the Little Oasis."

"Dara! You didn't go off alone with her?"

"Yep. And I'm still here." Dara swallowed the last of her tea and put the cup in the dishwasher.

"You amaze me. What does she want?"

"Just a friend, I guess." She turned to go.

Jane touched her arm, and Dara stopped. "Then she's found a good one."

Dara returned Jane's smile, averted her eyes, and left.

Erik's sermon proceeded like a freighter at sea this time. He made it through the whole sermon without stammering once.

The trick, evidently, was to fix his eyes on the clock above the sanctuary door, so as to avoid his father-in-law's incisive gaze on the one hand, and his grandmother's gleaming maw on the other. Of course, the clock was positioned near the peak of the vaulted ceiling, and this made him look like he was preaching to God himself. Judging by Erik's expression, God had pudding in his beard.

Una blasted her "amens" loud as ever, but Erik barged on through. Luckily, Dara had had the foresight to lead Sophie to a pew *behind* the bombshell.

Sophie fidgeted with her program through the whole service. When it ended, she scuttled out the door before Dara could usher her into the fellowship hall. So, taking a cue from Finis, Dara followed to fetch her back in.

But when she opened the church doors, she found that Sophie had already lit a cigarette. The woman sucked on it like it contained the first real oxygen she'd had all day. Dara stood outside the door staring walleyed, wondering what to do.

The door swung open with a force that swept Dara to the side. Una stepped out in her red dress and matching stiletto heels.

"Darlin', I'm so glad you didn't get away before I had a chance to meet you. I'm Una Gunderson." She extended a hand to Sophie.

The bombshell had on a push-up bra, Dara was sure of it. In this case it effected both a vertical and a horizontal cleavage.

Sophie shook Una's hand, blowing her smoke to the side.

"I'm Sophie." She glanced at her cigarette sadly, like she'd have to put it to sleep.

"Mind if I join you?" Una pulled a pack of Eves from her purse and lit herself one, sucking her cheeks in and tossing her head like Bette Davis. Sophie smiled and took another puff.

Dara could just see it. The next time the door opened to knock her aside, it would be Finis, and there she'd be with these two. She'd get a negative fifty by association.

Finis had taken to stopping by from time to time for "accountability sessions." While Jane hid in her room, he'd check Dara's charts, pat her shoulder, and counsel her in ways she could do even better.

She'd become a regular at the women's ministry meetings, and right this moment there was a stack of pink paper napkins on her dresser at home she'd promised to decorate with violet stickers before next Wednesday's tea.

Finis said she had done him proud.

But what if he found her with these two blondes who didn't even know to do their smoking *behind* the church? She fled inside where she could at least feign ignorance.

There was Amy in her powder-blue suit, lacking only the pillbox hat.

"Erik's doing better," said Dara, stepping up beside her.

"He's a brave man!" Amy laughed. "You know, I think Dad likes his preaching just fine. He's just so used to evaluating people, and he puts on those glasses and pulls out that pen."

Dara leaned closer. "Una's out there smoking with Sophie."

"I'm not surprised. I told her she should quit. She just said, 'How many years do you think I've got left, honey?' Oh, and she told me to leave her lily by the bed."

Dara rolled her eyes. "She's got plenty of years left."

"Well, I think that would be her point exactly."

Finis emerged from the fellowship hall. "There you are!" He strode with such force, Dara stepped back.

"Listen," said Finis. "Erik and I have a meeting in Crayton

tomorrow. I'll be gone till Tuesday. I've got just an hour to go over your charts before we leave, but you'll have to head home now."

Dara's hand moved toward her pearl, but she stopped herself before he noticed and tucked both hands behind her back.

"Oh, but Daddy …" Amy smiled. "Dara was going to come to my place."

"Well that can—"

"She's bringing Sophie, the lady she brought with her today." She wrinkled her nose and dimpled. "We're all going to have tea together and just the nicest time of fellowship." She nudged Dara, and Dara nodded.

Finis opened his mouth and shut it again. "All right, then." He kissed Amy's cheek. "You're a good girl." He walked away and opened the door.

Over his shoulder Dara saw a faint curl of smoke. Past his legs she saw Una and Sophie on the curb, getting on just fine. Una danced her cigarette to illustrate whatever story she was telling, and Sophie looked like any minute now she might crack a smile.

Finis turned back, opened his mouth, shut it again, shook his head, and left.

Whatever lace-doily sort of tea and fellowship Finis envisioned when Amy wrinkled her nose at him never materialized. What he likely feared once he opened the door and saw two blondes with their cigarettes—that's what came about, though Una and Sophie weren't the problem. It was Una and Jane. Dara probably lost twenty points just listening.

It started when Ivy suggested Sophie sit near the air conditioner. Dara looked and sure enough, Sophie's thistle hair had gone moist at the roots. Her face was rosy, with droplets coursing down her hairline.

"Sophie, honey, you look radiant," Una said. "Why don't you

trade places with me. At my age, refrigeration's not necessary."

Sophie blushed and shook her head. Jane extended a hand and coaxed her to her feet. "Really, we all understand. I once fancied I'd been called to minister in Siberia, since I clearly had the gift of spontaneous convection."

"The baby boom's the entire cause of global warming," Una declared. "The biggest generation in history, and half of them with hot flashes these days. Think that doesn't raise the earth's temperature a notch or two? The scientists just need to be patient. I'll bet Jane and Ivy have already cooled off considerably. Haven't you, girls?"

Ivy smiled. "Considerably."

"Please don't say that," said Jane. "It's too disheartening."

"I'm just talking about the environment, honey. Sophie, don't you worry. It doesn't take long."

Sophie took her seat by the air conditioner, and Una sidled next to her, still talking.

"Women are a vital part of bionomics, you know. Stop spawning little girls, and in fifty years, whole species will disappear, their habitats iced over to a sterile wasteland."

Sophie grinned, turning her face to the side, still quite red.

"What you need are lighter clothes," said Una, fingering the long polyester sleeve of Sophie's blouse.

It was one of two blouses she'd worn on alternate days since she'd first shown up at the Studmuffin. She'd pushed her sleeves up, but they were just too tight to push far.

"I didn't bring many clothes with me," she said.

"Well, come on then." Una stood. "Let's go see what I've got that'll fit you."

Sophie held back. Her eyes scanned Una's outfit, and Dara resisted a chuckle.

"Some of my clothes are quite ordinary," said Una. "Aren't they, Amy?"

"Just the ones you don't wear, Gram."

"Well, there you go, then."

Amy's place had the haphazard charm of a home furnished with yard-sale finds, but Una's piece of it left nothing to chance. The bed was covered in moss velvet to match the draperies. The headboard, dresser, and tables were all carved mahogany with flashes of gold touched to the rosebuds. She had an actual dressing table skirted in the same gold chiffon that filtered light between the drapes.

And by her bed was a crystal vase with a single white silk lily.

Una opened a dresser drawer and pulled out a sleeveless shell, soft blue. "This should do the trick," she said. "It's really too big in the top for me. I used to be bigger, but ..." She waved her hands around her two cleavages. "One too many trips to the knocker press!"

"It's what she calls a mammogram." Amy smiled.

Sophie chuckled, just a little.

"It's a better name," said Ivy, settling into the green brocade reading chair.

Una shook her head. "Take a warning from me, girls. You can't put these things through the pasta press and expect them to bounce back every time. One day they just give out, and what have you got but cooked lasagna to stuff in your brassiere?"

Jane sat on the bed. "I once heard of a woman who yanked herself out of the wicked contraption too quickly, and they curled up just like gift ribbon."

"Well, that would keep them off your knees, at least," said Una.

Sweet little Amy grinned like she'd hoped exactly this would happen.

Sophie had started laughing—holding her hand up, still hiding her teeth, but she was audibly laughing.

Dara caught her eye, and the two burst out in a mutual snort. Then Jane and Una snorted, and Ivy and Amy, and they had themselves a pig party right there in Una's boudoir.

"You can try that on in my closet, dear," said Una at last, indicating the blue shell still in Sophie's hands.

Sophie opened the closet door and stopped. Dara leaned

over to catch a glimpse. Sophie stood slack-jawed, scanning one wall to the other and back again. "Is this you?"

"It is." Una strode across the green carpet with the other women close behind.

There on the far wall of the closet were pinups of a goddess in her underthings. The bras were structured and comprehensive. The underwear extended from the tops of her thighs to an inch above her navel, with no high-cut anything. They were more decent than any bathing suit Dara had ever worn, only they were silk and chiffon, ginger and coral and jade and royal blue, and somehow they were far less decent than anything she had ever seen.

They were beautiful.

Una was beautiful. Her skin was fair, and her lips the color of cinnabar. Her hair curled around her face like spun topaz. In one picture she gazed at something above her head and to the left, with such a look of transport that Dara could believe the woman had just encountered a visiting angel while pulling on her stockings.

Dara looked from the pinups to the woman who stood beside her.

Una winked.

Flustered, Dara turned back to the closet.

Amid all of the photographs lambent with sensuality, one small three-by-five was different. In that one, Una simply laughed, her head thrown back, her shoulders hunched like a child caught up in a joke.

"That was Mike's favorite." Una smiled.

"Mike?"

"My husband. One wonderful man for fifty-two years." She patted Dara's arm. "Such things happen in this world."

CHAPTER 13

*F*ifty-two years! I didn't see her as the type." Within a block of Amy's house, Sophie had gone tense, knifing down the sidewalk in brisk paces.

Dara had never seen her this way. The corner of Cedar and Edison, where their paths would part, was just two blocks away. Somehow that seemed a relief.

"She's a good friend for you, don't you think? Her and Jane? They're *strong* women." She balled her fist. "Wish I'd been strong a few times. But they're good friends for you."

"Why just me? What about you?"

Sophie shook her head. "No sir, I'm going back home. It wouldn't work anyway. I don't know how to talk to people."

"That's funny." Dara shook her head.

"What?"

"You're talking fine now."

Sophie rummaged in her purse till she found her cigarettes, then looked hard at Dara. She started to speak and stopped. Lighting her cigarette, she started again. "I've got to find myself a meeting. Marie calls every night. She asks if I'm going, and I say I am. Truth is I haven't looked one up. But if I don't, little Sophie Jasso's apt to find herself right back in the gutter she crawled out from." She blew her smoke out in a thin white stream.

Dara frowned. "Sophie who?"

"Sorry. Jasso was my last husband. I forget sometimes."

Dara nodded.

"I want to make my life better, Dara. I've been to prison—don't guess you knew that."

"Nooo ..."

"Long time ago." She took a drag on her cigarette and puffed it out. "I mean to say—I can't be a Big Sister or anything, but I can do something good. There's a church near my house where they have a convalescent home. Pastor says if I get straight, I can come in on Tuesdays. Read to the old people who can't see, you know? I could do that, couldn't I?"

"Sure. You could do that. *Stay calm ...*

"I've never done one right thing in my life. But that would be something, wouldn't it?"

"Sure." Dara tapped a hand to her pearl.

They arrived at the corner of Cedar and Edison and stopped.

"Dara?"

"What?"

Sophie dropped her cigarette to the sidewalk, ground it out with her foot, then looked her in the eye. "Where did you live before Brittlebush?"

Dara hesitated while Sophie stood white-mouthed and still.

"Los Cuervos." Dara turned and started walking. She didn't look back till she'd rounded the corner and walked another block. Then, seeing no sign of Sophie, she ran.

In her trailer, down the hall, in her room, the door shut, the blinds pulled, Dara sat on the shadowed floor in the far corner. She held Algernon by the middle till he squeaked. She didn't let go.

"What was she talking about?" she asked the cat. "What does she want?" He squirmed, and she adjusted him to her shoulder but kept her hold.

"Stupid even to talk to her. It's not a safe world."

Algernon squirmed out of her hands and settled in her lap. She stroked his back, and he purred, gently clawing at her stockings. "What do you suppose she was in jail *for?*" She shook her head. "What was I thinking?"

Algernon lifted his nose to hers, and she rubbed her face against his. "She doesn't know where *I* live. That's good. I'll just tell Tom to send her away. He'll do it—he said he would."

She put the cat down and climbed to her bed. She picked up her red binder and placed her hand on her mother's picture. Closing her eyes, she repeated the invocation she'd learned from Finis, as she'd done for weeks now, morning and evening and several times in between. "Lord Jesus, I want you to give me my mother back so we can ..." She shuddered. "So she can watch *over* me and tell me what I should *do.* Please. *Please?*"

Surrounding the picture were cutouts of the Grand Canyon and Yosemite and various other places. Shaking her head, she slipped a hand into the plastic sleeve and pulled them out. She really didn't want to go anyplace with her mother.

One she left in. It was a picture of a house, cut from a *Better Homes and Gardens,* cute like the red and green one on Broadbent and Birch, only blue like the Rawlingses' house. It had a green lawn and a rose terrace, and a glider painted white on the porch. The article in the magazine described how the woman who lived there decorated her house on a budget, using things she'd made herself. There were pin-tucked and embroidered curtains and pillows, quilts for the beds, hand-painted cupboard knobs, even a hand-loomed carpet.

Dara smoothed the plastic sleeve over the blue house, imagining the dining-room table behind the bay window where she and her mother would spread a drop cloth and paint stripes and dots on porcelain knobs. She touched the porch swing where the two of them would read the newspaper in the evenings after work or watch the stars at night.

She opened the binder and turned to the tabbed section for her progress chart. The red line arced upward like a thunderbolt in reverse. She leaned against the headboard and closed her eyes.

"You could do better," she whispered to the dim light. "I'm doing my part. I don't need your flirts and kisses; I need *results* or … or at least *advice!* But you keep your own counsel."

She drifted to sleep.

"Dara! Dara!"

She heard the knocking and scrambled to her feet. Algernon bolted from the bed and dashed underneath. Dara reeled and sat heavy-headed on the edge of the bed. What had she been dreaming?

"Dara!!"

Sophie!

Dara sprang from the bed a second time and ran to the window to part the blinds. Sophie stood in the middle of the yard, her arms swinging loose as she spun, searching from the driveway to the yard to Tom's house. She darted up the steps to the house and pounded the back door. "Dara!"

Had Tom come home? What if Clemmie let her in? Dara ran to the trailer door, breathing the Lord's name in something between a curse and a prayer.

She opened the door. "Sophie, what are you doing?"

The woman hustled across the yard. Dara shrank back, then forced herself to step out and shut the door behind her. Better to be in the open.

"I have to talk to you," Sophie said.

"Have you been drinking?" Dara hurried off the steps.

"No, I haven't, Dara. Really." She came closer. Dara backed up, and she stopped.

"How did you know where I live?" Dara asked.

"You were married."

"What?"

"You were married, Dara. How did he treat you?"

"Sophie—"

"You have to tell me."

"No, I don't have to—"

"Did he hit you, Dara? What did he do?"

She stepped back. "Sophie—"

"Tell me. Tell me if he killed your father."

"Stop it!" Dara stepped backward to the driveway, lifting her hands to the sides of her face.

Sophie wiped her tears with the flat of her hand. "I won't hurt you, just please tell me."

"Dara!" It was Tom's voice. He charged down the driveway with Clemmie at his heels. He stopped and spoke to Clemmie, and she ran to the house.

"What's the trouble here?"

Sophie looked from Tom to Dara.

"She found me," Dara whispered.

"Found you?" He turned to Sophie. "How'd you find her?"

"I'm sorry," Sophie said. "I hired a detective. I had to borrow money to do it, but I—"

"A detective?" Dara pressed her back against the chain-link fence.

Tom stood beside her. "What do you want with Dara?"

Sophie wiped her tears again and shook her head.

"Go home, Sophie," Tom said. "I think you should go home."

Sophie turned, still weeping, and left.

Dara sobbed into her sleeve, and Tom led her to the yard. They sat on the trailer steps, and she cried against him.

"What was that about?" he asked.

She shook her head.

"She won't be welcome in the restaurant anymore. I'll tell her to stay away from you, or we'll call the police. Shhh." He stroked Dara's hair and waited.

At last, she rested against his chest. Her breath caught in spasms.

"I'll see that I'm in my house when you're at home, so you're not caught alone again. We can do our shopping together, you see? Like an old married couple. I'll be a gentleman. Brits make good gentlemen."

Dara smiled between spasms. "Tom."

"You know? I could get a mobile phone like Jane's. One for each of us."

"You can't afford that."

"Consider it a perk."

Jane walked up the drive and stopped. "Is this a private moment?"

Dara pulled away and scooted to the edge of the metal stair.

"Oh, Jane!" Tom scolded. "I was just convincing her to elope with me, and now you've ruined it."

Dara leaned her face against the rail.

"Jane?" Dara pushed on her shoulder that night and whispered. The duchess rolled over in bed, nestling her face in her silver hair. Dara pushed again. "Jane!"

She opened her eyes and squinted at the light from the open door. "What?"

"Please wake up."

"Dara? What's wrong?"

"I have to show you something. And I need your help."

Five minutes later they sat at the kitchen table. Jane pushed the gray strands from her face and peered. "What is it?"

"I know who Sophie is."

"Who she is?"

"I know why she's been watching me." Dara shuddered. "Or I don't know, but I …"

Jane looked hard at her.

"On the way home today, she said … a slip of the tongue, you know? She said she used to be Sophie Jasso."

"Jasso?"

"Her ex-husband. She—" Dara pulled the watercolor from her lap. "Look." She slid it across the table to Jane, who squinted like she was reading a map.

"Jane, look! SJ! See?"

"Sophie Jasso," she whispered. "Oh!" She leaned back in her chair. "But then, there's pages of SJ's in the directory, aren't there?"

"Yes. But none of them acting like Sophie." Dara zipped her pearl back and forth on the chain.

"No. No, I see that."

"Jane, she's been to jail." Dara whispered the news, pausing the pearl in its path.

"Jail? Why?"

"I don't know." She dropped the pearl to wipe tears from her face and picked it up again. "But she knows something. And—*jail*, Jane! Anything might have happened."

"Oh, Dara. We'll call the police."

"No." She took the watercolor back. "They'll need more than this."

"Well, what then?"

"I've got to go see her."

"Now? At midnight?"

"Today was terrible. She might leave, you know? And I don't even know where she lives. But she knows something!"

"Well, I'll go with you, then. But ..."

"What?"

"Shouldn't Tom come with us as well? Hooper might come sit with Clementine."

A cigarette point of orange light glowed through the motel window. "She's awake!" Dara whispered.

"Well, that's the idea, isn't it?" Tom spoke aloud.

"Knock on the door," Jane whispered.

The door opened. The woman's shadow stood in the darkness. "Hi," she said.

"Sophie," said Dara, "I need to talk to you."

"Yeah." Sophie nodded. "I scared you today."

"Of *course* you scared her," Tom began.

Jane touched his arm, and he stopped.

"I'm sorry." Sophie sniffled. "I've wanted to talk to you for so long." She wiped her eyes and forced a chuckle. "Listen. If I were you, I wouldn't want to be alone with me."

"No, she doesn't," Tom said.

Jane touched his arm again.

"Maybe we could walk across to Denny's, okay? I have something to say to Dara, but, you know, maybe if we sat in a booth, and you two just sat … nearby? Would that be all right?"

"I haven't been drinking." Sophie lit a cigarette when the coffee was poured.

"That's good." Dara sat forward, her hands pressed between her knees.

Sophie nodded toward the table where Jane and Tom sat. "He likes you, I think. Maybe he—"

"For heaven's sake, Sophie!"

"Sorry. I'm just nervous." She wiped her tears. "I told you I was in AA."

Dara nodded.

"And they've got steps we follow."

"Yeah?"

"Well, the eighth step says to make a list of all persons we have harmed and become willing to … to make amends."

"Okay?"

Sophie tapped her cigarette in the ashtray and took a deep breath. "And the ninth step says to make direct amends to all persons we have harmed, if …" She shrugged. "If possible."

"And you've harmed me?"

Sophie nodded and looked to Tom and Jane who quickly looked away.

Dara squeezed her knees tighter to her hands.

"I was never a good mother," Sophie said. "Just not a whole person, I guess. I needed too much."

Dara leaned forward.

Sophie held up a hand. "I'm not making excuses. No one made me do the things I did. I know that. I've made enough excuses for both of us."

"Sophie?"

"Things just got out of hand, but I … I let them, I know." She lifted her cigarette up but trembled so much, she had to catch it with her lips.

"Sophie, what are you saying?"

"I'm saying I'd never let anyone hurt my child on purpose. Please Dara, believe me!"

"But Sophie!" Dara shook her head. "Your eyes are the wrong color!"

"What?"

"Your nose is too … long, isn't it?"

"I don't—"

"Sophie, you're not my mother!"

"Your mother?"

"You don't look anything like her!"

"Why do you think I'm your mother?"

"I don't! Are you?"

"No, Dara, I'm not your mother."

"Then you know her!"

"Dara, I don't—"

She yanked the cigarette from Sophie's hand and put it out. "Stop playing games. You're SJ, and you know my mother!"

"SJ?"

"Sophie Jasso! SJ! Now tell me where she is!"

"I don't know." She shook her head. "It wasn't Frank Jasso."

"What?"

"It was Leonard Rogers."

"Rogers?"

Sophie picked up her cigarette, looked at the extinguished end, and put it down. "I had a kid, you know? And I was working at A&W making squat and about to lose even that because of the drinking." She leaned across the table. "Leonard was a *doctor.*"

Dara sat back and stared at her.

"What doctor would want me, right? But he treated me like a queen, never hit me or yelled, even when I was drunk." She rolled her eyes. "Never even tried to stop me; that was a clue, right? But I thought—"

Dara started to talk, but Sophie held her hand up. She picked up the cigarette, lit it, and looked at Dara without bothering to wipe the tears away. "It wasn't me he wanted, Dara. It was my son."

"Your son."

She nodded. "My son, and for four years I was too drunk to know." She wiped her eyes. "When Leonard went to jail, I went too, because they thought I ..." She choked and caught her breath. "Kevin went to a foster home."

"Kevin?" Dara pushed the pearl into her collarbone. "Kevin Brogan?"

Sophie nodded. She looked at Dara and nodded again.

Dara sank against the back of the booth and wept.

"I didn't know," Sophie said. "I never saw him till I heard his name on the television at the 7-Eleven, and I turned around. And there was his picture. And your picture."

Dara wiped her face and caught sight of Tom and Jane, who had dropped all pretense of not listening.

"Please forgive me," Sophie whispered.

"Forgive you?"

"Everything he did was my fault. He was just a little boy, and he was *beautiful!* And I didn't protect him." A squeak rose from her throat. Dara reached a tentative hand across to Sophie's.

Sophie pulled several napkins from the dispenser and gave Dara half. Feebly, she smiled. "Should have thought of these before."

Dara nodded and wiped her face.

"I've been all this time working up the courage to tell you. I was going to give up in the morning and go home, and just, well, mail you this." She pulled an envelope from her purse and handed it to Dara.

The envelope felt heavy. Dara opened it and pulled out a folded legal sheet. She unwrapped the paper and saw a stack of hundred-dollar bills.

"What's this?"

Sophie looked around, and Dara followed her gaze. No one but Tom and Jane were watching. "It's only a thousand," said Sophie. She snuffled and put her hand on Dara's. "I'm not saying it pays for your father or anything. Don't be insulted."

"I don't need—"

"I don't know how else to make amends. Please keep it. It's just a little bit, just a start."

"Sophie—"

"You've lost your father, and I was hoping …" She looked at her lap. "I was hoping maybe you would be like my daughter." She lifted her head. "Is that too ugly to think of?"

"No—"

"Because if it is, you don't have to see me anymore. I'll still send all I can."

"I can't keep your money."

"Please."

Dara was silent and finally shrugged.

"You could buy a wedding dress, maybe. Find someone to take care of you." She nodded ever so slightly toward Tom, who looked away.

"This really isn't the time, Sophie."

"Okay."

The two women wiped their eyes.

Sophie took a long breath. "They say he hit you."

The room reeled around Dara. How much more could she take?

"One newspaper said he beat you bloody from the day you were married." She wept fresh tears.

Dara gazed at her, the paleness in her face, the way she struggled to catch a trembling cigarette to her lips.

"Newspapers lie," Dara whispered.

"What?"

She held her gaze. "Kevin and I were very much in love."
Sophie leaned forward.

"My father's death was an accident, and so was Kevin's.
The papers lie."

"Oh, Dara!" Sophie squeaked. She put her cigarette down
and held Dara's hand in both of hers. "I was so afraid he'd gone
through life hating me, and that he did to you the things that I
deserved."

"No. Well, maybe, because he treated me like … like a
queen."

"Really?"

"He used to say he'd search for you someday. He told me
… He said he loved you."

Sophie's face saturated with tears. Dara looked to the waitress and nodded for the check, careful to avoid the eyes of Tom
and Jane. Then she handed Sophie another stack of napkins and
stroked her hand.

In the trailer Jane offered tea, a lavender bath, a biscuit, but Dara
refused them all. She walked into her room and sat beside
Algernon on the bed.

She picked up the red binder and stroked her mother's
picture. Then she opened the cover and removed the four-
color pen from the pouch. She turned to the progress chart,
traced the thunderbolt, and turned to the section for daily
scores.

What was a lie? Negative five? What about a very big lie, or
two or three or a whole string of them? She rolled the pen in
her hand once or twice before turning back to the chart.

She slashed a vertical line from the top of the arc to the
bottom of the page to the center of her gut. She stabbed it there
several times, hard enough to hurt, and cried aloud, then
checked herself, afraid that Jane would hear.

She wiped the tears with her arm. Then she ripped the

pages, handful after handful, from the binder, tore them in pieces, and dropped them to the floor.

When she was done, she pulled her mother's picture from the plastic sleeve and dropped the binder. She picked its frame up from the table and put the picture back inside.

Then she turned the light off and lay down without undressing. She wrapped her hand around her pearl and muffled her cries in her pillow until she fell asleep.

"Good morning, Finis!" Tom blurted. He stood gaping at the spatula Dara had thrust at him before she ran to the pantry for cover. Finis was the last person she wanted to see, now that she'd quit his program.

"Mornin', Tom."

Was Finis at the *counter?* The close-by pitch of his voice said he was, but he never sat at the counter! Clutching her pearl, she backstepped in the darkness.

"Dara here?" Finis asked. She held her breath, waiting for the answer.

"No! She left a moment ago. A bit ill, I think."

Ha! Good Tom! That was five points off *his* score for lying!

"Oh, sorry to hear," said Finis.

"What'll you have, then?"

"Nothing at all, Tom. Thanks. I'll stop in and see how she's doing."

The bell clanged over the restaurant door, and Tom sauntered to the pantry. "All clear."

She breathed a sigh.

"Now," Tom said as he handed back the spatula, "would you kindly turn those pancakes before the customers catch me cooking and leave?"

"Thanks." She brushed past him and glanced through the cook's window. Lonnie Santiago, the sheriff's deputy, sat at the counter, laughing.

"What?" she asked.

"You hidin' from Finis?"

She frowned and busied herself turning pancakes.

"You and Jane been dancing again? He told me about that."

"So is that illegal?" She shot him a look meant to shut him up. It worked well enough. He turned to his crossword puzzle and sucked his pen.

"Nope," he muttered. "Just stupid."

"Stupid is working crosswords with a pen," Dara grumbled under her breath. "Arrogant piece of—"

Tom chuckled.

"What?"

"I don't see the point," he said. "Finis is this very moment stopping by to look in on you. So what? He finds you gone and comes back here."

"He doesn't care enough to look in on me." She turned the pancakes and checked the orders on the carousel. "He only cares that I gave him back his red binder. And his pencil pouch. *And* his four-color pen!"

"You gave them back, did you?"

"Left them on his motor home doorstep, and he's lucky. There are other places I could've put 'em."

"Ah, Dara." He patted her shoulder and headed for the refrigerator. "It's good to have you back."

"Back where?"

"I imagine he got your meaning. No more to be said, right?" He returned with a cantaloupe and sliced it in two.

"Won't be enough for Finis," she said. "He'll want to hear me say I failed."

"You didn't fail."

"I failed." She slapped the pancakes and eggs onto three plates and handed them over. "I was doing so well, too."

"Were you?"

"Yes." She looked at him. "I was!"

"You think your little sin diet made you a better person than you are right now with all your thorns exposed?" He arranged orange and cantaloupe slices on the plates and put them in the window for Jane.

"Okay, so I was a failure from the start. Thanks for the encouragement. And stop laughing."

Jane appeared on the other side of the cook's window to slip an order on the carousel and take the plates. She looked from Tom to Dara, smiled one of her knowing smiles, and got back to work.

"Just tell Finis you graduated," said Tom.

"Graduated!" She checked the new order and cracked three eggs on the grill.

"Right. There you were, minding your own business, listening to the Bible on tape, knitting car covers with photo-realistic images of Jesus to raise funds for a new multimedia church auditorium with stain-free carpet, whilst simultaneously praying up at long last an end to the Middle East conflict. When suddenly, Michael the archangel appeared before you, saying, 'Hail, Dara, full of … of …'"

"Watch it," she said.

"'Full of some such thing, the Lord is with you. I've got your chariot of fire running at the curb to lift you in a whirlwind to heaven. For lo! The light of your countenance poses a serious risk of skin cancer to the lesser souls of Brittlebush.'"

Dara shook her head, but Tom continued.

"But you said, 'No, Michael, no! There are yet more women to whom I must show forth the grace of God! More women who just might find their way if I offer them one miraculous shred of kindness where they least expect to find it.'"

"Don't make fun of me."

"To which Michael replied, 'Verily, you've got a point!' And he shrouded the brightness of your face, and forever banished that smarmy-toothed grimace, so you could walk unnoticed upon the earth, God's wonders to perform." He handed her a bowl of pancake batter and bowed.

"If I graduated, I would have found my mother. But I don't see her anyplace, do you?"

"You will," Tom said softly. "Any day now she could stop by for pancakes, as easy as that. Don't give up." He turned to slice more cantaloupe. "And I wasn't making fun."

She looked the other way. "No more smarmy smiles for you, then."

"That's a relief."

She glanced up to lock eyes with Ivy, who stood grinning outside the restaurant window, her hand lifted to her cheekbone, waving her fingers. Dara flashed one of her practiced, perky smiles, breathing a curse at the back of her mouth, like a ventriloquist. "Tom!" she said through her grinning teeth. "Look what you made me do!"

He looked, just as Ivy walked through the door. "Ah," he said. "Remember—Michael the archangel!"

CHAPTER 14

*T*here you are!" Ivy called to Dara. "Finis said you were sick—are you feeling better?"

Dara nodded.

"I'm so glad to hear that," she said. "Tom? Finis and I were hoping we could talk with you this afternoon—just to firm up plans for Finis's birthday party."

"Certainly," said Tom. "Things should slow down around three. How about then?"

"Sounds perfect!" she chirped.

"Stacy still coming with her daughter?"

"Yes! Just two weeks! Two *long* weeks! How will I hold myself together till then?"

"With a cup of tea and the help of good friends. Dara's got some brilliant ideas for the menu she'll discuss with you this afternoon."

Ivy said something cheerful and breezed out. Lonnie lifted his head from his puzzle and snickered, but Dara hardly noticed. She glared at Tom till he looked her way.

"You can't hide from him forever." He shrugged. "The question is, do you want to face him down at three with Jane and me standing by, or do you want to worry till he drops by unannounced?"

"Well, no, but ..." She stopped, deflated. "But I don't have any brilliant ideas for the menu."

"Of course you do! Have you ever baked a cake?"

"Yes ..." She dragged the word out, rolling her eyes.

"What kind?"

"Pillsbury, Duncan Hines, Betty Crocker." She put her hands on her hips. "Oh, and I did make a really good peanut butter cake once, from a recipe in a magazine."

"Do you still have the recipe?"

"No. But it really wasn't a recipe. It was a boxed spice cake, with a few added ingredients and peanut butter in the frosting."

"There you go! Brilliant!"

It helped that peanut butter was Finis's favorite. He waited through a full half hour of party planning before bringing up the binder.

"I was going to give you a little blurb in my book," he said.

"Thanks," said Dara. "But I've had plenty of blurbs for one lifetime."

"So this means you're giving up on prayer?"

"I don't know, Finis—I'm just giving up on your plan. Go ahead and write your book. It's just not for me."

"But my plan is based on what the Bible says about prayer. And the Bible says righteousness is not an option if you want God's grace."

"Now, you know, when you put it that way, it doesn't make sense," said Ivy.

"'Course it makes sense."

"No. Because doesn't *grace* mean an unearned gift? So if you have to be righteous to receive it, then doesn't it become something you earn?"

Finis cast her an icy stare.

"You're not the only one who went to Bible college," Ivy said.

"No. Just the only one who paid attention." He chuckled and looked from Tom to Dara and Jane, and back to Ivy, who held his gaze. "I see what's happening here." He looked at Jane. "You been talking to her, is that it? Both of them." He nodded toward Dara. "All caught up in your spell. Una, too." He pointed to his wife. "I know the things you and Una talk about when you sit late nights on the back porch. I don't have to eavesdrop; I feel it when you come to bed."

"Finis," Jane began.

He held up a hand and continued. "It's just so much more attractive to think that God will answer your prayers just because he thinks you're pretty." He laughed, nodding at Ivy. "Before long, you'll be out in the desert," he waggled his hands, "just like Jane, out there cavorting with God like he's your sweetheart, deceiving yourselves to think he would meet you there."

"Finis, I think—"Tom began.

"Hold up, Tom," Finis said. Dara opened her mouth to speak but stopped when she saw the liquid rims of tears in his eyes.

"You see, I don't live in the world these women live in," he said. "I live in a world where terrible things happen. Where beloved young wives and mothers die for no proper reason at all." He looked to Dara. "Where little girls lose their mothers and daddies all in one young lifetime. I live in a world where my parents were both alcoholics, where I as a child trembled daily with the fear they'd kill each other in one of their fights. A world where my big brother marched off to Korea when I was sixteen and came home eight weeks later in a casket." He took several deep breaths while the rest of them waited.

"I live in a world," he continued softly, "where young girls like my daughter Stacy, *beautiful,* with all the brightness and potential you could imagine, where they get off on a wrong foot somehow and disappear down a cesspool I can't even bear to think about. And in the world *I* live in, you find out what it takes to get just a little tiny handle on things, and you grab that handle and you don't let go."

He stood so abruptly his chair fell over. "And you," he said to Dara, "you think it's cute to just leave the binder on the doorstep with no hi, bye, or how do you do. All I can suggest is that you go dancing off into the desert if you want to and worship some freewheeling God *I've* never met. Just let the world go to hell without you, if that's what you want to do." He took another deep breath. "Ivy, I'm walking home. You bring the car when you feel like it."

He started to leave, and then turned, weeping. "But I'll tell you this. Our daughter is cleaning up her life and coming back to us, and it's not because I got all mystical and starry-eyed. It's because I prayed. Because I cared enough to do the things I had to do to make my prayers mean something. You think about that." He wiped the tears from his face and left.

Even Jane stayed away from the desert after that. She and Dara said little beyond what was needed to serve the customers. Dara took to going to bed early, and Jane took up a habit Dara never expected: She started watching television late into the night.

Tom was quiet too, though he did offer an odd, unsettled smile from time to time. He watched the two women with a tenderness that flustered Dara. Jane returned his hushed affection, but Dara looked the other way.

Strangely enough, she found it easy to be good, now that she'd rid herself of the red binder and the progress charts. She watched the customers and wondered what pain they kept secret. She began to imagine she could see their sorrow if she watched long enough, and she smiled true, gentle smiles at them in sympathy for the things she didn't know. When Carol Greeley's baby cried waiting for its breakfast, she brought it a bowl of applesauce. When Peter Riley shorted her a dollar for his chicken sandwich, she kept her peace and put a dollar in the till when he left.

Wednesday night she delivered her pink napkins with the violet stickers and sat through the ladies' tea. She witnessed the sorrow in all the beaming faces and offered what kindnesses she could.

All the sarcasm was gone. She didn't think bad thoughts, say bad things, or lose her temper. She was a different person, and by the looks of things, the same was true of Tom and Jane. That was a good thing, wasn't it?

But she felt heavy, like her insides had turned to sludge.

Hooper didn't seem to like what he saw. "Who died here?" he asked when he came in for breakfast, and his voice sparked like a firecracker in the silence. He didn't get his answer. On Friday, he asked Jane out to a movie, and she declined. So on Saturday he insisted Tom stop by for coffee after closing.

When Dara quit Finis's program, she'd thought she'd stop going to church, but when Sunday came, she decided she might as well go. What else would she do with her time? She got up, picked out a dress, and hung it on the doorknob. Then she went to the kitchen for breakfast.

Jane sat at the table. "I made some tea."

"Thanks." Dara poured a bowl of Cheerios and sat down. She lifted a spoonful to her mouth and stopped.

Jane held the cat picture in her hand. Dara had left it on the window ledge behind the napkins the day she confronted Sophie. She'd forgotten it was there.

The duchess studied it, sipping her tea. Dara considered grabbing it away, but changed her mind. No need to snap at Jane. After breakfast she'd just put it away.

"I wonder why the cross on the cat's head?" Jane asked.

"Don't know." Dara shrugged and focused on her Cheerios.

"Some artists use the cat to symbolize the union of the physical world and the spiritual." She traced a finger over the black cross and the cat's outline, the white against blue. "There's an old legend that when Jesus was born, a cat gave birth in the same stable. Perhaps the artist had that in mind."

Dara slapped her spoon down and snatched the picture from Jane. She stopped herself, took a deep breath, and forced a smile. "I'd just rather not think about it now, if it's all right."

"Of course."

Dara took the picture to her room and tucked it under the sweaters in the bottom drawer of her dresser. When she returned, she heard a feeble knock at the door and answered.

There stood Ivy, in jeans and a yellow jersey with matching yellow Keds, her hair arranged in soft brown curls around her face. She gripped the handle of her shoulder bag like it was all that held her up. She'd been crying.

"Come in, Ivy," said Jane, and the woman stepped in without a word.

She sat on the couch and wiped her eyes with the tissue in her hand, nodding acceptance of Dara's offer of tea. Jane helped to carry three cups to the living room, and the women sat waiting till Ivy gathered her words.

"I need to go to the desert," she said. She swiped the tissue under her nose and looked at Jane. "Will you take me?"

Jane pressed her hands against her knees and stared at them a moment before meeting Ivy's eyes. "Of course," she said at last.

"Thank you!" Ivy smiled with relief. "Finis won't be happy, but he hasn't been happy with me for some time."

Another knock. Dara put her teacup down and got the door.

"Is she here?" Una stood on the step like a midwife who'd come an hour late. Amy stood behind her, biting her lip.

Dara nodded and stood back to let them in.

She'd never seen Una in anything but a dress and stiletto heels, but there stood the bombshell, tall and bony with her jeans tucked into her cowgirl boots, her chambray shirt tied at the waist. Amy just wore her sweats and running shoes.

"Are you going?" asked Una.

Ivy nodded, wiping her nose.

"Can we come?" Una rested her hands on her hips.

"Has something happened?" asked Jane.

"You know how Dad gets." Amy bit her nail. "Erik's okay with us going. He asked Mary Holbrook to play the piano."

Ivy sniffled.

Dara ran a hand through her hair and looked at Jane. "Let's get dressed."

They drove ten miles from town, onto a dirt road, and another ten minutes till the only indication they weren't on Mars was a string of power lines swagged across the valley. Jane stopped the car, and the women got out. The only one who took her purse was Ivy, who clutched it as though it held something dear.

They stood silent a long while in the rustling air. At last, Una brushed her hands on her jeans. "So. What do we do?"

Jane laughed. "I've never done it in a group before." She thrust her hands into her pockets and smiled. "I really don't have a technique."

The women still looked to her, and she laughed again. After a week of silence, Jane's laughter lifted Dara's spirit like a gust of wind. The duchess pulled her hands from her pockets and walked.

Standing together, the women watched as she proceeded to a small mound fifty feet away. She stopped with her back to them and soon began to flux and sway, and the next moment she raised her hands, palms down, as if on the lift of wind. She swayed like a bird in flight, she turned and spun with one foot flat and the other on tiptoe, and her silver hair trailed like a silk scarf.

The women now looked to Dara, and she shrugged. "That's how it's done," she said. She walked away to a clearing between the brush. When she got there, she turned to see that Ivy, Una, and Amy had all found their own places, and now stood waiting to see what she would do.

She giggled and turned away, and the wind played with her hair. She heard the old sighs, the whispers, and she closed her eyes for sheer pleasure. She lifted her hands above her head and felt the caressing breeze and the morning sun, and she swayed fluid as the grass.

"My Dara!" she heard. "My darling, my own!" and the wind brushed tears from her eyes.

How long did she stand there swaying? When she closed her eyes, it seemed the swirling wind lifted her, and she heard the supernal hush of blue air. She danced with no feeling of weight, until at once her legs felt liquid and weak.

She opened her eyes, sat on the sand, and looked around.

The area was flecked with women dancing, and she watched them, astonished at what she saw.

Amy moved like a sprite, light as an aspen leaf. It seemed she could float across the plain on the wind if she chose.

Una held more weight, as if her bones were greenwood. She swayed with stately grace, her arms to the sides, supple and strong.

They were all so intensely beautiful. She saw the reason Amy was a pastor's wife—not only because she'd married Erik, but because of the gentle acceptance that worked through her like the threads of a cloth.

And she saw that Una, somehow, was meant to wear those outrageous clothes and live that outrageous life, for reasons unknown. But real reasons, nonetheless.

She turned to Ivy, and a deep sorrow welled in her stomach. Ivy danced like a ribbon in the wind, but she wept old tears. It seemed to Dara that the woman's shoes ought not to match her blouse so precisely, that her hair should not be curled, but should hang straight and longish against her neck, free to tangle in the breeze.

Dara wondered who exactly had made her the Brittlebush fashion advisor, but there it was, this need to hand the woman some scuffed jeans and old shirts and to muss her hair.

She turned to Jane. The duchess danced, careening into the wind so that it seemed she would fall, but Dara knew she wouldn't. Jane was lovely beyond description, and Dara loved her friend with a joy that stunned her.

At last the women came together and walked side by side. They came to a rise that dipped and sloped to a long expanse of umber sand, and they sat on the ridge to rest. The sun warmed them, and the wind whispered behind them. Dara closed her eyes and wondered if they'd all go to sleep. But at last, Ivy drew a long breath and let it out in a quiet wail.

"I've spent my life agreeing with him," she said. "I have argued his side against my own heart time after time after time. I've loved what he loved and turned away from what he didn't." She wept, and Dara touched a hand to hers, while Amy scooted nearer to wrap an arm around her shoulder. "It's cost me so much!" Ivy whispered.

"He's a good man," she clarified, patting her daughter's hand. "I'm not leaving him, Amy. But when I prayed here today, it felt like a real prayer. You know what my prayers are usually like?" She laughed, wiping her tears, and rummaged in her bag. She pulled out a small brocade planner and held it up. "They're like staff meetings, where I hand Jesus his marching orders for the day." She turned the blue tab of her binder labeled "Prayer List."

"Look," she said. "I've got a page for every day of the week." She filed through, and Dara saw lists that covered both sides of the pages with tiny notes crammed in the margins.

"This one's Sunday," Ivy said. "On Sunday I pray for the church. Monday is for the mission field. Tuesday is for our country. Wednesday is for people who are sick or in trouble. Thursday is for people who are lost. Friday is for Finis, and Saturday is for Amy and Stacy and the rest of our family."

"Long lists," said Jane. "Very impressive."

"Aren't they? Don't I look like the CEO of heaven?"

"Which day's yours?" asked Una, and Ivy shrugged.

"Why not just chuck them?" asked Amy.

"Well, you know. What if I forget to pray for Caroline Rico's biopsy, and she turns out to have cancer?" She chuckled. "I used to be worse. When Finis and I were first married, I thought Janis Joplin died in her sins because I'd never thought to pray for her. That's when I started my list."

Una chuckled.

"Don't laugh."

"Not at you, darlin'," the bombshell replied. "When Billie Holiday died, I took full responsibility."

Dara shook her head. What would either of them do with something real on their conscience?

"Why don't we all just drag the whole phone book into our prayer closets?" Una suggested.

"Why only one?" asked Jane. "There are dozens at the library."

"I'd have to lock the door and never come out," said Ivy, "and you know? Right now that sounds like a good idea." She shut her planner and opened her bag to put it in. Her hand caught on the shoulder strap, and when she tried to free it, the planner slipped from her fingers. It scudded down the slope of the hill, over the top of a small boulder, and landed on edge. The rings snapped open, and as the planner continued to tumble, the pages scattered like a flock of birds.

Crying out, the women scrambled to their feet. They had just started down the hill when a gust of wind gathered the pages into a whirlwind of sand and white wings.

They stopped and watched them blow.

"My calendar!" said Ivy. "My shopping lists and cleaning lists and party plans!"

"Just like that," said Jane.

Amy was the first to laugh. But that started them all, and they staggered, cackling, slapping at each other, and wiping tears away.

"It's all right," cooed the small voice. "I won't hurt you."

Dara opened her eyes and rolled over in bed. There was no one there.

"Come on out," she heard. "It's all right."

She rolled once more to peer over the side of the bed. Emerging from beneath were two pink legs and the pads of two small feet, soiled gray at the bottoms.

"Clemmie!"

The girl backed out and sat up. "I want to see Algernon. He's under the bed."

"Well, have a good look."

"Will you get him out?"

"No. You broke into my house again."

"It's my dad's trailer."

"That *doesn't matter!*" She grabbed her robe from the foot of the bed.

"Got any breakfast?"

"I do if you like Cheerios."

"I like Lucky Charms."

"Then go home and get some."

Clemmie shook her head. "Daddy won't buy them."

"Guess your new favorite is Cheerios. Come on."

They headed toward the kitchen. The living room window was open where Clemmie had climbed in, and the breeze felt good. Dara poured two bowls of cereal.

"You've got to stay put at night," she said when they sat down. "You could get hurt. What if someone hit you, and you couldn't get away because they locked you in their house? Ever think of that?"

Clemmie frowned reproachfully as if she knew better than to believe such things.

"It's not a safe world, Clemmie. Your dad would feel terrible if anything happened to you. Everyone would. I'd feel terrible."

The child studied her in silence.

"Tell you what," Dara said. "You climb in my window anytime you want. Just don't go anywhere else. Okay?"

Clemmie nodded. "Would you make the kitty come out?"

"Can't promise that. But I'll play Memory with you."

"I'm tired of Memory."

"You and me both. What do you want to play?"

"Fish?"

"Fish is good. Do I have to show you all my cards?"

Clemmie shook her head.

Dara pulled the red Bicycle cards from the kitchen drawer. She let Clemmie deal the first hand—and regretted it, because she dealt slowly and precisely, pausing several times to recount.

Clemmie was a sore loser too. But when she won, she danced a fish-wriggling happy dance that made losing worthwhile.

When at last she tired of the game, she asked, "Want a treat?"

"What kind of treat?"

"Just say yes. Want a treat?"

"Yes."

"Smell my feet!" And she danced her happy dance, laughing at her own funny self.

She scrambled to the couch and patted the cushion beside her. "Read me a story."

"Can't. I don't have any storybooks."

The child frowned, and at that moment Algernon crept into the living room, as if to slip unnoticed to the food bowl.

He misjudged.

Clemmie sprang from the couch, squealing, "*Al*-gernon!"

The cat cowered, then scrambled out the open window, just in time.

"Go get him."

"Don't think he wants company." Dara got an idea. "I know a story I can *tell* you."

"About what?"

"About a pearl." She sat on the couch, patting the cushion beside her.

Clemmie took the offer, and she began. "Once upon a time …"

When she finished, Clemmie asked the question Dara had once asked her father: "What did the prince do with the pearl?"

"I don't know," said Dara. "I only—"

"I know what he did."

"What's that?"

"He hung it around your neck."

"Yeah." Dara touched her pendant. "I guess he did."

A piercing howl sounded outside. Both Dara and Clemmie scrambled from the couch. Dara checked out the window and saw nothing. She ran to the door and opened it. Algernon faced a white cat on the lawn.

"Algernon!"

He ignored her, preoccupied.

She ran down the steps and flipped her hands at the other cat. "Shoo!"

The cat sidestepped.

"Shoo!"

For the first time, the white cat turned to face her. On its forehead, as keen as if someone had painted it there, was a black cross.

Dara staggered backward and dropped to the step.

The white cat turned its attention back to Algernon, and Algernon howled. He stepped forward, and Algernon stepped back.

Catch him! She pulled herself to her feet and took a cautious step toward the white cat. He didn't notice, so she took another step, and another …

And caught a cold spray of hose water. She gasped, just as the two cats scrambled away, disappearing over separate fences.

"Clemmie!" she shrieked.

The girl doubled over, laughing, still holding the hose. "I got you!"

Dara ran to the fence where the white cat had escaped. He was gone.

She spun around, seething. "What were you doing?"

Clemmie dropped the hose and took a step back. "I didn't mean to."

"Yes, you did!"

"No," said Clementine. "I was making them not fight—the way Daddy does. You just got in the way!"

"Well, that's great," Dara said. "Now the cat's gone, all because of you!'

"What's going on?"

Dara turned to see Tom padding down the steps, barefoot and unshaven in his jeans and a torn T-shirt.

She strode toward him. "Your daughter climbed through my window. *Again!*"

"So what's the harm? There's no need to yell at her."

"Somebody's got to yell at her, and it can't be you, can it? Who could possibly expect you to discipline your child for running away at night? That would be too responsible."

He ran a hand through his hair and said, "Get inside, Clem."

The girl seemed eager to oblige.

He faced Dara. "So are you now an expert on child rearing? You know everything that passes between me and my daughter?"

"No, I don't know everything. I don't have to know everything to know it's not safe for her to climb in strangers' windows." She swiped the water from her face.

"You're not a stranger. It's never a stranger, it's Mrs.—"

"Tom?" Jane stood at the trailer door in her bathrobe. "What's wrong?"

"Why don't you ask Dara? I don't know!"

Dara looked to Jane and wept, staggering back again to the steps.

Jane took the step above and put a hand on her shoulder.

Tom walked across the lawn to stand near.

"The cat in the picture." She held her head. "He was here, white, with this black cross." She traced the cross on her forehead. "And Clemmie—" She cupped her hand to her mouth to muffle the cries.

Tom stepped closer, scratching his head.

"He's gone now, Tom. And I don't know where he went."

It was two hours past opening, and Tom hadn't shown up for work. Dara really hoped he was having a long talk with his daughter and not just sulking over the morning's argument.

Meanwhile, half the town had come for breakfast. Dara was left to chop all the fruit and vegetables, cook all the eggs, pancakes, and French toast, with no one to do the dishes.

Jane stuck three more orders on the carousel, flashing a smile that showed definite signs of strain.

A nice morning with Clemmie, and Dara had spoiled it. Over a cat. What was the point?

Why couldn't she just live her life and forget her mother? She had just begun to think she could be happy with her friends, her job, and Clemmie climbing in the window to play Fish. This morning it had seemed like enough. Until the white cat.

She'd figured out the scoop. Her mother had, for whatever reason, begun a new life, with a new family—Jefferson, Jacobs, or Johnson, maybe. And she'd had a child, maybe Sally, Susan, or Sam, who drew pictures of their white cat. And the new family didn't know about the old one, so she'd hid the photograph behind little Sammy's cat picture, till, fearing still she'd get found out, she had discarded it altogether.

End of story, right? Because in that case, her mother sure didn't want her knocking at the door introducing herself to Mr. Johnson. As for herself, she didn't really want to meet Sammy.

The bell rang over the restaurant door, and a large group walked in, at least seven or eight. Jane actually had to shuffle them off beside the door to wait for two tables to open up.

Dara cursed Tom under her breath.

She dished the eggs and pancakes onto plates as fast as she could and arranged the melons and oranges. She put them in the cook's window and checked the orders on the carousel. Ten more pancakes, four sausages, six eggs, and an omelet.

The back door opened, and Hooper rushed in and walked to Dara's side.

"Give me the spatula," he said.

"What?"

"Give it to me. I'm taking over." He snatched the spatula from her hand and nudged her aside. "Tom's outside, and you need to go with him."

"Why? Is Clemmie hurt?"

"No!" Hooper rolled his eyes. He spun her around, untied her apron strings, taking the apron for himself. "Would you quit your questions and just go!" He gave her a push.

She started for the door, backstepped, grabbed her purse, and walked outside.

There stood Tom beside his car, with the white cat slung over his shoulder.

"You found him!"

Tom handed her the cat. "He's very friendly, but he doesn't much like the car. Can you hold him?"

"Where are we going?"

"Get in." He opened the door. "I have an idea."

As they drove, he shouted over the cat's complaints. "He lives somewhere in our neighborhood, right? Or he wouldn't have turned up in our yard. I found him on Filmore and Birch, snoozing on someone's front porch, but it wasn't their cat. I checked."

"They were home?"

"Their neighbors were."

"So what do we do?"

"We go back to Filmore and Birch, we put the cat down, and we follow him."

"Oh." It was a novel idea. "But what if my mother's not home?"

"We'll take our chances. She could work nights tending bar for all we know, and that would make this a good time to find her."

"My mother doesn't tend bar."

"Sorry. Just a guess." He turned onto Filmore and pulled over. "Here we are."

"Here?"

"Yes, here." He got out of the car. Dara opened her door, and Tom ran around to help, as if she were holding a baby.

The cat leapt from his arms before he could put it down, then ran under the nearest parked car and hunkered down in the shade.

"He's going to wait till we leave," said Tom, "and he looks like a patient cat."

"So what do we do?"

"Wait here." He walked to the back of his Toyota and opened the trunk to rummage through tools and plastic bags and an old blanket. "Aha!"

"What?" asked Dara.

He emerged triumphant with what looked like a bazooka painted neon blue and green. A Super Squirter.

CHAPTER 15

*Y*ou're going to shoot the cat?"

"It's just a glorified squirt gun!" Tom hurried to a house across the street, turned on the side faucet, and positioned the gun's reservoir.

"Tom, they'll catch you!"

He was done already. He returned to squat at Dara's side, took aim, and squirted a powerful stream. The cat scrambled out. They chased him down the sidewalk till he darted into a juniper bush under someone's front window. Tom fired another round, and the cat ran across the street.

"Watch for cars!" Dara called.

The cat took cover under a Jeep wagon in someone's driveway, but Tom urged him out. The cat ran around the corner to dive under a lantana bush. Tom fired a round of water, and he darted away.

Dara kept up till they found themselves in someone's backyard. "What if these people have a dog?"

"They don't."

"This seems cruel."

"It's only water. With luck, he'll flee to the safety of his own house."

"How do you know this isn't his house?"

"He's not crying at the door." Tom peered under a boat tarp. "There he is!" He took aim, and the cat fled over the top of the fence into the yard next door.

Dara ran to have a look. "How can you be so sure he'd cry at the door?"

"Because it's logical. Did you see where he went?"

"Under a barbeque."

"Great. Watch and tell me if he leaves."

There were plenty of places to hide in this yard. Tom routed him from under the barbeque, but then he ran into a shed with an open door, behind the wooden bench by the back door, under a bush, and up a tree. From the tree the cat leapt to the yard next door. Dara followed Tom.

The cat escaped the yard and bounded across the street. He turned another corner, but they saw where he went: through a vent into the crawlspace of a brown stucco house.

Tom dropped to his belly and peered through the hole. He crawled twenty feet to another vent, looked through, and sagged. "He's just where I'd be, flat against this wall, out of sight."

"Can I help you?" A man in shorts and a polo shirt stepped off the porch.

Tom sat up. He rested the Super Squirter on his knees like a commando on watch.

"We're looking for a cat," Dara said.

"You're welcome to all you can take. There's four or five strays that make their home under there."

"We only want one," said Tom.

"You gonna coax it out with that?"

"We coaxed it *in* with this, I'm afraid."

"Why?"

"It belongs to, well, a friend of ours," said Tom. "She's been quite worried about her cat, and I know she'd be glad to have it back."

The man looked down at his clothes, which appeared clean and freshly pressed. "Even if I crawled in after it, I'd never catch it. Cats move a lot faster than I can crawl. Why not tell me what it looks like, and I'll be glad to give you a call when it comes out."

"It's white, with a black cross on his forehead."

"Oh! You mean Sybil Johns' cat."

"That would be the one." Tom winked at Dara.

"You know her?"

"She's a friend of my mother's," said Dara.

"Well, I'll just take him to Sybil when he comes out. That be okay?"

"Fantastic. By the way, Dara here can't remember. Which house is Sybil's?"

"Well, it's the second house from the corner down there."

"Of course." Tom leapt to his feet and shook the man's hand.

Dara hugged him when they got in the car. "You're a genius."

"Sybil Johns, and she lives two houses down from Filmore and Ash. Shall we go now?"

"No!"

"No?"

"I'm shaking."

"She won't notice."

"And I'm sweating from the run."

"You look fine. We'll just ask Sybil what she knows about your mother."

"But can you give me ten minutes at home to clean up? I should get the cat picture, anyway."

A half hour later they stood on the sidewalk before a pale gray house with a manicured lawn, fenced in by shrubs trimmed square at the tops.

"It's nice," said Tom, and it was. The door was enameled black with a brass handle and kickplate. The shutters were painted black to match, and to the side of the porch hung bamboo chimes, clacking in the breeze.

"Shall we go?"

Dara could only nod.

He took her arm, led the way, and rang the bell.

"Just a minute!" The lilting voice sounded from inside.

A window slid open ten feet to the left. "Almost dressed, Kathy! Just let yourself in."

Tom cleared his throat. "Not Kathy, I'm afraid."

"Oh," answered the voice. "Well, I don't have time for salesmen just now."

"Not salesmen, either."

"Well, who are you, then?"

"We have a personal matter to discuss with you."

"That sounds time-consuming." There was a pause. "You're not the police, are you?"

"No, ma'am."

"Well!" She sounded impatient.

A moment later the door opened, and a woman stood before them, short and round with silver curls. "I'm sorry, but I'm on my way out the door, and I already have a church."

Tom smiled. "Are you Sybil?"

"Oh!" She seemed relieved. "No, you've got the wrong house. Sybil lives over there, across the street."

Dara turned to look. The house she'd indicated was a strained mustard-gold, faded from what must once have been the color of the real thing, fresh from the jar.

"I didn't mean to be rude," said the woman, "but I'm on my way to a party, and I couldn't imagine who would call on me now when I'm in such a hurry. But Sybil lives over there. Do you know her?"

Dara nodded.

"Friend of her mother's," Tom explained. "Thanks for your trouble."

Dara started across and stopped in the middle of the road. Tom caught up and took her arm. "We've found her."

She nodded, vaguely troubled by the mustard house.

He looked down the road both ways. "Shall we go?"

She nodded again, and he led the way.

The lawn was dried to the color of wheat. Beside the door stood a rosebush, long dead, with a faded Twinkies wrapper caught in its thorns.

Tom knocked, and a peeled bit of veneer fell to his feet.

The window next to the door had its curtains drawn, but they heard a television inside, music, and a laugh track. No answer.

Dara turned to go, but Tom knocked again.

"Just a minute," they heard from inside.

The door opened a few inches, and they saw a face.

"Are you Sybil Johns?" asked Tom.

"Yes."

"Good!" He smiled at Dara and cleared his throat. "We think you may know someone we're looking for."

"I don't know anybody." The door began to close.

"But we have a picture of your cat," said Tom.

"Gabriel? What did you do to my cat?"

"Gabriel's fine," he said. "He's just down the street a bit. What we have is his picture." He nudged Dara. She retrieved the watercolor and held it out.

"That's mine," The face acknowledged. "I paint sometimes."

"Can we come in?"

They waited for an answer, till at last the door swung open.

All that lit the room was the television. Clothespins held the curtains together to banish any stray bit of sunlight. The woman settled into the chair and set her feet on the footstool. In the light from the television, her bare legs emerged thick and scaly from her housedress, her feet crusted at the bottoms. She rested her arms to the sides, and the flesh folded like bread dough around the elbows.

She watched the television, and they watched her.

Something smelled. Dara had the feeling, in this place, it could be anything. The floor was littered with newspapers and magazines. The coffee table was stacked with dishes. In making her way to the couch, Dara stumbled on a pair of shoes.

What did this woman have to do with her mother?

Tom cleared his throat again. "We'd like to ask some questions."

The biting voice on the television pronounced someone "the weakest link." Sybil made no sign she had heard Tom's question.

He crossed the floor to turn the volume down, then reached for the lamp in the corner and turned the switch. The dim yellow light did nothing to lift the gloom of this place—but it did everything to explain it.

The dishes stacked on the coffee table were all dirty—bowls half full of macaroni, or crusted with dried gravy, stacked one on top of the other. The cat box sat in the corner beside the television, filled to overflowing with old dung.

Sybil scowled. "Ask your question, then."

"We think you might know a woman by the name of Clara Murphy."

Sybil stiffened in her chair. Her lips parted, and she glanced from Dara to Tom and back again. "No," she said. "I don't know her."

"We have a photograph." Tom nudged Dara. She pulled the picture from her purse and gave it to him.

Tom held it up for the woman to see. She eyed it a long moment before her glance darted from one random spot in the room to another and rested again upon Dara. "I don't know anything about her." She turned away.

The movement Sybil made when she turned snagged something in Dara's memory. Her breath caught in an instant pulse of apprehension.

Tom handed the photo back to Dara.

She looked at the picture and then at Sybil. Yes! The same turn of eyebrow, the same set of the chin.

"Is that all you wanted?" Sybil demanded.

Tom stood and reached for Dara's hand.

She hesitated, glancing at the stacks on the floor. Several piles of *Air & Space*, some *Scientific American*, *Smithsonian*, *National Geographic*. Stacks and stacks of *Astronomy* magazine.

"Mama," Dara whispered. The woman swallowed, and Dara spoke louder. "It's you."

Tom slowly sat down.

"You're Clara Murphy," Dara insisted, louder still. "You're my mother."

The woman sat motionless.

"Look at me!"

Sybil's chest heaved, and at last she turned her head.

There was nothing in her face—no tears, no regret, no love. The woman stared through Dara over the folds of her bread-dough skin.

"Thank you." Dara's voice shook. She stood and stepped over the shoes on the floor, knocking the coffee table in her rush to leave. A bowl half full of dried beans fell to the floor. She stepped over it. The doorknob rattled in her hand when she turned it, but she opened the door and stepped out into the glare of the noonday sun. She rushed down the walk and across the street. While Tom unlocked the car door, she rested against the roof of his car and breathed great gulps of clean, innocent air.

"Did I mention Stacy likes ambrosia?" Ivy paced the restaurant, still wet from the rain, with her new little black plastic binder. "At least, that's what she used to like."

"You mentioned—lots of coconut." Dara flipped the switch on the coffeemaker.

This was no day to plan a party; it was a day to forget she'd been born. But Ivy looked brittle with anxiety. "We'll have the ambrosia," Dara said.

"And extra bananas, don't forget."

"It's on the list."

"Sorry. Since I lost my planner, I don't know what I'm doing."

"It's all going to be fine, Ivy."

The woman rummaged in her purse and pulled out a CD. "I bought her this. Would you play it?"

Dara read the title: *"Chicago 16."*

"Finis once had the kids burn all their records. He was worried that ... well, never mind. This was one of Stacy's favorites. Maybe she still likes it."

"Maybe."

"Will you play it?"

"Sure, I'll give it to Hooper. Will Finis mind?"

Ivy snapped shut her plastic binder and stuffed it in her purse. "It can't always be about Finis." She pulled up a chair. "My daughter's coming tonight, Dara. I haven't seen her in sixteen years. What'll I do?"

"You'll act happy to see her." Dara forced a smile.

"Oh, I'll be so happy to see her. I'll probably knock the wind out of her, just hugging her."

"That should do the trick."

"And Talia. My own granddaughter, and I've barely seen her. Do I look like a good grandma?"

"Sure."

"Tell me the truth, how do I look—well, not now, with my hair all wet—"

"It looks good that way."

"You're joking."

"No. I'm not." She looked the way Dara had imagined in the desert.

Ivy pulled out a compact and checked the mirror.

Dara fingered the wet hair and rearranged a few strands. "What if you let it dry like that?"

Ivy studied the effect and shyly smiled.

The question made her mad, and that was good. Better anger than the dead weight of grief she had carried to work. There was energy in anger, and the day flew by.

"What'll I do?" Ivy had wanted to know.

What *was* the proper thing to do upon meeting a long-lost daughter? Certainly not to watch television in a darkened room like no one was there, and lie when it came to the question. The proper thing was to act, above all, like it mattered.

Dara charged through the final cleanup, scrubbing tables at frantic speed.

Jane scurried to keep up. "I'll come with you."

"No. I won't be long."

"What'll you do?"

"I don't know. Talk to her."

"I'll drive."

"I'd rather walk."

"Then I'll walk with you."

"Don't worry, Jane. She hasn't got the spit to hurt me." She whipped off her apron and left.

Sybil hardly had the spit to answer the door. She slumped at the threshold, hair flat on one side and a crease on her cheek.

"The thing to do," Dara said, "when your daughter turns up at the door, is to act like you're happy to see her."

No answer.

"A hug might be in order, or a smile. Maybe even, if it doesn't give you hives, a question or two to show interest. Like oh, say, 'How's your life?' 'Are you happy?' *'How's your father?'*" She was in a fine mood to answer that last one.

Sybil didn't take the bait.

"Can I come in?"

She stepped aside.

Dara went straight to the window. "The first thing we're going to do ..." She yanked the curtains open, scattering clothespins to the floor.

Now she saw more clearly the dishes on the coffee table, the sand in the threadbare carpet. The stacks and stacks of papers and magazines, the clothes piled in the corner. The worn chenille on Sybil's chair to match the crease on her cheek.

Through an open door she glimpsed a bedroom, with the bed unmade, the sheets gray with dinge.

"You can't live this way."

"Disappointed?"

"Where's your kitchen?"

She nodded to a dark doorway. Dara lifted a stack of bowls with her fingertips and carried them in. She could only see the end of one counter, and it was cluttered with dishes and debris. She elbowed the wall for a switch and found it.

Every inch of counter space was piled with dirty pans, empty Coke bottles, cans of baked beans opened and half full. The sink was full of dirty dishes. There was no place to put the bowls in her hand. She set them on the floor.

"Don't you ever wash your dishes?"

"The sink's clogged."

"Must have been clogged a long time." She turned, thinking. "How about your bathtub? Is it clogged too?"

"No."

How would she know? The woman hadn't washed her hair in at least a month, and by the smell of her …

Dara looked under the sink for dish detergent, though she didn't expect to find any.

She was wrong. Sybil had two of everything, and if the bottle said it controlled odors, she had three. Dara selected a bottle of Joy and a can of Ajax.

She scrubbed the bathtub three times before she believed it was clean, then squirted a large puddle of Joy under the faucet and turned on the water.

She fetched the first stack of dishes. Sybil grabbed a stack and pitched in.

Dara knelt on the floor to wash, rinsing under the faucet. Sybil found a cleanish towel to dry with. They finished that evening at 9:20.

Dara rinsed the tub and stood, rubbing the small of her back. She put the plug back in the tub, squirted a little more soap, and started the water. She tested the temperature. "This is for you. Do you have any clean clothes?"

No answer.

"How about a washer and dryer?"

Sybil nodded, shrugged, and shook her head. "The washer doesn't work."

Dara eyed Sybil's stained housedress, the stiffened pile of clothes behind the bathroom door. "Why not just throw those away and start over? I'll bring some clothes tomorrow."

Sybil looked her in the eye. "You don't owe this to me."

"No," Dara said. "I'll see you tomorrow."

When Ivy came for breakfast, her hair lay soft and straight against her cheek. She wore an old pair of jeans and a rumpled green linen shirt. Somehow, she looked exactly right.

So taken was Dara with Ivy's new look, she hardly noticed the woman and the young girl behind her. But Jane ran to the three with arms out, crying, "There they are!" Ivy squealed, jig-dancing with joy.

Stacy stood a good five inches taller than Ivy. She had her mother's looks, only shamefaced, like a beaten dog. She looked at people out the tops of her eyes, when she looked at them at all.

Talia stood tall as Stacy, but only because of the thick black soles of her shoes. She had ringed her eyes with black shadow and painted her lips ice pink. A tiny diamond winked from the crevice of one nostril. She wore her jeans low, and next to her navel she sported a butterfly tattoo.

"Such a lovely girl!" pronounced Jane.

"I think so," said Stacy, lifting her head for just that instant.

Dara extended her hand. "Pleased to meet you."

"Where's the birthday boy?" asked Tom.

"He said he wasn't hungry, and that's fine." Ivy smiled. "Just gives me more time with my girls."

And more time was what she took. The three lingered for nearly two hours over cackle berries and skunk eggs, and lots and lots of coffee.

From where she stood at the grill, Dara witnessed the transformation: The women relaxed, their smiles softened to a natural glow. A mother and her girls, together at long last, and happy.

Dara arrived at Sybil's to find Tom's Toyota parked in the driveway. Good. She'd asked him to work on the kitchen drain.

What wasn't good was finding Clementine curled up with Sybil and a *National Geographic* on that filthy sofa.

"The telescope's made up of little mirrors," Sybil said, while Clemmie snuggled close.

"Nice to see you two getting along," Dara said without a shred of warmth. "I'll just be in here working."

She cleaned the bathroom and gathered the clothes on the floor into trash bags. She stripped the bed and remade it with new sheets, a new blanket, and bedspread. The old bedding went in the garbage, as well.

She cleaned the refrigerator, just tossed everything that was spoiled. That left Sybil with a bottle of ketchup, six kinds of salad dressing, and a gallon-sized jug of Hi-C.

"Here we are!" Tom turned the faucet on and stood back to demonstrate the unhindered flow down the drain.

"Great!" Dara smiled.

Tom loaded the soaps and cleansers back under the sink.

Dara moved close and whispered, "You really want your daughter curled up on that couch in there?"

"I'll give her a good bath tonight." He put the wrench in his toolbox and shut the lid. "Hooper knows a couple of newly-weds with two of everything, so they've got plenty of furniture to unload. Think she'd part with that chair?"

"I'll insist."

When Tom and Clemmie went home, Dara fetched from her car four bags from Time and Again, and three from Wal-Mart. "Your new wardrobe." She hung the dresses and blouses in the now-empty closet. She put the pants and four packets of under-wear in the dresser. "These should all fit." She turned around. "Sometime before the weekend, I want you to pick out your favorite dress."

"Why?"

"Because we're going to church."

"I don't go out much."

"I've noticed. *I* certainly haven't seen you around." She headed for the door and grabbed her purse. "See you tomorrow."

By Friday night, Finis's party felt like a rest.

It wasn't just the hard work of cleaning Sybil's house; it was the acrid feeling Dara hadn't yet put a word to. If that pathetic woman living in that dump really was her mother, then by gum she'd do something about it. She would simply make the home her mother *should* live in and *buy* her the clothes she should wear.

But it had all been so draining, and the party preparations were a welcome relief.

She checked the peanut butter cake in the freezer to make sure it was ready to frost. It turned out the only one who knew anything about cake decoration was—of all people—Hooper. Any minute, he'd show up to do the magic.

Dara stirred the tomato sauce on one burner, and the egg noodles on the other. She opened the oven to check the chicken parmesan and caught the warm scent of garlic and basil. They were almost done.

Perhaps she should set some dinner aside for Sybil, but Dara was sick of thinking about her. If the woman had said thank you or even complained … but she just stood by watching while Dara did the things she was supposed to do herself.

That piano Dara had been so sure her sainted mother would own? Sure enough, she found it—in the back shed, cracked, dusty, and out of tune. Hooper knew someone who could tune it, assuming it wasn't beyond repair. Tom had helped her lug it in, so now it occupied its proper place near the window, across from Sybil's new couch.

She'd hauled the television to the curb with the trash, but Tom fetched it back.

"There's nothing wrong with it," he said.

"Then you take it."

"It isn't mine to take. Nor yours to give. No need to be cruel."

Abandonment was cruel. And so, by the way, was indifference.

No gratitude for the new clothes. Sybil sulked in the corner, wearing a nice pair of jeans and a pink cotton blouse. Pouting, of all things, looking absolutely …

"What?" Dara demanded.

"Nothing."

"Tell me."

"I don't wear things like these."

"Then wear something else."

"I can't."

"Why?"

"You threw my old clothes away."

"With good reason. Wear something else I gave you."

Sybil shook her head.

"What? You don't like any of them?" Dara leaned against the sofa and crossed her arms. "Anything's better than … You used to wear things like that."

Sybil looked away. "I've gained some weight."

That was certainly true.

Dara gave up. She went back to Time and Again and got the baggiest shirts and dresses she could find, and several pairs of sweatpants. The same kinds of things she'd thrown out, only clean, at least.

No idea what Sybil thought of the haircut, but that was nonnegotiable. The woman's hair had all the color and style of compost. Dara cut it to a blunt shoulder length with a few layers on top. When she handed Sybil the mirror, the woman stared for several moments. Her eyes softened—did that equate to a smile?

She *had* to like it better. But to say so would have sounded like a thank-you, and Dara didn't expect one of those anytime soon.

On her way home, she stopped at Wal-Mart to pick up some hair color: Natural Light Brown, to match the woman she remembered, the one in the family picture.

But that would have to wait.

This day, she had a party to handle. Ivy and Finis were due with their kids in an hour. Where was Hooper?

She heard a sound and turned to see Hooper carrying what looked to be an old toolbox.

"Your cake-decorating kit?"

"It is. Looks manly, don't it?"

"The cake's in the freezer. How will you decorate it?"

"I'll improvise."

What he improvised was a spray of white roses, with a yellow ribbon spreading left and right. On the left the ribbon read "Happy Birthday, Finis," and on the right, "Welcome Stacy and Talia."

Finis showed up in a gray suit and tie.

Hooper handed him a dime-store cowboy hat.

"What's this?"

"It's a party, Finis, not a funeral."

He set it aside without so much as a smile. "Ivy has a new look."

"A very lovely one," said Tom.

And it was. She wore a sleeveless dress, sienna-brown silk, a few shades darker than her arms. With her softer hair and less makeup, she looked—what? Gentle. Ivy looked gentle.

Finis put his arms around Stacy and Talia. "Have you met my two girls?"

"We have," said Tom.

He narrowed his eyes. "Dara, I'd like you to meet God's answers to my prayers."

"I'm happy for you, Finis. I'll introduce you to my mother on Sunday." She met his gaze.

"I heard you'd found her. Call her up and ask her to the party."

"She doesn't have a phone."

It was true; she didn't have one. Hadn't had for some time. According to the phone company, she had a balance three years overdue.

"I don't get any calls" was Sybil's explanation.

Of course she didn't, not with a dead phone on the wall. But then, what would she need a phone for? To call her daughter?

It was a habit with this woman, not paying the bills. Dara had gone over the day before and found Sybil in her living room, curtains drawn, no lights, no air conditioner, no television. She just sat in the dark, sweat sliding down her forehead, soaking her new shirt.

The power company had shut her off.

"My check hasn't come yet."

"What check would that be?"

No answer.

"When?"

"Monday after this one."

"That's over a week!"

"It happens."

"But what about all the food I put in your fridge?"

"I can't pay what I can't pay."

So Dara paid.

By Sunday, with the help of that bottle of hair dye, she'd have a mother fit for church. Let Finis know she'd done just fine, on her own.

Once she and Tom set up the buffet, there was little to do. She sat with Jane.

Finis walked Stacy and Talia around, one on each arm, bragging about his answered prayer.

Stacy wore a pink dress with matching pink sandals and bag. She looked like she wanted to be Ivy—the previous, coifed and coordinated Ivy, the one Finis liked.

Talia, on the other hand, just pleased herself—or was it the DeBello boys, Mark and Ron? They glanced her way thirty times a minute, no matter where in the room Finis escorted her.

Once, Finis stared them both in the eye. They glanced

away like they'd been checking the clock. Ten minutes later, when Talia stood at the buffet, they got in line behind her.

She'd cut her T-shirt short and wore her jeans low enough to display her butterfly. Finis walked an odd dance, positioning himself between the girl and all lookers. When at last they sat to eat, he maneuvered Talia to a seat next to him. He fixed his eye upon the DeBello table. The two boys looked away.

It was—after that, and for a time—a good party. Dara had never seen Finis turn on the charm, but he had some. He even friended up with Una on this night.

Tom played the music Finis and Ivy liked, the Gaithers, Jim Nabors. Jimmy Durante singing "Tenderly."

Chicago 16.

On the first chord, Finis raised an eyebrow. "What's this?"

"One of my favorites, Mom," said Stacy.

"I bought it the other day." Ivy shifted. "Just on a whim."

Finis chewed his chicken and looked from one to the other. "Listen to what they're singing." He chuckled. "'Hard for me to say I'm sorry.' This your way of sending a message?"

CHAPTER 16

*I*t's an album Stacy liked," said Ivy.

"No. See, I know what you're doing. You're dropping a big hint for Dad on his birthday." He turned and shouted, "Turn it off, Tom. You've made your point."

The room fell silent.

"Finis, don't," said Ivy.

"A man can't stand up for himself?" He stood and leaned two fists on the table. "I want everyone here to know, I have nothing to apologize for. I see you all chatting up my Stacy, *my daughter*, congratulating her for 'overcoming,' and that's all well-deserved praise. What she doesn't divulge of where she's been, I'm sure you all can guess. But I didn't abuse my daughter. I didn't send her to any of those places she went to. Do you understand me?"

Stacy curled inward like a dry leaf and tugged at the hem of her dress.

"Now she's letting her little girl go down the same road she went. In fact Talia's got a head start. Showing parts of her body I never let my girls show. Tattooing herself so you know where to look. Well, go on then—have yourself a good look. Go ahead and watch her like some TV reality show where you tune in to watch people cheapen themselves, the way folks used to watch hangings, watching the downfall of people like it's enter-tainment, like it's not real people whose lives mean something to somebody."

"Daddy—" Stacy touched her father's arm.

He shrugged her off. "I don't think I can stand it, Stacy. I don't think I could stand to watch it happen again."

Finis looked away from Stacy, to Ivy, to Talia, to Amy and Erik, and at last to no one at all, to the walls and the ceiling. Then he pushed his chair aside and left.

Stacy looked around the room. People averted their eyes. She took her sweater off and wrapped it around her daughter, then stood, pulling Talia with her. She walked out while Ivy wept into her paper napkin.

Saturday night, Dara colored Sybil's hair. As usual, the woman acted like a pet fish, silently accepting whatever Dara did without complaint. But also without gratitude.

Gabriel, the cat, was more responsive. He rubbed against Dara's calves while she combed the applicator bottle through Sybil's hair. Finally, he leapt to the counter to watch.

"You let him up there?"

Sybil shrugged.

"Where did you get him?"

"Some feral cat had kittens in my backyard. Gabriel was the only one that let me hold him."

"And you called him Gabriel because of—"

"The cross." For the first time, Sybil smiled.

Maybe it was because the night before had been so terrible, or maybe it was the first crisp sparkle of an autumn breeze, but Dara felt good that day. She had walked to Sybil's, swinging her Wal-Mart bag full of Natural Light Brown, plus a tube of lipstick and a compact. This was the day she would bring her mother into focus.

While Sybil sat on a step stool in the middle of the kitchen, her hair reeking with purple slime, Dara started lunch. She put a quiche in the oven. She made a salad with artichoke hearts and a dressing of lime juice and olive oil. Then she put the salad into the refrigerator and motioned her mother to the sink.

The first tear fell as she rinsed out the colorant. This was her mother's hair in her hands, her mother's scalp beneath her fingertips. They were in the kitchen together, with a breeze blowing through the window, doing things women did together.

She nudged the tear away with her shoulder and turned the water off. She wrapped a towel around Sybil's head and sent her back to the step stool.

Dara plugged the blow dryer in and began. If she stood behind the stolid face and just watched the hair fall from the brush, she could pretend this was an ordinary day, with a mother she'd always known.

"How's it look?" Sybil asked.

"I'll hand you a mirror in a minute." She turned off the dryer.

She grabbed the compact and dusted Sybil's forehead, nose, and chin. Then she dabbed on the lipstick, pink, like she'd worn in the picture.

Dara squatted for a better look and willed herself not to cry.

It was her mother—broader in the face, but the *proper* face staring back, with such a look of bashful hope that Dara could almost love her.

She handed her the mirror. Sybil touched fingertips to her lips and closed her eyes.

Dara worried.

But Sybil studied the mirror again and smiled.

"Is it good?"

Sybil nodded.

"You like it?" Dara laughed. "Good." She went to the oven and pulled out the quiche.

The table sat in a small area off the living room. Dara cleared away the mound of junk mail and unopened bills, and set out blue placemats with matching napkins.

"Do you ever go out of the house?" Dara asked when they'd eaten half their lunch in silence.

Sybil nodded. "I deposit my checks, and I buy groceries."

Dara could guess. "You go just before the store closes, when no one's there. You drop your check in the night deposit."

Sybil just stared in reply.

"Why don't we take a walk after lunch? Just around the block. For practice?"

So they did. They walked side by side, in a friendlier silence than they'd known before. They walked past neighbors mowing their lawns or washing their cars, asking, "How do you like this weather?" like they were talking to friends. They walked on the parking strips around children chalking pastel pictures on the sidewalks. A black kitten sunning on a front porch bounded across its front lawn to greet them, and they squatted to scratch its head, to stroke the adolescent fuzz on its back while it quivered its tiny tail. "Not so bad?" Dara asked when they got back to Sybil's home.

"No."

"Then I'll pick you up for church at nine. Did you choose a dress?"

Sybil nodded.

Satisfied beyond all hope, Dara left and went home.

She arrived to find Ivy standing in the driveway, weeping. "It's happened again." She leaned against the side of Tom's house.

"What's happened?"

Jane emerged from the trailer. "What's the matter?"

Ivy wiped the palm of her hand across one eye and sniffled. "Stacy and Talia are gone. They never came in last night."

"Well, they've gone home, then. You can call them—"

"It's just the way she did it last time. She didn't say good-bye or leave a note. She just disappeared."

Jane touched her shoulder, and Ivy stepped into her embrace and sobbed.

"What do I do, Jane? Do I leave my husband?"

"Oh, Ivy."

"It's not fair. There's no right way to choose." She stepped away from Jane and folded her arms. "But I won't choose against my daughter a second time."

"Did you call the bus depot?" Dara asked.

"Of course I did. And the police, but they can't ..." She shook her head. "Finis just works on his stupid book. He thinks he can clean the whole world up, and if that means discarding Stacy like so much trash ..." She wiped her face against her sleeve. "I can't do it. I will not live another sixteen years not knowing where she is."

"Where's Ivy?" Finis was in a state after the service, and Erik and Amy got the brunt.

Word was, he had awakened that morning to find her gone—Ivy and Una, both.

Women in the church whispered prayer requests to anyone they could catch—because, well, wouldn't Finis be an easy man to leave?

Dara huddled with Jane and Sybil in the corner of the fellowship hall. Out of the way, but not out of earshot.

"I'm sure she's just running an errand." Erik sounded most unsure.

"So pleased to meet you, at last," Jane attempted, extending a hand to Sybil.

"An errand with Una?" Finis asked. "What did they do, run out for cigarettes?"

"They'll come back, Pop. Don't worry."

Sybil attempted a smile and shook Jane's hand.

"Perhaps we could visit over tea." Jane smiled. "Would you join us at our place?"

Sybil seemed glad to agree.

They had no sooner crossed the parking lot when the door swung open and Finis strode out. "You girls in on the secret? You know where she's gone?"

The next moment, Una's car pulled into the parking lot.

Finis ran to the place where she parked. Ivy got out on the passenger side. He ran to his wife, looking as if his knees might buckle. "Ivy, where—"

The car's back door opened, and Stacy and Talia stepped out.

Finis rifled his fingers through his silver hair. Stacy ran to her father. He took three steps to close the gap, and she wrapped her arms around his shoulders. He wept against his daughter in mewling, broken sobs.

Dara walked a beeline across the sand, alone. Without much trouble she'd found the spot she and Jane had come to the day Jane stood like a phoenix on the ridge. She climbed to the top and spotted the pomegranate rocks. She selected one a safe distance from the edge and rested.

Here in this place, there was peace. No Sybil, and no phone.

She had gotten Sybil's phone hooked up, and that was her first mistake. The woman called every day, at least twice.

The first day she wanted more cat food. Dara had bought her a bag three days before. What she didn't realize was her mother had started feeding every cat in the neighborhood.

Why not? It wasn't her money.

What was it after that? She had run out of chocolate grahams, so she called Dara at work. She had "forgotten" to pay her water bill, so Dara paid the bill *and* the penalty. Her toilet clogged up, so Dara had to stop by after work to use the plunger.

How did the woman survive all those years without Dara?

The worst was yet to come.

Sybil had gone out and gotten a box of red hair dye and put it in herself.

She couldn't leave the house to buy groceries, couldn't be bothered to pay her bills, couldn't deal with her own clogged toilet. But she could go out in the middle of the day and pick out a color her hair had *never* been.

Jane pronounced it "lovely," of course. Dara got a headache just looking at her.

She gazed, now, at the sloping plain in the deepening light. The sun had lowered midway past the far mountains and dazzled the clouds to embers.

The wind gusted up the slope and caught her hair, whipping it like a flame.

"Stop!" she said. She got up and walked.

She pretended not to hear the whispers. She shoved her hands into her pockets and kept her course straight. She wasn't dancing, not this night. She shouldn't have even come.

The wind tickled her neck.

"Stop it!"

She gathered her hair and tied it in a knot. No good. A few paces and it came loose. The desert sand danced around her, and she felt the brush of it against her arms.

"My own, my own, my beloved, my own!" She heard the song.

"You're not acting very God-like!"

And still it played.

She hurried back to the car. She started the engine and made her way down the dirt road to the highway. Once there, she picked up speed. Still, the lowering sun gilded every mesquite bush, every rock and pebble. It tinted the road before her and flashed in the windows of Brittlebush. The air whipped through the open window and tossed her hair.

When she got home, she ran up the trailer steps and opened the door.

And stopped.

Jane sat wet-faced in a circle of lamplight, her legs curled beneath her on the chair.

Dara knelt before her. "What's wrong?"

Jane handed her the folded piece of paper in her lap.

Jane and Dara,

I'm coming home next week, alone.

My gadabout has died. I'll make the funeral arrangements when I arrive, and will let you know.

I write this from Portland. We never made it
to Canada.

I'm afraid I've smeared the paper again.
Forgive me.

Love,

Harold

Dara slumped to the floor. She laid her head back and
wept as Jane stroked the tangles from her hair.

Harold called the next morning to say the funeral would
be the following Thursday. Hooper took time off to help Tom
while Jane and Dara attended.

Dara had not been to a funeral since her father's, but this
was not the nightmare his had been. She didn't hear people's
thoughts; she only felt their sadness.

The entire sanctuary of Grace Lutheran, arced and
wooden, like the hull of a boat, was full. Latecomers crowded
the door and lined the walls.

Four or five friends stood to speak, and they said the
expected things, that Glenda was kind, generous, and loving.
Then Harold took the podium and began:

"Glenda was a woman of great love—with twenty-four
hours a day like all of us, and a few less years. Did she know
that? Maybe, because she was very efficient—she managed to fit
us all in.

"But really I think she didn't know. I think she just
couldn't get enough of all the things that make life good. She
never stopped looking at the flowers in the garden, the sky, the
birds. I don't mean the way most of us look; I mean she never
missed a thing. Like the yellow pollen inside the iris. The rose
hips in winter—like tiny pomegranates, she used to say. She
never let me cut the rose hips.

"Because to miss the depths of all she saw would be a sin
to Glenda.

"And I hope this won't make you nervous, but she saw
into the depths of you. She saw the curve of your shoulder as

you stood before her in line at the grocery. And I think she knew where it came from, whether it was a job you just couldn't do well, or someone who wouldn't honor your love. She caught the sparkle in your eyes when you found something too scandalously funny to share. Don't worry, you shared it with Glenda, and she *was* scandalized!

"Glenda didn't know how long she had to live. But she always said, if you pay attention, five minutes is enough."

He drew a long breath while tears pooled in his eyes. "But thirty years was not enough for me. I paid attention as well as I could, but it could never be enough. My brave, beautiful wife."

He kissed his fingertips, extended them toward her body, and returned to his seat.

Beautiful?

Dara wiped her tears and stared at the porcelain doll in the casket. Her lips were the problem. Something about the way lipstick gathered in the glue between them. Glenda had tried so hard not to look sick, and now it seemed she tried not to look dead.

And it almost worked.

The next morning, she heard a knock at 7:47. She'd overslept. She sprang from her bed, grabbed her robe, and put it on while she walked to the door.

It was Tom, freshly bathed and ready for work. "Sleeping in today?"

"I'm not late yet."

He peered past her shoulder.

"What do you want?"

"I thought Clemmie might have stayed the night with you."

"No!" Dara said, fully alert now. "Is she missing again?"

"At the moment. She'll turn up."

"Tom, I can't believe you! Every time this happens, you act like it's no big deal."

"It's all right. Someone will call, and I'll pick her up."

She checked her watch. "It's almost eight. Whoever has her knows by now."

"*You* wouldn't have known." He walked down the steps. "I'll go listen for the phone."

"Tom!"

He turned.

"Do I have to spell out what could happen? There are people who climax themselves hurting little girls."

"Shhh!" He glanced toward the neighbors. "This is Brittlebush."

"Oh, and you think bad things can't happen in Brittlebush. Maybe Los Cuervos, which is half as big, but not Brittlebush."

"Open up the Studmuffin. When I've found her, I'll be in."

When he hadn't shown up by nine, Dara called.

He answered midway through the first ring. "Hello?"

"Have you found her?"

"No." His voice was so soft, she could barely hear above the noise of the restaurant.

"Has he?" Hooper called. Jane stood beside him.

Dara shook her head. "Tom, you've got to call nine-one-one."

"Right. I'll call them now."

Hooper was on his way out the door. "Shut the restaurant down. Meet me at Tom's."

Twenty minutes later Jane and Dara rounded the corner onto their street, right behind the police cruiser. They parked and entered through Tom's back door while he answered the front door.

Hooper had already gone searching. Dara knew the scene in Tom's kitchen all too well—the father sitting at the table with a policeman, filling out forms. She ran to her trailer, partly to escape, but also to be sure Clemmie wasn't under the bed with Algernon, laughing.

She wasn't.

Where had she gone before? The Baxters', the Gowers', Elma Price's. John and Bobbie Ruiz were out of town, but

Clemmie had gone to their place twice. Had anybody thought of that?

She ran to Tom's house and waited in the doorway, till the policeman noticed, and Tom turned, following his gaze.

"What is it?" he asked.

"John and Bobbie Ruiz are in Tahoe, remember?"

Things happened after that. The police located John's brother, Bill, who had a spare key to the Ruizes's house. Hooper had returned, and they all followed the policemen, all except Jane, who waited by the phone.

Dara rode with Tom and Hooper, the three of them almost giddy with relief that they had figured things out. Clemmie had to be there, right? Watching television, probably eating all their ice cream.

They gathered outside the green stucco house on Coolidge—Tom, Dara, Hooper, and the policemen. While they waited for Bill Ruiz to arrive, they knocked on the doors and peered through the windows. No answer, but that wasn't surprising. Clemmie would see this as a grand adventure. Tom swore he would convince her otherwise when she got home.

Dara rolled her eyes.

Bill Ruiz finally showed up, full of apologies and explanations. "Hard to break away from the job, you know?"

The two officers entered the house alone, while everyone else stood outside, peering through the door, still as statues.

Clemmie wasn't there.

Dara watched Tom pale while he took in the things policemen say at such times: what they would do to find his daughter; what Tom should do if she turned up. They gave him their business cards, and the younger one said, "Don't worry."

The older one clearly knew better.

That afternoon they took turns watching the phone while others searched door-to-door. Tom and Dara walked the streets calling Clemmie's name. Hooper called the local television and radio stations, asking them to make announcements.

Women from church brought casseroles. People they hardly knew joined in the search. The town was divided into sections, and maps were handed out so folks could mark off houses as they went.

Later that afternoon Dara sat beside Jane and Hooper in a silent living room. Tom perched on the edge of his armchair, with the phone under his hand like a pet cat.

Finis set about fetching meatloaf and scalloped potatoes from the kitchen. "Have something to eat," he said, and handed Dara her plate.

She fingered her pearl and stared, uncomprehending, at the food.

Finis knelt beside Tom. He spooned some meatloaf and offered, "Come on, pal."

Tom accepted the bite and coughed. He clenched his lips to his teeth, whimpered, and coughed again.

Dara clapped a hand to her mouth and shuddered. She felt a touch on her shoulder and turned to Jane. The two women leaned against each other and wept.

She wished she had never told Tom what people did to little girls. What else could he think of now? She wished she had never thought of it herself. For she pictured it all, the rough hand stroking the tiny shoulder. The white legs in red boots.

Clementine!

Hooper called a prayer meeting at the church that night. Finis stayed by the phone with Tom.

Dara had no idea what to say to a God who could dance in a world like this. But she was not above begging if it would bring Clemmie home.

The sanctuary glowed with candles, as people filed into the pews. She sat next to Una, and the woman took her hand. Dara was not used to such affection, but Una had a strong grip that discouraged her from pulling away. Still, the old woman's fingers felt like twigs in a silk bag.

Erik walked through the sanctuary doors and up the aisle. He stood under the one electric recessed light in front and motioned the people forward.

He reached out his hands, and they all formed a circle. Then they began with the murmurs, soft choruses, "Holy Jesus," "Blessed Lord," and "Oh, God." Dara opened her mouth to join in, but nothing came out. Instead, she heard the voice's whisperings, the tendernesses, not in the wind or the moonlit air, but in that deep buried place of sorrow.

In there!

She could point to the place it came from. She pulled her hands free from the circle and pressed them to her middle like a woman in labor. Then, like a siren, the wail rose within her and surged to the top of the pitched ceiling. She felt people staring, and breathed, frantically trying—*please, no!*—to stop, but the cry, shrill and clean, pierced through the ceiling and past the stars. Dara felt the others shatter, she heard their cries—the whimpers, the keening sobs. She fell to her knees and wailed.

When the tears quieted, there were bodies on the floor, breathing, but still as the dead, and as peaceful. Dara lay on her face, listening with odd curiosity to the voice singing inside her.

"I don't get you," she whispered. "I don't understand you at all."

After long moments she heard a rustle. She turned her head and opened her eyes. The spell had broken, and people stood to their feet. Dara stood with them. She looked around at all the sodden faces. Una and Jane standing side by side, Hooper beside Jane, and all the others.

There was a woman named Judy, whose ex-husband had sued for custody of their daughter the week before. As Judy returned to the pew she staggered a little and caught herself. Dara drew in her breath, startled, for she'd felt in that deep place a despair that was not her own.

She looked away and caught the eye of Mrs. Daly, eighty-seven years old, who had always reminded her of Connie MacAdam in her gullible kindness. But when she looked into

Mrs. Daly's eyes, she felt the intentional, stubborn credulity of one who had seen terrifying, shameful things.

The old woman turned and made her slow way to Dara. She placed a tremored hand on Dara's arm and recited,

> The Lord your God in your midst,
>
> The Mighty One, will save;
>
> He will rejoice over you with gladness,
>
> He will quiet you with His love,
>
> He will rejoice over you with singing.

What did that have to do with Clemmie? Did God rejoice over her, as well?

Dara pulled away.

❦

Sunday morning, Ivy noted Jane's cell number and took a turn at the phone so Tom could attend church.

Early in the service Erik called the family forward for prayer. Tom and Jane grabbed Dara's hands and pulled her to her feet.

To be counted as Clemmie's family! She went, feeble with gratitude and pain. Still, on the way forward, she braced herself. She would not repeat the disaster of the prayer meeting the night before. She would think of something besides Clemmie. She would slow her breathing and count each breath.

It seemed that hundreds of hands pressed her arms and shoulders, as if to hold her firm. As if to press grace inside. Dara breathed: *one, two …*

"Keep her safe, Lord Jesus!" she heard.

Three …

"Please God, bring her home."

Four …

"Jesus, with all confidence that you hear and answer our prayers ..."

Dara barely heard the percussive *whump* of the sanctuary doors. The hands on her shoulders went slack, and the pleadings quieted.

"Oh, praise Jesus!" someone breathed.

Footsteps brushed against the carpet as people parted and she saw.

Clementine walked up the aisle, hand in hand with Sybil. Tom cried out and ran to his child.

"Oh, Jesus!" Dara whispered.

Why it had never crossed her mind to check her mother's house, she didn't know. Maybe it was because Sybil lived two miles farther than Clemmie had ever gone. Maybe because the woman's house still, for all the cleaning, smelled of cat urine and mold.

The police located the couple who had canvassed the neighborhood around Filmore and Ash. Why hadn't they checked the second house from the corner? When Dara heard, it made perfect sense. The curtains were closed, and the yard was untended. They thought the house was vacant.

"Do you realize Tom could press charges?" she railed when she got Sybil home.

"The child's lonely."

"Lonely."

"She's just a little girl, and she's lost her mama."

An answer burned like poison in Dara's throat, but she held it in.

And what had the two of them done for two days? They had read *Air & Space* while Clemmie sat on Sybil's lap. They had eaten macaroni and cheese, and chocolate grahams. They had tied ribbons onto barrettes for Clemmie's hair and wrapped cotton around pipe cleaners to make tiny sheep. They had lain in the backyard at night, spotting meteors.

They had found the North Star.

Prayer was not all it was cracked up to be.

Perhaps if she had scored better on the Ten Easy Steps. She didn't know.

All Dara knew after two long days of anguish was that she was tired. She took her shower, pulled on her nightgown, and stumbled to bed with her hair still wet, determined to sleep long and well.

Much earlier than she wanted, she awoke. Her neck ached and so did her back and bent legs. By the feel of things, she hadn't moved all night. Groaning, she checked the clock. Almost five thirty.

She could sleep another hour, and it would do her good. She rolled to her back and shut her eyes. And lay that way, with a weight of sorrow pressing in. She felt pinched, head to toe, in a violence that didn't strike but pressed, and pressed ...

It weakened her, this feeling she knew so well. She had felt it as a child, when she drifted to sleep or woke up, a desecration that felt like grinding steel, blistering hatred and rape, even to a child untaught in such things.

She kicked the covers off and sprang to her feet. Just too gunmetal gray in the room, that was all. She went to the window and opened the shades.

The yard was washed in pink-golden light, still and silent.

It was the troubles of the past few days. It was the nights with Clemmie lost, it was Harold's tears, and Glenda's lips pasted shut. It was her mother, hand in hand with Clemmie. It was all the memories she had managed to file away for the past months, the pictures that no longer sprang to mind unannounced.

But they whispered. That was surely the trouble now.

She returned to her bed.

She had asked for her mother and gotten Sybil. Things were as bad as they could get, and there was a peaceful assurance in that. She rolled to her side, slid her finger along her silver chain till she found the pearl, and went to sleep.

CHAPTER 17

*T*he next night, she knelt on the floor of Sybil's closet, scrubbing the wood floor to a lather, breathing the smell of pine soap and wet wood. Jane had suggested she break for a cup of tea, but a break was the last thing she needed. She had to move faster than the pictures in her mind could flash, so fast the weight in her chest never touched the ground, because if it did, it would pin her there, retching and weeping till she died of the grief.

Sybil stood in the doorway.

"Why don't you go watch television?" Dara asked.

"There's nothing on but news."

"Then go make Clemmie's doll."

But that project was finished. Sybil had already given it to her: a white rag doll with red yarn for hair. A blue dress and red boots made from an old change purse.

Sybil left.

Dara sat back on her heels to rest and dried the floor with a rag. She stood to retrieve the standing wire basket she had pulled from the back corner of the closet. It overflowed with old papers, boxes, and trinkets, and when Dara lifted the basket, several fell to the wet floor. She bent to snatch up an envelope— a water bill, unopened, four years outdated. She clenched it to a ball in her fist.

Let no one say she's irresponsible. She never throws her bills away.

She lifted the basket to the bed and dumped it. She could probably throw most of this stuff away. She started sorting. By the looks of the pile, half of it was unpaid bills, some from collection agencies, all long outdated. She rifled through and pulled most of them out, starting a pile on the floor. There were ads for magazine subscriptions, video club packets never opened, campaign letters from two elections previous.

There were a dozen or so *Smithsonian* and *Popular Science* magazines, which she stacked to the side. There was a plastic packet of soy sauce and a pair of unused chopsticks. An old bottle of nail polish, separated to pink sludge on the bottom and yellow liquid on top. These she added to the discard pile. A dinner plate dirty with an unknown brown smear, she set on the bed beside her. That left a shoebox, an unopened packet of barrettes, and—she snorted—a pamphlet titled "How to Organize Your Home and Your Life."

She set the pamphlet on the stack of magazines, turned back to the dwindled pile of debris, and stopped. There, on the bedside table, was a photograph of Clemmie, in a gold-toned dime-store frame, behind a cracked glass. The photo was taken from a distance of perhaps a hundred feet and slightly blurred, but there was Clementine, chasing a puppy between two trees in a green park near the monkey bars.

When had she taken this picture? When Clemmie hid in her house for two days?

Dara didn't recognize the park. The play equipment at Lindbergh Park was red and yellow, vinyl-coated. The monkey bars in this picture were the old kind, tarnished steel.

She set it on the bedside table and brushed a hand through her hair. Were there other pictures of Clemmie? She spotted a shoebox on the bed. Deeply tired, she sat down and lifted the lid.

They were letters. Ironically, in a house that rivaled the city dump, these were neatly filed, like index cards. Were they in chronological order? Dara flipped the first one back to check the date. It wasn't a letter at all, but a Christmas card, with a Coca-Cola Santa. She pulled it out and read the inscription: "Enjoyed our talk. Happy Holidays—Maris."

January 10, 1986—not long before her mother had left. It was addressed to Clara Murphy, at Dara's house in Los Cuervos—729 Prescott. The return address was the house she sat in now: 420 Filmore, in Brittlebush.

She pulled out another envelope, and a photograph fell out: a Polaroid of a woman, fiftyish, with bleached hair cut short. She sat on a park bench in a green pantsuit, with feet and knees together, black shoes polished to a shine, black purse held firm to her lap. Her lips drew a red line across her face like an attempted smile.

Dara opened the letter and read:

Dear Clara,

Since our conversation at the park, you have been on my mind continuously. How strange when we've only met once, but I feel that I've known you a long time, in the way one who has suffered knows another. My hope is that you feel the same way, and that you won't think me inappropriate for begging you, as one who knows and loves you, not to do the thing you're planning. Men do not understand the minds of women, and they will not change because you want them to.

But I'm afraid that you will, with or without my pleading, so I will simply repeat in writing what I said to you that day we met: Keep my phone number in your pocket. When trouble comes, use it—call collect, and I will come for you. I mean this.

Love,
Maris

Shaking, Dara tossed the letter and the picture aside and pulled out the next. This letter hadn't been mailed. The envelope simply said "Sybil."

Sybil,

I didn't wake you this morning. You looked peaceful, and I knew it to be the first peace you had known in how long?

You are safe now, my dear, in your new life. People remember my sister from earlier years, so no one will suspect, and really, I think the name suits you. You are my prophetess, my Sybil, and I your Maris, your Queen of Peace.

Meanwhile, make this home yours. I'll be home tonight.

Maris

Dara ruffled through the filed letters and pulled another at random.

Sybil,

You make me so angry.

Do you remember what you said that day in the park, that you wished the world would stop so you could get off?

This has been all my effort since that day, to give you peace.

Let it go. You've been forgotten, and that's for the best. Look around at our quiet home, see it for the haven it is. See me for all I am to you.

Can't you just be happy?

Dara trembled, tight with rage. She balled the letter in her fist and hammered it into the box, mewling and grunting with each blow.

"Dara?" Jane stood in the doorway.

Dara took the box and pushed past her. She bolted through the kitchen, out the back door, to where her mother stood, dark against the stars.

"Who is *Maris?*" She shrieked and heaved the box at Sybil, striking her in the shoulder.

The letters scattered, white in the light of the kitchen window.

"Maris is dead. She had a stroke four years ago."

"You loved her? More than Daddy? More than *me?*"

The woman offered no answer.

"Your husband's dead. You've never once asked, so maybe you didn't know he was murdered. It was right there, all over the news, but maybe you turned it off because you couldn't trouble yourself to care. He's dead. And I'm as good as dead myself. I *wish* I was dead."

No response.

Dara shook her head. "You just stopped the world and got off. But I never forgot you, Mama, never once." She looked once more, hoping, but Sybil stood impassive as stone. Dara darted past Jane, through the house, and out the front door.

She drove, hardly mindful of where she was going. She struggled to calm the chaos, the pots and pans clamoring in her head. She turned onto a dirt road, and in a few moments she stopped. She got out and stood in the light of the half-moon, adjusting her eyes. She'd returned to the place of the pomegranate rocks. Dara charged up the hill and stormed to the ledge, to face the stars with her hands on her hips.

"Give me another world to live in."

Not a whisper in reply.

She sat down, her legs suddenly tired, and her shoulders, and her mind. So tired, too tired, and deadly afraid. Because what new distress might she face tomorrow, and the week after that? The raping hatred watched her, and she trembled beneath it. She touched a hand to the pendant at her throat, and then, quiet with a new idea, she fingered the pearl.

What happened when the prince finished striking away with his chisel? What had her father said?

There, shining in the chinks where the rock had chipped away, she saw a particular golden pink like the sunset on the first day of spring.

But when she put the question to him, he admitted, "I only know rocks."

She knew now. There was no pink pearl inside her, just the calcified remains of her painful life. And she couldn't stand any more.

She unfastened the chain, pulled it off, and refastened it. She held it up and watched the pearl gently dangle in the moonlight for a quiet moment before she extended her arm over the ledge and let go. She leaned to watch it fall out of sight. She didn't even hear it hit the ground.

There was a rock that extended over the ledge like a thumb. She stood. She could walk to the end as if it were a diving board, and there would be no slope to break the fall.

She crept along the ledge to the rock and pressed with one foot to test its strength. Then she walked out onto it. She had never learned to swan dive, but that would be the way.

A rumble of sand startled her. She looked at her feet. The rock seemed steady.

"Dara?"

Jane. She turned to look.

"Dara, come back, please."

She shook her head. "No."

"Oh God, Dara, don't. I'll help you."

She felt the pinching hatred against her skin. "You can't help."

"*Dear God*, what do I *do?*" The duchess held her hands to her head.

Dara watched her, stunned.

"Please, please Dara, don't do this! Please!" She staggered forward.

Dara twisted on the rock, stupid in indecision. Jane was in trouble. Dara took a step to turn around and nearly lost her balance.

Jane was at the rock in an instant, still trembling, but all business. She extended her arm. "Hold my hand."

"It's all right, Jane."

"Take my hand!" Jane stepped forward, and the gravel shifted under her foot. Dara tried to catch her, but Jane flung her arms above her head, and Dara missed. A stone gave way, and Jane slid, shrieking, down the slope.

Dara ran off the rock and turned to where her friend had gone, but it was dark. She heard a hiccup in the scream, and knew Jane had hit something hard. A shadowed figure bounced and rolled down the lower part of the slope. It came to a rest on the valley floor.

"Jane!" Dara screamed. "Jesus! Oh, Jesus!" She ran to her left till the hill sloped more gently and sidestepped her way down to the valley, sliding most of the way, catching rocks and stickers on her hands but ignoring them in her haste. When she got to the bottom she turned to find Jane, but there were rocks and bushes, all shadows, and in the moonlight, she couldn't see …

"Please!" she begged, and her eye caught a faint glow. Jane's cell phone! She ran toward it and nearly bumped into Jane, who lay still as the stones around her. The green light turned off. She scrambled to where she had seen it and snatched the phone up, then ran back to the body and knelt. "Jane?" she whimpered, but the duchess lay motionless, her face to the sand.

She touched a key to turn on the phone's backlight, and dialed.

Lonnie Santiago got ink on his lips as he sat in the cruiser with Dara. The little blue top was gone from his pen, and he sucked the liquid right up the barrel like it was a straw.

So just the moment Dara spotted the gurney on its way to the ambulance and glimpsed a lock of silver hair matted with sand and blood, she shuddered and turned away—and there was Lonnie, blue in the lips, hoping she wouldn't notice. But the place was lit up like a stadium, and she saw him, plain as day.

Lonnie didn't see anything past his own preconceptions.

Dara sat in his car, telling the story he would soonest believe, and he rolled his eyes, shook his head, and wrote it all down. "You two go dancing on cliffs, it's bound to happen sometime, you know?"

She nodded.

He licked a Kleenex. "You sure know how to pick your friends. You got Tom letting his kid climb in people's windows, and Jane out here …" He shook his head.

The ambulance pulled onto the dirt road. It flashed its lights and headed out.

"I hope *you* steered clear of the edge, at least. It's just a crazy thing to do." Lonnie kept his lecture short, no doubt desperate to rinse his mouth.

She nodded to everything he said.

When she got back to her car, she laid her head against the steering wheel and shuddered. "Sorry, so sorry, so sorry …"

She grabbed her purse and churned the contents. Where were her keys?

Her hands hurt from the scratches and bruises she had gotten skidding down the slope after Jane. She stopped and tried to think.

Jane's truck sat empty next to hers. Who would drive it home?

And Lonnie's blue mouth, what a sight. She chuckled a ragged breath and hated herself for laughing. "So sorry …"

She searched her purse again. Where were they? She dumped the contents on the passenger seat and rifled through.

"You okay?" A rescue worker squatted by the door.

Dara jumped. "What?"

The woman reached through the window, touched Dara's face, and felt her pulse. "I'll get you a blanket."

"No, I'm fine."

"Hmm, you're shaking pretty bad. Why not ride with us?"

She shook her head. "Jane's truck—"

"We found the keys in the ignition. Someone can come for it later."

The ignition! Dara felt beside the steering wheel. There they were.

A man walked up beside the woman. "She okay?"

"She's showing some signs. I think she should ride with us."

"No!" Dara softened her tone. "No, I'll drive myself. I'm sorry."

She turned the key and started the car.

The sound of her wheels on the pavement lulled Dara into a numb silence.

All too familiar, the fire trucks and ambulance, and the sheriff's deputy asking questions like the world hadn't frozen in place.

The first time was on Myer River Road. She had told the truth that day with nothing near the composure she had tonight, there in the car with Lonnie.

So easy, this lie.

The deputy back in Los Cuervos had been a Texan, quieter than Lonnie, but he asked more questions. "So you thought Kevin was fixin' to hurt your dad, and that's why you got in his truck?"

And then later, "Did you know Kevin was gonna run him off the road before you got in?"

And yet again, "Did you and Kevin conspire together ..."

The answers were yes, no, and no. But the truth was more painful in the telling than this lie she told tonight.

So much was the same. The fire truck, the ambulance, and the rescue team. And Dara in the sheriff's car, the deputy with his clipboard, wanting to know if the fall was her doing.

And it was.

She had done it again.

Tom and Hooper sprang to their feet when she walked in. She caught the look on their faces, the way Clemmie chewed her finger in the corner, and she knew that Jane was not awake. She clenched her face to hold back the tears.

Tom didn't even ask what happened. He wrapped his arms around her and pressed her to his chest.

"The rock gave way—"

"I know," Tom whispered.

He didn't know, and she should tell him. But right this moment, she needed him to hold her.

A white-haired doctor entered the room. "Jane Cameron's family?"

Tom let go. "I'm her brother, Tom Laurel."

"I'm Harry Janson, the on-call surgeon." He leaned forward to shake Tom's hand.

"Is she awake?"

"No." The doctor bit his lower lip, fanning the bristles of his beard. "She's in a coma, a result of a concussion from the head trauma."

"When will she wake up?" Hooper stepped forward.

"There's no injury to the spinal column, and I'm hoping for the best. Sometimes comas last a long time, but it could just as easily last a matter of days or even hours."

He took a breath. "Meanwhile, we're dealing with some fractures. The one to her upper left arm is already set; she's got a couple of cracked ribs and a broken clavicle. Those should heal without complications. Her right leg is more serious. She's got a compound fracture below the knee and a broken hip bone, and we're going to operate …"

Dara collapsed into a chair, hardly hearing the rest.

The doctor squatted before her. "Are you Dara?"

She nodded.

"She's lucky you were with her." He patted her hand. "You got help to her quickly, and she's in good hands now."

Dara glanced at his eyes and looked away, pierced and shriveled by his kindness.

Doctor Janson took her hands and turned them palms upward. They were skinned and blood-speckled. "Come on back with me. We'll get these hands cleaned up."

CHAPTER 18

*J*ane could die.

The knowledge moved like congealed blood in Dara's veins. She lay sleepless through the night, thinking half thoughts that stopped just short of impact. Her friend could die—and then what?

She got up, dressed, and went through the motions of her routine. She trudged through the Studmuffin's back door, slipped on her apron, and fastened the ties in slow motion.

Tom stood at the counter, fumbling through the prep work, breathing in soft whimpers, chopping onions at an uneven beat.

How would they get through this day?

Dara set up the coffee, wiped the counters with bleach water, and set out salt and pepper shakers. One step, one breath at a time.

She heard a knock at the restaurant door. There stood Amy with Stacy and Talia. They asked to speak with Tom.

"Hooper gave me the recipe for whistle berries, and Stacy here makes good muffins." Amy stuck her hands in her back pockets. "So why don't you two get over to the hospital and leave this place to us? You should be with Jane."

Which made nothing easier for Dara.

At the hospital Jane lay motionless, swollen, and discolored.

Dara heard a sound behind her and turned.

Finis sat in a corner, his head in his hands.

Hooper leaned against the wall, looking shriveled and tired.

Ivy walked in with a tray of coffee cups and passed them around to people too frightened to swallow.

Jane could die—and Dara began to feel the brunt of it. "So sorry." She brushed Jane's hand and wept. "So sorry, Jane."

Finis mumbled something to Ivy.

She gave him a long look and nodded. He walked to where Jane lay and whispered a prayer. Then he kissed his wife and left.

Tom sat beside Dara and stroked her arm, not knowing the wrong she had done.

"So late it's blue."

Those were her father's words for this time of morning. Dara lolled in Clemmie's swing, gazing at the violet sky.

Years before, when Dara was twelve, he had caught her reading by flashlight, wiping tears and snuffling—at four in the morning.

He wasn't mad, and that was a wonder because it was four o'clock *Sunday* morning, with church to go to.

"What are you reading?" He sat on the bed beside her and brushed the moisture from her face.

It was a book by Madeleine L'Engle called *A Ring of Endless Light*.

"Read it to me?"

"The whole thing?"

"Just the part you're reading now."

And so she did, and he smoothed her hair and wiped her cheek, and when she came to the part that made her cry, he wept tears of his own.

The story was about a girl named Vicky, who understood the telepathies of a pod of dolphins. Vicky, too, had taken the blow of too much death: a baby dolphin, her grandfather, Commander Rodney—who died saving Zachary, who tried to kill himself.

At twelve, Dara imagined she was Vicky—never dreaming one day she'd be Zachary.

In the blue light now, she whimpered. She missed the duchess and she missed her father's calloused fingertips against her cheek. It staggered Dara, the harm she had done to the people she loved.

She knew better than to face these thoughts head on.

How had the dolphins healed Vicky? She tried to remember.

No way that made sense. They lifted her between them in the water, they showed her snowflakes, raindrops, and stars, and they … What did they do? They leapt into joy. And they sang "Alleluia," again and again. *Alleluia. Alleluia.*

And it worked, in the story.

Tom's back door slammed open and he ran barefoot down the steps, across the yard toward the trailer, buttoning his shirt.

Had Jane …

"Oh, God!" she stood.

Tom spun to Dara—and laughed.

"Dara! Dara, she's awake!"

She sobbed. "Oh, that's so wonderful!"

He hugged her, pressed his face to her hair, and wept.

"You go on," she said, at last. "I'll get cleaned up and then come."

"No, you're fine the way you are."

She needed time. "I haven't changed since yesterday. You go. I'll be along."

He hugged her again and ran back to the house.

A moment later, she heard him drive away.

She stumbled back to the trailer.

How would she do this? She'd been so afraid Jane would never wake up, she hadn't considered what to do if she did. But now she imagined the scene at the hospital, and it twisted her soul.

How would Tom look at her? What would Jane say?

She could just leave now.

But she had to say she was sorry. Jane had to hear her say it.

"Heyyy!" Jane extended her good arm while Dara hesitated in the hall. The duchess smiled.

Did she not remember?

"There she is, you see? Right as rain." Tom reached for Dara. "Jane thought you had fallen, too."

Dara crept in, glancing around the room. Hooper was there with Clemmie on his knee, and Ivy and Erik. She kissed Jane and trembled, then dropped to the chair Tom offered. "How do you feel?"

"Drugged." Jane sounded weak. "I didn't dress for a party."

"You look fine," said Hooper. "A far sight better than you did yesterday."

Jane smiled and held his hand.

How would Dara say it? She tried to speak and managed a whimper.

"How's the restaurant?" Jane asked.

"Fine," said Tom. "Amy and Stacy have taken over, and Talia. We've all been here every day. So afraid for you, Janey."

"I'll be fine, Tommy."

Fine? Dara glanced at the cast on her arm, the long cast on her leg, suspended.

"I'm tired," Jane whispered.

"Right!" Tom stood. "We should go."

"Just promise to wake up." Hooper kissed her forehead.

"I promise."

Dara stood and followed Hooper. Tonight she would think of a way to tell them.

"Dara."

She turned.

"Shut the door." Jane motioned Dara near.

Trembling, she obeyed and leaned in to listen.

"Promise me you'll never do that again."

"Jaaane!" she wailed.

The duchess stroked Dara's hair.

"I'm so sorry!" Dara sobbed. "I'm so sorry!"

"I know, dear."

"So sorry!"

"Promise me."

"I won't."

"Promise, Dara."

She couldn't speak. Jane held her till she caught her breath.

"Promise."

Dara raised her head and nodded.

"Please."

"I promise."

A blue light flickered through Sybil's new curtains. Had she clothes-pinned them? They puckered slightly in the middle. Dara sat in her car, watching.

Jane had asked for a promise, and she'd given it.

She attended herself, as if at her own bedside. She listened to her breath, the inhale and exhale, felt the pulse that would continue on and on, with what to endure in between?

A solemn promise.

And meantime, a mother to face. She went to the door. Sybil answered her knock, a shadow against the blue light.

"Can I take you to dinner?"

They ate at Denny's, two burgers with fries—hold the conversation.

Sybil spoke, at last, in the car. "I didn't ask you to clean my closet."

Dara started the ignition. She had no will to fight.

"It was none of your business, that box." Sybil looked out the window.

"It was my business to know why you left."

"Maris wasn't why I left."

"Seems pretty obvious she was. You never gave another reason."

"You never asked for one."

"Okay, then. I'm asking."

Sybil wept.

"Daddy was a good man, Mama."

"He was."

"I was just a kid. Was I so bad?" She listened for an answer. The silence hurt.

At last Sybil said, "You never knew your grandpa Lanning, my father."

"No."

"We kept you away from him—your dad did. He kept us both away, because …" She sniffled. "He used to do things to me."

"He hit you?"

She nodded. "Other things too."

Dara pulled to the curb in front of Sybil's house and stopped.

"He didn't want me marrying your dad," said Sybil. "When I did, we didn't see him anymore. But then someone told me he had cancer, so I …" she shrugged. "I went to see him. He was all alone, and I didn't want him to die that way. But he …" She swallowed. "He grabbed me, and when I pulled away, he called me a …" She didn't finish.

"Mama, I'm so sorry." Dara wiped tears of her own, then pulled the Kleenex from the glove compartment and handed one to Sybil.

But it didn't make sense. That was why she left?

Sybil blew her nose and shrugged. "Maris was someone I met in the park."

Dara waited. "Yes?"

"She was lonely."

Dara couldn't believe she was hearing this.

"She offered me a place where I'd be safe."

Dara motioned toward the house. "That? That's your safe place?"

Sybil nodded.

"Mama, Daddy's home was a safe place!"

"No." She shook her head.

"No?"

"No. Your father blamed me for going back. He blamed me for it all."

An argument, that's all it was.

A terrible childhood, a few badly chosen words, and her mother had disappeared for fourteen years.

If Dara went home, she would only think thoughts best avoided. Besides, visiting hours would soon be over. She bought a potted mum at the grocery store and drove to the hospital.

She heard Jane's laughter when she rounded the corner in the hall, so raucous and strong, it rattled the walls.

Dara smiled, flooded with relief for her friend. Who was the duchess talking to? And what language? She peered into the room and realized it was Spanish.

A large black-haired woman sat with her back turned. She leaned toward the bed, whispering in a voice that rose to a treble and a laugh. And then there was Jane's giggle, and the woman reared back laughing, and Dara glimpsed Jane's silver hair.

She backed away.

"It's Lena," Ivy spoke behind her.

Dara turned. "Lena? Does Finis know?"

"Finis brought her."

"No!"

"My Finis brought this woman, and look!"

Dara peered into the room. Such happy Spanish chatter and such fun! She crept from view and left the flowers with the nurse.

Dara sat in her car, lost in thought.

That was the woman who taught Jane to dance. She had imagined a gypsy or a witch. A lithe, dark-haired goddess whirling in the wind across the sands of Mexico. But not this matron in polyester pants and scuffed tennis shoes.

Only once had she heard Jane laugh that way. Dara remembered the day in their desert, the day they laughed together at a wordless joke whispered in the air.

She rolled down her window. The moon was out, and the wind felt like autumn, cool and secretive.

The hospital's glass door opened, and a woman stepped out. Lena!

She stopped in the lamplight, then walked, not to the parking lot, but down the path to the left, past the fountain and the flowerbed, across the driveway, to an empty field beyond.

The car next to Dara's blocked the view. She slowly opened her door and stepped into the shadow beyond the lamplight to watch.

Lena stood with her face to the moonlight, whispering, Dara thought—though a breeze had picked up, and it was hard to hear. Then the woman raised her arms above her head and began to sway.

Dara quieted her breath, careful not to miss the—what? The music? Yes, maybe the music, sung by a silent voice.

Lena was a shadow in the moonlit darkness, barely a thought, but she moved like one of God's thoughts, like a newly created thing, like a freshly lit flame, and a ripple of water, and the world's first wisp of wind.

Something in Dara longed, and something pulled away. She got back in her car and eased the door shut. She started the ignition and left.

She badly wanted never to see Lonnie Santiago again. But he lived in Brittlebush, and he ate at the Studmuffin.

Dara handed him a menu.

"Hey, Tom! How's that sister of yours?"

"I hear she's awake," called a man in the corner she had

never even seen in the restaurant before.

"She's doing well, thank you," called Tom from the kitchen.

"Will Caesar never wonder." Lonnie handed the menu back. "I'll have pancakes and two eggs."

She wrote the order and took it to Tom.

"Dara here's gonna quit dancing round cliffs—aren't you, Dara?" He had turned to address the man in the corner.

"Is that what happened? She was dancing?"

"That's right."

"For who, for gosh sake?"

"For God, is what I hear." Lonnie laughed, nodding his head like a dashboard dog. "That who you dance for?" He gave Dara a wink.

The man in the corner chuckled.

Dara rushed through the kitchen door and whipped off her apron.

"Where are you going?" Tom left his work at the counter and followed.

"You didn't hear that?"

"Not everything. Why?"

"They're making fun of Jane's dancing."

"What?"

"They think that's how she fell."

"It is how she fell."

She whimpered and slapped a hand across her mouth. "It's not."

"What?"

She removed her hand. "It's not how she fell."

"Well then … how, Dara?"

"She was helping me."

"Helping you what?"

"She was pulling me away."

He stared. "I don't under— Pulling you away from … Why?"

She waited, till she saw that he knew. "You tell them. She deserves much more than their jokes, Tom. Tell them."

She left out the back door.

She threw the boxes on the floor in front of the dresser, opened the drawers, and started in. No time to fold; she had to leave fast.

She heard Tom's car in the driveway and groaned.

"Dara!"

With one arm, she cleared the stuff on top of the dresser into the box.

"Dara!" He pounded on the door.

She opened the closet and pulled clothes off the hangers.

Tom pounded on the wall outside her bedroom. "Dara, you let me in!"

She could go out the back door, but the fence was there, and she would have to walk around the trailer to the front. What would she do?

She heard glass break. The front door! She recoiled into the corner.

"Dara, you talk to me!" Tom was inside.

She had heard this kind of rage before (you slut!), and she crept into the closet (you piece of filth!) and cringed.

"Dara!"

She knew the truth of it. She had done this hideous thing to Jane, but she couldn't face Tom's rage.

She pushed herself into the darkest corner of the closet and shut the door.

Tom's footsteps approached in the hall, the bedroom door opened, and he was in her room. "Where are you?"

She whimpered.

She heard him take a broad step across the floor, and the closet door slid open.

She crouched, keening, with her hands across her face.

Tom collapsed to his knees. "Why would you do that?"

"I'm so sorry."

"Didn't you want to live for Jane or for Clemmie? Or for me?"

"I'm sorry, Tom."

He sat beside her in the closet. She leaned away from him.

"It doesn't have to be a romance. Maybe neither one of us is up for that, but we're friends at least …"

"I'm going away."

"No." He shook his head. "Not like this."

She stood.

"No!" He leapt to his feet and pulled a box into the closet.

"Don't!" She pulled it back. "I have to go."

"I'll call the police!"

She stopped. "Please, Tom. Don't. I need to go back to my desert."

His shoulders shook, and he wept.

She touched his arm. "I won't do it again. I promised Jane, and I won't. It's just, I hurt people, and people hurt me, and I can't take it. I need to go back."

He pulled her to himself and clung to her, and she held to him and promised again.

The mice had abandoned her desert home, having polished off the string cheese and Cheerios she had left in the kitchen cupboard as a parting gift. They had left a little something for her, though. Every drawer and cupboard was specked and yellowed with their leavings, which settled the question of what to do on her first day back. She started in with soap and water. In the farthest reach of the lower cupboard by the wall, she found their nest: a wad of grass and odd tufts of lint from who knows where …

Unless she did know where. She scrambled to her feet to check the couch and chairs, and the mattress on the bed.

They were fine.

When the kitchen was clean, she found her hammer and nails and sealed shut the leather mouse door she had made back on the day she started holding funerals for mice and giving them names. It had been a stupid idea to begin with. Besides, now she had a cat.

While Algernon sniffed out the living room, Dara settled into her chair to watch. He would be strictly an indoor cat now. "I hope you don't mind," she said.

He leapt to her lap and nudged his head against her nose.

"The animals in this neighborhood aren't like the ones in Brittlebush," she explained, stroking his back.

Indifferent, Algernon slipped to the floor and resumed his exploration.

She was back where she should have stayed in the first place. There would be no nonsense this time. No visitors, no dancing, no hearing what people thought or feeling what they felt, no caressing voice in the air or—for heaven's sake!—in the deep buried place in her gut. *That* place was barricaded, closed for business. "Trespassers will be shot," she muttered aloud.

She had cried more tears in the past year than any healthy person should cry in a lifetime, and that had to stop. She had every reason to grieve, of course, but so did everyone else—and the rest of the world didn't weep over every death and rejection and slam in the face. They licked their wounds and kept going. Well. This place was her way to keep going. This was her waiting place, where she would keep the promise she made to Jane and to Tom. She'd stay alive, safe and quiet, till she was dead.

The voice had to be dealt with. She had tried this before—how many times?—and ended up in Brittlebush, at the bedside of her broken friend.

When all she wanted was to be alone.

Alone!

It wasn't that the voice didn't listen. That would have made things easy. No, it listened. It heard the things she didn't say. It won every game before she knew she was playing.

Not this one.

She charged out the door, down the steps to the sand and brush. A breeze whispered in the sunset glow.

She ignored it. She would not be swayed.

She opened her mouth to speak—and stopped.

There was the bluff where she had first seen Jane, standing like Moses. In the embers of the day, it glowed like a dying flame.

Not far ahead was the place where Jane danced in the blizzard. And the very spot Dara stood on, she realized, was where she had argued with thunder and lost.

An ache rose in her throat, but she pushed it down. She had come to say something, and she had best get it out. She thrust her hands in her back pockets and began.

"I guess you know what I've come to tell you."

The breeze fell silent.

"I'm not cut out to be your mystic, your lover, not even your servant. You've got me wrong. I'm not a good person. I want to be. But I hurt people."

This wasn't going well at all. No use taking the blame to soften the blow. It just gave the voice a way in. There was plenty to be said, and this was the last time. She might as well get it all out.

"Not that you're all lily white. You ask too much. You expect trust when there's no earthly reason to trust you, and heaven forbid you should explain yourself. You took away my father, and you let Jane fall from that rock. You sent me Sybil, who is one poor sorry excuse for a mother, I've gotta say. You're like Kevin, whispering into my neck, drawing me close, and then slamming me to the wall."

She took several deep breaths and lifted her hands. "Okay, sorry. Maybe that wasn't fair." For hadn't she played her part in the fate of her father and of Jane?

But guilt was an emotion, and the voice had always gotten to her through her emotions: her longing for forgiveness, for love, and for one precious fleeting shred of transcendent joy. And these were offered like candy through a car window. But with them came all the rest.

She was past that now. She could accept loneliness and emptiness and even guilt, and keep going, if only she stayed in this place, alone and safe.

"We've got some loose ends to tie up. Just some responsi-
bilities I'm going to ask you to honor. You've got the resources,
and I don't think I'm asking too much. I want you to heal Jane.
She's a good woman—one of your faithful. She doesn't deserve
to suffer. I want you to take care of Clemmie. Surely you don't
need it explained to you, why children should be protected.

"And Tom. He's a good, kind man who deserves much better than he's gotten.

"And Hooper. And Finis, and Ivy, and Amy and Erik, and all the
rest. *All* the rest. All the people I know and don't know. You created
them; they're your responsibility. Take care of them! They're so wrong
sometimes, but so fragile, and so lost and sad ..."

She sighed. "And Sybil. My mother."

She shook her head, her face warming, the ache returning
to her throat. She clamped her lips to hold it back. She took
deep breaths. She calmed down.

"Of course, it's up to you. It always is. But if you talk to me,
I won't listen, I won't answer, and I will not dance." She turned
and walked back to the house.

In her bedroom, she pulled the baby clothes from the wall
where Jane had hung them, stuffed the lot of them into a
drawer, and went to bed in the fading light.

She knew the rattled hum of Hooper's Fairlane, and that was the
sound that woke her up. She kicked her way free of the bed
sheets and hurried into her jeans and T-shirt. When she opened
the door and squinted into the morning glare, Hooper stood at
the foot of the porch steps.

"Took me three hours to find this place," he said. "A
friendly, outgoing girl like yourself has no business—"

"You haven't paid attention, Hooper. I'm not friendly. Go
away."

"We could've called the police, you know that? In fact, that's
the decision I've come to make. Suicide's illegal. So unless you'd

care to keep company with the likes of Lonnie Santiago, I'd suggest you fix some breakfast. You know how I like my eggs."

Three deep breaths. She folded her arms, refusing to cry. "Tom knows how to cook them that way; I refuse."

"Then I'll take 'em any way you're eating 'em. The Studmuffin's closed."

"Closed? Why?"

"Jane's in the hospital. You're gone. Amy and them are making funeral arrangements."

Oh no. "Whose funeral?"

"Una's. She died last night."

Dara stepped back into the living room and sank into a chair. Hooper followed and shut the door behind him.

"What happened?"

"Nothing special. She paid a call to Jane at the hospital, drove home, and went to bed."

"Was she upset because of Jane, or—"

"Now there you go, making every bad thing that happens your fault. Kid, the woman was eighty-eight years old. She was ready to meet her maker. She even dressed for the occasion."

"With that lily?"

He chuckled. "Yes, with that lily, and her hair arranged just so."

Fanned out on the pillow like the Lady of Shalott, Amy had said.

"Don't suppose you'd come to the funeral?"

Dara rested her forehead against her hand. She'd promised herself she would stay in her desert this time.

"I didn't think so," said Hooper. "I guess you've seen enough funerals for now, anyway."

She didn't want to think about this anymore. "Tom could hire someone for the restaurant. Or you could help him."

"No, I've got you to check on. And after driving all over the countryside, I've worked up an appetite. How about those eggs?"

Fifteen minutes later, they sat at the kitchen table eating breakfast. Dara was going to skip it herself, but Hooper threatened again to call Lonnie.

"I'm not going to jump off a cliff," she said. "I promised Jane and Tom, and I won't do it. I'm fine now."

"'Fine' doesn't hole up out in the back of nowhere with no neighbors and no phone. Which reminds me." He pulled from his pocket a cell phone and charger. He plugged the charger into the outlet at his feet, attached the cell phone, and set it on the table. "You keep that, and you keep it charged."

"Why? I won't answer it. I won't use it." Hooper shot her a look, and she backed down. "Fine. But I can pay for my own phone."

"No, you can't," he said. "Not living off that little inheritance you got from your father. Wonder how he'd like you to spend it."

"I'll ask next time I see him." She picked up their empty plates and put them on the counter. "You satisfied that I won't do anything stupid?"

"Not a bit."

"Well I won't. I just want you to leave me alone."

"I think I'll check in from time to time, now that I know the way. When you make a run to town for groceries, you might stop in on one or the other of us, see how we're doing."

She didn't answer. Hooper swallowed the last of his coffee, put the cup in the sink, and left.

A week later she used that cell phone to call the hospital in Brittlebush. She asked if Jane Cameron was still a patient there.

"I'll transfer you," said the nurse at the desk.

But Dara's question was answered. She hung up the phone.

CHAPTER 19

She dreamt one night of Una in her blue silk underthings, young with amber sunlight in her hair. The bombshell leaned back in her chair and crossed her red stiletto heels on the porch rail. "What was it Glenda said?"

"About what?" Dara sat on the steps and sipped her tea.

"About life."

"She said she meant to use the time she had."

"Did she say that? That's good—but not what I meant. There was something else."

Dara grinned. "She said she liked Harold in black knee garters."

"Why not?" Una laughed, and her hair gleamed like sunlight through a honey jar. "But there was something Harold said—"

"I thought we were talking about Glenda."

"We are. Something he said at the funeral …"

Dara shrugged.

"If you … If you pay attention …"

"Five minutes is enough."

"That's it!" The bombshell slapped her knee, and sunlight spattered like rainwater from her skin. "That's good. That's very good."

Someone nibbled Dara's toe, and the dream wafted away.

She peered over the side of the bed where her foot extended. Algernon brushed his head against her heel and nibbled again.

"What do you want?" She already knew. He wanted breakfast. The cat and Hooper always wanted breakfast.

Hooper had come several times in the months since she

moved back, and their conversations had gentled down a bit. She'd almost come to enjoy his visits. As Hooper would say, he'd "had himself a life," and he told good stories. A one-time Oklahoma cowboy "just like Will Rogers," he'd ridden rodeo till a spinal injury convinced him to go into the printing business.

He'd been divorced twice before he gave up at the age of forty-three. "I've cleaned up considerably over the years," he'd told her once when they sat on the porch, watching a hawk spiral inside a thermal that traveled across the plain.

Something about the way Hooper dropped this bit of information made her feel he was applying for a job—or, more likely, a marriage.

"How's Jane doing?" she asked.

And he answered the same as always: "You want to know that, you pay her a call."

But she'd caught his suppressed grin when he realized she was on to him. She wanted to know if Jane was out of the hospital, if she was walking yet. But his smile told her Jane was doing all right, and that was enough.

"How are things at the Studmuffin?" she ventured.

"You want to know that—"

"Knock it off. Tom won't want to see me; I can't just drop by."

"What makes you think he won't want to see you?"

She snorted. The answer was obvious.

"He's not mad at you, Dara."

"I notice it's you coming to see me, never him."

"You want him to come see you?"

"No."

Hooper chuckled. "He's not mad. Just scared. What if he decided he cared for you? It's not been so long since his wife died."

"His wife was your daughter."

"Yep."

"So why do you keep coming out here? I've done terrible things. There's nothing to say I won't do it again."

"Nope. Nothing at all."

"Well then?"

"You think you're the only sinner in the world?"

"Don't get churchy on me. I didn't mean to—"

"You think you're the only *unintentional* sinner in the world? Exactly one and a half of my two divorces were my fault."

"So what are you looking at Jane for?"

"Did I say I was looking at Jane?"

She smiled at him, and he grinned. "Maybe I shouldn't," he said.

"I didn't mean it, Hooper."

"You suppose I ought to crawl in a hole someplace and give up?"

Dara looked away.

"In fact, that brings up a good question. What do you hope Sophie's doing right now? After all she's been through, and all she did to that boy you married, you think maybe she should hide out someplace till she finally kicks over?"

"Leave me alone," she said.

"Your problem is you have no faith."

"Maybe I don't. But what exactly would I believe in at this point in my life?"

"Oh, the usual churchy things. Jesus. Life after death. Life before death."

"I did all that. Back in Sunday school when I was seven, I asked Jesus into my heart the way they told me to. That was about a year before—"

"Good, start with that. What did you ask Jesus to do?"

"Come into my heart."

"Why was that?"

"Because he died for my sins?"

"And why did he do that?"

She sighed. "To make me right with God."

"And how does that work?"

"How does what work?"

"How does that work, that Jesus died for your sins, and that makes you right with God?"

"I don't know. Ask Erik. It just changes things."

"Changes things, or changes you?"

"Changes me, I guess."

"Presto change-o? You're a good person all of a sudden?"

"Obviously not."

"So how's it work? God becomes man, dies a terrible death, and then you say a little prayer, and now everything's different. How's that work?"

"I don't know, Hooper."

"Nobody knows, Dara."

"So are you saying you don't believe it?"

"Nope. I do believe it. I just don't understand it. But I'll tell you what else I believe. I believe something wonderful went on there, something wonderful enough to make the angels sing. Don't you ever feel that, Dara? That something mysterious and wonderful lies at the base of things?

She didn't know what to say. "How's Sybil?" she asked.

"Now that's one question you ought to be asking. And it's the one I couldn't answer if I wanted to."

"Why not?"

"Because the nut doesn't fall far from the tree, that's why. She's got her curtains pinched shut and her door on a chain lock. No one goes in or comes out of that place. She might as well be out here with you."

"It's no different than it's always been."

"Nope. It's no different at all."

After she dreamt of Una in her red stiletto heels, Dara fed Algernon, and prepared to take a drive into town.

It ate at her, this news about her mother. No doubt the house was back to the mess it had been before, and Sybil sat in her recliner, watching game shows in the dark.

Without bothering to explain to herself why she did it, Dara showered, dressed, and spent some time on her hair. Then she walked out the back door, got in the car, and drove the long road back to 420 Filmore in Brittlebush.

When she knocked, the door opened as far as the chain latch allowed. Sybil peered through the gap, then loosened the chain, and opened the door.

The house was clean. She'd pinned her curtains shut, but the lamps were on, and the tables were polished.

Dara stepped inside. "You look nice," she said.

"I've lost weight. I've started eating vegetables."

"I see that."

Sybil smoothed her blouse over her stomach and looked away.

Dara glanced into the bedroom. The bed was made and the dresser top was clear, except for a cotton runner and a small clock.

"I've been playing the piano," said Sybil. "Would you like to hear?"

Dara nodded.

She sat on the bench. "I'm a little rusty, still." She placed her fingers on the keys and played the intro to "April Showers."

Dara closed her eyes, crossed her arms, and struggled to hold herself together.

Her mother's playing was more than a little rusty, and her voice was not what Dara remembered. But the radiant instant of recognition she'd wished for at Shelly Rimes' recital came upon her now in a flood of emotion.

"It isn't raining rain, you know," went the song, "it's raining violets." Dara remembered a joke her mother used to tell about "acts of senseless violets."

She smiled.

Her mother finished the song and shut the cover over the keys. Without lifting her eyes, she said, "I've made you some things."

"What things?" Dara asked.

Sybil stood and led the way to the bedroom, and motioned for Dara to sit on the bed. She opened the closet door. The clothes hung neatly inside, grouped by type: first the blouses, then the pants, then the dresses. The floor was clear except for one box. Sybil pulled the box out and sat on the bed beside Dara.

She reached inside and pulled out a rag doll. She'd spent some time on this one. The doll's bobbed hairstyle was embroidered, strand by strand. The face too was embroidered, but rich with detail: irises and pupils in the eyes, shades of pink on the lips. The doll wore a handstitched bodice, and a skirt, cross-stitched with violets, top to bottom. Sewn to the doll's feet were a pair of satin lace-up dancing shoes.

"It's beautiful," said Dara.

There were other things. A wooden jewelry box she'd painted with stars and varnished. An afghan crocheted with soft yarn in the colors of a desert plain.

The last thing she pulled from the box was a photo album. Framed on the cover was the family picture her mother had carried with her when she walked out the door.

Dara swallowed, stifling tears, and turned the cover.

The top page held the photo Dara had found of Clemmie playing in the park.

She touched the picture, and looked at Sybil. "Where did you get this?" she asked.

"I took it, not long after I came here."

"Came here? Clemmie's only five."

"It's not Clemmie, Dara."

Not Clemmie?

"It's you."

Dara looked closer at the small girl in a blur of motion, running from a puppy.

She took a close look at the park in the picture. It had the old-style monkey bars, curved to a dome at the top, like … Oh! Like the bars in Landorf Park in Los Cuervos, before they bought the new ones.

"It's me," she said.

Sybil nodded. "You were a small child. I guess you looked a little like Clemmie." She turned the page. "I took others."

She had taken others, eight or ten of them, of Dara in the schoolyard, Dara walking home. Dara in the front yard with her father. "I almost got caught when I took that one," she said. "You never saw me. I wore sunglasses, and took them from my car—well, Maris's car."

"Why?"

"I missed you. Maris said you'd be okay, but I wanted to see for myself." She turned back to the picture of Dara in the park with a puppy. "This was the last one I took. You were playing and smiling that day, and I knew you were okay."

Dara whimpered, "I wasn't okay, Mama."

"Neither was I." Sybil pulled a tissue from her pocket and wiped her nose. "I didn't mean to stay away. I thought I'd come back when I wasn't ashamed, but it never happened. But I didn't forget you, Dara. I never forgot."

She returned home that evening to find her back door gaped open. Hadn't she shut it when she left? Dara pulled to a stop in the driveway and hurried up the step. She checked the latch. It failed to catch when she pushed the door shut. She rushed into the house, calling, "Algernon!"

She got no answer. She ran from room to room. She looked on the couch where he liked to sleep, on her bed, under her bed. In the bathtub where he drank from the dripping faucet.

He was nowhere.

She ran out the back door and down the steps.

"Algernon!"

She scanned as far as the front and back porch lights would show, but that wasn't far.

She got in her car and drove the dirt roads, even off road at times, with her headlights on high beam. She called out the window, "Algernon! Kitty, kitty! Algernon!"

She saw two cottontails, a jackrabbit—and one cringing coyote, darting sideways before her headlights and loping away.

When she had searched as far as she could see with her headlights—when she could hardly see at all anymore, tired as she was—she trudged through her back door and left it open, just in case. She collapsed on the couch in her clothes and lay there brittle and awake. After an hour she thought, since she couldn't sleep, she would get up and search.

And then she slept.

She woke when the gray light shone through her living room window. She wept. Her cat was gone, and it looked like rain. She wouldn't find him now, not in this wilderness.

Still, she trudged out to the porch.

And there he was. Her ample-bottomed cat, a hundred feet away, pouncing under a mesquite bush. She called to him, but he ignored her. She ran to grab her shoes. *Please, please.*

When she got outside he was still there, a bit farther away, licking his paw. She slipped on her shoes and set out.

It had been a while since the cat had been out in the fresh air, and he had never been outside in a place like this. He danced away.

"Algernon, come here!" But this was like play, and Algernon liked to play.

She ran. Algernon ran faster. She crept up on him. He waited till she stood within four feet and sauntered away.

And so it went. She followed him across the plain and toward the bluff, and then just the direction she didn't want to go.

"No!" she cried, but Algernon trotted into the gorge.

She walked to the entrance and stopped. "Algernon! Kitty, kitty!" She drew a breath and walked in.

"Algernon!" She crept between the white spires, whispering as though she might be heard. A blast of thunder sounded overhead. She pulled her arms close to her body, afraid for some reason to touch the walls. "Algernon!"

She stepped out on the other side as the first raindrops fell. She ran to the shanty church and stood in the doorway. "Algernon!"

And there he was, skulking and mewing. She squatted and held her hands out, and the cat, at last, seemed glad to oblige.

"You're all wet, and it serves you right." She pulled him inside and shut the door.

And turned around. She was back again, in the First Church of the Exceedingly Isolated Valley. She circled the room and, one by one, observed the stations of the cross.

There was Jane's Max. He was nothing like Hooper: a handsome man, debonair, able to take his tea wherever the situation warranted. Dara laughed, remembering that first night when the duchess said it. "Max and I would take our tea in the tops of trees." But she never explained why.

Max didn't seem the type to drive his car off a bridge on purpose. Maybe it really was an accident. But Jane didn't know for sure. What must that be like?

There was Lena, laughing with a mouth full of gold crowns. Why was she on this wall, where they had hung pictures of their pain? Was it the trouble she had sparked between Jane and Finis?

And the movie star man, whose name was … Dara thought back. Fernando. Why was he here? Had he died, or was there something else?

Strange, comprehending it all at once: There was pain in the duchess's life that Dara knew nothing about.

She walked to the next picture: Finis and Ivy in that terrible pose. With a good eye, you could see the pain behind Finis's forbidding gaze and Ivy's fatigue. But you had to know where to look.

With some hesitation she crossed to the other wall.

There was the picture of her parents on their honeymoon with their new kachina. She searched her mother's bright face. No sign of Sybil there—no sign that day of the pain she had known.

There was so much Dara didn't know. She wished she hadn't destroyed the kachina. She wished she could give it to Sybil, to remind her that she had been happy.

There was the nail on the wall where Dara's wedding picture had hung.

Was she ready for this one? She took a breath and retrieved the frame from under the altar, then carried it back to the pillows on the floor. She propped the picture on her knee. Her father's face had been gaunt with worry that day, and she had been too stupid to notice. Now she saw the thousand anxieties and burdens she had never seen before.

She looked at Kevin. In him, too, she saw so much more. Did it comfort Dara to know she had taken the blows he meant for Sophie? Not really, no, but even so, the memory had lost much of its power.

She set the picture aside.

Where was Sophie now? she wondered. Was she still sober? Tom had been convinced Dara had single-handedly given the woman what she needed. Sweet Tom. She wondered about him and winced at her last memory of his face, desperate, wet with tears.

The rain had stopped. She stood and hung the wedding picture on its nail, then lifted Algernon to her shoulder, and walked outside. She hesitated a moment at the entrance to the gorge, sighed, and stepped in. The place smelled of moist earth. She tilted her head to see the dappled sky between the white columns and felt a strange weight of heart. She walked slowly, stroking the sandstone with her hand. When she got to the other side, she turned to look back. All was silent.

As she walked home, the desert was quiet, as gentle as a sigh.

She got Algernon inside, made herself a cup of tea, and took it to the porch. She sat in the chair Una had occupied in her dream, and lifted her feet to the rail.

How to begin? The air waited, breathless and still.

What could she possibly say? Her throat tightened, and a

tear coursed down the side of her face, past her ear. She brushed it away.

"Please," she said at last. "Please talk to me."

The wind breathed a long sigh, and she heard it whisper, "My Dara."

The next morning she awoke to a faint sound, like distant bells. A slant of sunlight shone red through her eyelids. She opened them, and just as quickly squeezed them shut. There was the sound again! She got up and stumbled to the window, and saw something—what?—something red. She squinted—and in that bleary half-sleep saw a large flower, whirling into blossom a distance away.

A *very* large flower.

Impossibly large. She squinted again. Was it a flame? Had a mesquite bush caught fire in the storm? But the storm was long over. She wiped her eyes and focused once more. And saw the wafting, billowing folds of silk, orange and pink and red, with a drift of silver hair above, and two dancing feet beneath.

She clapped a hand to her mouth and sobbed.

Then she ran to the front door and fumbled with the knob. She scrambled down the steps and across the sand and caught the duchess in a wild embrace.

Jane shrilled with laughter as the silk floated down around the two of them, and the blossom closed.

Dara stepped back gingerly, allowing Jane to steady herself with her cane to the earth. And there stood the duchess, in her silk and beaded fringe, her jingling coins, her shawls and veils. Jane tucked something into Dara's hand.

Dara knew it was her pearl before she opened her palm. "How did you find it?"

"Tom helped."

"Is he okay? Is Clemmie?"

"They're fine."

"Are you?" She brushed her tears with the back of her hand.

With her cane to the sand, Jane twirled around it, and the two embraced again.

The night they'd met, the duchess had mentioned a belly-button ring. Dara had to know. When they pulled apart, she nudged aside the veil. A bit of dazzle, just above her waistband, gold and ruby-studded. There it was.

CHAPTER 20

*T*hat December, Dara sat on the edge of the bed, where her mother lay on her side in the lamplight, with Algernon at her feet. How had she slept through the noise? A houseful of people talking and Nat King Cole singing "A Cradle in Bethlehem" just outside the door.

Dara's desert home had never been so full. She smiled, taking in all the voices—Jane's British lilt, and Tom's. Hooper's twang. Finis and Ivy, Amy and Erik.

And Clemmie's carnival chirp: "Pick a card, any car-r-rd!" She had learned a new trick, but it started the same.

Sybil slept so soundly, Dara wondered if she should wake her. But dinner was nearly ready. She gave her a nudge. "Mama?" Sybil rolled to her back and opened her eyes. "How do you feel?"

"Like I'm catching a cold."

"Do you feel up to dinner?"

Sybil sat up. "Is it ready now?"

"About a half hour more—I thought you'd like some time to wake up. But I brought you a cookie." She extended the iced reindeer from behind her back.

"You made these?"

"Me and Clemmie. I think it's your recipe though, as near as Dad could remember. We used to make them at Christmas."

Sybil looked away. "He was a good father to you."

Dara felt sorry she had brought him up. She wanted to enjoy this night with her friends, with Nat King Cole singing about wise men following, through the dark, the star that beckoned them. "Yes," she said. "He was a very good father."

"So." Sybil smiled. "Jane and Hooper getting married before they move to Mexico?"

"Looks that way."

"What about you and Tom?"

"Me and Tom?"

"He kissed you right outside the window when I came in here for my nap."

"You spied on us!" Dara pushed her arm.

"I did not! I just heard you talking out there, and then you got quiet. I could tell you were kissing. So?"

"I don't know."

It was a frightened, tender, awkward kiss, from which they both had fled indoors. Dara shrugged.

Sybil nodded and looked away. Dara leaned to glimpse her mother's face. "Got time for a story?"

Sybil nodded again.

Dara positioned herself on the bed, against the headboard beside her mother and began:

"Once upon a time, there was a pearl …"

Everyone had gone home, except Sybil, who stayed in Dara's room. Together, they had made a bed for Dara on the couch, with sheets folded to hospital corners—at her mother's insistence. Dara hadn't even known what a hospital corner was before, but now Sybil wanted things just so. Dara laughed to herself and walked outside. A full moon slipped out from behind the drifting clouds, illuminating an alabaster gleam that extended for miles in the cool light.

Dara walked down the porch steps and listened. The silence drew her, and she followed, down the driveway, past the gate, past the mesquite bushes bent with white. Her feet crunched on the hardened snow. A breeze carried the scent of piñon pines.

She walked till she could see the light streaming from the room where Sybil lay clutching the pearl pendant—Dara's pearl, which she'd wrapped up as a gift for her mother.

When she'd finished telling the story, Sybil had turned her face to the wall. "Your father made that up?"

Dara handed her the package. "Merry Christmas, Mama."

Sybil pulled off the ribbon and paper and opened the box. "No," she said. "It's not for me."

"It is. Daddy would want you to have it."

"I don't deserve this."

"Wear it." She fastened the chain around her mother's neck, leaned back, and smiled.

But through the whole Christmas dinner, Sybil fingered it, like something foreign. Still ashamed.

Dara could tell her the story and give her the pearl. She could clean her mother's house and wash her hair. But she could not take her pain away.

She could attend Jane's wedding and see her off to Mexico, but neither she nor Hooper could keep her from dancing too close to the brink.

She could convince Clemmie to stay in her bed at night or Tom to lock the door, but the child would grow up and find her way—and who knew for sure which way she'd find?

And Tom. Dara remembered the way he trembled when they kissed, every bit as fragile as she was. What could they ever promise each other, really? What could anybody promise anyone?

Well. There was the promise her father had made to her mother, that Tom had made to Holly: the promise to stay. To love, despite the risk.

A light snow began to fall. It touched her face in a dozen tiny kisses, and she laughed. "I'm trying to think, here."

But joy flitted in the cold breeze and sparkled all around in the moonlit snow.

She turned and took in the white plain and the bluff, pulled into itself like a sleeping lamb. She took in the moon and the roving clouds, and between them, the clean ancient shining of starlight. It was so quiet, she heard her own breath, like music.

And then she heard another's.

She strained to listen, but it teased her. She smiled and stretched her arms outward. "What?"

The snowfall brushed her fingertips.

"Dance with me," whispered the silence.

And she did.

Author Interview

How did you start writing? What was your first piece of writing like?

I remember the day I composed my first short story about a girl and her dog. The moment must have impressed me because I can close my eyes and see exactly where I was, standing in the shadow behind the kitchen bar, black and white tiles at my feet, the long slant of light from the windows. I especially remember feeling enormously proud of my first work of fiction.

The story itself is sadly lost because I wasn't able to write it down. I was perhaps four years old and had not yet started school.

Why do you write fiction?

Some people encounter great doctors or teachers in childhood and end up following in their footsteps. For me it was storytellers. When I was eight, my mother read to me A. A. Milne's *Winnie the Pooh*, and I adored the things he did with words. When I was nine or ten she read to me *The Little Prince* by Antoine de Saint-Exupéry. I've read that book again and again at various times in my life. What magic, and what a lot to say in such a simple, fanciful story! I think maybe *The Little Prince* was the first book that made me want to write.

Why do people remember a story more easily than a sermon?

I'm not sure that's strictly true. Some of George MacDonald's *Unspoken Sermons* have made a great impression on me. In fact, the little story of the pearl embedded in *To Dance in the Desert* was inspired by a passage in his sermon titled *The*

Consuming Fire. Then again, MacDonald was above all else a storyteller, even in his sermons.

I think the best stories come from a deep place in the writer, and they speak to a deep place in the reader: the place where we care more about truth than facts, the place where we weep our hidden tears and cherish our dearest hopes, and the only place where true prayer is possible. It's the one place within us that really matters, and that's where storyteller and reader join hands. In fiction, as in all art, deep calls unto deep.

What do you hope readers will take away from your book?

I hope my readers come away believing that no matter what happens, at the base of all reality there is Emmanuel, "God with us." In the truest, most mysterious sense, life is very good.

Which character in the book is most like you?

I'd love to just jump right in and say it's Jane, but Jane is the freewheeling sparrow I wish I was. And on my best days I am like her, a little. On my worst days I'm more of a cornered little mouse like Dara.

What actor would you picture playing Dara in a movie?

Let's ask Winona Ryder. She's a wonderful actress who can show an amazing range of emotion in a single moment. She knows how to look very small and lost in a very big world.

Which writers have influenced you most?

Go get Walter Wangerin Jr.'s little book of Christmas stories titled *In the Days of Angels.* Open to the first one, "The Manger Is Empty," and turn to the passage where he introduces Odessa Williams. I don't have a coherent explanation for this except that it was a truly great piece of writing, but the moment I read that passage marked a major, emotional turning point for me. My writing changed dramatically after that, and within a week or so I started to write *To Dance in the Desert*.

Madeleine L'Engle has also been a strong influence, as have C. S. Lewis and George MacDonald. For as long as I have had faith, I've wanted to write about it, and these authors are the masters.

Describe your writing process.

Some writers spend weeks and weeks on a detailed outline and work very methodically from that. Others work by the seat of their pants, just making things up as they go along. I spend weeks and weeks on a detailed outline then toss it aside and work by the seat of my pants. When I get lost, I go back to the outline, rewrite it, then toss it aside again.

The important thing is to hold onto the emotional center of the story and to become my characters the way actors do. I'll know by intuition what they say and do next. When the writing goes well, I probably look like a dreaming dog, all full of twitches and grumbles. Twitching is a very good sign in a writer. Really.

Can you share a particularly memorable encounter with a reader?

To Dance in the Desert is my first book, so most of my readers have been wonderfully kind and encouraging friends. Author Sharon Souza became my friend because we liked each other's work. We and several other writers had exchanged chapters in preparation for a fiction clinic we planned to attend. Sharon sent me an e-mail, and the moment I read it was the first time I ever experienced knowing a *reader*, a stranger whose life had been impacted by something I wrote. It was unforgettable. I think the best thing

about publishing a novel is that I will have readers. I look forward to meeting them.

What is one fact about yourself that readers might find most surprising?

A question like this makes me want to run right out and take
up kickboxing just to have something surprising to report.
The urge passes, however, in the half-moment it takes me to
realize such a thing would involve getting kicked.

The truth is I am the least surprising person I know. I married
an amazing man with great stories (of course) who races cars
and builds flying model airplanes and sculpts things out of
stainless steel wire and who once, as a child, had the Andrews
Sisters for his babysitters. I have two incredibly brilliant
boys—don't get me started on them. As for me, I am a book-
ish, cat-loving, coffee-drinking homebody who reads much
too slowly for one with so many books. The most surprising
thing about me is that I wrote a novel. This is it.

Invite Kathleen Popa to Your Book Club
Transport your book club behind the scenes and into a
new world by inviting Kathleen Popa to join in your group
discussion via phone. To learn more, go to
www.cookministries.com/readthis or
e-mail Kathleen directly at kathleen@kathleenpopa.com.